An Understanding

To believe in legends, one needs to accept there are powers and beings capable of things beyond the human imagination. God, who created all, gave different abilities to different beings, angels, gods, humans, creatures, and mixtures of each, all lived as one, some mortal, some immortal.

Many millennia ago, humans started worshipping immortals, making them more significant than they were meant to be. For that reason, they were no longer able to live as one. Mortals always wanted what the immortals had, and the immortals began using them as their minions to wage and fight in wars, not their own. God separated them all into realms; immortals could no longer live with humans but were still tasked to watch over them when called upon.

Unfortunately, if together longer than necessary, the mortal becomes confused. Are they experiencing reality or fantasy, dream or wake, real or unreal? This otherworldly confusion often leads to insanity and sometimes death.

Can the forbidden love of a mortal and a god overcome the chaos caused and stop insanity from taking over, or will death claim another victim?

PROLOGUE

"Why?" Kallisto cried, heartbroken and angry, as she paced her bedroom floor. "I begged him to stay, and he went to sea anyway. Why didn't he listen?—Why?"

"I don't know, but I do know that he loved you and your mom more than anything, and taking care of you was his purpose. I'm so very sorry," Amanda answered Kallisto's pleas.

Two days after the storm Kallisto and her mother, Thia, received the news. Her father's fishing boat and all those aboard were lost at sea, presumed dead. The two stayed up all night crying and holding each other. Dawn came, and to Kallisto's disbelief, it had not chased the nightmare away—her dad was never coming home. She called Amanda, her best friend since elementary school, to come over and take her mom's place as consoler and companion as Thia went to the docks to see what the next steps were.

The day dragged by and was filled with anger, pain, and lots of tears. Most of the day, Kallisto sat dazed and unable to face reality. Her mother was in no better condition, and if it weren't for Amanda, neither would have made it through the first full day. Her usually snarky best friend must have honed in on her maternal and domestic sides. She cooked for them and made sure they both stayed hydrated. Dark came again, and each succumbed to sleep. Kallisto's nightmares continued. She woke screaming, with her mother rocking her and Amanda holding a cold cloth to her forehead. Grief showed in Thia's eyes as she consoled her daughter.

Once Kallisto realized she had been dreaming of her father's last moments and not actually living them, she took a few deep breaths to calm her racing heart.

"I'm sorry I woke you both," Kallisto apologized.

Thia helped her daughter up, "No need to apologize, sweetie."

"I'll go put on some water for tea," Amanda walked from the room.

Turning to her mother, Kallisto shook her head and sobbed. "I can't do this, mom. This hole in my chest hurts so bad."

"I know, but we have to. Your dad would want us to." Thia tucked Kallisto's hair behind her ears.

The good thing about the comfy sectional couch is it held three grown women comfortably. They drank hot tea, told stories about Kallisto's dad, and wiped tears from each other's eyes until morning crept through the windows, and they all fell asleep; each curled up with a throw pillow and fuzzy blankets.

Kallisto woke screaming—again.

⤙⤚⤛ ⤜⤝⤞

She was not Morpheus' usual dreamer, but a deal was a deal. He waited until Kallisto Nalani went to sleep. Her father was the reason he made the deal to help the young woman. It was rare for a mortal to call on the gods these days; nonetheless, one called on him to help a young woman through her grief.

Morpheus manifested in the bedroom of the sleeping mortal girl. His breath caught; she was stunning, with her long black hair splayed across her pillow. *She is mortal, Morpheus. Stop looking and get to work.* He thought.

He needed to gather some information about her to slip into her dreams. He noticed a framed picture of who must be her parents. Several books lay on her desk; all titles held the words *Greek gods* and *mythology*. That was not surprising, being she was half Greek. He could tell she loved her family and was interested in the myths. Grinning, he leaned over and whispered into her ear. Her eyes opened, and what beautiful eyes they were, aqua shining in the dark.

"Who are you?" Kallisto pulled her covers closer to herself and scurried to the top of the bed.

"My name is Morpheus, and I am a dream god, one of the Oneiroi. I am here to help you."

"How did you get in my room?"

"Dream god, remember? I am in your head," Morpheus reached out and lightly traced his fingers over her forehead. "Tell me a little about yourself, Kallisto." He could not believe how gorgeous she was. He touched her because he had to. Her eyes captivated him; her olive skin was flawless and smelled like vanilla. Unfortunately, she was mortal, and he was here to help her—because if she were not mortal—

CHAPTER I

Two Months Later

Kallisto woke with a thin sheen of sweat covering her body. Her dream felt very—very real. In it, she got frisky with a Greek god, hence the sweating. She woke before it was too late or, in her opinion—not late enough.

"Damn," she cursed, remembering the god's warm, inviting scent. "Why can't I let myself have any fun?" grumbling aloud.

Kallisto Nalani, daughter of a religious Greek mother and an overprotective Hawaiian father, was brought up to believe sex and all things considered *sexual* were meant for after marriage. That was all great unless you were a seventeen-year-old girl in the twenty-first century who seemed to be the only virgin over sixteen on the island of Maui. Kallisto tried very hard to hold onto their beliefs, but her realistic dreams were not helping her unsatisfied hormones. Family and friends told her that she was the most beautiful girl in Hawaii; however, guys never spoke to her, never asked her out, and vanished when she made herself present. Her long shiny black hair and extraordinary light aqua eyes proved too intimidating—so her mother said.

Kallisto let out a deep breath. She knew she couldn't persuade herself back to sleep, so she sat up, rubbed the sleep from her eyes, and tried very hard to remember what the young god in her dream looked like and what his name was. It was always the same. Dreams so vivid they left physical markers on her skin. Then she would wake frustrated, unable to recall the face of her dream man. Most mornings, she woke with the smell of honeysuckle and lavender on her body. This morning sweat was covering her, and she had slightly swollen lips. When the realistic dreams began, she thought she was crazy. After two months, she was resigned to the fact that she *was* crazy, but curiosity had set in—*What did he look like? Did he have a name? Should she give him a name?*

She looked around her bedroom, which was quite unlike most girls her age. Living in Greece until the age of seven, she was fond of the fabled legends. As a child, everyone called her Artie, which was short for Artemis, the goddess of the hunt. Kallisto's father started the nickname because the goddess was supposedly forever a virgin. Little did her dad know, Kallisto was an avid reader of fantasy and enjoyed a more modern take on the goddess than the stories of old. Her room, with its Greek decor, was much like a tribute to the gods in legends instead of the pop idol of the present. She knew she was different from the other teenage girls in school. While they were anticipating the prom, she was rereading the *Iliad*.

"Okay, I'm officially losing it," Kallisto murmured as she rose from her warm bed covered in a golden duvet and six haphazardly pillows strewn over its surface; creams and gold were everywhere. She looked in the mirror, *Oh!* She raised her hand to her neck, remembered the sensation of his lips, and then groaned.

"Why did you wake up?" She stared and criticized herself, not seeing the beauty many of her friends and family claimed her to be. She saw a tall awkward girl with full lips and unusual eyes.

While breathing in the scents from her dream, Kallisto felt the twinge she got so often—someone was watching her. A shiver went down her spine. Glaring at her reflection, she murmured, "Damn feelings." The "feelings" had steadily increased over the last seven weeks and were almost continuous, much to her dissatisfaction. With the constant feeling of being watched and the realistic dreams of a man she couldn't entirely remember, she again thought she might be losing it.

Before her sexually charged dreams started, she had horrible nightmares spurred by her father going missing at sea. He and his crew were presumed dead. Three days after his disappearance, the god started helping her with the nightmares, turning them into places with beautiful landscapes and laughter. Unfortunately, they never completely went away until a week later when miraculously, her father returned safely to them. It was the longest and most terrifying week of her life.

The nightmares slowly turned into the lust-driven dreams that consumed her most every night. Occasionally she and her god would spend time together on Mount Olympus, feeding the animals, swimming under a beautiful waterfall, or having a picnic. Other times they would start kissing, and she would quickly wake. As much as her dreams frustrated her, the feeling of someone constantly watching was unnerving.

"Okay, get a hold of yourself," she closed her eyes and shook her head. *I really need to get a life.* That was just what she was planning to do during spring break. She was leaving for Greece to stay with her grandmother. However, that was three long months away.

⇒⇒⇒⇒ ⇐⇐⇐⇐

Morpheus watched Kallisto through the orb until she entered the shower. Her body was much like Aphrodite's, the goddess of love and beauty—perfect. Hourglass curves and flawless deep olive skin set his body on fire. At 5' 10", she was beyond anything a mortal woman should be permitted. Being Greek, there was no shame in the naked body. However, he knew Kallisto did not feel the same and would never advocate his watching while she was "all natural." That was saying a lot since he lived on Olympus with the most beautiful deities of any pantheon.

"How is it you are merely human?" Morpheus asked aloud as he adverted his eyes.

"I am a god, and so are you. And that is why you should NOT still be going into the dreams of that mortal, and you definitely should not be watching her." Phantasos, Morpheus's oldest brother, walked in to see him standing next to the cobalt blue sphere. Phantasos stood 6'4" and had the body of a Greek god—literally. With his shoulder-length blond hair and a chest that surpassed the fittest human man, he looked to be in his mid-twenties—when in reality—he was well over five thousand years old.

"I want to go to her. She has no idea our times together are real, not figments of her imagination—and I want her to know," Morpheus replied.

"You know that is against all rules. Those of our pantheon and the Oneiroi."

"Like you care about the rules."

"I care about you; that is enough," Phantasos sighed. "I do not want you following in my footsteps." Phantasos was never one to follow the rules of dreams or sleep. His rule-breaking caused many problems between himself and their father, Hypnos. He, too, fell in love with a mortal woman through her dreams. The woman was unstable and killed herself while in her *dream* state.

She, of course, didn't realize she was not actually dreaming. By all appearances to her family, it was as if she died in her sleep—no known causes. Since that tragic night, Phantasos had not entered the dream realm. That was well over a century ago. He was a lost dream god, the only one of three Oneiroi who refused dreams.

"I will not be as careless as you," Morpheus countered.

"Then why are you still watching her? You were supposed to only help, and most of all, why are you bringing her here?"

"You know about that?"

"Of course I do. What would happen if her parents were to walk into her room at night and see her missing?" Phantasos was shaking his head in disgust. "Do you have any idea what it was like for me to watch Marissa kill herself here on this mount and then have to watch her family grieve? Father has not spoken to me in over a century. Do you want the same fate?"

"Father speaks to me only if he must. I am in love with her; can you not understand that?"

"Listen, she does not know you. You are nothing but a dream to her. If you were to go to her in the flesh right now, she would have no clue who you are!" Phantasos's tone was stern, almost desperate. "Humans cannot remember our faces—you know this. The Fates will never allow it. Look at the mess Zeus caused by his carnal knowledge of humans."

Morpheus knew his brother was right. He remembered that dark day Marissa died; it changed his brother in every way. Phantasos loved her, but she went crazy from being repeatedly pulled from one state of consciousness to another. Playing with the dreams of the gods could get dangerous, but the dreams of mortals—those dreams could become deadly. Humans could not comprehend the pull they were undergoing. There is a very thin line between reality and fantasy for a lot of people, and when the two lines are merged by a god, a person can easily snap.

"I know I should leave her alone, but I cannot find it in myself to do so," Morpheus admitted to his brother.

"We are immortal, they are not, and we are forbidden to mix with mortals. You must find the power to let her go," Phantasos's voice was quiet as he flashed from the room.

Kallisto stepped from the shower without the feeling of someone watching—*thank the gods*. She put on a little eyeliner, mascara, and lip gloss before heading for school. This was another *day of dread* in her week—day two of midterms. Thankfully, it was also the last day before Christmas break. She always loved Christmas. Her family mixed the ancient traditions of the Grecians with those of the Polynesians, making for a festive time in her household.

While backing out of the driveway, Kallisto again felt that nagging sensation of someone watching. There was only the elderly widow across the street out in the cool early morning air tending her landscape. The widow, Mrs. Bailey, became Kallisto's grandmother after moving to Hawaii. Kallisto only had one living biological grandmother, and she was in Athens, Greece. Mrs. Bailey had taken up the slack, being the best elderly maternal figure anyone could ask for.

Kallisto backed slowly from her driveway and then pulled into Mrs. Bailey's. "Hey Mama Bai, you're out early," Using her endearment for her grandmother, stand in.

"Oh, hi sweetie, I didn't see you come out this morning," Mama Bai's aged eyes were full of wisdom and love.

Kallisto hopped out of the car to give her a hug, only to tower over the elderly woman. Mama Bai stood a mere five feet and was like a small child next to Kallisto. It dawned on Kallisto that it could not have been Mama Bai watching her if she had not seen her until she drove up.

"Are you okay, Kalli?" Mama Bai asked.

"Yeah, I was just thinking about my midterms," *and my invisible stalker.*

"You'll do fine, sweetie. You always do."

"Thank you, Mama Bai. You're out earlier than normal."

"I couldn't sleep, so I came out about a half hour ago. Maybe I can get this flower bed seen about before my soap comes on," She said, mentioning her favorite pastime.

Kallisto leaned over and gave Mama Bai another hug, "I better get to school before I'm late. See ya later. Love you."

Kallisto returned to her car and drove off, still feeling someone peering at her. She turned around in her seat twice—once at a stop sign and again at a red light, to look in the back seat and see if someone was there. As quick as it had come, the feeling vanished. She always had an intuitive nature. So much so her mother listened to what she said whenever she got *those feelings*. Her mom listened not long ago when she told her not to go with her best friend, Lisa, on a shopping trip to California.

A fatal car wreck in Los Angeles had plagued her dreams for several days in a row, and Kallisto's only connection with LA was the trip her mother planned to go on with her friend. Kallisto begged her mother, with tear-filled eyes, not to go on the already paid-for trip. Lisa continued with her plans, not knowing of Kallisto's intuitions. A few days into the trip, she hydroplaned while driving a rental car, sending her headfirst into oncoming traffic. Kallisto's mother would have been with her friend if she hadn't followed Kallisto's intuition. It took her mother a long time to smile again after the accident. Thia blamed herself for not trying harder to get Lisa to stay home, but how could she have told her that her daughter had terrible dreams of a wreck and she, too, should not go on the trip? Fortunately, the crash only broke Lisa's wrist and bruised her up; however, if Thia had been with her, she would not have made it out alive—the car's passenger side was unrecognizable.

Kallisto's nightmares were why she and her mother was so concerned for her father when he was missing at sea. Anxious feelings made her have vivid nightmares. She could see the storm rising above his ship and the crew scrambling in terror. Wind and waves shredded the hull, and she knew no one could survive. That was her dream two days before the storm was to hit. When she told her father of her nightmares, he just said everything would be okay because they would be fifty miles further out than the reach of the storm. They were not. Kallisto knew her father's fate; unlike her mother, he wouldn't listen. The authorities told her and her mother there were no survivors, confirming her visions. What she had not anticipated was his return. To this day, her father has no idea what happened to him. He said everything went dark, and he found himself in a hospital eight days later with a wristband that said, John Doe. Luckily, when he woke, he was able to give the nurses all the information they needed to get in touch with his family.

The authorities said they found him lying on the coast on the north side of Kauai. That was strange since he had been over one hundred miles south of the Big Island. No one else from his ship survived.

Nothing about the last two months made sense. Her father's disappearance and survival, combined with her realistic dreams, were enough to make her go crazy if she pondered them long enough, but the sensation of someone watching her was beginning to take its toll.

Kallisto was turning into the school parking lot when she saw Austin Johnson standing dead center in her parking space. This baffled her. Austin was the quarterback and student body president, and she and he did not run with the same crowd. She didn't think he knew of her existence. In eighth grade, she had a huge crush on him. The schoolgirl crush had her writing his last name over and over in her journal and hoping the teacher would assign her seat next to his. With his newfound popularity in ninth grade and the ego to go with it, her crush vanished. Short dark-brown hair, sharply defined features, and brown eyes made him the most handsome guy in school, and not only was he naturally athletic; he was smart.

As she drove into her parking space, trying to avoid hitting Austin, he moved to the white line on the driver's side. Kallisto's face said it all— *What? Why?*

"Hey Kalli, how are ya this morning?"

He knows my nickname—weird!

She could only say, "Fine," while thinking, *Why are you speaking to me?*

"I was wondering if I could walk you to class."

"Why, did you lose a bet?" Kallisto knew as soon as the sentence escaped her mouth, her foot should take its place. They had never run with the same crowd, and for the life of her, she could not comprehend why he was speaking to her now. "I mean—how do you know me?" Still not the right words, she mentally rolled her eyes.

Stunned, Austin replied, "Everyone knows you're the beauty of the school. Besides, we've been going to the same school forever."

"I—" *did he say beauty?* "I just mean, well, we've never spoken to each other before."

"Well, it's never too late." His mouth turned up in a sheepish grin, and he motioned toward the side door of the school where the majority of the seniors usually entered.

Kallisto grabbed her backpack and fell into place by his side as they walked into the old brick building. The first person the two noticed as they entered was Elizabeth Cromwell, and she looked like daggers might start flying from her eyes. Elizabeth and Austin had been the school's hottest item for the last year until word had it he broke up with her at the beach two weeks ago. There had been several rumors about why, but Kallisto's favorite was that he found out she had to shave her face every morning. Juvenile—well, yes—but it did give a funny image. Finally, Kallisto came to her senses as Amanda, her best friend, came bounding up with a *what the hell* look, mirroring Kallisto's initial shock.

Kallisto glimpsed the amusement on Austin's face as he turned away from Elizabeth, who was still glaring daggers in their direction, to face her and asked, "I was wondering if you'd like to catch a movie tomorrow night?"

Both girls' mouths dropped open. Kallisto blinked several times and cocked her head to the side, ensuring she heard him correctly, then shrugged and said, "Sure."

"Great, I'll see ya in math then." Austin turned and walked to his locker, two spaces down from Elizabeth's, where she stood with one hand on her hip, glaring in their direction.

Kallisto could see the two arguing and wondered what Elizabeth had seen between her and the jock. Whatever she saw, she did not like. Elizabeth kept glancing in her direction with what was absolute hatred. Unfortunately for Elizabeth, the hate did nothing for her appearance. She wasn't eternally beautiful, but with her long strawberry blonde hair that hung in ringlets and her cherub face, she was pretty enough.

"When did you two hit it off? You failed to mention it on the phone last night," Amanda asked, confused.

Kallisto shook her head. "He was standing in my parking space when I arrived this morning; he asked to walk with me."

"You do realize Elizabeth might kill you and hide your body under a frilly pink blanket in the woods?"

"Uh—What?" Confused, Kallisto wondered—*what the hell.*

"She's crazy and seriously crazy about him. She knows you're not into pink frills, so I think she'll torture your dead body with pink ruffles."

Amanda had a different more morbid way of looking at things than most people. She and Kallisto had been best friends since Kallisto came to Hawaii. They met at the docks from where both of their fathers sailed. Amanda's father was a marine biologist and head of the science department at the local university. Kallisto's dad was a commercial fisherman. The two girls had shared a love of the sea, and they both knew what it was like not to have their fathers' home all the time. Amanda was a blonde, blue-eyed beauty with a seriously sarcastic attitude. Between Amanda's morbid outlook on all things and Kallisto's love of Greek tragedies, they forged a friendship that lasted for ten years. Amanda dated more than Kallisto and was a little worldlier with her hormone-induced body, but she was still a good friend and would do anything to help those who were incapable of helping themselves, as long as they could put up with her sarcasm.

"She wouldn't kill me, and why should I care what she thinks anyway?" that was the extent of Kallisto's defense.

Amanda reiterated. "She's crazy and vindictive! I don't care if Austin broke up with her—her claws are dug in. She's always been mean to you without any reason. Now, I'm thinking you'd damn well better watch your back."

Amanda was right. Elizabeth was mean to everyone who didn't consider her the—*all that*—she considered herself. When the bell rang, Amanda and Kallisto went their separate ways. Three of Elizabeth's friends converged on Kallisto as soon as she walked into class.

"Why were you walking with Austin this morning? You know he and Elizabeth are together." The trio stood with their arms crossed, glaring.

"I heard they broke up," Kallisto tried to be brave; confrontation was not one of her strong points.

"They will be back together by Monday," Ashley, Elizabeth's red-headed best friend of the three, stated.

The grin in Kallisto's voice was evident. "Really, since when did you become clairvoyant?" She knew it would take the three girls a minute to decipher her word choice.

Just before Ashley could retort, the teacher entered the room as the intercom with the morning news came on. Elizabeth's friends sneered at Kallisto before returning to *their* side of the room. Kallisto was confused by the morning's activities. Had she known her day would start with the best-looking guy in the school asking her out, she would have worn something a little nicer. She was sporting a white t-shirt she got online from a little Greek shop that she loved to frequent every time she went to Athens, called D.F.O. (Designed for Olympus), that said, *I Want to Start My Own Pantheon.*

Kallisto's first class for the last day of finals was English, which she loved. They were writing a historical fiction short story for their semi-final, and she had convinced her teacher to allow her to create a story about the Greek gods. Since this was not actual history, she argued that in her homeland of Greece, the legends of the gods were a profound part of their history. She had used the "I would like to bring my culture into my writing" ploy, and it worked.

She had written down her outline the evening before and could not wait to write her story. The story had to be written in two hours and be grammatically correct. Kallisto, being the decent writer she was, wrote two pages in thirty minutes. The words were flowing far easier than usual, even for her. She realized her story was eerily similar to her dream last night. Writing the outline before she fell asleep must have been what inspired her dream. She was writing about her god standing with her in a beautiful great hall, its walls adorned with gorgeous paintings. Of course, she left out the part that woke her in a frustrated sweaty state, which may be too much to ask of Mr. Andrews to grade. She read over her six-page short story and realized she had not described *her god*. She still had fifteen minutes to create an image to fit the Greek god of her dreams.

"Okay, Kallisto—think," she murmured under her breath. Just then, a chill ran down her spine as the feeling of being watched came on her again. She looked around and only saw her classmates with expressions splayed across their faces ranging from satisfaction to pure misery. Marc Lindsey was about to pull the front of his hair out as he concentrated on his paper. Kallisto could tell he had only written half a page, *Poor guy.* She shook her head, trying to dislodge the feeling of being watched, to no avail, and willed herself to come up with a worthy god image. Gradually the image of what her god would look like came to her. She began writing.

I assess his appearance. His blond hair hangs to his muscled, tanned shoulders and frames a chiseled face with deep-set crystal blue eyes circled by long black lashes. At least 6'5", he mastered a confident swagger.

Now, that should do it.

That was what she wanted her dream god to look like. While she could always remember bits and pieces of her dreams, she could never remember his face or name.

Maybe tonight, my subconscious will use this image in my dreams.

Morpheus grinned at what Kallisto wrote about her fictional character. She was very intuitive. Maybe Phantasos had been wrong; maybe subconsciously, she remembered what he looked like. After all, her description was spot on. He watched as she turned in her paper, walked to her locker to grab her math book, and headed to her next test. He sneered as a guy approached Kallisto and gestured for her to sit by him. It was not the gesture; it was the hungry look in the boy's eyes. He knew that look—it was the same one he wore. The floor in Morpheus' room began to shake, and a statue of his mother fell to the floor, breaking into pieces. His eyes went from crystal blue, to black, then red, in a split second. Jealousy and anger streaked through his veins like acid. He closed his eyes, trying to calm his rage or at least stop himself from destroying his bedroom. Unusual, he was never jealous, but he had never felt the same with the nymphs or the daemons he used to consort.

By the time he calmed down a notch, Kallisto's class had started, and she and the boy were no longer engaged in conversation. He could, however, see that the boy was still watching her. He resisted the urge to shock the young man's ass with a bolt of lightning or engulf him in flames. Tonight he would ensure the boy's dreams were anything but good. Morpheus allowed himself a half grin at the thought of the boy running through briars—naked.

He watched as the bell rang, and Kallisto and the boy walked together to her locker. Austin propped his hand against her locker above her head and leaned slightly toward her. He was talking to her, but Morpheus knew the boy's stance meant more than his conversation.

Unable to take it any longer, as any young jealous god would, he made the boy's head ring with sudden pain. Austin grabbed his forehead, letting out a small cry of agony. Morpheus laughed aloud.

⋙⟫ ⟪⋘

"Are you okay, Austin?" Kallisto asked in a concerned voice.

"No," he was clutching his head. "I think I need to go to the nurse."

"I'll go with you—you don't look so good."

Kallisto led him one hall over to the nurse's station. She told the nurse he was fine, joking and laughing when he suddenly grabbed his head in pain. The nurse looked him over, gave him two Tylenol, and sent him home.

Kallisto stayed with Austin until the Tylenol kicked in enough so he could drive himself home. "If you don't feel like going out tomorrow night, I understand."

"Are you kidding? I've been trying to get the nerve to ask you out for the last two years. It'll take more than a headache to stop me now."

Kallisto blushed. She had never had anyone say something so sweet, not in real life anyway. Her god was always kind, wonderful, and sexy, but those were dreams, not real, she reminded herself.

Kallisto went to her third-period class, economics, which was already halfway through the midterm. She gave the teacher her late pass and sat at an empty desk. Luckily, she was able to complete her test before the bell rang while the haunting watcher still loomed; it had been a feat. She went to lunch and sat in her usual spot beside Amanda. While giving Amanda the low down on what had happened to Austin and, most importantly, what he had said to her in the nurse's office, Elizabeth marched up to the two of them.

"I don't know what you think you're doing with Austin, but you'd better stop, or you'll wish you had," Elizabeth threatened.

"I told you; she'll wrap your body in a frilly pink blanket," Amanda said.

Kallisto rolled her eyes and sneered back at Elizabeth, "What I'm doing with Austin and what I plan on doing with Austin is none of your damn business."

Elizabeth glared, threw her nose in the air, turned, and stomped from their table. Amanda and Kallisto could not help but laugh. They had taken a lot off Elizabeth since seventh grade when she decided that she was the best thing walking, and they were—well—what she walked on. She had made them the butt of her jokes and sneers for the last five years, and having this little piece of glory was fantastic.

Amanda was both surprised and pleased. "Okay, Kalli, where did that come from? I mean, you don't ever stand up to people. That's usually my job. I'm not complaining 'cause now my life's complete, but you—? You have seriously pissed off Medusa. The way she looked at you—you could've turned to stone."

"I know. What if she found out that Austin was trying to get the nerve up to ask me out the whole year they were going out? And as for me taking up for myself, I've decided Elizabeth will never again make me feel like I'm not good enough." Kallisto's eyes shimmered with self-confidence.

⇜⇝ ⇜⇝

Morpheus watched as the rest of Kallisto's day played out, and she returned home. He was contemplating whether or not to make her take a nap. He needed to see her. The image of that boy leaning over Kallisto at her locker was still in his head. The glass in his hand shattered as he recalled the memory. He was just about to say the words that would make Kallisto's eyes so heavy that all she could do was sleep when his brother reentered the room.

"I thought I told you to stop watching that mortal girl."

"I—I was—just making sure she was okay."

"I hope you heed the warning I gave you earlier," Phantasos went to the orb. "I give it to you, brother; she is the most beautiful girl I have ever seen."

"Never let Aphrodite hear you say that," Morpheus smirked.

"What did you say her name was?" Phantasos asked.

"Kallisto Nalani. Why?"

"No reason. I just thought she looked familiar."

"Do not look too close big brother. I might have to zap you too."

"Too? What did you do?" Phantasos asked.

"Oh, nothing. Where have you been?" Morpheus quickly changed the subject.

"I went to see Phobetor."

"How is our lone-wolf brother doing?" Morpheus asked.

"Great for Phobetor. He never changes. He leads that dull life of safety unless he gets mad, then the nightmares he comes up with are just not right."

"You know something, Phantasos? I do not get you. You do not want me to have any fun, yet you think Phobetor is too dull."

"I think you are young and playing with fire by messing around with a mortal's dreams. Even worse, you have been bringing her here to Olympus. Mortals are not capable of processing that kind of reality."

As his brother lectured—again, Morpheus strained to keep from rolling his eyes.

"Okay, I get it. Calm down." Morpheus did get it, but he was too far gone to stop.

Chapter II

Movies

Once home, Kallisto stretched across her bed with her journal and pen and wrote about her day, reeling from its strange events. She first tried rewriting the description of the Greek god she came up with in English. Closing her eyes, she tried to see the man in her mind as she had put him on paper, to no avail. Instead, she opened her eyes and wrote about Austin and how mad Elizabeth was—she couldn't help but grin. Kallisto had just finished her journal entry and homework when her mother called for her to help unload the groceries.

She passed her mom, who carried several bags, through the garage and into the kitchen. Kallisto's mother, Thia, was beautiful. Her hair was a little lighter than Kallisto's, and her eyes were blue instead of Kallisto's aqua-green, but their facial features were virtually the same. Aside from the minor differences, they looked much like sisters. The years had been kind to her mother—she didn't look a day over twenty-seven. Whenever she introduced Kallisto to people as her daughter, their reaction was always the same, "You don't look old enough to have a daughter her age." "You look like sisters instead of mother and daughter." "What's your secret?"

As she pulled groceries from the minivan, a hand grabbed her shoulder. Startled, Kallisto gasped, "Damn it, Amanda, you scared me. Don't you know not to sneak up on someone who had their life threatened by a scorned, crazed teenage girl?

Laughing, Amanda grabbed two grocery bags, "Sorry, didn't mean to scare ya, but you have to admit—that was funny."

"For you, maybe. I've been having this weird feeling that someone's watching me. It comes and goes," Kallisto led the way through the garage to the kitchen. "I even checked my backseat twice on my way to school this morning. I think

I'm losing it." Kallisto gave a half laugh. "You almost gave me a heart attack before I realized it was you."

"Well, from the sound of it, Austin's been eyeing you for some time," Amanda gave her a slight bump with her hip.

"Austin, who?" Thia asked, very interested.

Amanda grinned mischievously at the invitation to tell Kallisto's mom the story. Kallisto, not amused, rolled her eyes and put the cheese in the refrigerator. The three women spent the next ten minutes putting the groceries away as Amanda made sure she embarrassed Kallisto by giving her mother all the details of her daughter's new admirer. Thia's smile widened at Amanda's animated antics as she told of Elizabeth's jealous tirade in the lunchroom.

"Well, honey, it sounds like someone is finally showing appreciation for your kindness and beauty," Thia said teasingly. "I knew it would happen sooner or later. I was hoping it would be later—maybe—let's say, after college."

"Thanks for the embarrassment," Kallisto chided Amanda once upstairs in her room. Actually, Amanda had saved her from having to tell her parents about her date. She was dreading the look on her father's face. After all, he'd made it midway through Kallisto's senior year of high school, never having to worry about young men groping his daughter. He couldn't stand the thought of her dating. Why he was so worried, Kallisto didn't know.

"I knew you'd be worried about telling them, so I thought I would come over and help you out. Besides, we could chill out, paint our nails, and watch a chick flick," Amanda said sheepishly. "What about it?"

"Sounds good to me. Let's go to *Flicks* for a movie." Flicks was a novelty movie and vinyl record shop that was all the rage. Being the shop was new, she was able to talk her dad into purchasing a DVD player a couple of weeks prior. This would be their second time using it. Kallisto grabbed her purse and told her mom of their plans as the two girls ran out the door and hopped in Amanda's car.

Once at *Flicks*, Amanda jumped out of the driver's seat and ran in the opposite direction. Kallisto rolled her eyes as she watched her cross the parking lot to a group of guys from school, most of which Kallisto didn't know very well.

"I'll meet you inside," Kallisto yelled after Amanda. Amanda, unlike Kallisto, had no reservations about speaking with the opposite sex, even while they stood together in a cluster.

Kallisto moved up and down the aisles reading the movie cases when the feeling of being watched came over her—again. Thinking it must be Amanda, she turned around and bumped into a guy who had his back to her as he read the movie titles on the other side of the aisle. She felt dizzy, and a warm tingle spread over her when her body brushed his. The sudden smell of lavender permeated the atmosphere around them.

"Sorry, excuse me," Kallisto said.

"No problem," the man answered in a deep, accented voice, still eyeing the movies.

Those two words caused a chill to travel down her spine and across her ribs. She followed him, pretending to read the movie cases. They made it down two more aisles when she noticed his long, blond hair and incredible height. *It couldn't be.* Just then, Amanda came bounding up, beaming with excitement.

"Michael Wells just asked me out for tomorrow night." Michael had been on her "top ten guys I must date before the end of high school" checklist. In fact, he was one of only three left to check off.

"That's great. Now, who's left on your list?" Kallisto asked, distracted. She rose on her tiptoes to peer over the movie stands, but he was gone, and so was the feeling.

"Who are you looking for?" Amanda asked. "I just told you some kick-ass news, and you aren't listening."

"I'm sorry, I just thought I saw someone I know, that's all." Kallisto grabbed the movie, *How to Lose a Guy in Ten Days,* "What about this one?" She hoped to distract Amanda from her interrogation since the film showcased her favorite actor, Matthew McConaughey.

Amanda eyed the case, "Oh, I love that one! Let's get it."

Kallisto let out the air filling her cheeks for two seconds before Amanda responded. She did not want to try and explain to her best friend that she thought she just saw the "Greek god" from her dreams for the last two months. Not to mention that she didn't actually see the stranger's face, but just had an unusual feeling when she bumped into him, and he smelled familiar, and he made her knees buckle with his voice; and oh yes, she also thought he was her "invisible stalker." Nope—that would make her sound absolutely crazy.

They paid for their movie, and before they left, Kallisto made one last scan around the store to see if her "Greek god" was still there. He was not. *Yup, I've snapped,* she thought.

Kallisto knew her house was a home away from home for Amanda, so she sent Amanda to put the popcorn in the microwave while she started their movie. Kallisto's father came into the TV room agitated. He was a very handsome man who, at forty-one, had the look of a man ten years younger. The only thing that let on he was not in his early thirties was the slight gray peppered throughout his hair. Mom said it made him appear distinguished. His hair had always been jet-black up until he turned forty. It was then the twigs of gray began to show. His eyes were light brown, and his black eyebrows were full, making his eyes appear deep-set. A sharp jawline and a continuous five o'clock shadow graced his face.

"So Kallisto, your mother tells me you have a date with Austin Johnson tomorrow night. Where's he planning on taking you?" Her father cut right to the chase. Kallisto stiffened at his question, knowing he would only consider the worst no matter what she said.

"He asked me to a movie Dad. No need to get worried. He seems to be a nice guy," Kallisto was trying to defuse any situation that might set her father off into a speech about how boys are after only one thing. That was a talk he had given her when she turned sixteen. Thankful he never went into what the "one thing" was. He had just wanted to make sure she knew what "slime balls" boys could be.

"Yeah, well, your curfew is 11:00," he said as he put a hand up to advise against any protest. "I am being generous. I wanted it to be 9:30, but your mother thought I was being absurd, so she talked me into 11:00. It's against my better judgment, so don't argue about it, or I'll go back to 9:30, my original plan."

Opened mouth as if about to say something, Kallisto just nodded. She knew better than to argue with her father, even though all her friends stayed out until midnight or after.

"Yes, sir."

As Amanda came in from the other side, her father walked from the room. "Was that your father, I heard?" Amanda's face showed concern.

"Yes, he just wanted to let me know my curfew tomorrow night was eleven. He said that he was going to make it 9:30, but mom stopped him."

"That's okay. If you want, we could double and come in early. That way, Austin assumes we have other plans and not that you have an overprotective dad." Amanda always knew what to say or do to make things easier for her.

"That sounds great; let me call Austin and see if it's okay with him." Kallisto grabbed her cell phone and looked up Austin's number. She turned the volume on the television down since the looping menu for the movie was playing, and she could barely hear.

After only two rings, Austin answered. He sounded a little disappointed but agreeable. They only talked for a couple of minutes to pin down the logistics. Once she gave Amanda the information, Amanda called Michael. He would meet her and Amanda at her house at six and then swing by Michael's to pick him up.

The two girls watched the movie, ate popcorn, and painted each other's fingernails and toenails. Kallisto told Amanda about waking up sweating and very frustrated from her dream the night before.

"My dreams are so real lately. I can smell the fragrances from my dreams cling to my body and my room," Kallisto admitted.

"You just need more excitement in your life. All you do is read about ancient Greece and its legends. You need to learn to live in the 21st century," Amanda's teasing was always the same.

"Hey, don't knock it," Kallisto said in mock defense. "The gods know how to live. I've learned more about life through their stories than I'm willing to find out on my own or that my dad will let me."

"It's gone too far if you're "trying" to have fun in your dreams, and you wake up frustrated and covered in sweat," Amanda giggled.

Kallisto stuck out her tongue. "Let's hit the hay; I'm tired." Grinning and wiggling her eyebrows, she added, "I didn't get much sleep last night."

Amanda rolled her eyes and followed Kallisto upstairs, where the girls took turns taking off their make-up and putting on their pajamas. Kallisto had a twin bed, so her mother set up an air mattress for Amanda. Depending on whose house they were crashing at, the other would sleep on an inflatable mattress on the floor. This was how they spent at least one night a weekend for the last ten years.

❧⟫⟫⟫ ⟪⟪⟪❧

Morpheus went to his orb to check on Kallisto. He decided to overlook his brother's suggestion to stay away from the mortal, or as he liked to call her, his "earthly goddess." Through the orb, he could tell the two girls were about asleep. Once sleep took them, he would go into Kallisto's bedroom and say a few words in Amanda's ear to keep her asleep when he took Kallisto. After all, to wake up and your friend nowhere to be found would be a shocker. Morpheus had forced Amanda into deep sleep several times over the last two months. She was always around at some point, and he would not miss time with Kallisto if he could help it.

Morpheus had just seen her; after all, where else would a dream god go to pick out a movie? Knowing she must have felt the sting of electricity when she brushed against him, he dared not look at her, fearing she would link him to her short story. Even though he had touched her hundreds of times on Olympus and in her "dreams," she had thought those encounters were just dreams. This time their touch was in her realm of reality; her awareness was spiked by being fully in one domain, not in between. He could feel her eagerness pulse through her as she followed him from one aisle to another.

Waiting for sleep to take Kallisto and Amanda, he decided to make a couple of "dream calls." Life cannot be all fun. After all, even dream gods must do their duty.

Morpheus closed his eyes and listened for those who needed his help or, *wait a minute...* an evil grin spread across his face. Suddenly he remembered the promise he had made to himself to call on a certain teenage boy, one who had been leaning a little too close. He closed his eyes once more and envisioned the boy's face. As he did, he received the confirmation of sleep he needed in order to join the young man in his dreams.

Making sure to stay in the shadows, Morpheus entered Austin's dream state. The boy was dreaming of football and cheerleaders. Morpheus rolled his eyes. *Now for some fun!*

Abruptly, Austin's predictable dream became nightmarish. He stood in a dense forest surrounded by leafless trees and damp fog with the musty odor of rotted leaves and moss drifting up from the forest floor. The full moon's white face shone through the bare limbs, casting shadows around him. He stood still, afraid to move, sensing he wasn't alone. Off in the distance, a ghostly howl broke the silence. Something furry crawled over his bare foot, but he was still too terrified to move. Then a deep voice rang out above the howling creature in the distance.

"Stay away from her."

Morpheus's eyes glowed a crimson red out from the trees. Shaking, Austin hit the ground and curled up, lying on his side, knees to chest and head bent, covered with his arms. He jerked awake still in the same fetal position as he had been in the forest, with sweat clinging to his body and pains surging through his head as they had in school. He could still smell decayed leaves and moss and looked around his dark bedroom, afraid of what he would see. *Nothing!* Austin sighed with relief, seeing his room as he had left it. The dream was over—except for the lingering smell of decay.

Through his orb, Morpheus watched Austin's confusion. He thought Austin would think twice before touching Kallisto. At least, he hoped he would; he did not want to have to escalate his warnings. Morpheus was not a god to be messed with. Not even the gods of Olympus, aside from Zeus and The Fates, would ever dare to cross him. He was the god who controlled all *types* of dreams, and he carried a power no other Oneiroi had, the ability to render a god powerless. Mortals could be driven mad over time with just the right sort of dream, but a god could be rendered powerless while in their dream state, and then they could be tortured. No god ever wanted to be without their powers, so they made it a practice never to anger Morpheus.

CHAPTER III

WATERFALL

The orb showed Kallisto awake but sleepily grinning at her ceiling. Morpheus had a few choices. Go to her in real form while she was awake—*probably not the smartest move*. Make her sleep, then bring her to Olympus—his favorite idea since it would be the fastest, or he could wait for natural sleep to consume her. In the end, he decided to wait for her natural sleep since it was the safest. Making a mortal repeatedly fall asleep could mean they depend on an unnatural method to sleep or wake. Worse, when a person is pulled from their realm of consciousness to another under the disguise of rest, the mind and body continue to contradict each other, causing a mental breakdown. The human mind was not designed to take excessive tampering. That's why the sleep gods were never to stay with someone past what was considered necessary. Kallisto's father had been home for the best part of seven weeks, which meant Morpheus had interfered seven weeks more than was necessary. He could tell Kallisto's energy was waning, but she seemed mentally strong and was sure she would continue to be.

Kallisto stared at her ceiling and thought about the day's events. She had a "real" date for the first time and was confident in her test-taking, especially on her English paper. Thinking of the English paper caused her mind to wander, and a smile spread across her face as she thought about the description she came up with for the god in her story. For some reason, this time, the image was vivid. Toying with her description, she mentally manifested an image of him lying on a blanket by a beautiful waterfall. She memorized that image, with his blond hair and crystal blue eyes, secured the well-developed figure into her head, and drifted to sleep.

Morpheus felt the instant Kallisto fell asleep. With a grin, he flashed himself into her bedroom. Quietly he walked over to Amanda, where she snored lightly on an air mattress wrapped in the gold blanket. He leaned down to brush the hair from her ear, and she stirred as his hand grazed her cheek. He whispered the few words placing her in a deeper slumber. This was a dream god's tool to help someone in desperate need of healing, the kind needed to heal a person from physical or mental trauma, but only he and his brother, Phobetor, could actually heal a dreamer while they slept. Healing sleep could only be used on mortals; gods were immune to this Oneiroi ability. As the words left his lips, he could see Amanda's body relax beyond that of normal rest. He entered her mind and made sure she was okay. Before she could wake, the spell would have to be removed.

Morpheus pulled from Amanda's dreamless state and turned to Kallisto, marveling at her beauty. *Aphrodite has nothing on you.* He stood over her and knew he had entered heaven, and with a touch to her hand, they were both on Mount Olympus.

Kallisto woke and sat up on the thick grass beside the pool below the towering waterfall. She had become acquainted with her new location since she visited it quite often. A tall, elegant doe with her spotted fawn drank from the flowing blue stream just down from the pool where water cascaded from the cliff.

I'm alone.

She stood and went to sit on the ancient rocks by the cool water. The giant hardwoods' leaves blew gently in the wind. Treeless spots in the distance where thick grass and wildflowers grew brought back memories she and her god had shared. She could write about this place and never truly capture on paper what she saw with her eyes.

"Kallisto, I was hoping to see you today." It was "her" Greek god. "You look beautiful."

Kallisto worried about what she might be wearing. To her relief, she wore a white peplos trimmed in gold piping with golden olive leaf clips on the shoulders holding it together. She stood up and ran into his arms.

"I'm sorry I left you the last time—well, I'm sure as— frustrated as I was," Kallisto apologized with a flush.

Morpheus just smiled as she stumbled over her words. She was trying to apologize for having him worked up, and she could tell he was amused when she admitted to her own frustrations.

"I mean," Kallisto continued, "I didn't mean to leave in the middle—well, in such haste."

"Yes, you did leave me—frustrated, but it was probably for the best. After all, you should keep your virtue intact," his crooked grin made her cheeks redder.

He took her hand and led her to the water. "Would you like to swim with me?"

"Are you going to behave yourself?" Kallisto grinned.

"Probably not."

She took his large, tanned hand and walked to the spot where the ground gave easy access to the pool of water below the falls. This was Kallisto's favorite place on Olympus. It was where her first dream of Morpheus took place. The first time was amazing and surreal. Her dream became even more awesome when he told her she was on Mount Olympus. Morpheus removed everything except his undergarment and dove headfirst into the pool. Kallisto watched how gorgeous the man was, tanned and incredibly tall, with hard lean muscles. Her heart skipped a beat when he broke the surface and shook the water from his hair. His signature devilish half grin and a motion of his head beckoned her to join him.

Kallisto followed suit, thankful she had on undergarments. She heard Morpheus' audible intake of breath when she removed the peplos revealing her lacy bra and panties.

She returned his flirtatious grin with a very seductive one of her own. Then, she, too, dove headfirst into the water. She surfaced to find him beside her. Once she had taken a couple of breaths, Morpheus grabbed her by the waist, pressed her against his rippled body, and stared deep into her beautiful aqua eyes.

"I missed you my *dea femminile.*"

"I missed you too," Kallisto said, loving his deep-set eyes looking into hers and how his hands felt sliding over her body. "You know it's very hard to be virtuous when you look at me that way."

Morpheus' body twitched, "Who says I want you virtuous?"

Kallisto knew better than that, but his statement, coupled with his thick Greek accent, made a chill run through her anyway. *Who knew words could affect someone so?* After all, he was the one who always put a stop to their most heated moments.

"Did you make me wake up early this morning?"

"I knew you would be upset had we *explored our horizons* any further," he answered.

"I'd be okay; after all, I was only dreaming. Why she held onto her virginity in her dreams was beyond her. *If I can't consciously allow myself to be sated—why not subconsciously.*

"Whoever said you were dreaming?" Before she could reply, he captured her lips with his.

"You know, even if I wasn't dreaming, I wouldn't mind my 'virtue' becoming a little tarnished," Kallisto's lips brushed his as she spoke.

Morpheus playfully splashed her with water, and she returned in kind. He suddenly stopped to watch as Kallisto retreated, swimming to the cascading water, and stood up, letting it consume her. She was the most stunning creature he had ever laid his eyes on. The water running over her body was just about as much as he could take. He knew he could never let her go. To calm himself, Morpheus extracted himself from the pool. He knew she would regret their being together, especially if and when she realized her dreams were real.

He manifested two white terrycloth towels. Explanation of his abilities was never necessary; after all, Kallisto thought she was dreaming. He decided to give himself a loose, long-sleeved button-up and jeans instead of the robes he had been wearing. For Kallisto, he supplied new hot pink undergarments and left them waiting for her on the rocks. *Yes, being a god has its advantages.*

Not taking his eyes from Kallisto, he watched as she swam over to the edge and walked out of the pool. Morpheus came up behind her and wrapped her in one of the towels.

"What are you thinking, my *dea femminile*?" Morpheus whispered in her ear as he continued to hold her.

"I'm letting my senses take in this peaceful place. There's something so calming about the water falling and hitting the pool, the birds singing, and the scents of lavender and honeysuckle hanging in the air. I wish I could stay here with you forever."

"I, too, wish we could stay together," Morpheus whispered as he claimed her mouth again.

"No!" she protested, eyes still shut as he pulled away. "You don't have to stop."

"Believe me, I do." Morpheus bit his lower lip, trying to calm down as he took two steps back, willing his body to obey the command from his brain instead of the one from his heart.

"I have given you dry clothes," he pointed to the hot pink bra and panties he had conjured moments before. "I hope you like them—I do." He winked. "Go behind the rocks and change. I promise I will not look."

⤜⤜⤜ ⤛⤛⤛

Kallisto could have sworn he said, "This time," under his breath. With clothes in hand, she made her way behind the rocks, still contemplating what she thought were his whispered words.

"No," Kallisto shook her head, realization dawning on her. "Can't be."

She slipped on the clothes, which felt magnificent against her body; soft warmth dispelled the chill from the cool water. After coming from behind her changing area, the two walked hand and hand the short distance to the meadow, where their picnic blanket and basket waited for them. The wildflowers splayed over the ground like a kaleidoscope scattered its contents as far as the eye could see. As they sat there, he entwined his fingers with hers, and she closed her eyes, trying again to immerse herself in the ambiance.

"Morpheus," Kallisto took on a more serious tone.

"Yes?"

"I want this to be real. I feel so safe and whole in your arms. What if I was never to wake up? Could I stay with you?"

Alarm and regret spiked through him. *She cannot think this way.* She was not sleeping. This was reality. She just did not know it. He wanted to tell her, but doing so would mean dooming himself to torture, something Hades enjoyed doing whenever a god broke the rules. Even though Hades was accommodating to his dilemma before, he was unlikely to turn down the enticement of inflicting pain now. Also, if she stayed, her parents would think she had been abducted or had run away—*no—I have to think of something.*

"Kallisto, I would like nothing more than for us to stay together, but the reality is waiting." This was not a lie. He was a god, and she a mortal—that was reality as much as he wanted it to be otherwise.

"I know. Why can't I remember what you look like when I wake up? I can smell you on my skin but can't remember your face."

Instead of answering her question, he tapped her temple, "You are trying too hard. I am always here."

"Maybe so; I just want to remember, that's all."

Morpheus placed a grape between his exceptionally white teeth, half in his mouth and half out. He leaned down to Kallisto's mouth, and she bit into her half of the grape, momentarily removing all conversation about her inability to remember his face, especially as his hand ran up the side of her body, resting itself in the curve of her waist. Reluctantly, he pulled back again before having to stop the encounter altogether.

"You were a little worried about your tests last night. How did they go?"

"I think I did well. Something happened in English, though, but for the life of me, I can't remember what." Puzzled, Kallisto leaned back and sat on her knees. "I needed to remember something, to see it for myself—but I don't remember what that something was," she squinted trying,g to recall.

Guilt engulfed Morpheus, knowing it was his tampering that caused her confusion. It caused The Fates to block her from connecting the fictional god of her short story and the god from her dreams as one and the same. Oneiroi were meant only to be dreams. The rules of the Oneiroi were simple. Help the dreamer stay in the shadows as much as possible; your face will never be remembered. Mortals could only understand one reality, one realm, and one dimension of time—the one in which they lived.

These ancient rules were The Fates' way of keeping mortals balanced. Morpheus knew Phantasos was right; she was on the verge of a new realm of reality, which mortals should not enter.

"What else happened today?" Morpheus tried to distract her, plus he wanted to know what was up with the Austin boy.

"Well, I almost feel guilty."

"Why would you feel guilty?" He knew what was coming.

"I have a date tomorrow night with this guy from school," she blushed.

Morpheus' jaw worked as he ground his back teeth. He inhaled sharply, "You do?"

"I actually thought about telling him I was taken," she laughed at the idea.

He knew he had no right to be angry or jealous, but he didn't seem to be able to help himself. "Why did you not?"

Kallisto was stunned, "Well, it's not like I can cheat on a dream, man, can I?"

He gave a low hiss, "I suppose not."

"Morpheus, I'm in love with you, my *dream man*, and that's not a cliché either. I have fallen in love with a man that I dream about every night, not just any man; no, I had to go and make him a Greek god," Kallisto rambled anxiously.

"Shhh, all is okay. You go and have fun with your mortal date," he stood up and pulled her to her feet. "I will visit less often and let you have a normal life." He hugged her tight and kissed her on the nose, fading before Kallisto could protest.

⇝⇝⇝ ⇜⇜⇜

Kallisto woke crying, "No, don't go—please don't leave."

"Kallisto, are you okay?" Kallisto's verbal cries and Morpheus' release of the spell woke Amanda.

"Yeah, I had a bad dream, that's all," Kallisto choked.

"Cheer up! We have dates tonight," Amanda grinned and stretched, "I had the best sleep. You know somethin'—I always sleep better when we have our girl's nights. I'm goin' to put on some coffee. You want some?" Amanda darted out the door before Kallisto had time to answer.

Kallisto would never understand how Amanda was always so cheery first thing in the morning. She sat up in bed, looked around at her Greek-inspired bedroom, and tried very hard to recall her dream. She could smell the familiar honeysuckle and lavender on her skin, and her mouth tasted of him, but specifics were not coming to her. Strange, she always remembered her dreams, maybe not his face, but usually the dream itself. Why couldn't she remember the one that had her crying so loud she woke Amanda? She padded into the bathroom and turned on the shower waiting for the hot water to make its way up the pipes. Finally, she was without the feeling of spying eyes. When her reflection showed a hot pink lacey bra and a pair of lacey hot pink panties to match, her blood ran cold. She didn't own any hot pink lingerie.

"What the—," and then she remembered.

"Damn it, Phantasos, where are you?" Morpheus beckoned his brother.

"What has you pissed off this time?" Phantasos appeared in front of Morpheus wearing a long white robe open with a pair of baggy white linen pants, no shirt. Morpheus knew he had interrupted his brother's leisure time.

"I am going to ask Zeus if I can go to earth for a while," Morpheus stated.

"What?" His brother exclaimed.

"I am going to Kallisto." Morpheus held up a hand, stopping his brother's protest. "I know it can't be forever, but I have to let her know I'm real. I know she senses it. The Fates are fighting her instincts to keep her safe, but I feel she would be okay with the truth."

"It is out of the question. You are not allowed to tell her anything." Phantasos scolded.

"I know—believe me, I know, but I also believe she will figure everything out on her own in time. I truly believe she is strong enough to handle the reality of things. She half believes in the legends anyway."

"Why now—why the hurry?" Phantasos asked.

"There is a mortal who is infatuated with her," Morpheus paced. "I refuse to watch her fall for anyone else. I am going to make a deal with Zeus."

"And when he refuses your deal, what then?" Phantasos questioned.

"I will ask Hades."

"Are you serious?" Phantasos looked stunned. "You know what it is to make a deal with Hades? He will have your soul."

"Well, let us hope the big guy takes pity on me and gives me the deal of a lifetime."

"If you are so dead set on this, why did you summon me? It does not look like I can talk sense into you. I know how you are."

"I was wondering if you would do me a favor?" Morpheus's eyes were pleading. After all, his brother was a lost dream god, so this was a big ask. "Will you take over my dream duties until I return?"

"What? You know better than to ask such a thing of me," Phantasos protested.

"Please," Morpheus begged. "I have a better chance with Zeus if I tell him my duties are covered. Besides, you are the only one I trust with my mortals."

"I cannot, and you know why," Phantasos felt pulled by his guilt over Marissa and the need to help his little brother.

"I need someone I can trust to pull me back if I cannot make myself leave," Morpheus was still pleading. "I trust you to help me, no one else. At least think about it."

"I will think about it but do not get your hopes up. You may want to ask Phobetor." Phantasos shook his head in disbelief.

Amused, Morpheus countered, "You have to be kidding. I do not want the mortals to be bored to death; besides, he does not have the—influence to pull me back if need be."

"I said I will think about it. That is all I am willing to give you at this moment," Phantasos faded.

Chapter IV

Crazy

Kallisto finished her shower and returned to her room, where Amanda was waiting with two warm cups of java.

"What does my room smell like to you? I know that's a strange question, but just humor me."

Sniffing the air, Amanda answered, "Coffee, lavender, and a sweet, flowery scent, sort of like—honeysuckle. Why?"

Kallisto's eyes widened, "What did you say?" She asked again.

"I smell coffee, lavender, and honeysuckle. It must be your lotion."

Kallisto slowly shook her head, "Nope. I left my lotion at your house last weekend, besides it's raspberry and vanilla. This is going to sound crazy, but I woke up this morning wearing a bra and panties given to me in my dream last night," mostly to herself, she said, "and you can smell it too." Realization was beginning to set in. "He's real." With that, she sat on her bed wide-eyed and began trembling.

"Are you okay, Kalli?"

"I've gone crazy." Kallisto kept repeating the words as Amanda sat on the bed beside her and wrapped one arm around her best friend, trying to lend comfort the best she could, not understanding what was happening.

Tears trickled down Kallisto's face. She knew Amanda must think her crazy; after all, she felt like she was. She had never held anything back from her best friend except this, the craziness since her dad returned. She wiped her eyes with the sleeve of her bathrobe, took a deep breath, and gave Amanda the rundown of madness that had plagued her for the last two months. She began with the dream of the storm hitting her father's fishing boat and ended with the dream she had just had, driving home the fact she was wearing clothes she hadn't owned before she went to bed. She talked to Amanda for over two hours, thankful her friend listened intently without question nor the slightest expression. Once she fully explained all the oddities of the last couple of months, she stopped and watched Amanda contemplate it all.

With downcast eyes, Kallisto said, "I know you think I'm crazy. Amanda—I think I'm crazy. Sometimes I remember things, and sometimes I don't. I'm not explaining it right."

"Why would I think that? Is it a little hard to swallow?—Well, yes." Then, out of nowhere, she smiled, "I guess it's good you have a certifiable nut for a best friend who believes in all things supernatural."

Kallisto hugged Amanda, "I need to figure this out. Could I have been around someone who could've hypnotized or drugged me?"

"I prefer to think you have a real honest-to-goodness Greek god myself," Amanda wiggled her brows.

"But how—and why can't I place his face?" Kallisto sighed, then shrugged.

"Maybe he's ugly," Amanda grinned, and Kallisto playfully stuck out her tongue.

Kallisto remembered, "I wrote about a Greek god in my short story yesterday. Maybe he looks like him. He was the vision I fell asleep thinking about."

"So, you're sticking to the Greek god theory?" Amanda grinned devilishly.

"You're incorrigible," Kallisto rolled her eyes. "All I know is that we both can't smell the same odors from *my* dream, my father cannot just show up several hundred miles further north than he was supposed to be, and I can't just conjure new lingerie out of the air. Not to mention the feeling of being watched all the time."

"You're the authority on Greek gods and legends," teasing Amanda continued, "and sounds like you'd be even more of an expert if you had—carnal knowledge."

"Amanda, honestly, is that all you ever think about?" Kallisto reprimanded. Both girls broke into laughter. "But what if he's a crazed lunatic that has me under some kind of hypnotic trance?"

"So, you believe some crazed lunatic brought your father back from gods knows where?" Amanda debated. "Highly unlikely, and I seriously doubt a crazed lunatic would have that good of taste in lingerie."

"But it's so outrageous, and my brain's in overdrive. Maybe honeysuckle and lavender are natural aromas from—" spotting the object by her pillow stopped her mid-sentence.

"From—?" Amanda prodded and followed Kallisto's eyes. "What is that next to your pillow?"

Kallisto stood up, walked to the other end of her four-poster bed, and picked up a beautiful pink wildflower. "Do you see a flower in my hand?"

Amanda laughed, "Well, that does it. If you're crazy, then we're mutually crazy—literally, we're seeing and smelling the same illusions."

Kallisto sat back on her bed with the flower clutched to her chest. "This is all so weird. I have spent my entire life wanting to believe in the mythological tales my grandmother used to spend hours telling me. Now, I—" Kallisto's voice cracked, and her aqua eyes filled with tears. She could not finish.

"Kalli, listen to yourself. Aren't you the one who's always saying that every legend is rooted in something real? Who's to say the renowned legends of the Greek gods aren't real?" Amanda sounded more convinced than Kallisto that Greek gods existed.

"Okay, say you're right, then why would a 'Greek god' come to me in my dreams?" Kallisto countered.

Amanda raised one eyebrow. "Have you ever looked in a mirror with your eyes open? Don't you see the people whispering and pointing when you walk by? Oh, or my favorite, when you walk into a restaurant, or anywhere for that matter, everyone goes quiet and stares at you? Just a little heads-up, Kalli, it's not because you have a booger in your nose. You're the epitome of grace and beauty." Amanda had been doing a great job containing the sarcasm, but sometimes it took a smartass to prove a point.

Kallisto scoffed. "Then why haven't I ever had a date?"

"Because guys are scared of you."

Kallisto's eyebrows shot up, "Thanks a lot.

"I mean, they're intimidated by your beauty, and when they become acquainted with you, you become even more intimidating because that beauty goes beyond skin deep." Amanda was trying to be kind; being the queen of cynicism, she was doing very well.

Kallisto didn't have a reply to that. She didn't see herself the way her friend had just described her. Throughout life, she had always seen herself as somewhat of an outsider. She loved fantasy and had a strong sense of family. She was a helpless romantic living in, as her mother always told her, the wrong century, possibly the wrong realm. Kallisto was most happy while in Greece. There she felt truly at home.

Finally, she spoke, breaking the silence. "Things like this," she waved her arms to acknowledge everything happening, "do not take place in real life."

"Maybe, but real life is relative. If you never experience *something*, that *something* doesn't occur to you. That doesn't mean it doesn't take place for others." Amanda stated.

"You sound like an oracle," Kallisto laughed.

"That's my point right there. What seventeen-year-old girl refers to someone as sounding like an oracle? I bet only a handful of the senior girls know what an oracle is." Amanda did make a valid point.

"Yeah, point taken; I read way too much mythology," Kallisto sighed with the flower still clutched to her chest.

"And you say I'm incorrigible," Amanda shook her head.

For the next three hours, the two girls played with the idea of there actually being a Greek Pantheon led by the all-powerful Zeus, who reigned on Mount Olympus, where he and the other gods led lives rivaling today's reality shows.

As Amanda started out the door on her way home to get ready for their double date, she turned, grinned, and asked, "Will you make a mental note to ask your *Greek god* if he has a brother, cousin, or friend in need of company? I could add them to my list."

Kallisto laughed and agreed to do so before she closed the garage door. She then let out a heavy breath and closed her eyes. Standing in the garage, she decided she would not think about the strange happenings in her life until after her first date, which would start in about four short hours.

She ran upstairs and made her bed, placing all the pillows just right. Then she looked around at the mess she and Amanda had made while playing with hairstyles they thought would look good when they dined with the gods. Not at all productive, but it had been a lot of fun and cheered Kallisto up. Amanda had a way of making Kallisto feel better when she was down and out; that was one of the many things that made them best friends.

Always well organized, Kallisto knew what she would wear within five minutes of accepting Austin's invitation. She would wear a short well-fitted black dress with a v-neck low enough that she knew she needed to be out the door before her father got home. The little black dress was casual enough to wear to a movie or dressy enough to wear to a fine restaurant; it depended on the shoes. She had kept her hair up, the last way Amanda had fixed it, loosely with ringlets hanging down in precise intervals around her face with pearl picks placed throughout to add a little spark to her onyx hair. Amanda had also applied her makeup; she had to confess—she looked first-class.

As she waited for time to pass, she decided to write her day's events down in her journal. She made sure to include every detail of her last night's dream, which she could conjure anyway. She mostly remembered his closeness, what the waterfall and meadow looked like more than his appearance, and what their conversation fully entailed. She decided to take a nap when she had written as much as she could think to put down. As she walked over and sat on top of her bed, she realized she had not had the feeling of someone watching her all day. That had been the longest she had gone in two months without the ominous feeling creeping up on her, sometimes at the most inopportune time, like while she climbed in her shower.

Morpheus gave Phantasos a couple of hours before flashing to his home on the hill next to Aphrodite's mansion. He then proceeded to flash from Phantasos' front door to the great hall where his brother sat on a large black leather sofa playing video games. Even the gods enjoyed technology from the mortal world.

His brother didn't look up but knew who had just entered his home.

"I've thought about this, and I'm going to do it for only one reason and with a few conditions."

Simultaneously, relief and worry crossed Morpheus' face, "What are the conditions?"

"Let me give you my reason first," Phantasos beckoned Morpheus to sit on the massive couch. "I do not want you going to Hades. And I believe Zeus will be more apt to help if your dreamers are covered. As far as the conditions...well, they are more like rules. First, you can only stay for two months, no more; second, you cannot acquire carnal knowledge of this mortal woman.

"What!" Morpheus interrupted loudly.

"Third," Phantasos continued as if not interrupted, "you cannot tell her who you are or what you are unless—" he held up his hand to Morpheus, stopping another interruption, "she asks you directly if you are Morpheus, the Greek god.

"How the hell did you come up with such outrageous conditions?" Morpheus asked in outrage.

"The Fates, little brother, The Fates—ask no more questions; these are the rules if you wish to go. Well, Zeus may have more rules to go with these three. I will cover for you only if you agree to the rules."

"No carnal knowledge?" Morpheus gave his brother a pleading look.

Morpheus knew he had no other choice and knew there was no arguing with The Fates Three. If he was going to be with Kallisto for more than a few hours at a time and be in a more realistic atmosphere for her, he needed to make these rules work. He had heard tales of the gods bringing mortals to live on Olympus, but those were accounts told to young gods like fairytales were to mortal children. Morpheus planned to explore this possibility and make it happen for him and Kallisto.

Swallowing hard before his reply Morpheus said, "I will do what I must, brother; thank you for helping me. I know you think I am foolish, but I prefer to think of myself as passionate."

"When will you petition Zeus for the privilege to go to the mortal realm for more than the usual hour or so?"

"I plan to go in the morning. I have asked for an audience with him first thing. I only hope he wakes in a good mood." Morpheus had devils in his eyes when he then asked, "What would you say to a little venture to make sure your little brother meets with a well-rested god in the morning?"

"HELL NO! Are you completely mad?" Phantasos exclaimed. "Do not answer that. I already know the answer. I will not enter Zeus's dream state to ensure your meeting with him goes well. I suggest if you are that worried, you should ask The Fates if they can give you a heads up on when the best time for you to meet with the big guy is. He gestured with his finger out the window toward Zeus's marble mansion that towered over everything.

"You cannot blame a guy for trying." Morpheus shrugged innocently.

"Go home, Morpheus," Phantasos said. "But do not depart without coming back to see me if he gives you the go-ahead."

"Sure." Morpheus turned serious, "Thank you, Phantasos." The look he gave his brother was of great appreciation. He turned on his heel and flashed himself back to his bedchamber mid-stride.

He needed a plan. How would he get close to Kallisto, become someone she could trust, and make her fall in love with him as a man, not a god? He could hardly walk up to her, lay a searing kiss on her perfectly formed lips, and tell her that he was the Greek god of her dreams. That sounded like one of the world's most sordid pick-up lines. He laughed as he conjured images in his head of Kallisto slapping him. No, he would formulate a plan, and with luck, one even The Fates might like. Morpheus sat down and racked his brain as he tried to devise a foolproof plan of action. He could not have her perceive him as a stalker. He needed to appeal to her on a level that would not seem invasive or just plain strange, and he needed a place to live. Not having gone to his orb all day, trying not to pry too much knowing Kallisto was going out with that mortal, he was finding himself very restless. In the last few months, he had not gone more than a couple of hours without at least observing her day by way of the orb.

"That is it," Morpheus proclaimed aloud. "I will join her in the part of her world that is the most unstable environment I could enter— high school."

Morpheus grinned as he formed his plan. He could easily pass as an older teenager up to about twenty-three. Gods aged very slowly after the first true seventeen years of their lives. It took centuries to reach the age they decided would be where their appearance spent eternity. His eldest brother looked around twenty-seven, and his father only looked to be in his early thirties. Zeus was tens of thousands of years old and only looked to be in his mid-forties.

As Morpheus thought about his plan's logistics, a chill came over him. The one he usually received when Kallisto fell asleep. He walked to his orb and peered to see if he was correct, and of course, Kallisto lay on her bed napping. *Should I?* He could not resist. This time he went to her, took her hand without waking her, and manifested the two of them back to his luxurious temple.

⋙⋙ ⋘⋘

Kallisto woke to find herself stretched across the largest bed she had ever seen. It looked walnut, almost black, and about three feet off the floor. The sheets were gold and red satin with a down-filled comforter inside an incredible golden duvet. He, too, had more pillows than were necessary, even though the bed could have comfortably slept an entire family of six.

Waking up to find yourself somewhere you had never been before would unnerve most people, but not Kallisto; she had become a pro in extraordinary happenings. This time when she sat up, she was greeted by Morpheus propped on one elbow as he watched her.

"I was beginning to think you were so comfortable that you would not wake up," Morpheus grinned.

Kallisto grinned back and looked around the lavish room with its fifteen-foot ceilings and twelve-foot windows. The furniture was a mixture of both ancient and modern. She had never seen furniture so large or gorgeous.

"Where are we?" She asked.

You, my *dea femminile*, are in my bed-chamber," with that, he wagged his eyebrows the way that always made her heart stop and her desire rise. Combined with his sexy half grin, the two became a lethal combination against her self-control.

"You sure know how to give a girl an intense nap," she laughed.

Morpheus leaned over and gave her a warm sweet kiss on the tip of her nose. "I just wanted you to know something." She was about to ask when he placed his index finger to her lips so she couldn't interrupt.

He continued tracing her lips ever so slightly. "I want you to know that I am in love with you, Kallisto Nalani," and with his whisper, he kissed her.

Kallisto pulled back breathlessly after a few moments and looked deep into Morpheus' eyes. "I know this is real, Morpheus."

The stunned look on his face said it all. She knew she was right before he could deny it. "I also know you are a dream god, one of the Oneiroi, who visits when I sleep. I just don't understand how it all works or, most importantly, why you would want to spend so much of your time on me?"

It took him what she thought was forever to answer. Before he did, he sat up straight, never breaking eye contact.

"You are indeed most astute. I am bound by rules, Kallisto. Please understand all I have ever truly wanted came into my life two months ago. That was you. I adore you more than you can possibly understand. I want to be with you, and I will find a way to make this work if you, too, desire me." He appeared more intense, not the lust-filled look he previously wore when she woke, but one of determination and distress.

Kallisto sat there awestruck at his sudden declaration of love and the fact he had not argued with her over her newfound presumptions. Her eyes burned with the onset of tears, and she hugged him tightly, not wanting his beautiful words and the warm feel of him to ever disappear from her memories.

"Yes—I mean—I feel the same," Kallisto admitted.

"You also need to know that some things are about to change. Strange things are going to happen," he warned. Pulling back from her and looking into her eyes.

"Stranger than usual? Boy, I'm in for a treat," Kallisto grinned.

Morpheus laughed. "I just want you to try and do something for me."

"Anything," Kallisto urged him on.

"I want you to remember, no matter what, I love you and am trying to be with you, even when I am not physically present. Remember this encounter vividly. Fight the blocks that keep you from remembering everything." Morpheus' pleaded.

Kallisto was confused. "I thought you said I'm trying too hard."

"Maybe you are trying too hard when really it is quite easy, and all you need is faith," Morpheus offered the tip. "Now you have a big night and need to wake from your nap. Here is something I want you to have. Please give me your right hand." When she did, he placed a beautiful golden band around her ring finger. Engraved in glorious script were the words, *My Dea femminile*.

She threw her arms around him, "Oh, Morpheus, it's divine."

"No matter what, I want you to wear this and think of me whenever you look at it," Morpheus smiled. He kissed her passionately one more time. Growling when she groaned, he managed to pull back, placing his palm on her cheek, and whispered. "I will have you one day, Kallisto."

She knew his declaration held a double meaning, sending a chill up her spine. She closed her eyes and woke from her nap, saying, "I love you too."

Looking around, Kallisto found she was back on her not-so-vast bed, in her small bedroom, on planet earth, feeling refreshed and content. She remembered dreaming of a beautiful bedroom but couldn't remember anything else. Thinking intently about her dream, she stood up and went to peer out her second-story window. Something caught her eye when she reached for the latch to open the window, hoping the fresh air would help with her thoughts. On her right hand was a beautiful gold ring with the inscribed words, *My Dea femminile*.

Suddenly, her dream was clearer, except for his face, never his face. He had given her a ring, and she remembered the fantastic words that sent her heart fluttering—again. She raised her hand to her lips and remembered his warm touch and moist lips on hers. Once again, her skin smelled of lavender and honeysuckle. The ring was more undeniable proof that her world was not as black and white as she had thought. She had always loved the legends her grandmother told her of the Greek gods. She often fantasized the myths were real. Her grandmother taught her there were gods for everything, including sleep and dreams, known in lore as the Oneiroi. They controlled the dreams of mortals and immortals.

"Wait a minute, why haven't I thought of this before?" Kallisto declared audibly. She ran to her desk and turned on her laptop. She closed her eyes and bounced her knees up and down in anticipation of her findings. *Why does the computer seem to take forever when you need it to hurry?*

Once *Google* appeared, she typed in Oneiroi. Three names came up under the search subject; three brothers who made up the dream gods and were sons of Hypnos, the god of sleep. Their names were Phantasos, Phobetor, and the most powerful, Morpheus. Fear and excitement consumed her like fire, starting at her head and traveling the entire length of her body. "Morpheus, that's him—that's my Greek god."

Now she knew the truth of her "dreams," and she was almost positive he was the one who watched her. Her lips gave a slight twitch of satisfaction. She knew she was right.

Chapter V

Dating

Kallisto went through her closet again, trying to find something to wear. She just found out her mother had taken the little black dress she intended to wear to the cleaners and had not picked it up. Amanda came bounding up the stairs in her flared-leg, hip-hugger blue jeans and a black low-cut top that showed just how good puberty had been to her. She left her long blond hair down and rolled the ends to give it a little body. She looked great and well put together. On the other hand, Kallisto was still sporting a green tank top and a pair of purple bikini panties.

"I like the look Kalli, and I'm sure Austin will," Amanda tried not to laugh.

"Shut the hell up and help me!" Kallisto sounded stressed. "What do I wear on a date? It's not like I have much experience."

"Whatever you're comfortable in," looking Kallisto up and down, Amanda added with a snicker, "just not that comfortable."

Kallisto stuck her tongue out at her friend, turned back toward her open closet, and combed over what was a garment graveyard; everything was old and void of life. She had the remains of half a dozen or more outfits sprawled on the floor around her feet and on the back of the chair where her gray cat, Barnabas, usually made his bed.

"Well, are you going to show me the ring?" Amanda asked eagerly.

Kallisto had called Amanda after her nap to enlighten her about the gold ring with its inscription and the *dream* in which she received it. She also told her about searching the internet and finding out what her god's name must be if mythology had it correct—Morpheus. To Kallisto's amusement, Amanda was not surprised over her latest bizarre occurrence but was more eager to discover that Morpheus had two brothers, which she decided should go on her date list. Kallisto shook her head, laughing at Amanda's ever-predictable nature.

"You know, Amanda, leave it to you to believe in legends just so you can fill your social calendar," Kallisto held her right hand out to Amanda. "See, it says *My Dea femminile,* meaning my goddess."

"That is gorgeous. So, you remember him giving you this ring, but you cannot remember his features?" Eyebrows furrowed in confusion. Kallisto could tell Amanda tried to grasp how the visions, dreams, hallucinations, whatever they were, worked.

With a sigh, Kallisto attempted to explain. "Have you ever had a dream where there was someone in it that you knew and loved, but only the essence of them was what you could remember in the morning? I can remember his warm lips and how he smells, and I can sometimes remember what he tells me, but his face is not recallable. He's become part of me, but I can't tell you what he looks like—and it's very disconcerting."

"What are you going to do?" Amanda asked.

Replying, Kallisto gave a half-hearted laugh. "What can I do? I'm not the one in control here. He comes to me when he wants to. I don't even know for sure I have his name right. Morpheus just *seems* correct."

"But you were so sure about your findings when we spoke on the phone earlier. Why are you wavering in your assurance now?" Amanda asked. "You need to believe what your subconscious is telling you. For some reason, you've had a major brain block here lately. Correct me, Kalli, if I'm wrong, but aren't you the insightful one?"

"I have always known what to expect from my feelings. Whether they came to me in a dream or while I am driving down the road in a vision or feeling, I always know what is happening or going to happen." Kallisto was deep in thought as she spoke. "Things have been so different since Dad's disappearance. I don't seem to have clear visions in my head. Things are somewhat—" she stalled, trying to find the word "—blurry."

"Well, let's try to figure this out tomorrow. We need to go out and have fun tonight, but first, you need to get some clothes on your body instead of on the floor and in the chair." Amanda giggled at the mess.

The girls waited downstairs on Austin. Kallisto's mother came from the kitchen to hug and say goodbye to her daughter. "You girls look nice tonight." Her eyebrows rose, taking in her daughter's attire.

Against her better judgment, Kallisto wore a short, light pink skirt and a white fitted button-down with a pink lace-trimmed tank underneath. She was overjoyed that she was able to wear three-inch strappy white heels. This was something she rarely did because of her height. Amanda had insisted on them, telling her to "Live a little and show some leg." Too tired from exploring the desolate confines of her closet, she gave in to Amanda's peer pressure and wore her thigh divulging skirt. Kallisto was just grateful that her father was still at the docks. He, unlike her mother, would not have held his tongue.

"You girls have a phone?" Kallisto's mother asked.

"Yes, ma'am, we both do," Amanda replied, using the southern bell charm passed down from her mother.

"Good. You know to call if you need to?" This was a statement rather than a question

Kallisto resisted the urge to roll her eyes, "Yes, Mom, we'll be okay." The doorbell rang, and Kallisto jumped. She found the closer rendezvous time came, the jumpier she became.

Amanda grinned at Kallisto's apparent discomfort. She had waited a long time for her best friend to join the dating circuit. Amanda was sarcastic through and through but always a good friend and there whenever the occasion called for a backup.

Kallisto walked slowly to the door and closed her eyes, concentrating on what to do next. With a deep breath, she opened the door to find Mrs. Bailey smiling sweetly up at her.

"Hi Mama Bai, how are you? Come in." Kallisto stepped back and held the door open, giving Mama Bai a big hug as she stepped over the threshold. Just before Kallisto could close the door behind Mrs. Bailey, she saw a big black Ford Expedition pulling into the driveway. Her shaking was somewhat controlled after the initial scare from the doorbell but returned when she eyed the vehicle pulling behind her mother's mini-van. *"Crap!"* She thought.

Austin emerged from the SUV wearing faded blue jeans and a navy-blue polo. He was very handsome, and it didn't pass Kallisto's notice that he looked quite sexy, even if he wasn't a deity. She also noticed he looked her up and down. The devils dancing there were nothing to the mischievous grin that donned his face. For someone who had taken two years to get up the nerve to ask her out, he sure didn't seem the least bit intimidated by her now.

"Hey—you look beautiful," Austin's smile was wide as he gave her a peck on the cheek.

"You don't look too bad yourself," Kallisto returned. "Come in, and I'll get Amanda and let you meet my mom."

When she closed the door and turned around, her mother, Mama Bai, and Amanda were standing in a semi-circle, ready to converge. "Austin, this is my mother, Thia, and my adopted grandmother and neighbor, Mrs. Bailey, more commonly known as Mama Bai. You already know, Amanda."

Austin shook Thia's and Mama Bai's hands, "It's very nice to meet you both." He, too, was a charmer. Kallisto wondered briefly if he had a southern background as well.

"Well," Kallisto's mother said as she clasped her hands together. "I guess we had better let you three get going so you can pick up Michael."

The three teenagers didn't have to be told twice. They were out the door and in the vehicle in seconds. "Well, ladies," Austin began, "where does Michael live?"

Amanda gave him the directions as Kallisto assessed the situation. The hungry look in Austin's eyes unnerved her and seemed inconsistent with his story of having a tough time getting up the nerve to ask her out. She also felt *him*—watching.

Once the four of them were in the SUV, Amanda asked, "So what's on the itinerary tonight, guys? We need to be back by eleven. We've gotta get up early."

Both guys looked disappointed. "What about a quick bite to eat and a movie?" suggested Michael.

"Or if you want, John Branson is throwing a party at his place tonight," Austin suggested.

"If you don't mind, I'd be more comfortable if we just went to eat and to a movie. I don't run with that crowd, and Elizabeth has given me a hard enough time without me showing up where she and her cronies are sure to be."

"Elizabeth's been harassing you?" Austin asked.

Kallisto could see a smirk on his face and wondered what he was thinking.

"Yeah, surely, you're not surprised. The two of you dated for a long time," Kallisto answered.

"Dinner and a movie it is, then. What would you ladies like to see?" Michael chimed in.

"How about the new one, the one with Chris Hemsworth?" Amanda suggested—pleaded. Chris Hemsworth was her second favorite actor.

"Sounds good to me," Kallisto also had an affinity for the middle Hemsworth brother. They continued to converse and decided on a small Italian restaurant where the wait was minimal. The four teenagers were chatting and laughing when Austin laced his hand with Kallisto's. She felt a little uncomfortable with the gesture, but it was nothing to the sudden sensation of rage around her. She could have sworn she heard and felt a growl of discontent, obviously, not from her three visible companions but from the air itself.

⟫⟫⟩ ⟨⟨⟨

Unfortunately, self-control was not a virtue easily obtained, even after a couple thousand years. Morpheus' eyes, red with jealousy, scrutinized Kallisto beside the hormone-laden mortal. He would not let that mortal "boy" interfere with his plans. He watched and listened.

"What the hell does that boy think he is doing?" Morpheus watched Austin slip his hand around Kallisto's. He felt the telltale burning red in his eyes that signaled the beginnings of his loss of control. Old, to mortal's standards, he might be, but young in his realm, he was. Once a young god lost control, all sorts of hell could occur.

⟫⟫⟩ ⟨⟨⟨

Kallisto felt a little uneasy sitting so close to a guy; after all, she thought her previous interludes with a man were mere dreams. It didn't help the deity who shared in her uneasiness watched her. She wondered if she would be as comfortable with "her god" when she returned to him, knowing on some level, which she didn't fully understand, it would be real. Would she be able to look him in the eyes, knowing he watched her date someone else? What would he do if Austin kissed her? Would she let him kiss her? Would her "god" still love her? As the questions entered her mind, she felt the anger in the "air" grow. She half smiled, half grimaced and took this overwhelming feeling to signify that her deity only wanted her mind on him.

"Kalli!" Amanda prompted.

"Uh—yeah?" Kallisto pulled herself from her daydream, slightly embarrassed at being caught. "Sorry, I was in my own little world." She knew Amanda would understand.

"We were wondering about getting ice cream at The Creamery on Main Street after the movie," Amanda repeated.

"That sounds awesome; I love that place. They have the best homemade waffle cones," Kallisto licked her lips and could have sworn Austin's eyes darkened.

Once they pulled into the parking lot of the little Italian bistro, Austin leaned over to whisper into Kallisto's ear. "How about we take our ice creams to the park, and we can go for a walk, just the two of us?"

Kallisto was taken a little off guard at his request to "be alone." She still wasn't comfortable with boys but didn't want to look too apprehensive, afraid he would assume her anxiety to be a lack of interest.

"Sure, I will have to walk barefoot, though," pointing to her heels.

Morpheus did not like the hungry look in Austin's eyes as he pulled back from whispering in Kallisto's ear. He knew all too well what that look meant. Austin needed a reminder. Giving Kallisto his ring served more than one purpose. Yes, it was a constant reminder of him and his world, but it was part of his world, deeply connected to his abilities as a god. He could wield power through the ring and Kallisto if necessary, as long as she wore it.

Not thinking, Kallisto placed her right hand on Austin's upper arm to get his attention when a current of electricity shot through her and into Austin...hard.

"Ow! You shocked me." Austin rubbed the spot Kallisto had touched.

"Sorry, static electricity?" She shrugged guiltily. "I was going to ask if you'd excuse us while we go to the lady's room. You know girls always go in pairs," Kallisto smiled and gave Amanda a desperate look.

Once inside the restroom, Kallisto raised one finger to Amanda, suggesting that she wait while she looked to see if the room was free of ears that might think her insane. "He's watching me again, and I swear the ring shocked Austin."

"What? You're telling me that your god is watching our date and shocked your date?" Amanda laughed.

"How is this funny?" Kallisto demanded.

"Are you sure your father didn't hire this god?"

Kallisto couldn't help but smile. Amanda's way of looking at things sometimes found humor where humor didn't usually exist. Her dad would go to any means possible to keep his little girl...little forever.

"All of this is just so weird. He is watching me as I speak. I can feel him, and I swear I heard a growl when Austin put his hand in mine in the car."

"Maybe you have a jealous god," Amanda interjected.

"Must be. I also wanted to tell you that Austin wants to go to the park to eat our ice cream after the movie; so we can have some "alone" time. You need to slow down with Michael. I'm not comfortable enough with Austin to hold his hand, and you are well on your way to—"

The restroom door opened, and four girls about a year younger than Kallisto and Amanda came streaming in, talking animatedly and giggling. Sighing, Amanda gestured toward the door for them to return to their dates.

The girls returned to their seats and waited only minutes before their waiter took their orders. Surprisingly, the four of them found plenty in common to talk about. Among the topics of interest were school, graduation, what colleges they were applying to, and music. Time went by much faster than Kallisto would have expected. Before she realized it, she had forgotten about her god and plunged herself into the camaraderie of the evening. She was finding that she enjoyed the lively conversations.

⇝⇝ ⇜⇜

Morpheus became increasingly irritated as Kallisto smiled with pleasure. Brief moments at a movie store or standing in a crowd would not get him what he wanted—Kallisto permanently on Mount Olympus. She was smart, and his plan relied heavily on her ability to see through the dream ruse. He needed her sanity undamaged if he was to convince the big guy. Unfortunately, this was not a subject the gods took lightly; mortals were not meant to dwell with the gods.

Somehow Phantasos convinced The Fates, also known as the Moirai, to let Morpheus go to the mortal realm for an extended period. This gave him hope since the three sisters controlled the past, present and future—maybe things would go his way. There had been times when very powerful gods, namely Zeus and Hades, had strong-armed them into acting against destiny, but there was always a price to pay for such influence. Hades had to allow his wife to stay with her mother half of each year, unable to see her. Zeus, well, he had many obstacles to overcome from his heavy-handed ways. The only ones who understand the price paid are The Fates and the deity who was dumb enough to square up with them. The price was often an emotional toll—for life. Threats and coercion were not taken lightly by the Moirai. Zeus might be physically more powerful, but his daughters had time and destiny on their side. Desperation was the only motivating factor Morpheus could think of that would make a god try to intimidate the sisters.

What Morpheus needed now was a plan. Once in her world, then what? After that, how would he convince the Moirai and Zeus that love should be enough to allow him and Kallisto to be together?

Once they finished their meal, the girls excused themselves to the restrooms again. Michael and Austin waited for the return of their cards taken by the waiter. "Hey, Michael," Austin grinned. "What do you say about us going to the park with our ice cream tonight? I thought you and Amanda might want some time alone."

"Sounds okay to me, but I think Amanda and Kallisto are enjoying us all being together," Michael commented. Michael liked Amanda a lot, but he felt Austin's plan was a little too blatant.

"I'm sure between the two of us, we can make 'em happy to separate for a while," Austin said, still grinning.

About that time, the two girls returned with fresh lipgloss and smiles. "You guys ready to go see the movie?" Amanda asked.

Just as the four were about to leave the restaurant, Kallisto got an overwhelming urge to look behind her. She felt like someone was standing extremely close to her back, but no one was there.

Michael held the door open for the girls while they exited the restaurant. Kallisto was in such deep thought as she looked behind her and ran into him. Kallisto apologized. "I'm sorry, Michael."

"In your own little world again, Kalli?" Amanda teased.

Kallisto playfully rolled her eyes and shook her head.

They made it to the theater just in time to see the previews. Kallisto and Amanda sat side by side, and the guys sat outside the duo. About halfway through the movie, the water from dinner had Kallisto needing a restroom. She hated to leave in the middle of the showing, but she couldn't wait any longer. Once in the lobby, she quickly made it to the restroom. On her way back to the theater, the feeling of being watched came over her, and it was stronger than usual. Kallisto began looking around, trying to see if any eyes were looking in her direction. A handsome guy with shoulder-length blonde hair and a tight black t-shirt leaned against the wall on the other side of the theater lobby. Their eyes met across the vast room, and a chill ran down Kallisto's spine.

"Kallisto," Austin said from behind her. She jumped and turned around anxiously.

"Sorry. Just headed to the restroom and saw you standing here," he gestured toward the men's restroom.

"Okay, I'll wait for you?" Kallisto offered.

"I wouldn't want you to miss Chris Hemsworth any more than you have to," Austin grinned. "I'll see ya in a minute." He turned and disappeared behind the restroom door.

As soon as he was out of sight, Kallisto spun around to see if her blonde-headed admirer was still on the other side of the room. He was not. *Could that have been?* "Damn, why can't I remember?" Kallisto stamped her foot in frustration and returned to the theater. Under her breath, she muttered, "At least I still have Chris."

After the movie, the four went to the Creamery and purchased their personal decadence. Both girls indulged in All Things Chocolate with waffle cones, and the guys chose sundaes. Once they had their desserts, they headed to the park with its romantic walkways lined with soft lights.

"Would you like to walk with me? The trails are lit?" Austin asked Kallisto.

"Sure," she answered warily. She looked to Amanda, whose look screamed, *you'll be fine*. So, she removed her heels.

Austin opened Kallisto's door. "Madam," he gestured with his palm up and slightly bowing.

Kallisto could not help but giggle as she took his hand and hopped barefoot out of the SUV.

"I'm glad you came out with me," Austin stated. "Not that you wouldn't have."

"I know he did not just say that," Kallisto thought to herself.

"That sure of yourself, are you?" Kallisto acknowledged his statement with a raised brow. "I almost said no, but I felt that any guy bold enough to stand and wait in my parking spot deserved a break."

He brought them to a stop on the path, taking her arm and turning her to him. He looked into her eyes and grinned. "I've never been turned down," and before she could comment, he leaned in and pressed his unwelcome lips to hers.

A menacing whisper sounded through the slight breeze, "I told you not to touch her, mortal."

Kallisto's ring felt like a circle of lava around her finger, and Austin screamed in pain. He grabbed his head and sank to the ground moaning and grunting in agony. The distress in his cries scared Kallisto. She knew her young god had caused this. Even though a small part of her felt Austin deserved a little discomfort for his arrogant and sudden rude behavior, she didn't think he deserved the anguish he was enduring. She had no idea how far a disgruntled dream god would go once provoked into a jealous tirade.

"Morpheus, stop!" Kallisto yelled at the dark sky. As soon as his name left her lips, her head began to ache, and she felt a little dizzy.

Just as sudden as Austin's pain started, it vanished. Austin got to his feet and began backing away from Kallisto, glaring like she had caused his pain.

"Where did that voice come from?"

"What voice? How dare you kiss me without invitation," Kallisto started rambling as she rubbed her head. "I was under the misconceived notion that you were a nice guy."

"I'm leaving. Are you coming?" Austin turned on his heel, still rubbing his head, and started back. He looked over his shoulder and eyed Kallisto as if she was some unfamiliar creature.

Kallisto followed, perplexed, rubbing her finger and then her head. *How did this happen? The night was going so well?*

Morpheus watched the orb with his mouth open in astonishment. "Not only did she remember my name, but she responded to me from her dimension," *That was not supposed to be possible.* This gave him an edge of unforeseen hope. Had his pep talk on faith helped?

Chapter VI

Zeus

Morpheus was both bemused and elated by his discovery. Elated for obvious reasons and perplexed how Kallisto made such a connection while in her realm. This was an unheard-of occurrence between their two worlds. Mortals had an easy time relating to the unexplained as long as their subconscious was making the connection, like while dreaming. A human being should not be able to remember his name, much less speak straight to him, command him even, while conscious. *What does this mean?* His thoughts raced, trying to come up with a rational explanation.

He continued to watch the four as they left the park. Morpheus saw Amanda's concern for her best friend, but what really got to him was the occasional silent tear that slipped down Kallisto's cheek. She was trying hard not to allow one of the droplets to sabotage her composure. Pain was etched across her brow, and he wondered how much he had put there. He mirrored her pain and could not wait until she slept. Yes, he would go to her in her dreams tonight, not taking her into his reality. Unlike the actual trips into his world, staying in her dream meant just that, her dreams. Whatever took place would remain, for her, only a dream.

Austin took Michael home first. Amanda got out with him, leaving Kallisto alone with Austin. A person could have cut the air between Kallisto and Austin with a knife. The animated talk and light humor between the four throughout the night abruptly halted.

When the door shut behind Amanda, Austin tried to make nice. "I'm sorry this was not the night we had both hoped it would be."

"And what did you hope it would be, Austin? Did you think I was going out with you because you're on the football team and popular? I thought you were nice and not a jerk. Your head hurt, and you blamed me, not to mention your audacity before that," Kallisto's voice cracked.

"I thought you were into me, that's all," Austin tried to make light of the situation, to no avail.

"Whether I am into you or not is irrelevant. I must hand it to you, though; you had me fooled. I thought you were a nice guy," Kallisto spat the words. "I'm not an easy date, Austin."

"It was just a kiss," he said.

About that time, Amanda and Michael immerged from Michael's front door onto his porch. They were laughing and then kissing. *Crap, did she have to do that in front of us? Now?* Kallisto rolled her eyes and crossed her arms over her chest.

She thought she heard Austin utter under his breath a sigh while saying, "I picked the wrong girl."

Finally, Amanda unlocked her lips from Michael's, and they headed back to Kallisto's. Austin did, at least, walk the girls to the front door. Amanda excused herself, entered the house, and left Kallisto on the front porch with Austin to fend for herself.

"Austin, I want you to know I was having a great time until the park. You'll not always be the quarterback or the most popular person, so maybe you should try and figure out who you truly are and just be you," Kallisto offered, sounding beyond her years.

Austin looked perplexed at Kallisto's revelation and only managed a half smile, "I'll see you at school." Then he left.

Kallisto opened the door to find Amanda pressed so close to it she should've stayed on the porch. "What happened?" Amanda was eager to hear the whole story—not through a door.

Kallisto went through the entire story from beginning to end. She made sure to add how Morpheus came to her rescue, so to speak, on the trail. "The worst part wasn't Austin's arrogance. He made me feel like a conquest he didn't have to put much effort into—an easy win. He played all sweet, then, boom, jerk. What kind of guy acts like that?"

Amanda wrapped her arm around Kallisto and apologized. "I'm sorry, Kalli; maybe tomorrow will be better. Let's go watch a movie with real gentlemen in it."

"<u>Pride and Prejudice?</u>" Kallisto asked, knowing this was their *why can't men really be that way* movie. Jane Austin knew what a man was supposed to be like.

"Mr. Darcy is sure to make you feel better," Amanda said, and the two girls headed upstairs. Halfway through the movie, both girls were uncharacteristically asleep.

Once Kallisto was asleep, Morpheus entered her dream. She was dreaming her feet were being splashed by the waves of the ocean as she watched a beautiful sunset. Morpheus walked up behind her and put his hand on the small of her back. She turned, immediately knowing who it was, and wrapped her arms around him. She buried her face in his chest and inhaled the lavender and honeysuckle.

"I was hoping to see you tonight," she said.

"I just wanted to make sure you are okay. I am sorry your date," Kallisto could hear the acid in his voice, "did not go so well. I am here only for a moment. I have some very important business I need to attend to. I'll come back to you soon. Try and remember—I love you."

Kallisto woke, with her head aching, and found she was still in her bedroom. She tried to remember what the man in her dream looked like but came up with nothing. Frustrated and tired, she grabbed one of her many pillows and curled herself into it. Sighing, she went into a dreamless sleep for the first time in weeks.

Morpheus lay in his vast bed wishing he could have brought Kallisto back with him. Why did the most potent relationships through time and literature need to be fought for and through improbable odds? He fell asleep with no dreams for himself, for who would have given them to him?

The following day Morpheus woke early to meet with Zeus. He paced the floor of his bedchamber, trying to decide what angle to go with. *I am in love with—I need—She's everything to me—I know I shouldn't still be in her dreams, but—*

"Maybe I should just beg," he said aloud.

Instead of materializing in the marbled mansion on the hill, Morpheus decided to walk; after all, Olympus was beautiful—no flaws. Just like the gods that dwelled there, the only imperfection was the lack of imperfection. Never a tempest, no wind, and the temperature resided at a perfect seventy-five degrees. Morpheus breathed in deep, honeysuckle fragrance thick in the air. The smell of honeysuckle was always there; no breeze to bring it, just the pleasant smell of the perfect world in which he lived. Stunning giant green foliage all around and never a parasite to bother. The animals that lived on Olympus did so in complete harmony. Absolute perfection, no need to leave, unless there was something or someone so compelling that living a life in complete perfection was not enough.

Walking gave Morpheus time to think. He felt even more compelled to go to Kallisto, having experienced her newfound awareness of him. Could he possibly get what he wanted...Kallisto forever? She made a connection once thought impossible. In legend, the mortals brought to Olympus to live were brought to stay and were never pulled in and out of realms through the cover of dreams. They were never allowed back into the mortal realm and were not subject to the going mad factor since they stayed continuously in one realm. However, that was rare, so rare Morpheus had never known a mortal to stay on Olympus.

He decided to lay his entire story on the line; after all, Zeus, too, had been compelled by mortals, so maybe he would have some sympathy. This was, after all, a sore spot in his marriage. Zeus' wife wasn't fond of Zeus' exploits with mortals, not that she was an innocent spectator; she too had her moments of infidelity. Beings of outward perfection, the gods love the fanatical behavior they bring on themselves. Always better than a reality show; in short, they thrive on drama. Scandal, after all, is what breaks the monotony of perfection. Free will is the one thing that made Olympus as imperfect as the mortal world.

One of the many servants of Zeus beckoned Morpheus into the enormous atrium. The entrance was more of a long vast room lined with sculptured images of various gods and nymphs. On the left was the marbled stone figure of his body, just as perfect as it was in real life. Only the most prominent gods lined this entry. The vast entrance hall's ceiling was thirty feet high with pallid marbled floors and walls. Everything about the mansion exemplified power and affluence. Even though the home of Zeus would be overwhelming to most, Morpheus was not impressed. He, too, had vast wealth. He was the chosen one of the Oneiroi, the most powerful of all dream gods. One would think the way his brothers treated him, being the youngest, he was inferior. They knew who commanded the power—they just wanted to keep him honest while they could. Phantasos kept him grounded as much as possible. Phobetor treated him as if he were any other being on Olympus—he only showed allegiance to his father, Hypnos, and Zeus.

Once again, free will was not easily contained. Morpheus was an imperiously powerful god of dreams and one of the few gods who commanded a presence and authority gifted to only the most influential. He was also young and bound to mischief. Containing this power and controlling his tomfoolery was the responsibility of his family and sometimes the entire pantheon.

"The master will see you now," Morpheus looked down to see a nymph motioning him into another room that paled to the atrium.

Morpheus walked behind the servant, trying not to appear nervous. He could always blackmail Zeus into giving him what he wanted. Not even Zeus wanted a disgruntled dream god against him. But, by the same token, Zeus was not a deity you wanted as an enemy. It was understood that he ruled those of Olympus, and even if you were a god, such as The Fates or Hades, who wielded so much power, you were expected to respect his authority.

"Morpheus, my son," an endearment Zeus used for all the gods on Olympus, "what has you here so early and with an appointment?" With that Zeus grinned and cocked one eyebrow. The supreme being that sat upon what could be described as a throne but was much more with its high back that towered over the seated god, and the arms of the white marble carved with the story of creation looked amused by Morpheus' apparent uneasiness. Zeus wore the appearance of a more mature being. Most gods chose the eternal appearance of their twenties or early thirties. Zeus chose the slight graying look of a man in his mid-forties. Even though he looked fortyish with his lightly salted hair and beard, he had a body that very few mortal forty-year-old men remembered from their youth, let alone possessed. He stood at least six feet eight inches. His presence alone commanded authority.

"I have come to ask permission to dwell on earth for a couple of months," Morpheus stated. He was trying not to sound too eager. Wagers with gods were dangerous ventures. If he made a deal with Zeus, it had better be worth whatever penance was rendered. The more enthusiastic he seemed, the worse the recompense would be.

"Oh?" With sudden interest, Zeus perked up.

Morpheus knew Zeus would love to have a dream god at his beck and call. Dreams were a way to give and receive information from a person or a deity. This was a power very few gods had, three to be exact, and to possess it was an exceptionally powerful tool in one's arsenal.

"Why would I allow you such a thing? You can enter that realm through dreams. Why would you want to go in the flesh to a place where you will not be appreciated for what you are?"

"I have a personal mission I need to see to," Morpheus answered, trying to stay composed so as not to seem overzealous.

"Why would a dream god have a personal mortal-bound mission? Again, why not just venture through dreams?" Zeus asked curiously.

"I—I need to meet someone, a mortal, in their realm," Morpheus responded reluctantly.

"Really, why?" Zeus persisted.

Morpheus closed his eyes and sighed. "I am in love with a mortal woman by the name of Kallisto Nalani. Thia, her mother, called me to her daughter's dreams to help her through a tough time. I fell in love with her, and she with me." As Morpheus made his profession, he noticed Zeus go rigid.

"Repeat the mother's name."

"Thia...Thia Nalani, why?" Morpheus was taken aback by the question.

Zeus was momentarily deep in thought but composed himself quickly. "The name just sounded familiar. You said the mortal loves you as well?"

"Yes."

"How can that be? Mortals have no memory of their sleep or dream gods," Zeus pried deeper. "How do you know she's in love with you?"

"I have been bringing her here—to Olympus after she falls asleep," Morpheus confessed hesitantly. "For a long time, she thought herself dreaming. Then she began to put the truth of the realms together on her own. I cannot explain it because it has never occurred before, and it's not supposed to be possible. She has figured everything out—the only thing left unknown to her is my appearance. I want to go to her world and see if she can love me, not her dream god that visits only to fulfill her desires," Morpheus, against his better judgment, laid everything on the line.

"You know what you ask for is forbidden. You are not supposed to deal with mortals in this manner. You have broken the rules—laws—and to break more would be unfathomable. This girl could go insane from your obsessive actions—pulling her from one realm to another," Zeus shook his head as he berated Morpheus. "Am I supposed to believe you could love this human when you failed to consider that you could be causing her irreversible harm?"

"I have been careful. I am not my brother. I would never allow her mental state to suffer to the point of no return," Morpheus defended himself—however, he felt a twinge of guilt for his actions.

Truth be known, she was addicting, and he needed to see her in her world to keep from pulling her back and forth. She had more trouble in the last few weeks since she started putting the two realms together. Mentally, she was not getting any rest. Her mind had figured out that it was in a constant state of alertness. Morpheus could give her body and mind the illusion that she was sleeping when in actuality, she was going from one realm of consciousness to another without slumber. Her own body was turning against her, and mentally she was suffering. He knew she was on overdrive and wanted to ease the tension, but he did not want to let her go.

"Is this the girl for whom you made a deal with Hades to save her father?" Zeus asked.

"How did you know about that?"

"My brother and I may not be the best of friends, but he does divulge when deals are made between any god of Olympus and himself. Let us just say it is one of his many ways of infuriating me. Be lucky that your end of the deal was not painful—most usually are." Hades loved to make deals with the gods of Olympus, and when the deal went awry, he exercised power over Zeus.

Morpheus knew Zeus sensed his desire to do anything for Kallisto. For a god to chance a deal with another god over a mortal was one thing, but gambling with two gods as powerful as Zeus and Hades over the same girl was akin to insanity.

"I guess I am lucky Hades loves his wife, and being separated from her half the year, dreams are his best way of seeing her while she is with her mother," Morpheus said." Furthermore, I suspect Hades would never be so reckless with his dream state on the line. Wagering with a dream god can be valuable if done positively or—agonizing if not."

Morpheus knew Zeus heard his subtle threat, but the powerful deity stayed composed enough not to let it show.

"You said this girl's mother is Greek, and her name is Thia?" Zeus questioned again.

"Yes, they moved back to her father's homeland of Hawaii when she was seven or eight years old. That is why she has a Greek first name," Morpheus was tired of the questions. He was not used to asking anyone for anything.

Zeus' eyes narrowed. "What about your responsibilities as a dream god while you are out playing Eros? You have a job that requires you to help not just the occasional mortal but gods and goddesses."

"My brother, Phantasos, has agreed to cover for me," Morpheus answered Zeus' question as if it was not a big deal.

Shocked again and with an eyebrow raised, Zeus questioned, "Really? I thought he was lost to the dream realm. What could ever have made him consider going back?"

Morpheus answered with only two words, *The Fates*.

He walked over to Morpheus and glared into his eyes. He was deep in thought, and Morpheus could tell he was trying to decide what it would hurt to allow a powerful god of dreams to visit the human realm, or at least that was Morpheus' guess.

"Very well, I'll give you a chance, but you must follow some rules, and of course, you owe me a debt," Zeus grinned.

"I figured, what are your rules? Phantasos already gave a few himself," Morpheus scowled in remembrance of his brother's three ludicrous rules.

Zeus smirked at that. "You will report to me every week."

Morpheus' brow furrowed, "What could you possibly want me to tell you?"

"I will ask the questions," Zeus spat back. "Second, you will take two of your servants and two of mine." He snapped his fingers, and two servants that looked to be in their late forties appeared beautiful and statuesque in front of Morpheus. "These," Zeus motioned to two servants, a man, and a woman, in a peplos and a white chiton, "will be your parent figures on earth. You will obey what they say, for I will give you instruction through them."

Morpheus closed his eyes, hoping to calm himself before he raged. "Let me get this straight. I am to obey these servants and report to you once a week?"

Zeus grinned and nodded his head. "These, plus the time frame I am sure Phantasos set for you. And, as you know, the rules that plague you as a god are still bound on earth. You are not to reveal who you are."

Morpheus interrupted, "Unless she specifically asks me if I am the dream god Morpheus, and I am to have no carnal knowledge of her."

He knew Zeus could hear his ire as he reluctantly spat the last rule out.

"Ouch, I would not have been that cruel. Third," Zeus continued, "you are not to speak of this to any other god except Phantasos, especially not Hades or Hera. Is that clear?"

"What is my debt?" Morpheus was eager to hear his fate.

"You will not ever bring her to Olympus again, and you will let her go after the time allotted to you by The Fates," Zeus finished with genuine sadness splayed across his face as he turned to pier out the wall of glass overlooking Olympus.

"What?" Morpheus shouted. He could not believe this. "Why—why would you give me such stipulations? Hades himself would not do that. He would be more than happy to torture me physically, but this." Morpheus began shaking, and so did the vast room.

"Enough!" Zeus' boomed. "You will take what is offered or nothing at all, young one. I am not keen on any of this. You have no idea what you are about to get yourself into. You are playing with things you will not know how to deal with once unleashed. You will obey, or you will lose yourself to the underworld. Is that clear?"

Morpheus tried with all he had to stop the quaking from engulfing him and threatening his surroundings. He could not believe what he was hearing. He forced himself to think rationally. "If I continue to see her as we are now, she may go mad. The only thing I can do to protect her is leave her alone." *What is the point of going to earth if I have to leave her?* Morpheus was speaking more to himself than to Zeus.

Zeus interrupted Morpheus' reasonable analysis. "That would have been the best route for her if she had not begun to differentiate between dreams and reality and the fine lines that separate them. Once a mortal understands these things, they will either accept it as reality or they will go mad. There is no in-between, and there is no going back. Not even The Fates can change what the human mind can and cannot contain or perceive," Zeus explained.

"What are you saying exactly?" Morpheus knew the answer but needed confirmation.

"It is too late? Her mind has comprehended too much and cannot turn back, and she needs more clarification, so she does not succumb to the madness teetering between realms causes. Humans have been diagnosing their "knowledge" of the realms for centuries as mental instability. According to humans, reality is only fact if it is logical. Anyone who believes otherwise is considered fanatical at best and insane at worst," Zeus continued with his lesson.

"Is there hope for her—if I go and explain?" Morpheus was stunned and felt sick. What had he done to Kallisto? This was his fault, and he might never be able to fix it. It was bad enough Zeus took away the possibility of him having a life with Kallisto; now she may not have a life worth living because of him. *How could love be the source of such pain?*

"There is always hope. That is what mortals live for," Zeus was not going to answer his question. That was a question for The Fates and a question they would most certainly not answer. "You have no choice now. The Fates require your presence in her life for reasons only known to them. Morpheus, it is not up to me anymore, the rules The Fates and I have given, must be followed. I advise you to try to distance your feelings and do the job you must do."

"And what would that be exactly, rip open my heart and doom Kallisto to a mental breakdown?" Anger cut through Morpheus' voice, and his hands balled into fists.

"You are going to try and put things in order. Your Kallisto has found favor with The Fates, but as I said before, they cannot keep her sane. Only you can convince her she is of sound mind and that sometimes legends are real," Concern was evident in Zeus' voice for what or whom Morpheus did not know. "Now, I suppose you have questions only The Fates can help with, so I will see you out."

Morpheus' mind reeled as the servant accompanied him to the atrium and out the door. Deciding to leave the conventional way for a god of his stature, he vanished and reappeared in his bedchamber. He sat on a plush leather chaise, put his head in his hands, and thought. *What have I done to the woman I adore more than any other being? She is so clever and beautiful and does not deserve a destiny of madness or premature death because I, the infatuated god, drove her insane by playing games with her psyche.*

Morpheus laid back on his chaise, closed his crystal blue eyes, and imagined the woman he had possibly destroyed with his antics. He could see her without the orb if he allowed himself to relax. He could experience, touch, and love her when he allowed himself.

He was with her in strictly a dream state. Six hours prior, he had left her, and she was now sleeping completely undisturbed, with no dreaming. This connection was strictly for his benefit. He had an overwhelming urge to be near her and a desire to protect her from any more mental abuse. So, he just watched her while his arms ached to hold her. He contented himself with the memory of her soft skin, the smell of wildflowers in her hair, and the warmth of her body when she pressed against him for a kiss. He opened his eyes, bringing himself swiftly back to his domain. He pinched the bridge of his nose. How could their love possibly cause such pain? Kallisto needed to understand the fantasy she believed in was real. Convincing a mortal that such things as gods, centaurs, and Medusa were real would not be easy, especially when he was not allowed to tell her anything unless she asked. Dreamworld and reality were about to crash for Kallisto. Morpheus hoped she would survive the fallout.

As he sat there, depression consuming him, he could not believe his ears. *Morpheus, where are you? Come to me.* Kallisto called to him from her dream state.

He could not fight the urge. The passion of her unconscious calling, produced from deep within her dream state, was impossible to resist. He closed his eyes and joined her in her dream. They were lying on clouds high above what looked like Greece and she was dressed in an almost sheer gown that accentuated her curves perfectly. He gulped audibly and decided to conjure her a robe to help keep himself honest.

"What—do you not like my gown?" Kallisto taunted him.

"It is not that I don't like your gown—it is just that I," his eyes looked her up and down with longing, "don't believe I trust myself to behave gentlemanly. If I do not put boundaries up—not that the robe would take much longer—" He didn't finish his sentence—he just gaped.

Kallisto closed the gap between them. *She is so elegant and graceful, he thought.* She stopped a foot from him and took his hand into hers. Taking one step, he closed the space between them, seized the back of her head with his free hand, and pulled her to his lips. Her scent set his body on fire, and the warmth of her mouth was almost more than he could endure. Being a gentleman, or at least trying to, he let go of her and stepped back half a step, just enough he could still feel the warmth radiate from her body.

"Okay, I need a cold shower and," Morpheus gave her a half grin, "I need to talk to you about something very important."

Kallisto pouted at his retreat. Morpheus noted her face and, under any other circumstances, would get her anything she wanted.

"What would you like to talk about?"

"I know when you wake, you cannot remember my face. I need you to try. Just trust me on this. I may not be in your dreams much in the next couple of weeks— Shhh!" Morpheus placed his index finger over her lips so he could continue without the interruption he saw she was preparing. "I just need you to have faith and believe me when I say I have not left you. Remember me, Kallisto," he was begging.

"You'll come back to me, though, right?" Kallisto's voice shook with trepidation. "My life seems centered around you now. I'm not sure how to describe it, but I need you.

He wrapped his arms around her waist and pulled her into a tight embrace. They stood there, just the two of them holding each other. Morpheus knew he had to try to make this work, not only heal her mental state but find some way for them to be together. He also knew she would need to wake in a couple of hours, so he whispered the words into her ear, making her sleep a deep rest from which he would have to wake her. Back on her bed with her many decorative pillows and the white and gold duvet, he wrapped his arms around her and stayed, smelling her hair and feeling her body curved into his until it was time for her to wake. When dawn came, he whispered the words for her to wake and finished by saying, "remember me." He then vanished before she could open her aqua eyes.

Chapter VII

Painting

Morpheus watched through the orb as Kallisto woke. He now had some decisions to make. Free will was a powerful right, but could that right overpower pantheon rules? Could her calling him by name be a coincidence? If he left her now, as difficult and possibly impossible as that would be, could she mentally mend from his invasion of her consciousness, or was Zeus right? Should he continue his plan, go to her, and trust The Fates?

In the beginning, he went to Kallisto intending to heal her grief. After days of enduring her sorrow-filled nightmares and finding himself incapable of altering them—he gave back what she had lost, fixing what caused her so much pain, even in sleep. Within a few days of watching all her pain unfold, he decided to make a deal with the devil. Morpheus went to Hades and asked him to give Kallisto back what she had lost, her father. Being the god of the underworld—of all the dead—Hades was the only deity you could negotiate with to bring back the departed. Entering into a deal with any god was beyond foolhardy, but one with Hades was reckless. Especially if it was to save someone you barely knew—and a mortal at that. After Kallisto's father came home, she was elated, and her dreams became the best of his long existence, the dreams he should never have stayed around to watch. He found true love, made a deal with the devil, and was tempting The Fates—all for one mortal girl—could he just walk away?

Kallisto stretched and yawned as she woke from her slumber. *That had to be one of the best, most productive nights of sleep I've had in a long time.* She lay there and tried to remember if she had any dreams. The morning came for the first time in months without the scent of lavender or honeysuckle. Her brows furrowed as a sense of emptiness filled her. Her thoughts chased each other through her head as she tried desperately to remember whether or not her Greek god had visited. She closed her eyes and spoke his name in a barely audible whisper, "Morpheus?"

With a rush, she remembered two things; standing on what seemed to be clouds wrapped in his arms and the two words he spoke, *remember me*. With that thought, she knew her sleep had been filled with him; he had not abandoned her.

Amanda had beaten her to the bathroom, so she bypassed it and followed the scent of coffee to the kitchen. There she found her parents eating breakfast; her dad had returned early.

Her mother spoke first. "Good morning, sweetie. How did your evening go?

"Well, it was going great until I found out my date is an arrogant jerk. I really don't think I'm cut out for high school boys, and their, *I am a jock, hear me roar*, arrogance."

Thia laughed at her daughter's bored mockery of her date, and her father frowned.

"What did he do?"

"Oh, it's nothing to worry about, dad—he just thought I should be overjoyed to go out with the quarterback. I, unfortunately for him, didn't think he was as important as he thought himself to be, so I told him so." Kallisto grinned.

"Talking about "Austin the Great" are we?" Amanda interjected as she walked into the kitchen, towel-drying her long hair. "He really should develop a bigger chest if he were going to go all high and mighty with a date such as Kallisto."

"Well, it seems you girls haven't been damaged," Thia giggled at the girls' sarcasm. Kallisto's father shook his head and excused himself from the kitchen.

The three women continued to bash the male gender over pancakes and sausage. After breakfast, the duo returned upstairs to prepare for a day of shopping when Kallisto's cell phone rang. To grab it, Kallisto hopped over the clothes, which were still scattered on the floor from her scavenger hunt the night before.

"Hello," her eyes went wide when she heard the voice on the other end. "Well, I suppose. I don't know about that, Austin. I thought you were dif—"

Kallisto stopped. Amanda sat on the bed, waiting as the silence from Kallisto's side of the conversation filled the room.

After several minutes, Kallisto said, "Okay, one more chance."

"What the hell!" Amanda protested.

"Tomorrow then, okay," Kallisto said into the phone just before she hung up.

"Please tell me that was not what I think it was," Amanda begged.

"He apologized, told me he was wrong, and has been thinking about what I said when he brought me home. I'm giving him a second chance."

"I cannot believe this. He's a jerk, and you know it." Disgusted, Amanda walked from the room.

Kallisto ran to the bedroom door and asked, "Aren't we going Christmas shopping this afternoon?"

"Yes, I just need coffee. I'm sure after a gallon; this will make sense."

Morpheus spent the morning thinking of his shortage of options. With a heavy heart, he decided to go to his brother and iron out the logistics of his extended visit to the mortal realm. He had decided not to speak with The Fates. They were like talking to oracles, but at least an oracle gave you a riddle; The Fates Three just said a lot while saying nothing.

Phantasos sat in deep thought, enjoying the shade of a large weeping willow on the edge of a great koi pond surrounded by waterfalls. All gods enjoyed their places of refuge; for Phantasos, that was his gardens and ponds.

"I am leaving today," Morpheus stated without any other explanation.

"I suspected as much," Phantasos sighed. "You will have two servants that will answer to Mom and Dad, and you will work in the *Gallery of the gods* in the outdoor strip mall a couple of blocks from Kallisto's home. It is the family business you will inherit."

"Is that the same gallery franchise Hermes set up in Greece about two hundred years ago to give mortals a more *realistic* view of our world?" Morpheus asked. "Ironically, the paintings and sculptures in his galleries are exact replicas of our world, yet most mortals have no idea the legends are true."

"Yes, the truth in the art is overlooked as just beautiful masterpieces from anonymous artists. It's incredible how much information we put in front of them, and they still believe us to be mere fantasy." Phantasos laughed.

"Hermes is quite the entrepreneur. His galleries are now worldwide. Too bad he has no need of money," Morpheus stated. Grinning, he continued, "Looks like I am now an employee of Hermes. Maybe he will dream of giving me a raise."

Ignoring his brother's jest, Phantasos continued. "You will live in a large home in a gated community. We will place a daemon at the gatehouse while you are there to avoid a mortal seeing anything suspicious. The story will be that your family owns the company, and you are working on opening the Maui gallery. You are a senior at the local university and will begin classes after Christmas break as a transfer. The school will be getting your "transcripts," Phantasos made quotation marks in the air as he said this, "from your previous school in Athens, Greece. To the mortals, you will have a profound Greek accent."

"Looks like you have thought of everything, brother. Out of curiosity, how do my transcripts look?" Morpheus winked.

"You are at the top of your class as an ancient history major. I wanted to put you in the bottom twenty percent but decided that would get you nowhere with your woman." Phantasos looked smug, trying hard not to laugh.

"Actually, my favorite subject would be anatomy," Morpheus raised his eyebrows and smirked.

"That may be little brother—that subject has homework you do not need to work on," Phantasos jeered.

The two brothers continued their bantering for a few more minutes trying to delay the unavoidable. "Do not forget to watch over my dreamers. I will contact you when I can."

Phantasos nodded, and Morpheus vanished.

After about fifteen minutes of binging coffee, Amanda returned to the bedroom. "Goodness knows I've dated some creeps—I guess it's your turn. I just don't want you to make the same mistakes I made." Amanda confided to Kallisto. "Besides, what about your dream god?"

Kallisto eased over to her friend and gave her a big hug. "I know, but if I don't, I'll wonder if he was serious about his apology. What if he does mean it and becomes the person I thought he was before he turned into a jerk? After all, we all make mistakes. And as for as my dream god goes—he's—let's say—not of my world."

The girls went to the strip mall to get the last of their Christmas shopping done. It was now the twenty-first of December, and time was ticking. Kallisto finally found the fishing cap her father wanted.

"Hey Amanda, let's go look at the new art gallery. I hear it has sexy paintings of Greek gods."

"Sure, I could use some Greek god eye candy about now," Amanda said in a monotone voice. The lack of inflection in her friend's words was funny, and Kallisto snorted before she could compose herself.

"I want—no—I need an unnaturally beautiful Greek god to kiss me most passionately and give me incredibly gorgeous hot pink lingerie." Sarcasm exuded from every syllable as Amanda rolled her eyes and clasped her hands to her chest.

Laughing, they made their way through the thick holiday crowd to the gallery. Kallisto eyed a painting of a beautiful waterfall that made her stop and gasp.

"That's it."

"What's it?"

"See that painting of the waterfall?" Kallisto pointed.

"Yeah—Why?" Amanda asked.

"That's it, our waterfall—on Olympus—it's there."

"The one from your dreams?

"Yes, that's it." Kallisto's mouth opened in awe. "Amanda, there is a spot right here," Kallisto points to a spot on the painting, "where you can easily enter the pool, and running along the stream, deer and other animals come to get their fill. I wonder how much they are asking for it?"

"Sir, do you know where or if that waterfall exists?" Kallisto questioned a sales attendant as he was walking by.

"On Mount Olympus, of course," with a slight accent and a wink, the salesman, with a name tag showing John, answered.

"How much is the painting?" Kallisto asked, not taking her eyes off the falls.

"That particular painting is $45,000," the salesman informed her.

Kallisto tried very hard to keep astonishment off her face. "Thank you."

She turned to Amanda, mouthed *shit,* and then beckoned her to follow her back out to the sidewalk. "Damn, did you hear him? They want $45,000 for that painting."

Amanda, wide-eyed, said flatly, "Wow. I guess you'll have to settle for the real thing—darn it."

That made Kallisto laugh, and the girls set off again to finish shopping. The day was perfect. Christmas decorations graced every corner and storefront. Under the gazebo in the courtyard were carolers singing all the Christmas classics, wearing short-sleeved colorful button-down shirts and grass skirts. The smell of cinnamon and evergreen leaves hung in the air. The décor, songs, and smells made up for the lack of frigid temperatures and snow synonymous with the season.

"How could someone not enjoy this time of year?" Kallisto asked. "Isn't this beautiful?" The two of them sat on benches around the gazebo and listened to the carolers sing, ironically enough, *"White Christmas"* by Irving Berlin. "

After completing their gift list, the girls returned to Kallisto's. Amanda pulled into the driveway to let Kallisto out.

"I'll call you tomorrow to see if you have come to your senses about going out with that *"god wanna be,"* Amanda scowled but followed it with a grin.

"I thought Austin was a jerk, and you didn't enjoy his company," Thia asked when Kallisto walked through the door.

"Well, hello to you too, mom," Kallisto let out a breath through her nose and hoped her mother did not find her as gullible as Amanda did. "He called and apologized and then begged for a second chance to make up for being such an ass last night."

"Well," her mother pondered momentarily, "they say that forgiveness is divine. I just hope you know what you're doing."

Still lugging shopping bags, Kallisto said she did and excused herself from the room, wanting to relieve herself from her burden.

In a couple of hours, Kallisto managed to wrap all the gifts she had purchased and set them under the ten-foot tree towering over their living room. The tree was decorated with a mixture of Hawaiian and Grecian cultures. One could find figurines of St. Nicholas on a fishing boat and Santas wearing colorful Hawaiian shirts with leis around their necks. Kallisto's parents worked hard to educate her in both cultures. As with Greek custom, a shallow wooden bowl with a wire holding up a cross wrapped in rosemary sat on the dining room table. The rosemary was dipped into the holy water, housed by the bowl, and the holy water was sprinkled daily throughout the house to ward off bad spirits. Her father's ukulele propped against the wall. They loved to gather with friends and sing Christmas songs in Hawaiian as her dad played the ukulele.

The decorated room made Kallisto's thoughts return to last Christmas when her grandmother flew from Greece to spend three weeks with them. After sprinkling the Holy water each evening, her grandmother told them stories of the gods. Her tales were often different from those you would find in books. She told them as if they were real. The gods were portrayed as helpers to man who possessed unique abilities, combined with the infidelity of so many deities, made for very complex fantasies. Kallisto's favorite stories were of Zeus, Hera, and Hades, which covered most stories about the Greek Pantheon.

Her grandmother's stories were always told with great emotion, and she never spared the details that made you feel like you were a part of that divine world. Kallisto grew up loving all her time with her grandmother, particularly the ones in Athens. When she was in Greece, sitting with her grandmother, looking over the beautiful city, she always felt like she was in the world of the gods, more comfortable than anywhere else. Kallisto smiled as her memories raced through her head. The painting of the waterfall in the gallery made her feel the same way—like she belonged. She closed her eyes and remembered how the water felt cascading over her body and the smell of the honeysuckle that lingered in the air. She could feel the tingle her god's eyes gave her as he watched her enjoy the waterfall. Remembering her dreams made her feel as comfortable as being in Greece with her grandmother.

Chapter VIII

Accent

Monday morning came and went as Kallisto helped her mother prepare for the holidays. They went shopping for the ingredients to prepare their Christmas meal as well as a few last-minute gifts her mother needed to pick up. They returned home and together baked a variety of bread and made cookies to wrap and give to friends. Around five o'clock, Kallisto excused herself to get ready for her date with Austin. Not wanting to give the wrong impression, she chose a more modest outfit of blue jeans with a cute t-shirt from D.F.O. that said, *Got Ambrosia?* She guessed the humor would be lost on him.

Austin was on time, six o'clock on the dot. To her humiliation, Kallisto's father answered the door. He did not try to hide his displeasure with Austin. He even asked if he had learned his lesson and could mind his manners. Kallisto rushed him out the door before her father could humiliate her further.

Once in the car, Austin began with a reiteration of his apology. "I'm sorry for my behavior the other night. Your dad has every right to be disgusted with me."

"That may be true, but he should be polite," Kallisto said.

"Where would you like to go this evening?" Austin asked.

"How about a movie?" Kallisto was very eager to start over from scratch. She was always willing to give second chances, but no more than that.

"There's a great comedy out; let's see when it's playing."

"Sounds great to me. Let's go to the one at the outdoor mall. We can eat in the food court and look around until our movie starts." Kallisto suggested.

She wanted to make sure they were around a lot of people, not completely trusting him after their last date. Second chances are great, but you never repeat a mistake by walking in the same footsteps as your first blunder. This was good advice given to her by Mrs. Bai when she was younger, and she and Amanda's friendship with Elizabeth were over.

They talked animatedly, and to Kallisto's astonishment, she enjoyed- their conversation. He asked her about her hobbies, and she admitted she was a geek who loved to read and enjoyed studying mythology.

"My mom is from Greece, where I was born. I love to visit my grandmother whenever possible. She's the one who got me fascinated with mythology."

"That's cool. I've always lived in Hawaii. My dad is a botanist, and where else can one study some of the most fascinating plants this country has to offer?" Austin seemed more talkative than he had on their previous date.

Time passed rather quickly as they talked, without any awkward silences. The marquee showed the next showing beginning at 7:45. Deciding to eat at the mall gave them an hour and a half to eat and look around. "Sounds good to me. I'll go ahead and get our tickets." Austin said as they stood in front of the box office.

"What hobbies, other than football, do you indulge in?"

"I love all sports, and I have a thing for physical science. I know that doesn't sound fun to a lot of people, but I'm good at it, and I'd love to teach high school one day and maybe coach the football and basketball teams."

Kallisto was beginning to see Austin in a new light. *Maybe we can become friends after all.*

They threw out their paper plate and Styrofoam cups and walked through the mall, peering into the windows while enjoying the Christmas atmosphere. Kallisto kept her arms folded, not ready to have him hold her hand, which was still too intimate for her. She also felt a little guilty for being on a date—again. She felt like she was cheating on her dream man.

"Kallisto?" Austin had been saying her name as she stared into space, her mind clearly on other things.

"Oh, I'm sorry. I was just thinking."

"No problem. Do you care to go with me into the sporting goods store?" Austin asked.

"No, that's fine." They still had forty-five minutes until they had to be back at the theater.

Austin ran into some school buddies. Kallisto stood in the shoe department for fifteen minutes, waiting for him to introduce her—which never happened. She decided to wander around the store. On a good note, she found a pair of light brown hiking boots she would love to have. She laughed since the only hiking she did was in her dreams—on Mount Olympus—*I'm so not normal!* She continued walking around until she saw the art gallery just a shop down from her. They now had only twenty minutes until their movie began. She walked over to her bad-mannered date and interrupted.

"Austin, I'm going to check out the *Gallery of the gods.*" She pointed in the direction she was already walking without looking at him.

"Okay, I'll be there in a minute," He went back to talking with his friends.

As soon as Kallisto stepped into the gallery, her skin was invaded by chill bumps, and she could've sworn she smelled honeysuckle and lavender. She shook her head to clear it and made her way to the painting she couldn't stop thinking about since she and Amanda had been there the day before. The painting took her breath away the way it did the first time she saw it. She stood there with closed eyes, leaning her head back just enough to soak in the imaginary aroma that seemed to be coming from inside the store. Behind her shut lids, she replaced the painting with the actual memory of the waterfall. She remembered the doe and its fawn drinking from the pool and how the water felt cascading over her body, and how being held by—

"May I help you, miss?"

Kallisto jumped and opened her eyes as a heavily accented Grecian man interrupted her thoughts. It took her a minute to focus on the exceptionally hot Greek. Chills went up her spine.

"I am sorry for startling you. Do you like the painting?" A boyish smirk played across his full lips.

All Kallisto could do was stare open-mouthed at the Greek beauty standing before her. She would have categorized him as a Greek god. His long blonde hair was pulled into a ponytail at the nape of his neck, and his crystal blue eyes held some purpose she couldn't place. They reminded her of someone or somewhere.

"Uh—yeah, I mean, it's beyond beautiful." Kallisto was unsure if she was answering his question or referring to him. "You could say it's a place a person could only dream about."

"It is said to be the largest waterfall on Mount Olympus." He gave her a grin that came dangerously close to stopping her heart. As he stared straight into her eyes, he moved close enough she could feel the heat of his body and added, "If I did, I would give it to you. Someone as beautiful as you should be immortal."

Cocking her head to the side, she asked, "Excuse me?"

Not stepping back from her, he nodded toward her shirt, "Your shirt."

"Oh, yes. You're probably the only person within a hundred miles of this mall who understands it. Have we met before?"

"Hey, Kallisto, sorry, the guys were catching me up on Branson's par—" he cut his sentence short when he saw his date standing inches from the sales attendant. "Excuse me, am I interrupting something?"

"No, he was just telling me about the painting." Kallisto didn't look from the man's eyes and didn't point, so Austin had no idea which painting she was referring to. She shook her head, trying to dislodge the trance. Clearing her throat, she turned to Austin. "Is it time for the movie?"

"Yes, we really need to head over to the theater." Austin didn't remove his eyes from the man scowling at him.

Kallisto took one last glimpse at the Grecian "god" who gave her chills. She said goodbye, turned, and then left with her date.

Morpheus stood there grimly as he watched the woman he loved, in her natural, fully conscious state, walk out the door with another man. *When had he come back into her life?* In a whisper to himself, he stated, "This was not part of the plan."

"Who was that guy back there?" Austin asked as soon as they were out the door of the gallery.

Kallisto had no idea how to answer this question. *Just a guy selling paintings—A really gorgeous guy with a hot body that gets my shirt—I don't know—The sexiest guy I've ever seen*—all honest answers, but none she wanted to give.

"He was just telling me about a painting I've been eyeing." Truth, sort of.

"He seemed to know you."

"What makes you think that?" Kallisto asked.

"The way he looked at you, and he was almost on top of you. He also looked like he could kill me for interrupting."

Kallisto was relieved the theater was close to the gallery. She turned the interrogation around on him.

"I was wondering why you didn't introduce me to your friends."

"You go to school with all of them. I thought you knew them." Austin answered.

"Well, I knew one of their names was Mark, but that was it. I had no clue who the other three were, and the only reason I knew Mark's name is because he's always on some school ballot that we're encouraged to fill out."

"Sorry." That was all Austin said before handing his ticket to the ticket taker and ushering Kallisto to the correct theater.

The rest of the evening was spent in that awkward silence. After the movie, he took her home and left without so much as looking back.

Kallisto ran into her house and up the stairs, unable to contain her enthusiasm. She dialed Amanda's cell.

"Are you at home?" Kallisto asked.

"Yeah, why are you? I thought you had a date with Mr. Conceit."

"We ate, looked around the mall, and saw a movie. Then he brought me home because I'm in love with an art gallery worker." Kallisto was waiting for Amanda to respond to that.

"What did you say?" Amanda asked.

"I met a guy, well, sort of. Anyway, he's so hot, and he understood my "Got Ambrosia" t-shirt. Best of all, he is Greek!" Kallisto was bubbling over with excitement. "Can I come over and stay the night?"

"Of course. Maybe you'll explain things face-to-face better than you're doing over the phone. See ya in a few."

Kallisto ran back downstairs and knocked on her parent's bedroom door. "Come in." Kallisto's mother's gentle voice came from behind the thick wooden door. Kallisto went in and told her parents she had a good time on her date. Her father felt like she had made a mature decision by coming home earlier than her curfew and telling her so.

"I'm going to spend the night with Amanda. Is that okay?" She asked both of her parents, who each had on their reading lamps with their books lying across their laps, giving her their full attention.

"Sure, just be careful," Thia said.

Kallisto kissed her parents on the cheek and left, trying to hold in her excitement, hoping not to give them any reason to question her further about her evening.

Arriving at Amanda's house a short while later, Amanda opened the door before Kallisto had time to get up the front steps. "Tell me all about this guy at the mall, and then if we have time, you can tell me about your date—what's his name."

Amanda's house was cozy, with family portraits from years gone by hanging throughout. Her mother was quite the decorator, being from The South, where homes are a fashion statement, but despite its trendy décor, it always felt like home. Both her parents were already in bed, so the girls went to Amanda's room to gossip about the scandal of the evening.

Kallisto, like her grandmother, could spin a good story, so this was the first time Amanda had ever seen her tongue-tied. Basically, all she was able to convey was a guy that worked at the gallery was absolutely gorgeous, and only because she used those exact words and nothing else. Even with her short description, Kallisto's eyes and lack of ability to put her findings into words gave away how enamored she was with the man from the Greek art gallery.

Kallisto woke well rested on the morning of the twenty-third, but still, no dreams. She was careful not to wake Amanda and tiptoed out of the room to grab a bowl of cereal. Her heart was heavy, and she felt lonely for the first time since Morpheus entered her dreams. She recalled the past several days. This was the second night in a row with dreamless sleep. The good of it was she didn't feel as tired or as fuzzy-headed as she had been over the last several weeks. She vaguely remembered Morpheus telling her to remember him. Closing her eyes, she tried to connect herself to the memory of that day, the last time she was with him. She could remember his pleading with her to try to remember what he looked like. It seemed there was more, but she couldn't put her finger on it.

"Morning," Amanda stumbled into the kitchen, rubbing her eyes and yawning. "What's on the agenda for today?"

"I'd like to go back to the mall and see if that Greek salesman is working," Kallisto grinned.

"Sounds good to me. I had a strange dream last night. There was a man; I couldn't make him out. He told me to watch out for you, that you were—emotionally and mentally fragile," Amanda sounded concerned. "The dream was so real. It kinda freaked me out a little."

"I wonder if it could've been Morpheus?" Kallisto thought aloud.

"I don't think so, but I could be wrong—actually, I'm not sure why I don't think it was him. I'm sure it was just a dream. I was worried about you going out with Austin again. Maybe my subconscious was telling me to get you away from the jock." Amanda was rambling uncharacteristically, much like

Kallisto always did when she was anxious. Trying to lighten the atmosphere, she grinned, "I told him you were always mental in some way."

"Thanks a lot; with friends like you—" Kallisto began, but Amanda's cell phone rang.

"Hello," Amanda answered, grinning back at Kallisto, "well, I can't today—how about the day after Christmas? Yeah, okay, see ya then."

Kallisto grinned at Amanda as she hung up from a brief conversation of plan-making.

"That was Michael; he wanted to catch a movie today. I told him we would the day after Christmas."

"You don't have to go with me to the gallery. Call him back and go to the movies. I really don't mind." Kallisto really didn't mind. She wanted a chance to think and possibly talk to the salesman at the gallery.

"Are you sure you don't mind? I like him. We've been talking a lot on the phone, and he came over last night and watched a movie with me and my parents. How crazy is that?" Amanda beamed.

"Of course, I'm sure. " Go call him back, and I'm going to go home and get a shower," Kallisto spoke as she stood. "Call him," she gently pushed Amanda toward the phone and left.

As Kallisto walked out to her car, she got the familiar feeling of someone watching. This time her lips turned into a grin instead of the usual grimace she got whenever the pestering sensation came upon her. She now knew who was behind the chilling feeling.

She climbed into her car and, buckling her seatbelt, said, "Come see me, Morpheus."

She knew he would, she didn't know how she knew, but she did.

On Olympus, Morpheus went to his orb and watched as Kallisto walked out of Amanda's front door. Seeing her last night had made him more than anxious. He spent the night between a cold shower and beating the hell out of his punching bag. The shower was to tame his wild insatiability where Kallisto was concerned. The punching bag was for the anger built up between his disgust at finding her on the arm of that louse, the gods and goddesses playing games with his love life, and his rage for putting the woman he loved through possible mental anguish that could one day drive her mad.

He noticed her grin when she felt his presence, and his body reacted. Then she sent him into complete overdrive when she asked him to come to her.

As excited as he was about this new development, he was also shocked. *How can she know?* He did not know the answer to that, but he felt her ability to acknowledge his existence while she was awake had to be a step in the right direction. This task may be easier than he thought. Maybe if she could, without reservation, accept fiction as reality, the gods would let the two of them be together.

"If I go see her, I will surely need to bathe in ice water—cold showers are no longer cutting it," Morpheus said aloud.

Chapter IX

Athens

Kallisto made it home and quickly ran inside.

"Hey, mom, I'm home."

"Hey honey, I thought you were spending the day with Amanda," Thia said.

"She received a call from Michael, and I insisted she go to a movie with him. So, here I am." "I'm planning on going to the outdoor mall later this afternoon to look at a painting I've had my eyes on." Kallisto was in a hurry to get to her room.

"Your dad and I are going out tonight. We're meeting the Williams for dinner. Will you be okay here by yourself?" Her mother always worried about leaving Kallisto at home alone at night.

"Yes, mother. You know that I'll be going off to college soon, and I'll be alone at night all the time?"

"I know. Let me be a worried mother for just a little longer. It's my right of passage, after all."

Kallisto smiled at her mom and kissed her on the cheek, "I'm going to spend some time reading and maybe even get in a nap before I go to the mall. See ya before you go out?"

"Sure."

Kallisto ran upstairs, taking them two at a time. She could still feel him watching her. She was wondering how long it would take to make herself fall asleep. *I bet I won't be able to.*

"Can you help me sleep? Legend says you can," Kallisto said aloud to her spying god.

Again, her ring heated. This led her mind in all kinds of directions. She had so many questions to ask him. *Would he answer them? Could he answer them?* She wanted to know why he had not been in her dreams for two days in a row, why can she not remember his face when she was awake, but most of all, what did he want from her?

Morpheus knew making her sleep was not the wisest of things to do. He noticed she went back and forth on whether or not she was sane and whether or not to allow herself to believe in the stories her grandmother had told her since she was a little girl. He also knew if she believed enough to communicate with him verbally while awake, then she was much closer to accepting legend than he or even Zeus had thought.

"Okay, I need to take a shower. That means you need to stop watching me," Kallisto was very aware the ancient Greeks had no reservations about public baths, but she did.

"Just give me an hour, please," she begged.

She momentarily felt the ring heat again, and the feeling of being watched was gone. Kallisto felt euphoric at her ability to communicate with Morpheus and got quickly into the shower.

For the first time, Kallisto worried over the small details, like her appearance. She brushed her hair and put it in a ponytail, then applied her makeup and put on a silky white sundress with a sweeping neckline and a hem trimmed in cream lace. She liked to wear it when she needed to feel better about herself or just plain sexy. To be honest, she didn't know why she was doing this. She had been going to sleep and dreaming of him for a couple of months now.

Once satisfied with her makeup, she let her hair down and brushed it until it looked like black satin cascading down her back and over her shoulders. She stretched across her bed and waited for her admirer to return his gaze. The clock said she had about ten minutes before the hour she asked him for. As she lay there, she started feeling silly. Had she wanted the fantasy world she had grown up hearing about so badly that she had gone mad? She actually dressed up to take a nap.

Kallisto heard about people who role-played, getting so caught up in the game, and with their character, they went mad and sometimes committed suicide. Those people usually had other problems, mental or emotional, that plagued them before they ever started the games. What they had in common with her was they were so caught up in their fantasy world they could not discern between it and reality. Role-playing had nothing to do with their deaths; their inability to differentiate between the flight of their imagination and reality due to their emotional state. Would this be her destiny? *Am I insane? What about the facts? My lingerie, the ring on my finger, the scents on my skin—*

Kallisto yawned as her mind turned over with its yet unresolved chatter. She was weighing the facts and had decided to put everything down in black and white on paper so she could look at it. She thought to get up and retrieve her journal when her lids felt heavy. She closed them for just a moment—

Morpheus went to her bedroom and watched as she slept. She was so stunning lying on her bed in her silky white sundress, and her ebony hair pulled to one side draping over her shoulder. He noticed she had donned makeup. He drank in her appearance and reveled in it. *Aphrodite had nothing on this woman. Where to take her? Greece?*

He leaned over her body and brushed his lips over hers. She stirred slightly as he whispered the words in her ear that would take them to where she would wake.

Kallisto stretched, and her eyelids flittered open.

"Morpheus?"

"I'm here, my *dea femminile*," Morpheus grinned mischievously, making him sexier than usual, which said a lot. "We are in your homeland. I thought you might enjoy the trip."

"We're in Greece?" Sitting up, Kallisto was in awe of the view. Her eyes drank in the scenery from the hillside, and her nose filled with the familiar smell of sea salt. Tears filled her eyes. This land was in her blood, part of her soul. This was home.

"Would you like to take a walk around the city with me?" Morpheus asked.

She closed her eyes as he spoke. With the slight breeze, the smells, and his accent, she felt she had died and gone to heaven. She didn't want to wake.

"Is...is...this real?"

"Yes, it is very real, and I am breaking all the rules by telling you this."

"Why would you do that?" Kallisto asked.

"I fell in love with you the first time I entered your dreams. I have told you this before. Because of the rules, sometimes you cannot remember things about me, like what I look like. You may not even remember this conversation. Taking you as I have and like I am now can cause irreversible damage to your psyche."

"Taking me? Like, I'm actually here?"

"Yes, when I said real, I meant it. You and I are physically in Greece."

"How?" Kallisto whispered more to herself.

"I merged the realms for you, and by doing so, your subconscious is being pulled in different directions. I am a being who can take anyone, anywhere, while they dream. I can choose to take them in a dream or take them physically. Sometimes I keep you in the dream world. Most of the time, I do not. Sometimes you remember, most of the time you have no recollection."

Kallisto felt panic setting in. Morpheus must have noticed because he began rubbing her arm gently—a calming motion.

"I used to remember more about my dreams than I do lately. Why is that?" Kallisto asked.

"The Fates will do what they can to keep you from making the connection complete; however, for some reason, they, along with Zeus, have given me a chance to help you out mentally so you do not have a breakdown. I am not supposed to tell you these things," Morpheus confided.

"If you are breaking the rules, maybe you should stop telling me."

"I needed to get this out, and you will not remember when you wake. The best I can hope is you remember bits and pieces."

"How about that walk?" She desperately needed to be on her feet to think. "If I'm going to be with a Greek god in Greece, I want to remember something about it."

❧ ⟫⟫⟫⟶ ⟵⟪⟪⟪ ❧

Morpheus stood and reached his hand to Kallisto. He pulled her up to his body, and the two stood on a ridge overlooking the incredible sight of Athens below.

He bent his head and captured her lips with his, very gently at first, knowing he had to maintain his composure. Getting his body to cooperate was difficult; he, too, was going mad.

He was the first to pull from the fierce kiss beginning to develop. With his eyes still closed, he committed the taste of her lips to his memory. Kallisto just pouted.

"Don't look at me that way, I cannot break any more rules, and I am not allowed to have carnal knowledge of you. I decided kissing would be okay since different kisses have different meanings."

Kallisto eyed him with a raised brow.

"Okay, I know the kiss we shared has only one meaning, but I need some latitude. I have taken enough cold showers in the last two months to last me for the next decade," Morpheus admitted.

Kallisto giggled, "I'll try and leash my desire while in your presence, sir."

They walked along the docks holding hands and talking about their lives. He told Kallisto about his brothers and why Phantasos didn't want him to get close to her. He could see she was in deep thought as he told her how Marissa had gone mad from the pull on her psyche.

"She could not take it anymore, the not knowing. So, to prove that she had been sleeping the whole time, she killed herself on Olympus, thinking it was a dream. This was an unheard-of feat since it had always been thought a mortal being could not die on Olympus. That day it was found mortals could die anywhere. Her parents thought she had died in her sleep. Phantasos had to return her body to her bed before they woke. Between watching her drink the vile of poison, carrying her lifeless body back to her realm, and watching her parents hold her body while screaming and sobbing, Phantasos became lost—a lost dream god. He could no longer go into dreams, even to help an individual in desperate need. This drove a wedge between him and our father, which has gone very deep and is not likely to repair itself for some time—if it ever does."

"Is he still lost?" Kallisto asked.

"He is, but he is working on it, something he has not done in over a hundred years."

"A hundred years?" Kallisto was stunned. "How old is he?"

"I stopped counting centuries ago, but it is somewhere over five thousand years now," Morpheus answered her question as if it was normal to live thousands of years old.

"Wh—What!" Kallisto gave an audible gasp. "How old are you?"

"Is that important?" Morpheus asked hesitantly.

"Well, I just can't wrap my mind around this. Please tell me."

Morpheus took a long heavy breath, "I am three thousand seven hundred five years old and still just a juvenile in our realm. If it makes you feel better, they all say I am hot-headed because of my youth. "A very teenage trait—no?" Morpheus grinned.

"Yeah, young." Kallisto was stunned. They continued to walk silently for a couple of minutes.

Morpheus wanted her to get used to one shocking revelation at a time, so he gave her a few minutes to process the information.

After a few minutes of deep thought, her reply was nothing more than, "Wow."

Morpheus could not help but laugh at her surrender to this new knowledge. "That went better than I thought it would.

In a very logical voice, Kallisto gave him her reasoning, "Well, the legends of gods are just that, legends, myths. I've always said myths are started from sparks of truth; for those legends to have any truth, the gods would have to be immortal and have lived for thousands of years. It's only logical, even though it's hard to imagine living so long."

"I, on the other hand, cannot fathom aging and dying," Morpheus replied.

"Can gods die?" Kallisto questioned.

"It is very rare. There are many fallen gods, but to no longer exist usually only happens with wars between pantheons. That was one reason immortals used mortals to wage war, to keep entire pantheons from collapsing. Usually, the catastrophic storms that consume so many lives are due to feuds between gods. Most of those feuds are domestic."

"You live in a supernatural soap opera." Kallisto gave Morpheus a half grin.

He halted their stroll and peered down into Kallisto's eyes. He looked past his reflection through her pupils and straight into her soul. He could lose himself there without a second thought of going back. Back to the realm where she could not remember everything they had said to each other and where she could not recall his appearance. He traced a warm finger down her temple to the line of her jaw. With his thumb, he lightly mapped out the curves of her full lips.

"If The Fates don't want me to go mad, why don't they just let me remember?

"Because that is a realization you must come to on your own. We have laws that even The Fates must adhere to."

Kallisto went very still as he caressed her lips with his, momentarily forgetting to breathe. Morpheus pulled from their kiss and told her again...

"Remember."

Kallisto suddenly woke with the smell of lavender and honeysuckle. She looked at the clock; her nap had lasted well over an hour. She laid back on her pillows and closed her eyes, trying to recall her dream. She remembered being in Greece, the touch of his lips to hers, and the talk of rules. *What rules, though?* She spent most of her concentration on trying to remember his features. *How can I be in love with a face I don't know?* She strained her memory.

She gasped as memories of her overlooking Athens, kissing him passionately, and how strong and warm he felt in her arms, but still...not his appearance.

To her astonishment, she looked in the mirror and saw smudged lip gloss around her slightly swollen lips. Her reflection smiled back as she felt around with her extra awareness to know if he was still watching. He was not.

After getting her lips smudge-free, she left to run a couple of errands before she headed to the gallery, excited to see the painting of the waterfall and wondered if the young Greek salesman would be there.

Kallisto believed deeply in monogamist relationships, *but does that count when the one you love you cannot remember? At what point do I give up my childish fantasies and deal with the fact I cannot have a relationship solely in my dreams?*

She finished her mother's errands and checked her bank account, trying to decide if she had enough money to eat out at the mall. Her account held 153 dollars and twenty-three cents.

"Crrrap!" Exasperated at the lack of funds.

She hadn't had a job since the summer when she waited tables, but not very well, and what little savings she had acquired, she had spent on gas and Christmas presents. She had hoped not to have to get a job until after she came back from her trip to Greece over Spring break. Now in order to have spending money to shop at her favorite boutiques, she would need to acquire an after-school job. *Maybe the Gallery of the gods will be hiring.* After all, if anyone knew about the Greek or Roman gods, it would be Kallisto.

She drove, deciding to check out the job prospects at the mall while scoping out the Greek hunk. As she drove, she glimpsed her ring. She grinned wryly as it reminded her of her dream. With that came the memory of her and her Greek god looking over the city of Athens with the breeze flowing through her hair and his warm, soft lips caressing hers. Suddenly she heard a car horn and realized just in time that she had swerved just over the line into the adjacent lane. *Damn, Kallisto, get a hold of yourself!*

Her heart was still pumping hard and fast as she pulled into the mall parking lot. She sat in her car trying to calm her nerves when she thought she saw the good-looking Greek from the gallery walking to a convertible. This did nothing to help her heart. In fact, she was sure that it sped up considerably.

⤜⤜⤜ ⤛⤛⤛

As Morpheus climbed into his car, he felt eyes rake over his body. With a grin, he turned and winked at his admirer, *Kallisto.* Knowing that she was looking at him gave him a deep desire to go and pull her to him as he had mere hours before in Greece. Knowing that would only get him slapped; he grinned even wider. What he wanted was to go to her and explain himself. How would it look if a stranger ran up to her and proclaimed to be her dream god? That was sure to drive Kallisto's sanity over the edge.

He was going home for the rest of the day to map out how to help Kallisto remember. Plus, his masquerade as the son of a very wealthy family had its drawbacks. In the masquerade, he was the owners' son, but in actuality, he was the one doing the mundane public relations work known simply as "PR," another "gift" from Zeus—*Work.*

⤜⤜⤜ ⤛⤛⤛

As she watched the Greek magnificence reach for his car, he stopped, turned, looked straight at her with his penetrating eyes, and gave her the sexiest smile she had ever seen and winked. With that wink came the telltale chill down her spine. Her ring became hot, so hot she gasped and looked down to ensure her finger was okay. *Morpheus knows I'm looking at another man.* When she looked up, the Greek had disappeared into his car and backed out of the parking space. Kallisto noticed the further away the black Mercedes got, the cooler her ring became. Once the vehicle was out of sight, her ring was back to normal. Was her Greek god jealous—*again?*

Kallisto got a large French fry and ice water to save from spending too much money. Once done with her snack, she began looking on the doors and windows of the shops to see if anyone had a Help Wanted sign. She was able to find two department stores that needed someone, so she put in an application at both. She managed to waste well over an hour and a half eating and applying for employment, trying to gain the courage to go to the *Gallery of the gods.* She couldn't decide if she wanted the handsome man to be there again or not, so she played different scenarios in her head.

Number 1: If I go in and he is there, he'll surely think I came to see him. After all, I could never afford anything in there. Number 2: He would not believe that since I saw him leave. He would think that I thought he was gone. Number 3: But it was almost two hours later. He may think that I waited to see if he would come back. Number 4: He would think I have money and get his hopes up, thinking I might buy the 45,000-dollar painting. Ugh...why am I overthinking this?

Kallisto sat on a bench, watching shoppers pass while she got the nerve up to go to the gallery. She could see the excitement of the upcoming holidays in the eyes of the children as they walked hand in hand with their parents looking at the decorations. She could hear children laughing as they rode the beautiful carousel just south, where she procrastinated on the bench. Two sea birds strutted alongside the flow of the pedestrians as the shoppers talked and pointed at the beautifully decorated windows displaying Santa in Hawaiian swim shorts. The colorful Hawaiian button-ups combined with Christmas decorations and Maui's continuous slight breeze bringing in the smell of salt water and eucalyptus made it harder for her to leave her bench of safety.

Somewhat reluctantly, Kallisto stood and demanded her feet take her to the gallery whether the rest of her wanted to go or not. Within moments she was standing in front of the *Gallery of the gods* with shock on her face. The sign on the door stated in bold red letters, Help Wanted. She entered the store to find the same man as the day she and Amanda stopped by. Kallisto looked around at the paintings until the employee finished with his customer. She came upon one of Zeus, the ruler over the gods of Olympus. The painting was huge. Zeus was life-size and looked exceptionally powerful, portrayed in oils. She stared at the painting for a moment. Were his eyes green, almost an aqua green? Or were they more on the blue side of aqua?

"May I help you?" The salesman politely asked.

Kallisto jumped, "Oh! I'm sorry, I was deep in thought. Isn't he magnificent?" she motioned to the painting of Zeus.

"He is a sight to be reckoned with," answered the salesman.

"The painting looks so real. It's as if he is watching me from whichever direction I stand."

"It's been said that Zeus himself posed for this painting." The salesman grinned and watched intently.

"Who owned this painting before the gallery?" Kallisto asked.

"It is said to have once hung in Hera's bedchamber. The legend is that she was upset at Zeus because of his many infidelities and sent the painting from her sight by way of a servant."

Kallisto could tell the salesman loved to tell the tales of his people to the Americans.

"I love the legends of old. I was born in Greece. I moved here ten years ago. My grandmother still lives in Athens and *loves* the tales of the gods. You could say that learning and telling the legends is like a hobby of mine." Kallisto was in her element. "That's why I can't seem to stay away from this gallery. I noticed you are looking for help." She hoped the position hadn't been filled, and they had just forgotten to remove the Help Wanted sign.

"The owner's son is getting the store up and running. We are having our grand opening on New Year's Day," he said something about hiring someone for twenty hours a week to help get the PR for the store underway.

The salesman reminded Kallisto of herself—a rambler.

"Is he the man that I asked about the waterfall painting yesterday?" Kallisto asked.

"Yes, if it wasn't me, it must have been him. Are you talking about the largest waterfall on Olympus?" The salesman pointed.

"Yes, that's the one," Kallisto answered.

"Ambrose sold that one last night."

"Really?" Kallisto hung her head in disappointment. She would not have been able to purchase such a thing if she had saved for twenty years and knew it, the painting was an important piece of art to her, and she was crestfallen never to see it again.

"Were you interested in purchasing the painting?" The salesman asked.

"Oh, no. It was more than a little out of my price range. I just thought it was extraordinary, that's all."

"Here," the salesman handed Kallisto an employment application, "fill this out, and I'll give it to Ambrose when he comes in."

Kallisto filled out the application, putting not only her home and cell phone number on it but also adding Amanda's with a note that if the other numbers failed, they could most likely get her there. She returned the application to the clerk and left the store giddy over the prospect of working around so much Greek mythology and beautiful art. The idea of being around the owner's son didn't dampen her spirits either.

The following day Kallisto woke without the familiar smells she had become accustomed to, nor was there any recollection of a dream. She sat up, took a deep breath through her nose, then hopped out of bed and went down to the kitchen. She felt slightly lonely from the lack of her usual illusions but didn't have a headache and felt well-rested.

"How was your night?" Kallisto greeted.

"We had a great time. You slept in this morning," her mother raised an eyebrow in amazement.

Kallisto never slept late. She was usually the first to rise in the morning, with the exception of her father when he went to the docks.

"What time is it?" Kallisto hadn't looked at her alarm clock and didn't realize it was late until her mother brought it to her attention.

"It's 10:30. Here; you had a phone call." Thia handed Kallisto a sticky note with Gallery of the gods and a phone number written in blue ink. "The young man that called seemed amused when I told him you were still asleep. He actually laughed."

"I applied for a job. What better job for me than one where I'd use my otherwise useless knowledge of Greek gods?" Kallisto made a case for herself knowing her mother wouldn't be thrilled about her getting a job while in school.

"Well, I hope that you can juggle a job with school. It won't be easy. You need to call the Gallery back." Thia turned and strolled from the room, handing her daughter the phone as she passed.

Kallisto dialed the number while she fixed herself a bowl of cereal. Three rings later, a man's impressively alluring Grecian voice answered.

"Gallery of the gods, Ambrose speaking."

Kallisto couldn't speak. His Greek intonation was sultry, sexy, and mesmerizing, sending chills over her body.

"Yes, uh," she stumbled, "this is Kallisto Nalani. I had a message that you called me this morning."

Morpheus, aka "Ambrose," knew as soon as the phone rang, the voice on the other end would be his *dea femminile*. He had not gone to her last night in her sleep knowing that after being awake for so long the night before, she needed to sleep without disturbance, not to mention he didn't think he could have made it another night being so close and alone with her without—

"Yes, I am the one who phoned you this morning. My name is Ambrose, and I was hoping you could start work the day after Christmas. It will be a hectic day, so I need extra hands to run errands and answer the phone. We can properly train you for the position starting the twenty-seventh."

He was straight to the point, but Kallisto felt compelled to continue the conversation.

"Don't I need to be interviewed?"

"No, I am sure you are the one we have been looking for. John, our store manager, spoke with you yesterday. He told me I spoke with you the other night about the waterfall painting. You liked that piece?"

"It was my personal favorite. It reminded me of a—uh—a dream I once had," Kallisto turned red as memories filled her.

Morpheus grinned mischievously, then closed his eyes and planted a vision in Kallisto's head of what might have been the night he sent her back sweating.

Kallisto immediately gasped and went very quiet.

Morpheus' smile grew wider, "Are you okay, madam?"

"Yes, I was just distracted, sorry. What time would you like me to come in on the twenty-sixth?" Kallisto was trying to control her strange onset of emotion and the arousal his accent had over her.

"We open at 10:00, so if you would be here by 9:00 so John can give you a few brief pointers."

"You won't be there?" Kallisto closed her eyes at her stupidity. *Why did I ask him that?*

Morpheus was split between being pleased she wanted to see him and jealous that Ambrose was the one she wanted to see.

"No, Kallisto, I will be in later that day. I will see you then."

There was something about the way he said her name that felt familiar.

"Thank you for the job, Ambrose—goodbye." Kallisto reluctantly hung up.

Chapter X

Gift

The next couple of days went by in a blur of Christmas rush. Kallisto and her mom finished wrapping gifts and cooking. Austin called her twice, and both times she gave her mother the *please don't make me talk to him look,* so her mother made up a story each time. *"She's gone off with Amanda,"* and Kallisto's favorite, *"She's washing her hair."*

As far as her Dream god, well, he was nowhere to be found. The last time she'd seen Morpheus was when he had taken her to Athens. *When I dreamed of going to Athens,* she corrected her thoughts. She needed to stop her delusions—wanting something or someone so badly she thought her dreams were real. *Hadn't they been?* Her ever-present watcher was suddenly MIA; her ring was now just an ordinary piece of beautiful jewelry, and she was sleeping soundly with no remarkable dreams to speak of—*had she been in some sort of delusional trance for the last two months?* Kallisto opened the top drawer of her dresser that housed her intimate apparel. A pair of hot pink boy-cut panties and a matching bra lay on the very top. She sighed and closed her eyes, trying to capture the exact memory of the day she was given them. The memory made her smile, and her eyes began to burn. A tear fell from her face onto the lingerie. She needed to see him, touch him. *Where have you gone?*

Kallisto allowed herself a couple of tears, then wiped her eyes and went to shower. It was Christmas morning, and she wanted to be with her family and Mama Bai. She wanted to sit around the table passing the delicious meal, in its formal dishes her mother used only three times a year, Thanksgiving, Easter, and Christmas. Amanda and her parents were supposed to stop for dessert and coffee that afternoon.

Kallisto stepped into the shower as feelings of loneliness and confusion consumed her. Not having *dreams* of Morpheus wasn't agreeing with her heart. After a long hot shower and donning comfortable clothing, she stalked downstairs, looking to see if her parents were up yet. They were sitting at the table enjoying pancakes and bacon. She walked in, and her mother handed her a plate.

The doorbell rang as Kallisto began eating the Christmas pancakes her mother was so gracious to make.

"I'll get it," Kallisto's father called. He left the kitchen as it rang again.

"I wonder who that could be at 8:30 on Christmas morning," Thia pondered aloud.

"Maybe it's Santa," Kallisto joked halfheartedly.

"Kallisto, it's for you," her father yelled from the other room. Kallisto could hear the bewilderment in her father's voice from across the house.

She shrugged at her mother's quizzical stare, "I have no clue."

Deep down, there was only one person—*dream*—again, she mentally corrected herself—she needed to see, and he was not about to show up on her doorstep Christmas morning, ringing the doorbell. Kallisto giggled as she walked toward the door and thought how funny it would be if she were wrong. *Aren't knights in shining armor supposed to ride up on white horses? Well, if knights ride up on horses, I wonder what a Greek god would show up on.* Kallisto shook her head, dispelling those crazy thoughts as she opened the door.

There, in the doorway, stood her father and a delivery man. The man was quite handsome in his brown and tan uniform. She did not recognize the GG logo with a lightning bolt through the letters on his shirt. This was not a delivery agency that she knew of.

"Kallisto Nalani?" the man asked as he gave Kallisto a questioning look.

"Yes, that would be me."

"Special delivery. Could you sign here, please?" He asked her as he handed her a clipboard with paperwork that donned the same logo as his shirt.

"Sure." Kallisto took the clipboard from the delivery man's hands and signed on the line marked *Delivery Accepted By*.

"Who is this from?" Kallisto asked as her eyes trailed over a vast, flat object wrapped in brown paper. She could tell by how the man handed the package to her father that it was heavy and fragile.

"Sorry, ma'am, we aren't allowed to give out that information. He showed Kallisto a piece of paper showing the words, Sender Information Concealed.

"So, the person who sent this to me doesn't want me to know who they are?"

"Yes, that's correct, sorry," The delivery man apologized.

Kallisto's father gave the delivery man a cash tip, and he went back to his very nice, red sports car.

"Isn't that a strange delivery car?" Kallisto wondered.

"Here, let's get this giant package in the house," her father said, picking up the heavy parcel and following Kallisto into the kitchen.

"Looks like our daughter has a secret admirer," her father scowled at the package he sat in the kitchen.

"Another one?" Thia giggled. "Is this going to become an epidemic?"

"What do you mean by another one?" Her father asked.

"Oh, Dad, she's talking about Austin. He mentioned that he had liked me for a while and had just gotten up the nerve to talk to me. As we can see, he was obviously lying," Kallisto made light of the situation.

"Well, open it, kid. We're curious what this monstrosity is," Kallisto's father said.

Kallisto walked slowly over to the brown-papered object and meticulously tore away the ugly wrapping. This was one of the strangest things to happen to her while she was awake. Before she could get very much brown paper removed, she stopped. That all too familiar feeling of being watched came upon her. Kallisto smiled and thought—*about time.*

Morpheus couldn't help himself. He had to see her reaction to the gift. This was something he knew the moment he saw her look at it...it would be hers. Not just any ordinary gift; this was a proclamation of their times together. This was one of the ways he could show Kallisto he was real, which connected his reality with hers. He watched her through the orb while smiling with anticipation and excitement.

Kallisto gasped. "Oh. My. Goodness. Who—how—why?!" She rambled as she felt the blood drain from her face.

"What is it," her mother asked.

Kallisto turned the beautiful painting of the waterfall, *our waterfall,* around so her parents could see it. The colors of the painting were magnificent, and the golden frame alone was exquisite. The work of art before the three of them was worth more than her parent's first house twenty years ago.

"This is the painting from the gallery, the one I fell in love with. The owner's son sold it the night Austin took me to the movies. Mom...this painting had a price tag of 45,000 dollars. I can't accept this."

Kallisto's voice shook, and her parents gaped at the sight of such a present.

"I have to call the delivery company back and tell them I cannot accept this; it's too much and must be a mistake."

Kallisto leaned the painting against the wall and went to retrieve her phone. She returned to the table where her now cold pancakes sat and proceeded to look up the company's phone number. She searched to no avail. Google failed her.

"Mom, I can't find that delivery center anywhere. What am I going to do?" Kallisto pleaded with her mother to give her answers."

"Have the people at the gallery tell you who they sold it to. If someone purchases something this size, they're bound to have a record with a name, number, and address."

"Well, I don't like this, Thia. No one has the right to spend such money on our daughter. She's only seventeen. What kind of weirdo throws money around like that? What's she going to do with it anyway?" Kallisto's father ranted.

"Love it," Kallisto said in a dreamy voice as she looked at the painting, remembering that very place. Remembering the way it smelled, the sound of the water hitting the pool under the cliff, and the way Morpheus' lips felt against hers. "Yes, I'll love it."

She knew, in her heart, Morpheus, her dream god, had sent the gift to her. *But how? Yep—I'm going crazy.*

The rest of the day went in a blur. Mama Bai looked at the painting and told her she should sell it for college money. Her dad seconded the vote.

Amanda and her parents finally made it to Kallisto's for dessert.

Amanda went ashen when she walked into Kallisto's room, "It was him—wasn't it? Who else can afford such?"

Kallisto told her friend how "the feeling" had returned after several days.

"After I brought the painting to my bedroom, the feeling went away as fast as it came."

"All I can say is you better make all kinds of nice with him...he has brothers," winked Amanda.

"Incorrigible!" Kallisto shook her head.

The night ended with everyone singing Christmas carols and drinking hot chocolate around the tree.

Amanda whispered her congratulations to Kallisto as she started out the door, "Only you could turn a man's head to the point he would dig 45K out of his pocket just to put a smile on your face. Maybe he'll end up being a Greek god or something."

"Shut up and go home," Kallisto giggled as she pushed Amanda out the door.

Kallisto couldn't sleep. Lying in her bedroom surrounded by books, pillows, and the gorgeous painting hanging on the wall, she felt utterly alone, with no feeling of being watched. The events of the day—no—the last two months weighed heavy on her mind. She couldn't decide if she was insane or merely in a long-drawn-out dream in desperate need of being woken before she did go insane. Trying to wrap her human mind around everything was not proving easy. Every explanation she came up with was over the top.

Mere feet from where she lay hung the magnificent painting. The streetlamp beamed through the window, making the waterfall shine. Who had given her such a gift? Who but Morpheus, would understand what that particular painting meant to her? How could a Greek god purchase a forty-five thousand dollar painting, much less have it delivered to her on Christmas Day? Why couldn't she put a face on the man she thought she loved? For goodness' sake, she could remember his touch, lips, and smell so vividly, but she could not pick him out of a lineup. How could her heart have fallen for someone she doesn't really know? All she had were a lot of questions and no real answers to any of them. *Sleep, Kalli; tomorrow, you start your new job.*

Chapter XI

Gallery

Kallisto woke again without dreams and was a little tired from the difficulty she had falling asleep. Excitement won the battle as she thought about the paintings and sculptures she would learn about. Mostly, if she were honest with herself, she was anxious about the dreamy Greek man whose father owned the gallery. She remembered his proximity and how his warmth and accent made her feel the evening she met him. *Oh, that accent!*

Kallisto arrived at the mall ten minutes before Ambrose had told her to be there. She felt it best to be early for her first day. John, the manager, was at the desk filling out paperwork when she knocked on the door and put on the happiest face she could muster since butterflies were flitting around in her stomach.

John smiled back and opened the door. "Hey, I'm glad you accepted the job. I need someone who knows mythology. Let me show you where you can put your things."

Kallisto followed John while sneaking peeks in the two office doors in the back, trying to see if anyone else was there. The coast looked to be clear of any Greek hunks. She spent the next hour learning about the paintings and sculptures and where everything was. She was glad she already knew most of the legends that went along with the paintings and knew of all the gods depicted in sculpture. The only problem was the abrupt chill she felt when she walked to the front of the gallery. After her third time making the rounds looking over the artwork, she decided it was the bust of Hera, making her uneasy as its eyes followed her. *Maybe it will sell soon.*

Learning the ropes made the early morning fly by, and she forgot about her anxious stomach. As she retrieved a stack of paperwork from the floor, she felt someone looking at her, and the ring on her long finger warmed slightly.

Kallisto grinned, believing her Greek god had decided to check in on her. Holding the stack of papers, she turned and ran right into the chest of a different Greek. Papers went flying, and Kallisto's cheeks went scarlet.

"I am sorry for scaring you—again. It seems I have an uncanny knack for making you jump."

"I'm. So. Sorry," Each word separated in mortification.

Great, he's going to think I'm a klutz. Oh, snap out of it, Kallisto; he's only gorgeous beyond belief and richer than Croesus—and his father owns your place of employment. Rambling thoughts assailed her.

They both bent over to pick up the scattered papers. When they grabbed the same piece of paper, their hands touched. That telltale chill went up her spine as she felt like she was gazing into the eyes of someone familiar.

"Kallisto, oh, I'm sorry. I didn't realize you were here already, Ambrose," John announced as he entered the small office, trying to see if Kallisto had found the papers. "Will you be working with us for a while today? We could use an extra set of hands."

Kallisto looked at John, still mortified—John looked at their hands, one on top of the other—Ambrose—well, he still looked at Kallisto, and he didn't remove his gaze as he answered John.

"I will be here until lunch. I will help you open and show Kallisto some paperwork as you work the floor."

Kallisto suddenly noticed she had not removed her hand from under Ambrose's. Again blushing, she pulled her hand away, letting the Greek pick up the popular yellow piece of paper. *After all, it is on his side; what was I thinking? I was thinking, damn, he's gorgeous.* Kallisto smiled slightly as her thoughts returned to his face, body, and accent...*Oh, that accent. Someone seriously needs to make a hormone control pill for times like this.*

❧⟫⟫⟩ ⟨⟨⟨❧

Morpheus allowed himself to read Kallisto's thoughts and could not help but raise an eyebrow and grin. Never taking his gaze off her, he took the stack of papers from her hands, combined them with the ones he retrieved, and handed them to John, finally releasing Kallisto from his gaze and turning his eyes to the man standing in the doorway.

"I guess we are open since it is five after nine?" Ambrose questioned.

"Yes, I just opened the front door before coming to look for Kallisto. I'll work the floor. Are you sure you don't mind showing her the paperwork?"

"No, go ahead. I will make sure she knows everything."

There was a definite underlying meaning in his words. He was going to make sure she knew precisely—everything. Hopefully, it would not take too long, either. Morpheus wanted his time in this world to be of her knowing who he truly was and not who he portrayed himself to be.

The following two hours were spent with Ambrose leaning over Kallisto, explaining the calendar of events to begin the New Year. The Gallery was having an exhibition of *The Paintings of The Fates Three*; three paintings were "supposed" to be exact versions of the goddesses themselves.

"The trio of paintings is worth a combined 750,000 dollars, and the need for security is great. These paintings have traveled from Greece to every store my father owns. They will be here for two weeks. There will be an unveiling and a formal dinner in January to celebrate. You will need a dinner gown," Ambrose smiled. "We have three weeks to prepare. Some preparations have already been made, but I will ask you to help with a few last-minute details—we can talk about that later."

He offered his hand to help Kallisto out of his chair so that they could help John.

The morning proved to be both scary and stimulating. During the last hour Ambrose was at the gallery, Kallisto showed off her knowledge of mythological deities by answering questions on the phone and the gallery floor. When on the floor, she caught him looking at her. Having Ambrose so close to her proved to be a little overwhelming. She had to concentrate on keeping her senses calm. His body was excellent, his eyes mesmerizing and familiar, and he exuded major masculine sexuality. Not to mention his thick accent made her weak in the knees. *Down girl. What is wrong with me?*

Morpheus found it difficult to keep a straight face. Struggling to keep out of her thoughts, he tried to concentrate on selling art. He constantly had to remind himself that she was obsessing over him—Morpheus, even though she thought he was someone entirely different. Could he be jealous of himself? He convinced himself that deep down, she knew Ambrose was he and not an ordinary mortal Greek man. She seemed drawn to him as a human and a god.

"Well, it's time for me to go. I'll leave the gallery in the hands of you and John."

Morpheus needed to keep up the appearance of a rich guy trying to help run a business. Plus, if he spent much more time watching Kallisto's beautiful body flow gracefully around the artwork and listening to the rambling thoughts in her head of how sexy he was, he might go over the edge—then there would be no telling how many rules he would break.

"Oh, Ambrose, I was wondering if you could give me some information." It was Kallisto's last chance to ask him about the painting.

Ambrose raised both eyebrows in response, "I'll try." He knew she was going to ask about the painting.

"Please tell me who you sold the Olympus waterfall painting to?"

Ambrose raised one eyebrow and gave a mischievous half-grin she had seen before.

"I am not at liberty to say.".

"Why not? I'm an employee."

"Yes, you are, but that does not change the fact I cannot answer your question. I wish I could." Ambrose spoke with finality and asked, "Did you like your gift?"

He continued to smirk, making Kallisto wonder if he knew why the waterfall was important to her. Kallisto shook her head...*That's crazy; no one could guess that.*

"I am sorry. Did I say something wrong?" Ambrose asked.

Kallisto studied his face. He didn't look sorry. In fact, he looked quite impish with the smirk splayed across his sensuous lips. *Stop looking at me that way! I'm definitely in trouble here.*

Ambrose's smile widened as the thoughts ran through her head as if he could read them.

"No," she lied. "I just can't accept a gift of such magnitude from someone I don't know."

"Oh, I am sure you know him."

There was that smirk again. *What does he know that I don't, other than the identity of my admirer?*

"So, it was a male?" Kallisto pursed her lips in thought.

Ambrose's eyebrows shot up. "You cannot convince me that you do not know who would send you a painting worth 45,000 dollars. How many people do you consort with that would or could do such a thing?" He almost sounded irritated.

Kallisto's ring heated up. She looked down at it, as did Ambrose. Just as fast as the ring heated, it returned to normal.

"I don't know," Kallisto snapped. Why she snapped at him, she didn't know.

"I have a meeting. I need to get going. Let me know when you think you have figured out who your secret admirer is. Maybe he thought you would know immediately who was behind such a gift."

Ambrose turned and walked out of the office, sounding almost frustrated.

Weird. Why would this be a big deal to him? Maybe he knows her admirer. The only one it could be—couldn't be—because he just wasn't able—was he? Damn, Kallisto, you sound crazy in your own head.

The rest of the day was packed with after-Christmas shoppers. John was shorthanded because the only other employee was an older woman who did little things like dusting and answering the phone. Unfortunately, she was on vacation until after the first of the year.

"You never realize how much it helps to have someone do things like answer the phone and keep up the housekeeping until they are not there to do it," John said as he was tallying up the deposit for the day.

"I know I'll be of more help once I have learned the ropes. I feel like I learned a lot today, though. Thank you for this opportunity. I love mythology, and now I have an excuse to surround myself with it. Not that I have ever needed an excuse," Kallisto grinned.

She made a sale and was quite proud of herself. She sold that menacing bust of the goddess Hera. She was glad to get it out of the gallery. For some reason, Hera had never been her favorite goddess. She was too cunning for Kallisto's taste. Kallisto wanted to feel sorry for her, but if you asked Kallisto, she deserved her heart aches where Zeus was concerned. In a fictional sense, it was true that Zeus stepped out quite often during his marriage with Hera. But, in Zeus' defense, Hera was a manipulator and untrustworthy in her own right. The bust made Kallisto uneasy, and she felt like it was looking at her whenever she walked to the front. She often felt that way when studying or reading about Hera and Ares, Hera's son, the god of war. The gods who made most people uneasy, like Hades, were always fascinating to Kallisto, but Hera was too crafty for her liking.

Hera waged wars among humans, using them as her pawns, making sure she received the outcomes of her liking. She turned the tables in favor of the Greeks in the battle at Troy, even though Zeus had forbidden interference from the gods. Zeus was on the side of the Trojans, and Hera favored the Greeks. By seducing Zeus, Hera kept his attention from the battle and ensured a result more to her liking. She had always been the type of goddess to get her way at any cost.

Selling the bust of the beautiful yet cunning goddess gave Kallisto breathing room. Not only had she gotten a great first sale, just over five thousand dollars, she no longer felt uneasy when she walked to the front of the gallery. For the life of Kallisto, she couldn't understand why anyone would want Hera's head and shoulders sculpture, even if she were the goddess of matrimony. Of course, Kallisto was also sure few people would understand her fascination with the waterfall hanging in her bedroom either. *To each their own.*

Chapter XII

Visitor

The following two days passed in a blur with no dreams and no Morpheus. Her heart was in physical pain, and every time she thought about Morpheus, her head began to ache, and since most of her life was spent thinking about him either consciously or subconsciously, her head hurt most of the time. She was beginning to feel the dreams were, well, just that, dreams. She had a vivid imagination, may have developed short-term memory loss, and failed to remember buying a hot pink bra and panties. No otherworldly dreams and not waking with the aromas of honeysuckle and lavender on her body made her feel so empty. She also hadn't seen Amanda in a few days. Of course, they spoke at least twice every day, but with the last few days consumed with work and Amanda being with Michael a lot, their usual weekend girl's night had been put on hold.

On the bright side of the equation, Kallisto was spending a lot of time on her favorite hobby. She'd acquired so many exciting stories about the sordid lives of the gods. She learned even more about the mythical gods of old and couldn't wait until Spring break to share them with her grandmother.

Ambrose hadn't been around very much either. He came into the gallery to check over the books but never stayed very long. He did wink at her and gave her a very sexy once-over as she walked in this morning. She did not feel watched anymore and now felt that telltale butterfly feeling in the pit of her stomach when Ambrose was around. Was Ambrose the reason she hadn't dreamt of her god in days?

A sense of sadness came over her. Had she replaced Morpheus, an imaginary god, with a sexy human Greek man, who happened to be her boss? *Damn, my life is becoming a reality show. Well, at least my show is all in my head and not splayed all over the television.*

While posing as Ambrose, Morpheus had a tough time around Kallisto. Unable to tell her who he was, proved challenging. When he sat with her too close, the heat of her body tempted him, so he decided he could not stay around her for too long, or he would be in danger of breaking several rules. The Fates could be cruel, and he did not want Kallisto or himself on their bad side if he could help it. To top it off, he had an issue with her attraction to Ambrose. Yes, he understood it did not make sense. *I am jealous of myself.* Phantasos would have a field day with this one.

"Kallisto may not be the only one in danger of losing her mind over this situation," Morpheus said aloud as he turned off the shower and stood propping one hand against the tiled slate of the walls. "How can I make her see me? She has to figure this out." He shook his long blonde hair and stepped from the shower.

Morpheus was getting ready to give the almighty Zeus, he thought with a roll of his eyes, an update on his position with Kallisto. *There are a few positions I want to have with her, but they are all forbidden, and those are not the ones Zeus wanted to know about. Maybe I need to step back into the shower and take a cold one this time.*

Zeus would want to know if Kallisto was staying mentally stable and whether she had figured out Ambrose was her dream god. For some reason, Morpheus could not shake the feeling that there was more to Zeus' curiosity about his and Kallisto's relationship. Zeus had been with countless humans, even fathered children with them. Why was Kallisto so different? He knew being a dream god made a difference to some degree, but Kallisto was much stronger than the average human woman. At least, he thought so.

That line of thinking made Morpheus muse over a sudden idea.

Aloud to himself, Morpheus pondered, "What if I asked Zeus to meet her? He could go to earth since I cannot take her back to Olympus."

"Hey, little brother." Phantasos interrupted Morpheus' thoughts.

Morpheus went rigid at his brother's voice. "You could knock, you know," Morpheus wrapped the towel around his lean waist and walked from the vast bathroom to his bedchamber.

"Now, what fun would that be? Someone has to keep you on your toes. This way, you never know who is around." Phantasos' grinned, showing perfect white teeth framed by full lips.

Morpheus was annoyed that his train of thought had been interrupted.

"I have an idea," Morpheus said as his towel vanished in thin air, and loose white linen pants and a baby blue long sleeve appeared. He looked like a tanned, ripped, and wholly sensuous Greek god.

Phantasos looked just as appealing in his "god gone bad," holey faded blue jeans and a tight white t-shirt that said in black letters; *I am not just a dream, I am a fantasy*.

"What is that?" Phantasos asked.

"What if I convince Zeus to meet Kallisto?"

Phantasos raised his eyebrows as if to question his brother's sanity.

"Just hear me out," Morpheus needed his brother to side with him. He needed hope. "I know he would change his mind about her. He would see how strong she is and that she can take our relationship and the truth about the myths she grew up loving."

"How do you purpose to make this miracle happen? You know Hera would have a goat if he went to earth, and neither The Fates nor Zeus will allow Kallisto on Olympus."

"Well," Morpheus began trying to persuade his brother. "I will give him a couple of updates, and then I will ask. I have a little time to think about it. Maybe I can get him to observe her through an orb, or maybe he will defy his wife and come to the gallery one day or even the gala promoting the three paintings of The Fates."

"I know why you are a dream god, Morpheus," Phantasos shook his head while staring at the marbled floors of Morpheus' bedchamber.

"Why is that?" Morpheus asked.

"Because you are one of the biggest dreamers I have ever encountered," Phantasos laughed and vanished.

Morpheus flashed himself into Phantasos' home, following his brother. He was not about to let the conversation end with that.

"I do not know what to tell you, Morpheus. The Fates have no intention of you *keeping* this human you allowed yourself to fall in love with. They are not easily swayed when their minds have been made up. Zeus himself has very little say when it comes to fate. If he had, do you not think he would have changed a few of his mishaps over the centuries?" Phantasos reminded Morpheus.

"I refuse to let her go, Phantasos. I will leave Olympus for good before I let her go," Morpheus admitted to his brother for the first time that he was considering giving up his godhood to be with a mortal.

"What?" You would give up your lineage and duty for a mortal who cannot remember what you look like?" Phantasos exclaimed.

"Yes." Morpheus stood directly before Phantasos, crystal blue eyes looking deep into his brother's onyx ones. He wanted Phantasos to hear the seriousness in his words.

"Well, little brother, it seems our only choice is to try and convince three unpersuasive goddesses and the leader of the Greek gods to allow you to bring a mortal woman here to Olympus to live with you until she grows old, withers, and dies; while you stay forever young to choose someone else to love." Phantasos tried to show logic where it did not exist. "Let me know what I can do to help you convince The Fates Three or the big guy. I will stand beside you."

"That is all I ask," Morpheus vanished back to his bedchamber, needing time to think before he went up the hill to deliver the news of "no news."

Morpheus looked over at the orb lying on his bedside table. He knew that Kallisto should be home from work by now. He wanted desperately to go to her. Instead, he watched her for a while.

❧ ⌘ ❧

Kallisto stopped dead in her tracks as she crossed her bedroom, looking at the waterfall. Her eyes began to burn as she remembered the many times she spent lying by the pools, swimming, and having picnics with Morpheus, surrounded by the scenery now beautifully displayed by her bed. At that moment, Kallisto realized how much she missed her god, whether she was crazy or not. She had placed barriers trying not to let his absence destroy her.

As a tear ran down her face and fell undisturbed to the floor, she had that haunting familiar feeling of being watched. Kallisto wiped at another tear falling unchecked down the opposite cheek hoping Morpheus wouldn't see her distress.

Morpheus felt her intense pull and knew she needed him. She was getting stronger with her mind. He would not let anyone come between them, not even if it meant his godhood, a decision he finally made. He sent her to sleep moments after her head hit her pillow.

Kallisto "woke" in her room with Morpheus propped on an elbow, looking down at her and stroking her long black hair. She rolled over to meet the gaze of his incredibly gorgeous crystal blue eyes and gasped, "I am in my bedroom with you?" It was a question. She wasn't entirely sure she was truly in her room or *dreaming*.

Morpheus just nodded his head slowly and smiled lovingly down at her. He closed his eyes and breathed in her scent deep through his nostrils. It had been just under a week since he had been with her as himself and not as Ambrose, and he needed to feel her warm slender body alive in his arms and smell her sweet scent that meant one thing to him, love. He needed to take in her essence. Even though he was with her as Ambrose almost daily, it was different from being able to hold or enjoy her as he could by being himself. Being with her as Ambrose was the hardest thing he had ever done, and when one lived centuries, that said something. Every time he saw her, his arms ached to hold her, but he mostly ached to tell her the truth. He knew in his heart she would be okay knowing her *dream* god was real, but he also wanted her to understand other realms exist.

Kallisto's eyes widened, and she sat up. Then she all but jumped into his arms. Her physical hold on him was almost as tight as the hold she had on his heart. Morpheus was grinning until he realized that the slight shaking of her body was due to sobs she desperately tried to suppress by burying her face into his chest.

"Kallisto, my love, why the tears?" Those tears were breaking his heart.

She did not answer. Instead, she pulled him tighter, if that were possible, and continued to cry. She no longer tried to hide her traitorous tears—he knew she was crying, so she let him console her.

Five minutes passed before Kallisto pulled her face from Morpheus' well-defined chest and wiped her face with her fingertips. She took a deep breath and apologized to him for getting mascara, one of the only makeup products she wore, all over his button-down.

"I'm sorry about the black streaks."

Morpheus rolled his blue eyes and shook his head, "It would be just like you to apologize to me for something so easily fixed." Then with a wave of his hand over the dark gray stain in the middle of his shirt, it became as clean as it had been before Kallisto rained tears upon it.

He then sat up and pulled her close to him. He framed her face with his large hands and tilted her chin up with his thumbs so that he could look deeply into her watery aqua eyes. "Why are you so sad?"

His question was no more than a whisper, but the pain over her sadness and the concern he felt was evident in those five questioning words. *Has my invasion of her life caused her this pain? Is she closer to breaking than I thought?* Questions were reeling through his head as he waited for her to answer.

"I have missed you so much." Lowering her eyes with her face still framed by Morpheus' warm hands, she continued, "I was not sure whether I would ever see you again."

Kallisto had missed Morpheus desperately, but it was not until she looked at him that she realized how much she had been suppressing by keeping herself busy at work and home. It wasn't that she shouldn't think about him. It was because her heart was breaking, and her head was in self-preservation mode. Her heart was breaking, and that was the reason for her headaches.

Morpheus let her face go and used just one hand under her chin to return her gaze to his. "Hear me now Kallisto Nalani. I will never leave you. If I have to become a mortal man to be with you, to stay with you, I will. You are my life."

With his words, Kallisto's eyes filled with tears once more, but this time underneath the tears was the soft smile on her lips. Morpheus could not help but lean down and kiss her lightly.

Before he could stop himself, he deepened their kiss and worked both of them into a frenzy. His hands entwined in her long black hair. Every time he moved her hair, the sweet smell of her shampoo and the scent of Kallisto engulfed him, making him want her even more.

Kallisto pulled him as close as she could, wanting to feel his muscled body against hers.

When Morpheus heard the sensual moan escape her as she exposed her neck to his lips, his body reacted like a magnet to hers. He knew then he had to stop this part of their reunion before Phantasos, or even worse, The Fates, popped in and *fixed* him for good.

"Kallisto," he said, moving back up to her mouth. "We must stop." Those were the words he used, but his body was saying something completely different.

With her lips still hovering on top of his, she answered. "Yes?"

"Yes—We must stop."

"Why?" She pulled back just slightly, only enough to let the whisper escape. Then she returned and deepened their kiss. He smelled of lavender and masculinity, and she would not give up on getting what she wanted. *After all, it is a dream.*

Morpheus pulled Kallisto's shirt over her head and began kissing her neck. Just as a shiver went up Kallisto's body and Morpheus gave a low chuckle, the room turned freezing. Not just cold, but cold enough that their rapid breathing came out as vapor when they pulled apart from one another.

Goosebumps assailed Kallisto's skin, and Morpheus was suddenly not so "magnetic" as before. Morpheus looked skyward and said in a low hissing voice through clenched teeth, "I get it, now fix the temperature, Phantasos."

"Phantasos?" Kallisto asked, surprised, "Your brother, Phantasos?"

"Yes. He is reminding me of a few rules, that's all." Even though there was a scowl of irritation on Morpheus' face, he knew deep down that this was for the best.

"Are you telling me that your brother could see wh . . . I mean, he . . . Oh my." Kallisto's hands went to her mouth as realization spread over her face. She went red and looked shocked as if someone had slapped her. "I'll never be able to . . .," and she just cut her sentence off right there because three things happen simultaneously.

Her shirt reappeared on her body, the room returned to its normal temperature, and the mythical god Phantasos himself appeared at the foot of the bed they were *wrestling on* moments before.

He bowed slightly toward Kallisto, acknowledging her with respect, and then looked not so happy at his brother, who still had his hands wrapped possessively around Kallisto's waist.

"You need to control your urges, young brother, and remind yourself of your purpose. Oh, Zeus will see you in half an hour."

Then, just as fast as he appeared, he vanished. The silence was thick and filled the room like white noise. Morpheus was going to have to explain a few things to Kallisto. He knew Phantasos counted on him to ensure Kallisto would not remember his interference, let alone the strange one-sided conversation that had just happened. There was one problem with that—he did not intend to make her forget. There would, of course, be parts she would not remember—just because The Fates had specific "bound" rules dream gods could not change—like remembering his features. He wanted Kallisto to remember everything she could about their times together. He mostly wanted her to remember him completely. He wanted her to remember what the lips that made her shiver looked like and what color the eyes that adored her were. He ached for her to notice who he was when he walked into the gallery, and they could start working on staying together instead of staying apart. *I need her to remember.*

"What the hell was that all about?" Kallisto turned her head and then adjusted her body to be able to look at Morpheus. She could tell he was dreading the interrogation.

"I will give you a choice, Kallisto. If I tell you, you will not remember when you wake up. If I tell you and The Fates hear or find out, then I could get in serious trouble," he put his hand up to stop her interruption.

"I don't wa—" Kallisto started, then stopped at Morpheus' hand.

"Let me finish." Morpheus knew he had to finish before he thought better of it. "All they can do is make me stay away from you and make my life seriously suck if I stay a god. I have already told you; I will choose to become mortal if I have to."

"I don't want you to become mortal for me, Morpheus. I want you the way you are," Kallisto replied.

"I want more. I want us to be together for eternity." Morpheus watched Kallisto to see when his carefully delivered words hit home.

"Together for eternity?" Kallisto asked slowly, with her brow furrowed in concentration.

"It is like this. I want to have you come live with me on Mount Olympus."

"What?" Kallisto couldn't control the reflection in her voice.

"The Fates do not want me coming to you anymore. Coming to you the way I do—he looked at the bed and grinned, giving her the meaning of his comment without going into detail. "And as often as I visit, it is dangerous for you, for any human. I could be risking your life. That is why mortals cannot remember what their dream gods look like. I broke the most important rule of all the gods—I fell in love with a mortal—a mortal I was merely supposed to help through a tough time. Phantasos did the same thing over a hundred years ago. The girl killed herself while on Olympus." He knew Kallisto's shaking head, a furrowed brow, and look of utter confusion were due to the overwhelming information and lack thereof.

"Wait—too much—too fast," Kallisto thought a minute before continuing with her many questions. "Are you telling me that this "girl" who was mortal physically went with your brother to Olympus and killed herself in the most beautiful place next to Heaven itself? It had not dawned on her that she had been physically on Olympus. How did he take her there?"

"The same way I took you," Morpheus said each word slowly, trying not to scare or upset her.

To Morpheus' surprise, Kallisto did not yell, faint, cry, or grab her head as if the information had caused her to go completely over the edge. Instead, she looked from him to the painting hanging by her bed and then back to Morpheus. She reached out and cupped his face in her hand.

"You sent me that painting. You took me physically to Olympus. You are real—we really went to Greece." Kallisto just continued as if a light bulb had been turned on.

"I'm not dreaming—am I?" Kallisto asked Morpheus.

It was then that Morpheus saw a shadow of fear on her face. He sat there trying to decide how to tell her. *How do you defy the realm of reality ingrained in the mind of a mortal?*

"You are in a type of dream state. You would not have been there if your parents had entered your room while I had you on Olympus. You were with me, body, mind, and soul. If your mother were to walk in here right now, you would appear to her to be daydreaming. I would command you to wake, and you would. When I release you from this state, you will not remember everything, just bits, and pieces, and you will still not remember what I look like." Morpheus paused, assessing the situation before he continued.

"I have told you most of this before. When I took you to Greece—search your mind, Kallisto. You have to remember what I tell you when we are together. Rules bind me, and for me to tell you everything, you have to remember some things on your own. You are still suppressing things when you are awake. Your mind keeps the two realms we live in separate, even though it knows they are connected. You are fighting the suppression placed upon mortals millennia ago. You must try my *dea femminile.*"

"I have no trouble remembering how you smell or how your lips feel to mine. Why can't I remember things like this or how you look?" She wiggled her way back into his embrace with her back against his chest. She could feel the warmth of his body through their clothes and smell the lavender and honeysuckle on his skin.

"Your mind is protecting itself. Morpheus had seen it hundreds of times. Mortals have a kind of built-in safety measure. When something they see or experience is too much for them, they suppress it. The brain locks it away."

"Well, keep me here with you," Kallisto demanded.

Morpheus tightened his embrace and answered, "I wish I could." As he pressed a kiss into her silken hair.

"I love you, Morpheus. I want to remember. I know you are real. Amanda does too. Why can't I overcome this mental barricade and remember what you look like?"

"Part of you still has a hard time believing, and The Fates have put up more barriers, it seems than usual, where you and I are concerned," Morpheus answered her while his head rested on the top of hers and his eyes remained closed. He was taking in all he could to sustain him until he could be with her again.

"Can you not come to me in my realm, you know, on earth without the "dream"?" Kallisto asked, making quotes in the air.

"That is a question I cannot answer, but I can tell you this. I am glad you like the painting—it is my favorite place." Morpheus turned her to face him. "Ask yourself how this," he pointed to the painting hanging next to her bed, "came to be."

"I must go. I have a meeting with Zeus," Morpheus looked sad. He wanted more than anything to stay with her.

"You really have a meeting with Zeus?" Kallisto's eyes went wide, and out of all the things he had told her, this was the one thing that seemed to surprise and shock her the most.

With a soft laugh at her enthusiasm, Morpheus answered, "Yes, and he does not take kindly to lesser gods not showing up on time. I might wake up in the morning as a frog or something."

"I would still kiss you," Kallisto giggled. "Maybe my god would become a prince, and my fantasy would turn into a fairytale."

They laughed at her words' imagery and hugged each other tightly. Morpheus leaned over and kissed Kallisto ever so slightly on her lips.

"Morpheus?"

"Yes."

"Could you give me something to make me remember that this dream was real?" Kallisto asked.

The mischievous little boy became apparent in Morpheus' eyes as he grinned. "I could give you a love mark on your neck" he smiled that half grin.

"You wouldn't dare," Kallisto grabbed her neck.

Morpheus dove on top of her, flipping her over onto her back, playfully trying to pull her hands away, which were grasped protectively around her neck. "I would, and Austin would have to get over it."

"Forget Austin; who cares. What about my dad or my boss at work?" Kallisto managed to get out the words as she giggled and laughed as the two of them really wrestled on the bed.

"Your dad would ground you, meaning no dates for a while. And I am sure your *boss* would not mind," he laughed at his own words as if laughing at an inside joke.

"Oh, you think not. He might get jealous." Kallisto raised one brow, trying to provoke Morpheus into a bit of jealousy of his own.

"Your boss would not get jealous. He would probably imagine what a wonderful time you must have had," his grin widened even more, showing his beautiful white teeth.

"You wouldn't want to embarrass me like that, would you?"

They wrestled for about five minutes, and Morpheus pretended to be defeated by a mortal woman. "I give. I will not mark you, not today anyway," he smirked playfully. Your virtue with your boss will stay undamaged for now." His grin looked almost devious.

"You are not right," Kallisto said jokingly as she slapped his arm.

"I love you, Kallisto."

With those words, he gave her another token of his love. Instead of the "hickey" to go, along with the ring and the pricey painting hanging on her bedroom wall, he wrapped a bracelet with the word, REMEMBER, engraved in both English and Greek.

As Morpheus clasped the bracelet to her wrist, he said, "I want you to look at this and do as it says—try—for me." Then his lips gently touched hers.

Kallisto woke and called out with a soft voice. "Morpheus?"

He was gone, and her bed looked like a wrestling match had taken place, and her lips felt slightly swollen like they would after being kissed passionately for a long time. She looked immediately at her right wrist, and there it was, the bracelet with the word REMEMBER inscribed across it in both English and Greek.

As she looked at the love token given to her, she began to remember her dream with more clarity than she had in a long time. The memory of Morpheus telling her he had broken the most important rule of the Oneiroi, he had fallen in love with her, and she remembered him talking about his brother, but could not remember what he said or which brother it was. She remembered their wrestling match and, with a smile, put her hand up to her neck. She breathed in deep through her nose, savoring the smell of lavender and honeysuckle.

Kallisto turned over in her bed, wishing she could hear the water in the painting hanging silently on the wall. She closed her eyes, concentrating on the water falling into the pool, making it foam. She breathed deeply, using her senses, letting the smells of lavender and honeysuckle help her to recall her dream. As fast as the image flashed in her mind, it went away. She couldn't make out any actual features, but she knew she saw a well-muscled man with long blonde hair. *Morpheus?*

Chapter XIII

Return

Morpheus flashed himself straight into the atrium of Zeus' massive residence. His mind was consumed with worry. He feared Zeus would pull him back before his two months were over. A servant girl with long golden hair and beautiful deep-set eyes, a daemon, beckoned Morpheus, waving both hands, to follow.

"So, Morpheus, what do you have to tell me?" Zeus asked as Morpheus entered the garden off the back of the mansion.

"I come to let you know Kallisto has yet to figure out that I am Ambrose, and she seems mentally stable. Only sometimes does she second guess herself." Morpheus began answering Zeus with short answers, not wanting him to realize how much Kallisto knew or did not know of the actual existence of gods and mythological creatures.

Zeus stared for what seemed to be forever, "you say, second guess. What do you mean? Does she believe gods to be real or not?"

"She believes us to be real, and I want her to," Morpheus replied with certainty. "I know you do not want me to be with her. I am not altogether sure why, though."

"We have no right as gods to invade and take over a mortal's world. It is not right to covet what should not be yours." Zeus replied, thinking this had been a difficult lesson for himself.

Morpheus' eyes widened with surprise. "You, the god that is known for "playing" with human women, is standing before me telling me that "we" have no right to a relationship with mortals?"

Zeus understood Morpheus was not questioning him out of disrespect but out of confusion. "I have not been with a mortal woman in more than a century. My wife does not—appreciate it." Zeus suddenly looked sad, and

Morpheus barely took in what Zeus said after that since he said it more like a whisper to himself, but it sounded like—*"My heart could not take another break."*

"I need you to please let me try. I will stick with the rules placed upon me by The Fates, and I promise not to bring her here to Olympus. Please, I love her," Morpheus begged, and Zeus knew that begging took a lot of humility, especially for a dream god as powerful as he. This was something the young god had never done before.

"I will not pull you back before the allotted time The Fates have bestowed. Remember, you must not tell her who Ambrose is. She should figure things out for herself for this to be destined. This situation is more fragile than you think, Morpheus. This mortal woman is young and very vulnerable, "Zeus turned his back on Morpheus as he spoke.

Zeus looked forlorn as he watched the water spilling over the top of the massive fountain in the garden where they stood.

"Depart from me. I will expect you in a week for another update." With that, Zeus waved his hand, and Morpheus found himself in Hawaii.

Morpheus turned the ruler's odd behavior over in his head. He had never seen Zeus so full of emotion. The Olympian King had always been a carefree being. Taking whatever and whomever he wanted, and to hell with the consequences. Yet now, he seemed emotional and distant. There was something to this situation that Zeus felt compelled to deal with personally. He never interfered with the soap opera lives of the gods unless he had to save one from Hades. *Why is he so troubled over my relationship with a mortal? Or is he so concerned about my choice of mortal—Kallisto herself? But why?*

Morpheus called for Phantasos. It took his brother five long seconds to answer his call. He needed a sounding board, someone to bounce his concerns off of.

"So, did you see the big guy on the hill?" Phantasos asked as he leaned his masculine body against the pillar in the middle of the great room. He seemed unnaturally at ease.

Phantasos was not usually as comfortable on earth as Morpheus, but for some reason, Phantasos did not let it show as he usually did. Most of the time, he would look around nervously to make sure he was not about to be jumped by mortals. He had always been anxious and eager to return to Olympus, wanting to spend as little time as possible surrounded by people, and in a world where it was imperative, he acted mortal.

Phantasos had only come to earth if his work required it of him or when he was very young, and a mortal woman caught his eye. *He then only spent enough time to sate his and her desires, then he would return promptly to Olympus. Most of his fooling around was done with nymphs, goddesses, and the occasional demigod or daemon. Morpheus could only guess that by Phantasos doing his work for him, which consisted of many mortals, he had become more complacent with his earthly visits and possibly with people, maybe even a few mortal women.*

"I did, and he has granted me the right to stay for the two months The Fates allotted me. I was worried he would make me return." Morpheus walked past his brother, who was still lounging against the large white pillar and opened the French doors that led onto a balcony overlooking his backyard. The yard had a large kidney-shaped pool fed by a natural waterfall cascading over smooth rock. It was relaxing for Morpheus to listen as the water made its way over the rock and spilled into the depths of the blue water. The waterfall was the reason the mansion was built in that precise location. The calming effect of the running water would make the most stressed being relax. Broad green-leafed foliage and ferns growing in the shady areas created by the large boulders and moss-covered trees bordering the pool gave the feeling of being far from reality. The waterfall reminded Morpheus of his and Kallisto's spot on Olympus, only much smaller. Morpheus reveled in the slight breeze by lifting his chin into the air and closing his crystal blue eyes. The gardens were nearly as perfect as Olympus itself. It was amazing what manufactured gardens could look like when no expense was spared.

Morpheus stood there, letting the sounds and smells of nature help calm his need to go to Kallisto and demand she remembers and show her who he was. Even with his eyes closed and most of his concentration on the world around him, he could feel his brother's eyes pierce his back. He did not flinch; instead, he waited for Phantasos to come to the balcony with him.

Morpheus stood there, taking in the breeze and scents, for ten minutes before his brother decided to join him. "Morpheus, I have never seen you this way. Where is my carefree younger brother?"

"Maybe when I have what I want, and she is safe, you will get him back," he lowered his chin and opened his eyes slowly to peer into his brother's darker ones.

"You cannot let this mortal woman consume you like this. The Fates are not easily dealt with and do not like being challenged. You had best try and secure this situation and stop fueling the fire you are building between you and this woman." Phantasos was trying one last time to talk sense into his youngest brother.

"You will either side with me, Phantasos, and help me, or you may leave me and not return. If you choose to leave, I will stay on earth and give up my divinity...and by the way—that woman has a name—it is Kallisto," Morpheus spoke softly but with much conviction. "I will not be played with, I will get my way, and I will have her."

"I just wanted to try one more time, little brother. You know I am with you. If nothing else, I have no desire to keep your job. I have become accustomed to my lazy ways, and you know how much I detest earth." Phantasos was trying to make light of the tension in the air. Morpheus had always been carefree and fun. He looked worried as if he was about to lose his best friend.

"If you are going to stand with me on this, then I need you to find out why Zeus is so committed to taking care of this situation. Also, why are The Fates so interested in my love life."

"You know why little brother," Phantasos began, "you may very well drive this woman crazy like I did, Marissa. We cannot have that happen again." Phantasos went from a matter of fact to low and sad when he mentioned Marissa's name. "Our people cannot lose another dream god, especially their most favored and powerful."

With that, Morpheus allowed himself a sly grin. "Are you admitting that I, Morpheus, am a greater dream god than the *Almighty Phantasos?*"

"Hey, you know I will do anything, even lie, to get you to see things my way."

Phantasos met Morpheus' grin, and the air finally became somewhat lighter between the two gods. They stood there conversing for over an hour.

Phantasos left, going to the dream of a mortal. He rolled his eyes and gave a small mock giggle like a love-deprived teenage girl while batting his eyelashes and said, *"Oh, I will just die if Mike is with that other girl. How could he do this to me?"*—"How in the hell do you stand it, Morpheus," and he vanished.

Morpheus went to his bedchamber to rest. The only problem was that he could not relax. Zeus had been troubled and was too interested in his love life. Morpheus could sense he was missing something, and it was driving him crazy. *But what?*

He lay there for hours with his muscular body stretched across his bed. The memory of Kallisto's mouth, her body, and her unique smell that sent him reeling raced through his thoughts. He had grown to love her in their two-and-a-half months together. By going into her dreams, he saw the life she led. Her childhood in Greece, her relationships with family and friends, her—*Wait a minute, her childhood in Greece.* "That *has* to have something to do with this," he said aloud.

Morpheus closed his eyes and allowed himself to go into the dream Kallisto was having. He made sure to stay as mist in the background, not to alert her to his presence. The last thing he wanted was to further confuse her with the obvious difference between natural dreams and the reality of their relationship. He was looking for something that might help him figure things out. He had the power to push her dream in the direction of his liking. With that thought, he grinned at the possibilities. *Kallisto is right—I am incorrigible. I could always plead the fifth.* Morpheus knew of the mortal saying, not knowing entirely what it meant, but he got its jest, and it could be used in his defense when he was standing before the Three Fates and Zeus, explaining why he had carnal knowledge. With that, he laughed and returned to the "real" task.

Kallisto dreamed of riding the winds on the beautiful stark white Pegasus with its powerful white wings beating a consistent rhythm and its long flowing mane blowing in the wind beside her. He would have to remember this dream of hers. Kallisto laughed as her ebony hair flew out like a curtain, and her aqua eyes danced with joy when the winged horse spiraled into a powerful yet graceful dive. Pegasus landed on a beautiful meadow. Not just any field, their meadow, and where along the tree line a fine mist gathered. She and Pegasus stood among the same kaleidoscope of wildflowers he and Kallisto had picnicked two weeks prior.

Morpheus was confused. This was not just any dream—it was *Real!*

Morpheus' heart almost stopped. He looked around frantically. *How is she on Olympus without me taking her? Who is doing this?*

He felt sick inside. *Could it be Phantasos? No, I would know my brother's work. How?* The question was a scream in his head.

"Don't fret, Morpheus, I brought myself," Kallisto said aloud, even though he was cloaked as mist.

Morpheus' mind frantically searched for answers. He shimmered into sight and strolled over to Kallisto as she dismounted Pegasus, naturally as if she had grown up around the magnificent creature.

CHAPTER XIV

PEGASUS

As soon as **Kallisto's feet hit the soft ground** of the meadow, Morpheus had her scooped up into his arms. He was rarely surprised, but this time he had no explanation. She was not supposed to be on Olympus, but since he had not brought her here, could he be held responsible?

"How?" he asked.

Her aqua eyes took his breath away. They were like beautiful seas, deep, gorgeous, and full of uncharted territory. Lost in them, he lowered her to the ground and lightly caressed the side of her neck with his lips. As he recovered his composure, he searched those aqua depths for answers.

"When I woke, I didn't remember much at first. Then memories began flooding my head all at once. I remembered everything except your face. So, I decided to fix that by coming to you."

"How only the Greek gods are allowed to appear here on their own," Morpheus shook his head.

"To be honest, I'm not quite sure how this happened. I was determined to see you, so I stared at the painting for a long time. Then, I closed my eyes, remembered, and wished. When I opened them, I was standing beside the waterfall. Pegasus was drinking from the pool. In awe, I momentarily forgot I was looking for you," Kallisto blushed.

He loved the way she was wholly candid yet innocent in her honesty. She exuded happiness. How could he ever feel anything but love and admiration and, at the moment, complete confusion?

"I know this is a wonderful, beautiful, magnificent dream, but I want to enjoy every minute of it. So, let's get on Pegasus and soar through the air."

She thinks that she is in a dream. How can I convince her she is not?

Morpheus needed to figure this out, but the pleading on her face made him want to move the heavens and earth to make her happy. He feared The Fates or Zeus would find out she was on Olympus—again. Even though he was not directly to blame, would he be held responsible? If he was held accountable for her being on Olympus, would they make him come home to stay? Not that he would. It would just mean the end of his immortality.

Morpheus smiled his boyish grin and whistled for Pegasus. The winged creature had wandered several yards from them while grazing on the lush grasses of the meadow. The horse trotted to their side and waited for them to mount. Morpheus helped Kallisto up and then, with great power, leaped onto the horse behind her. Being Pegasus didn't have a saddle and, by human standards, was a good eighteen hands high, Morpheus leaping onto its back was a feat unto itself.

Morpheus wrapped his arms around Kallisto and pulled her close to his body as he whispered into her ear, "Hold on, I am going to give you the ride of your life."

He grabbed her hands and placed them in Pegasus' white mane. He, too, grabbed a handful of mane and kicked the winged horse into flight.

The bright yellow and orange from the sunset on the horizon was beautiful. Cradled between his arms, Kallisto leaned back onto his chest and closed her eyes, committing everything to memory.

Morpheus decided to savor this time with her in his realm. He made good on his promise and spoke into her ear to remind her to hold on. With a well-placed kick of his heel, Morpheus had Pegasus spiraling in the air. The horse's momentum kept them seated on its back even as it rolled, turning them upside down. Kallisto squealed. Pegasus banked sharply to the right and dove, flying feet above the ocean's surface. They could see dolphins, and as they moved back closer to land, the coral reefs.

The sunset before Pegasus returned them to the meadow.

"Morpheus, how do I get back? I mean, how do I wake?"

Good question. He thought.

"Don't get me wrong; I don't want to wake up. It just hit me that I don't remember ever falling asleep."

"You should come home with me and lie on the couch or bed to see if you can fall asleep."

"I don't know if *sleeping* is what you have in mind."

"Well, I have to admit that under any other circumstance, you may be right, but it is about to be morning, and you need to go, I mean, wake, before you "sleep" the day away." Morpheus knew she was not dreaming, and if her parents were to go into her bedroom, they would not find her.

"I'll come to your home, but you must do me a favor."

"I can do nothing but whatever you desire of me," Morpheus grinned.

"Come see me in real life, in my world," Kallisto pleaded.

Morpheus grinned at his chance. He could promise, as he was there until the end of February.

"I could, but how will you know it is me?"

"Well, that's a good question. What if you pull me tightly into your arms and kiss me? I would know your kiss anywhere."

With his newfound knowledge, Morpheus wished they were back at the gallery as Ambrose and Kallisto. *Would that work?*

"Morpheus?" Kallisto waved her hand, then snapped her fingers in front of his face as he stared off in deep thought. "Hello, are you in there?"

"Oh, sorry, I was just thinking about that kiss," he grinned.

Kallisto could tell there was more than kissing on his mind but didn't press the subject. Before she could open her mouth to comment about "the kiss," she was standing in his bedchamber.

"Uh, how did we get here?"

"Hey, this is your dream, you tell me." That was not entirely the truth, he brought her there with a thought, but it was her "dream." He was still perplexed at that fact.

This is the bedroom of my dreams. Kallisto laughed at the irony of her thoughts. She loved the large furniture with its gold embellishments and the sizable windows that looked over the most amazing lands so fantastical they took her breath away. The air smelled of honeysuckle and lavender, the scents she associated with Morpheus. She closed her eyes and took a deep breath through her nose, making a memory, one she hoped to keep this time.

"Morpheus, I don't want to leave. Please, don't make me go back. I feel like I belong here, I can't explain it, but I have never felt like I belong in my world. I belong with you—I can feel it."

He closed his eyes as she pleaded for him to keep her. If she only knew how hard he was trying to do just that—and how much he wanted her to stay. "My *dea femminile,*" he traced her jawline with his index finger, "if I could keep you here with me—I would." The pain in his voice shocked even him.

"I am tired of not remembering things. Why do I remember everything you told me the last time, but only while I'm with you?" Kallisto asked.

"Well, that is an improvement—I am not repeating the same story as I used to each time we were together. I have to believe this will work out. Now, work on remembering me when we are not together. I cannot. . ." Morpheus broke off his sentence. "Were you expecting anyone to visit you tonight?"

Kallisto's brows pulled together at his question. "No—why?"

"Because your mother just let someone in, and they are coming up the stairs."

Dizzy, Kallisto shook her head, now standing before her painting. She took three steps back and sat dumbfounded on her bed. She hadn't been asleep. Her mouth fell open. In the sky overlooking the beautiful waterfall was a white Pegasus.

"You know, you could swallow a fly that way," Amanda crossed her bedroom.

"I—just—had," Kallisto couldn't get her words out.

"You just had what?" Amanda prompted, looking concerned, and sat down on the bed beside her friend. Amanda followed Kallisto's gaze to the obvious focal point of her attention.

"Was Pegasus in the painting when you saw it last?" Kallisto asked.

"No, but now that you mentioned it, I don't recall that mansion way in the background either." Amanda stood up and pointed out the mansion in the background.

Kallisto gave an audible gulp as she walked slowly to the work of art with her hand stretched out in front of her. Very carefully, she traced the Pegasus and the mansion with her finger.

"I did it."

"Very good, Kallisto, you touched the painting."

Kallisto turned and glared at her friend, knowing Amanda could not help herself.

"No, I went."

"Where did you go? You aren't making any sense, Kalli. What is going on."

"I stood here—what time is it?" Kallisto spun around to the clock on her nightstand.

"Oh, now that you have cleared that up," Amanda rolled her eyes.

"I was standing here two hours ago. I closed my eyes and wished myself to Olympus."

"And," Amanda prompted again.

"And, I went." Kallisto touched the painting again.

"Well, hell, wish me one of those gods you're always interacting with," Amanda said, not at all taken aback by her friend's proclamation of having gone to a non-existent realm where all things immortal resided.

Kallisto turned to Amanda. "So, you believe me?"

"Of course, remember, I'm the crazy one of this dynamic duo."

"I was just in his bedchamber, and he said that mom let someone in the house to see me, and I had to go, then I was dizzy and standing back in front of the painting. Two hours passed, Amanda—Two. I know I wasn't standing in front of the painting for two hours, but when I—*came to*, I was standing in the exact spot; the only change was Pegasus and the mansion," Kallisto wiped her tears.

"Kalli, what's wrong? You have this sort of thing happen to you all the time." Amanda hated to see her best friend cry. It made her heart ache.

"I went there, by myself, with no help from Morpheus. I rode on Pegasus and went to his bedchamber again."

"Again? Has my girl finally—"

"Amanda, is that all you think about? And, no. The answer is still no. Apparently, even when controlling my fantasies, I seem to fall short."

"You said that you rode Pegasus. How amazing was that?" Amanda smiled.

"It truly was one of the most miraculous things to ever happen to me, and that's saying a lot." Kallisto giggled through her tears. "Flying through the air on a mythological creature with a god protectively around you as you fly higher and higher—"

Amanda interrupted, "and here I was feeling sorry for you. I want to meet his brothers. I already have them written down on my list." With that, both girls burst into laughter.

"If I ever get to spend time with him when I'm "awake," maybe we can talk about your list. I can't remember everything when we're together."

"Hormones, they are to blame. At least that is what my mom says anytime something is amiss with her," Amanda said.

"Where is Michael?" Kallisto asked.

"He went out with some of his friends tonight. I insisted because he's making me claustrophobic."

Kallisto had wondered how long her best friend's infatuation with the sweet guy would last. However, she had to give her friend credit; Michael had held her attention far longer than her regular interludes. He was just too nice for her, and in the end, Kallisto knew her friend would get bored before too long.

Kallisto spent the last days of her winter break between Amanda and work. She managed to learn all the legends she needed for the art pieces in the gallery and couldn't wait to tell her grandmother. She missed her grandmother more than usual since she started working around so much Greek history. The gallery reminded Kallisto of her every time she walked its floors.

Kallisto woke New Year's Day to the familiar smells of lavender and honeysuckle clinging to her body. Her dream was of her and Morpheus walking the halls of a building with white marbled walls and unreachable ceilings. They talked while walking hand in hand. This discussion was about her family, her grandmother in particular. She knew the conversation stemmed from her ache to see her grandmother. The two of them were kindred spirits. Kallisto was a younger version of her grandmother. Kallisto's skin was a bit darker, but she, her mother, and her grandmother looked remarkably alike. Her personality was most like her grandmother's, though. Thia once told her that living with her was like living with her grandmother all over again. She took that as a compliment.

Today was the gallery's grand opening. She had to admit. She didn't realize that grand openings often happened days and sometimes weeks after a store opened, giving it time to establish itself. Big sales, refreshments, and news crews often attended. Kallisto was anxious to get to work because she knew Ambrose would be there all day—because of her anxious state, she felt a twinge of guilt. *There I go again, feeling guilty for wanting to see an ordinary, mortal man while my immortal Greek god waits for me in my dreams.* "Yes, I definitely need therapy."

Kallisto talked John into letting Amanda come in with her for the day to answer the phone, so they could stay on the floor helping customers. Ambrose would be there for PR and help on the floor. Amanda would do the things the other employee, who Kallisto still needed to meet, usually did.

Kallisto rummaged through her closet again for the "perfect" garment. Amanda cleared her throat, and Kallisto jumped.

"Damn it, Amanda, you scared me." Kallisto scolded.

"Sorry, but I come bearing a gift."

Amanda held the black dress Kallisto planned to wear on their double date—the one her mother took to the dry cleaners.

"Where did you get that?"

"I dropped by the cleaners yesterday after I left here. I knew you'd be frantic this morning, so I made life a little easier. Now all you have to do is get through the day with that Greek hunk by your side," Amanda grinned as she handed over the dress.

"Well, I was about to hug your neck and thank you until you said that."

The girls arrived at the gallery at the same time as John, who was even more nervous than Kallisto, but she was for completely different reasons. He took Amanda to the back of the gallery and showed her all she needed to answer telephone calls. A price list, information about the upcoming gala, his personal cell number for "special" customers, and a list of art pieces coming into the store over the next month.

Kallisto straightened already straight pictures and dusted clean tabletops. The large clock over the desk in the back of the gallery counted the minutes until Ambrose's arrival. *I am acting like a young schoolgirl with her first crush.* As that thought went through her head, the ring on her finger heated. As soon as it did, in walked Ambrose. Her heart skipped a beat. With him was a gorgeous man who looked to be in his mid-twenties with long blonde hair worn loose around his shoulders. He resembled Ambrose with his sharply defined features and stood about 6'4".

Before Kallisto had time to be introduced to the Greek beauty, Amanda rounded the corner and said under her breath, "Oh baby, please tell me he is for sale."

Kallisto bit back a laugh. She tried to ignore Amanda's ogling, but it was hard since her tongue was practically hanging out. If anyone could make her blush, it would be Amanda.

"The one with his hair pulled back is mine," Kallisto whispered.

"Fine with me; as far as I can see, it's a win-win situation."

"Ambrose, this is my best friend and partner in crime, Amanda."

Amanda's eyes left the newcomer's face just long enough to say hello to Ambrose and shake his hand. To Kallisto's amusement, the blonde-haired "deity" looked at Amanda with the same enthrallment.

Ambrose shook Amanda's hand and introduced his companion. "Hello, Amanda, this is my brother Christos. He will be helping us out today as the muscle of the group."

Ambrose winked at Kallisto, then arched a brow as he saw the mutual interest on the faces of the new help.

Morpheus convinced his brother to meet Kallisto and see what was so appealing about her that he would consider giving up his immortality and power. It took him several hours of persuasion to get Phantasos to join him for the day in Hawaii. Phantasos hated being in a place where he could not act as a god, but to Morpheus' delight, he saw mutual interest in his brother's eyes for Amanda—*quite fascinating.*

Kallisto giggled as Ambrose excused himself and pulled her to the back office.

"I'm afraid of leaving your poor brother with Amanda, she could easily eat him alive, and he'd never see her coming." Still giggling, it took the entire trip down the hall to realize Ambrose was holding her hand. Not just leading her but having each of his fingers intertwined with hers, a more intimate grasp.

"Believe me; he's very capable of giving her a run for her money," Ambrose grinned.

Once in the little office, Ambrose turned to Kallisto and dropped her hand. He had forgotten he was Ambrose and not Morpheus. He needed to be more careful.

"I was wondering," Ambrose swallowed nervously before continuing, "would you go to the gala as my date?" He was anxious to get this night nailed down. This would be the night Kallisto saw him as a god, not a man.

"I'm somewhat involved with someone right now, but since he won't make it to the gala, I don't see any reason I can't go as your date." Kallisto felt guilty, but she needed to be realistic. She knew she needed to start living in a world of reality instead of fantasy.

Ambrose grinned at her declaration of belonging to someone. "What is the lucky man's name that holds your heart?"

Shoot, he would ask me a question like that. Not one to lie if she could help it, she changed the subject. "Did you just hear Amanda call my name? I better check and see." And out the door, she went without answering his question.

What he would have given for her to have said his name.

⟫⟫ ⟪⟪

Kallisto grabbed Amanda from what looked to be an intense conversation with Christos and told her what had transpired in the office.

"My boss just asked me on a date, sort of. He wants me to go to the gala with him as his date."

"I hope you said yes. He is as close to a Greek god as one can get here on "planet earth."

"Stop it. I told him I'm taken, but my significant other wouldn't be able to make the gala, so I could go with him."

"What did he have to say about that?" Amanda looked amused.

"He asked me the name of my boyfriend, and I said that I thought I heard you calling for me." Kallisto bit her upper lip.

"Girl, you have to be the most interesting friend a person could wish for. By the way, I think his brother is delectable if he would keep his mouth shut." Amanda stated as she looked back at Christos, who spoke with Ambrose and John.

"Why should he keep his mouth shut?" Kallisto asked.

"Because he has to be the most sarcastic man God ever made, my equal, and I'm not sure that I like being bested—ever."

Christos had an aura that radiated raw power and masculinity. Where Ambrose was more refined with his blonde hair pulled to the nape of his neck, leather tie, and dress slacks, Christos wore his long blonde locks free, a t-shirt that said, "*Pinch Yourself, I <u>Am</u> Real,*" and faded holey blue jeans.

"He is just so—" For the first time Kallisto could recall, words failed her best friend.

Kallisto could only cover her mouth and laugh at her friend. She knew that Amanda needed someone to give her a run for her money and keep her on her toes. To see Amanda struggle for words was indeed a moment to be remembered.

"You, my friend, need to be bested on occasion."

Once the store opened, everyone was so busy all bantering and ogling stopped. Between Kallisto and Ambrose, artwork all but flew out the door. They began competing to see who could make the most sales by the end of the day. Of course, Ambrose had all the women flocking to him, but Kallisto made the very last and most profitable. A well-groomed man who radiated money and power took a fancy to Kallisto. She used his admiration to her advantage and sold six pieces for $208,700. That brought her total for the day to $300,855, and Ambrose's was $289,090.

"Ha! I won!" Kallisto boasted as she shot Ambrose an evil grin and took off running to the back of the store, waiting, hoping he gave chase. Just as she peeked around the corner, she saw the man she last helped, who purchased the six pieces. He came back and was now talking with Ambrose. *Crap, I hope he is not bringing something back or complaining about me.* Kallisto's mind reeled as only her mind could. *Should I go out there? No, if Ambrose needs me to confirm something—gods forbid—apologize for something, he will come for me. I'm going to stay here.* She should be moving things around to accommodate the new pieces. Amanda, John, and Christos were in the storeroom uncovering paintings and sculptures that had just arrived so they could take inventory.

"No, Kallisto is in the back working, but I am the manager and my father is the owner, so if there is anything you need, I am sure I can help." Morpheus did not like the look in the man's eyes when he asked for Kallisto—by name. He could tell his return to the store was not business related, and he wanted the man to leave before he was forced to look like a madman.

"Well, she was so nice and seemed very knowledgeable about the history of the artwork. Maybe she could advise me on where to display these pieces in my office. It's just off of Main," the man confessed.

"We do not send our employees on decorating assignments," Ambrose responded.

"You wouldn't have to pay her. I would be more than happy to compensate her expertise—monetarily." The man continued.

Now Morpheus was getting angry. He could read the man's intentions and would not allow him to ever be around Kallisto again. "May I be so bold, sir? Kallisto is taken and does not need to work, even for me. She will be married by the end of the summer, and she will not come to your office or your home."

"Young man, I spent a lot of money here, and I demand to see the young woman who helped me, and she can tell me no herself."

Morpheus spoke through clenched teeth, "I do not give a damn how much money you spent here. I will gladly return your money when you bring the pieces you bought back." Then, eye to eye with the arrogant human, Morpheus said, "She is mine."

He knew by the man's reaction what he had seen. The man stumbled back and turned very pale with his eyes wide. Morpheus' eyes tended to go very crimson whenever he was indeed angered. The graphic thoughts the man was entertaining of Kallisto were enough to provoke the dream god to madness.

"I'll keep the pieces." The man turned on his heel and left.

It took Morpheus a minute to compose himself. When he turned, Kallisto stood in the hallway. "Have you been standing there long?"

"Not too long. What was that all about?" She didn't want Ambrose to know she heard him say she was his. The fact was, she was not his—her heart belonged—hell—her heart belonged to a dream. *Maybe Ambrose was trying to get rid of the man. Yeah, that's it. He was saving me from a crazy rich man who must have taken my kindness to mean something much more than an employee helping a customer.*

"I am sorry. I was trying to get rid of the man. He seemed to have taken a liking to you and wanted you to come to his office. " How do you say it—he weirded me out," Ambrose explained.

Kallisto couldn't help but giggle at Ambrose's attempt at American slang. He sounded so cute with his heavy Greek accent.

"I hope I didn't do anything wrong. He seemed to like all the pieces he bought."

"That is not all he liked. I just let him know that some things are not for sale." Ambrose then grinned. "What was that you were saying about winning?"

Kallisto's eyes widened, and she turned to run, giggling playfully. Before she could get two whole steps, she felt his hand snake out and wrap around her waist. He pulled her to him and said, "No one has ever outdone me before my dea. . ." then he froze. *Shit!*

"What did you say?" Kallisto shook her head. *No, surely he wasn't about to use Morpheus' endearment.*

"I was going to say, my dear one," Ambrose smiled and released his hold on her waist.

Kallisto felt something was going on here, and she couldn't shake it as they finished the inventory. Everyone laughed and cut up the rest of the evening. Amanda and Christos seemed to have developed a love-hate relationship. John seemed interested in Amanda, and the two guys bantered with one another just as much as Amanda and Christos were.

Kallisto would catch Ambrose watching her. Amanda had always told her men watched her when she wasn't looking, but this was the first time she could remember it happening. Unbelievably, his watching her made her feel good about herself, which was rare. Morpheus was the only other "watcher" that made her feel anything close to good about herself. *How strange.*

The following two days went by in a flash. Kallisto hadn't seen Morpheus in two days and saw very little of Ambrose. She and Amanda had spent time watching movies and talking about what their lives would be like after graduation. They were planning on going together to the University of Hawaii in Honolulu. Their parents were looking into housing for them. They were thinking about a two-bedroom condo that could be sold and profit made once the girls graduated college. Kallisto had also been trying to get Amanda to go with her to Greece in March. Amanda wanted to, but she was supposed to go with her parents on vacation to Alaska.

School was starting in the morning, and Kallisto wasn't ready to go back and see Austin—even worse, Elizabeth. Austin had not called since her mother had told him that she was washing her hair. He seemed to finally recognize the obvious shun. *Would he be back with Elizabeth?*

As the trivial life of a teenager went through her mind, she thought she heard the doorbell ring. About two minutes later, her mother knocked on her bedroom door and told her a young man named Ambrose was asking for her.

"Are you sure? I mean, that's my boss."

"Your boss, is that very handsome, very young man standing on our stoop?" Thia arched her brow in surprise. "He looks more like a model or a g—"

"Mother." Kallisto grinned. "I don't want the other analogy that was about to come out of your mouth."

Thia grinned back, "Well, don't keep the "Greek god" waiting."

"What did you call him?" Kallisto raised a quizzical brow.

"I just finished that analogy that you didn't want to hear. Honey, he looks as good as any deity in those books you're always reading."

Kallisto stood unmoving in her bedroom. Her mind reeled as it did when she was nervous and desperately needed to think. Unfortunately, she needed to let her boss in first. *Boss—Ambrose can't be older than 22 or 23, and, as Mom said, gorgeous—I've got to stop thinking of him as anything other than my boss. Why would he come here?* "Kallisto, stop it, get a hold of yourself, and go let him in."

She reprimanded herself and tried to control her thoughts as she fought back the butterflies that once again set up shop in her stomach.

Chapter XV

Hera

Kallisto stood in front of the door and took a deep breath, willing her heart to stop pounding. After all, she saw him daily, and her knees had never felt this weak. Yes, she sometimes got the sick feeling that great anticipation and desire caused, but this—she was visibly shaking. *What is wrong with me?* She closed her eyes and counted to ten—*one Mississippi, two Mississippi, three—*

On ten Mississippi, she flung the door open before her courage waned. Unfortunately, it looked like she flung it open out of excitement and realized it when she saw the devilish grin he got whenever he one-upped John or was bantering with her or his brother. *Oh great, now I look eager.*

Morpheus grinned even wider as he read her mind. He suddenly remembered that she thought him to be someone other than the person he was. A surge of jealousy struck him, and he had to remind himself she was attracted to him, no matter his name.

"Well, this is a surprise. Did I do something wrong?" Kallisto made light of her early eagerness.

"No, all is well at the gallery unless there's something you want to tell me?" He chided playfully. "I was in the neighborhood; *after all, Olympus was close, for a god anyway,* "and thought I would stop by and maybe see if you wanted to go for coffee?"

Coffee with the boss. "You aren't firing me, are you?"

Ambrose laughed at her conclusion. "Hardly." He reached his hand out, an invitation for her to take it.

Kallisto looked at his hand and then gulped. She took his hand, and chills traveled up her spine. She turned her head back and raised her voice so her mother could hear, "Mom, I'm going with Ambrose for coffee. I'll be back in a little while."

"Do you have your phone?" Thia yelled back across the house.

"Yes." Kallisto smiled and rolled her eyes, "Always the worry wart," she said to Ambrose.

She allowed Ambrose to playfully pull her to his car and open the passenger side door. As he jogged around the front of his car, Kallisto made a mental observation. *Man, he looks so good in Oakley's. I swear I've been around Amanda too long.* His faded holey designer jeans and loose white button-up were not lost on her either. He looked great! *Yep, I'm going to kill Amanda.*

Morpheus grinned as he crossed the front of his car, listening to Kallisto's thoughts. He had come to love the way her mind whirled out of control, bantering with herself whenever she was anxious. Since he would be giving Zeus another update in two days, he thought it best to talk with Kallisto and see what she knew. Plus, he was curious about her appearing on Olympus and why she had not returned. He hoped spending time with her would pave the way for her heart to recognize Ambrose as her "dream god."

"Where to?" Ambrose asked.

"We're always at the mall, so let's go to that new little coffee shop down the street from the park," Kallisto suggested.

"Sounds good to me."

Kallisto laughed the entire way to the coffee shop as Ambrose told her about his brother's frustrations with Amanda. They had gotten under each other's skin on New Year's Day, and both had complained to Ambrose and Kallisto about their need to put the other in their place.

"You should have heard Christos describe Amanda. I told him he was describing himself, even down to the long blonde hair," Ambrose laughed.

"What did he say about that?" Kallisto questioned.

Ambrose grinned, "He shot me a Greek "sign of affection" that would have made a grown man blush."

Once they pulled into the coffee shop parking lot, Kallisto's cell phone rang. To her astonishment, it was Austin. *Crap.* Embarrassed, she told Ambrose she should probably answer the call.

"No, I'm busy this weekend. Well, I've already made plans, not that it is any of your business. Look, Austin, I thought you got the hint when—"

Before she could get another word out, Ambrose snatched the phone from her hand and said, "Look, Kallisto told you she has plans this weekend. That is none of your business. She will have plans next weekend as well. Goodbye."

Kallisto had only heard Ambrose's side of the conversation, but she could only imagine what Austin had said. "What was that all about?" Kallisto glared at Ambrose's childlike grin.

"I know I have overstepped my bounds, but—"

"You think!" Kallisto interrupted.

"I remember that guy from the first time I saw you, and I overheard you talking to Amanda about him. I cannot stand to see a nice girl treated wrong. Forgive me?"

At least he had the sense to apologize.

"I can't believe your audacity." Kallisto was irritated, but at least her words were no longer dripping with acid.

"Again, I am sorry. I should not have. I could call the boy back and apologize if you would like?" Ambrose offered.

Truthfully, Kallisto was glad; she didn't want to keep avoiding Austin like the plague. Maybe if he thought she was seeing another guy, he would stop harassing her. Why he continued to call, she had no idea, but stranger things happened. *Like standing in the middle of a coffee shop parking lot with your sexy boss, arguing over a phone call from an infatuated boy from school who couldn't take a hint. Yes, stranger things have happened.*

"Look, Ambrose, I'm a little confused about all of this," Kallisto motioned between them.

"I just wanted to get to know you before the gala. I thought we could talk a little about ourselves and the preparations for the exhibit. If I offended you, please forgive me."

Morpheus knew he had overstepped the line when he interfered with Kallisto's phone call. Morpheus could get away with that, but Ambrose could not. *Damn, I need to get a hold of myself.* The truth was he could not stand that Austin kid and was ready to be done with him. *There is nothing more lethal than a jealous god.*

Kallisto knew better. Her instincts told her he was interested in her and had been since they met at the gallery the first night. She knew the "coffee date" was more than discussing the gala. What she failed to understand was, *why her?*

"You probably saved me a lot of calls and lies, but let's get something straight. Never do that again." Kallisto tried to suppress a smile.

The rest of the day was great. After coffee, they went for a walk in the park and discussed everything from the weather to their childhoods and school, his graduate classes, and her senior year, topics not usually discussed with your boss. They never held hands or even touched. She felt strangely comfortable with him. Their stroll reminded her of her picnics with Morpheus on Olympus. As she thought of him, she became quiet and a little withdrawn.

"Are you okay?" Ambrose knew her mind was on Morpheus.

"I'm just missing a good friend of mine. You remind me of him," Kallisto answered.

"Really," Ambrose grinned, "is he smart and incredibly good-looking?"

Kallisto playfully slapped at his arm and rolled her eyes.

"Yes, he is very smart and incredibly good-looking."

"I knew it." Ambrose's smile widened.

"You're as bad as your brother."

Morpheus felt elated. *I remind her of me. Okay, now I sound like the one going crazy. This is getting too complicated. I may be the one to go insane over all of this.*

As they headed back to the car, Kallisto reminded Ambrose they needed to discuss the gala. Not once had it come up, just as she thought.

Ambrose grinned, knowing he had no real intention of discussing work, but he needed to come up with something to save face.

"Most of the inventory will arrive at the showroom the morning of Saturday, the 14th. If you could, I would like you to be at the showroom and tell the delivery men where to set the pieces to make the best exhibit."

"What time should I be there?"

"Eight o'clock should be good. John will be at the gallery controlling everything on that end, and I will make sure the paintings of The Fates Three are delivered and well taken care of."

Not far from his car, they stopped on the trail while discussing the gala. They went on to discuss décor and who would work the door. Once everything was final, an awkward silence stretched between them. They were standing very close to each other. Close enough that she could feel the heat radiate off his body. Next thing she knew, he was leaning down to kiss her—and her phone rang. *Damn it!*

Ambrose jerked his head up, mentally cursing at the interruption. He had not kissed her in days and never as Ambrose. He was curious to see if she recognized his kiss, but Amanda just had to call. He took her hand as she spoke to her friend and led her back to his car.

Still talking to Amanda, Kallisto followed Ambrose, feeling very bereft by the interruption and guilty for feeling so. She wanted him to kiss her; after all, who wouldn't? But the guilt that hit her was just as unexpected as the "almost" kiss.

What about Morpheus? That thought made her angry as one thought spiraled into another. *He hasn't been around in days. He just came into her life whenever he desired. I guess he hasn't desired in several days.*

"Sorry, yes, I'm here. Can I call you back, though? We're about to leave the park, and I want to say something to Ambrose before we leave. He's going around to get in the driver's seat. See ya later, bye." Kallisto hung up with Amanda, wondering what she would say to Ambrose.

To her astonishment, Ambrose slipped into his seat and apologized for his lack of restraint. "I am truly sorry. I do like you—a lot. I enjoyed hanging out with you today, and I messed things up by, well—" He started the car and backed out of the parking lot. "Please don't hold this against me?" Then he began to laugh.

Heat started up her neck. "Did I do something that amused you?"

"No, I was just thinking about how pathetic I am. I have begged your forgiveness twice since we have been together today."

"There is nothing for you to apologize for this time, Ambrose. I'm a big girl, and if Amanda hadn't called, I would've kissed you back." She blushed.

"Well, then, I am sorry Amanda called." He spoke in his deep, sexy Greek accent.

When they arrived at Kallisto's, he walked her to her door. "I had a great time, Kallisto. I would very much like to spend time with you this weekend."

"I'd enjoy that." She smiled and hoped he would kiss her.

Morpheus leaned down and kissed her cheek. "I will see you later then."

Kallisto stood there dumbfounded. *He kissed me on the cheek. How sweet—damn it.*

Morpheus' mind was turning over his almost perfect *human* day. He was so confused. He was Morpheus, no matter what he called himself. He was the dream god that had fallen in love with a mortal woman. Trying to court her as a human man, one she had no clue was her dream god. He held the same feelings and knew all that had been between them. She did not realize Ambrose was who she swam under waterfalls, had picnics in gorgeous meadows with, flew over Olympus on a Pegasus, and with whom she traveled the world. Kallisto thought those memories belonged to her and another. Morpheus no longer wanted her to consider being with another man, not even if the other man was him. *I need some time just to be me, whoever that is, and maybe some therapy.*

"Phantasos!" Morpheus yelled in his brother's entrance hall.

"You do not have to yell, little brother; I am a god—remember?" Phantasos smirked. "You have been playing human so much lately; I am sure you have forgotten you, too, are a god. A powerful one."

"Well, that is sort of why I am here." Morpheus went on a tirade. "I think I am losing my mind. I cannot remember my own name half the time. I am calling *people* I do not know, mom and dad, and I have to pretend I do not know Kallisto the way I know Kallisto. To top it off, Hermes is taking full advantage of my employment, and I have to truly perform as the manager/owner of this god-forsaken gallery. The only solace I get is when Kallisto is around. Even that is tainted when I cannot hold or speak to her as the god I am. I almost screwed things up twice today. TWICE!"

"Calm down, Morpheus. You should talk to The Fates and see if there is any hope," Phantasos said.

"I have a meeting with Zeus in a couple of days. I will spend my time between now and then figuring out why my relationship with a mortal woman has some of the most powerful gods of our pantheon in an uproar. Plus, tomorrow I have school."

Phantasos walked to his game room and motioned for his younger brother to follow. "Let's play a couple of rounds of basketball and get your mind cleared out."

"How are my dreamers doing?" Morpheus asked with a complete change of subject. He did miss the dream realm, much more than he thought he would, not that he would ever let Phantasos know that.

"They are all doing well. Hera beckoned for you, though. I told her you were in the dream of another god and would come to her soon. You must go to her before you return to the mortal realm. " No other god is supposed to know of your arrangement for some reason," Phantasos stated as he dunked the ball.

The two gods played for a couple of hours. Sweat was dripping from Morpheus' hair as he relieved stress.

"I better get a shower and go see Hera. See you later." Morpheus turned to leave, then remembered. "Phantasos, I mentioned to some people you will be going to the Gallery's exhibit on the fourteenth of January. Be there in a tuxedo," and he vanished before Phantasos could peg him in the head with the basketball.

Morpheus waited, not so patiently, in the throne room of Hera's palace. The room was exquisite with its crystal walls and gold ceilings. Her throne, a gift from Zeus, was made of diamonds.

"Morpheus, I am so glad you came," Hera glided into the room and greeted him as if they were best friends. Truth be known, he hated her. She was the cause of a lot of his mother's heartache. His father, Hypnos, had an affair with Hera just after Morpheus' birth. All he knew was that his mother hated her.

Hera was beautiful, as were all the Greek gods and goddesses. She wore gold bands in her long dark brown hair, and her gold-lined white robes clung to her elegant curves. Even though she was beautiful, she did not hold a candle to Aphrodite or even Kallisto.

Morpheus bowed from the waist in respect for the wife of Zeus. "Where else would I go when you are in need of me? I am just sorry I could not come to you last night." Morpheus could be very charming when he needed to be.

Even though Zeus and Hera's relationship was rocky at best, Zeus would kill any mortal or immortal that so much as looked at her with malice. She was the "love" of his existence. Well, myth stated it that way. In truth, their relationship was a very passionate love-hate relationship. Morpheus was more practical and sought a calm monogamous relationship. He wanted to love only one woman and spend an eternity finding different ways to love that woman. Zeus and Hera had a very different kind of union. They spent as much time betraying one another as they did loving each other. Each had children by different lovers, and each accepted that fact. Not Morpheus; he could not stand for that Austin boy to get anywhere near Kallisto without the green eye of jealousy rearing its ugly head.

"I am having family over soon, so I must make this brief. What I am about to ask you for is between no other but you and me. Understood?" Hera stared straight into Morpheus' eyes.

"Of course."

"My husband has been sleeping restlessly. I want to know why. I think it has something to do with you." She glared.

"Why would Zeus be restless because of me? He has not summoned me to his dream realm. I know nothing of his trouble sleeping," Morpheus defended himself.

Hera made a complete circle around Morpheus before she commented. "I did not say you caused his restless dream. I believe you are the reason he sleeps restlessly." Hera looked at Morpheus as if trying to detect an untruth.

"Why would he have bad dreams about me?" Morpheus asked, completely confused by her interrogation.

"I do not know, but I will find out. He has not been himself lately, and I know you have not been the one helping your dreamers. I also know you brought a human girl to Olympus. Who is she?" Hera pressed.

"She was one of my dreamers. I enjoy her company, that is all." Morpheus skirted the truth, remembering Zeus' warning about not telling Hera.

"Why is it that the men of our pantheon have a "soft spot" for the women of the human realm?" With the corner of her top lip raised in revulsion, Hera mused more to herself than Morpheus.

"Zeus has reprimanded me, so with all due respect, I do not think I need to rehash my dealings with the mortal woman. She is no longer a factor." Morpheus was angry, and it took all his willpower to keep his composure. He knew Hera, and she could not be trusted.

"Well, I have a job for you, dream god. I want you to find out what is going on with my husband. He spoke your name aloud in his sleep. Why? Find out. If you betray me by telling him, you will pay. Do you understand?"

Morpheus could take no more. "Never threaten me, Hera. I may not be as wise as many of the gods in this pantheon, but I wield a lot of power, more than even you. I will look into your husband's situation as is my duty to you as a dream god, but you will never threaten me." Morpheus' eyes went crimson, and the room shook ever so slightly.

A brief moment of fear crossed Hera's face before she composed herself.

"Do not make threats, young one. You cannot conceive of the power I have in my possession."

"Just remember, Hera," Morpheus grinned evilly, "you would need to rely on those you consider loved ones or those indebted to you. Do not screw with me. I only have to look to myself for power. I have told you I will help you but don't ever think of me as your puppet."

"Fair enough, but remember to whom you are talking. I will get my way, dreamer." Hera matched his grin, trying not to show the fear she had moments before. "I'll see you soon." Hera vanished.

CHAPTER XVI

SECRET,

Kallisto woke with her alarm clock blaring 3 Doors Down's "Let Me Go." She thought it a strange song since it had to be from the early 2000s. The lyrics played in her head as she showered and dressed. It made her rethink her current situation. The words stopped playing on repeat when the familiar feeling began. *Where have you been?*

To her astonishment, she felt his answer. *I am always with you.*

Kallisto stood before the painting. *I wish I had time to see you. Promise me you'll come to me tonight. I tried to go to you, but it didn't work.* She felt his answering smile like he was there with her.

Kallisto arrived at school, and to her horror, Austin was standing in her parking space—again. *If I hit him, how many points would I get?* The "point system" was a game she played with Amanda. It was a silly game with no rules, but it had brought them many laughs over the years.

He, again, moved to her side of the car as she pulled into her space. *Just a mental note, please switch spaces with Amanda tomorrow. She will run over him.* Before Kallisto opened her car door, she thought about the excuses Amanda would undoubtedly come up with if given the opportunity and laughed.

"Austin, I do believe you are a glutton for punishment. What are you doing in my space this morning?"

"I wanted to walk with you into school. Is that such a crime? Will your new boyfriend not allow you to have a guy friend?" Austin smirked.

"First, Ambrose is not a boy. He's a man. Second, he doesn't allow or forbid me anything."

"Oh, come on, Kallisto, lighten up," Austin said as he wrapped one arm around her shoulders.

All Kallisto wanted was for Austin to get lost. She resigned to walking with him inside so she wouldn't be late for history class. She knew Austin wouldn't leave her alone until the bell rang. As they entered the door, she thought she saw—*no, can't be. Why would he be here?* Before she could wiggle out from under Austin's arm, the "vision" vanished around the corner. She didn't have time to chase after her illusion.

"I'll see you in math," Austin said.

"Can't wait." Kallisto rolled her eyes. *Where the hell is Amanda?* Just as she thought it, Amanda came running through the door.

"Where have you been? You're never late." Kallisto asked.

"I overslept."

"I've got so much to tell you. Guess who came to my house yesterday and took me for coffee and a walk in the park?" Kallisto grinned.

"Please, Kallisto, tell me that rat Austin did not—"

Kallisto interrupted Amanda, "No. Ambrose."

"Get out! Your boss? Did you ask for a raise?" Amanda laughed.

"I swear, Amanda, you need a daily ice water bath."

Both girls giggled and bantered until Mr. Wright, their history teacher, came in. "I'm glad to see everyone back and well rested." I have a guest who will be with us for two weeks. He'll be working with me on a new project, and I'm going to ask you to join us. He'll be teaching us about the history of his land. He has a bachelor's in Greek History and is working on a dual master's in Greek mythology and ancient history."

It was then Kallisto knew the man she thought she saw in the hall was not an illusion.

In walks Ambrose. "Class, this is Ambrose Xanthopoulos. Please give him the same courtesy as me or any other teacher."

Kallisto's face started burning as fury and embarrassment rolled through her body. How dare he take me out on a date, almost kiss me, and ask me out this weekend. He's now my teacher and my boss. Damn him," Kallisto whispered to Amanda.

Amanda started giggling and raised her hand to excuse herself so that she could find composure. While Mr. Wright was busy approving Amanda's bathroom break, Ambrose's eyes locked onto Kallisto's.

He saw the shock and anger in her eyes, but what got to him were the tears she was fighting back. He had not told her. He figured if he had, she would not have gone out with him. The fact he was her boss further complicated the matter. Would she forgive this? *Probably not.*

Mr. Wright kept the class quiet, and the couple's eyes stayed locked. A few of Kallisto's classmates started noticing their locked gazes, but before anything was said, Amanda re-entered the room, bringing everyone's attention to her. Ambrose cleared his throat and began telling the class a little about himself.

Amanda mouthed, "Are you okay?" to Kallisto.

All Kallisto could manage was a shake of her head. She felt betrayed, and she wasn't sure why. Yes, he should've told her, but he was nothing more than her boss. So—what—they were just wrapped up in the moment yesterday? *It would not happen again.*

—In Greece, I studied and continue to explore the connections between true Greek history and the mythological tales told by our people through the centuries. Here I will be shameless and plug my parents' gallery—they own the "Gallery of the gods" at the outdoor mall. " Everyone but Kallisto and Amanda laughed.

One hand in the back went up, and Ambrose nodded for them to ask their question. It was Melissa, one of Elizabeth's friends. "How old are you, and are you taken?" All the girls giggled.

You would think they were twelve-year-olds. Kallisto thought.

"I am close to your age and dating someone." Locking eyes with Kallisto as he said it. His gaze was evident to everyone and made Kallisto blush.

The bell rang three short times, stopped, and was followed by three more short rings. "Fire drill," Mr. Wright stated.

"He's dating someone, and he asked me out? He almost kissed me!" Kallisto said to Amanda.

Everyone went outside for the second time this school year. The new advanced chemistry class was notorious for *creating* experiments. The building smelled of rotten eggs for days after their last experiment had gone wrong.

Seamlessly filing in with the crowd, Ambrose made his way to Kallisto, grabbed her arm, pulled her to his side, and waited for the last students to leave. Amanda gave Kallisto a questioning look, and Kallisto nodded, letting Amanda know she would be okay.

"You can release my arm." Kallisto snapped.

"Please, walk with me outside. I want you to know that my being here has no bearing on us."

"There's no *us*, Ambrose. You are my boss—nothing more. Yes, I agreed to go to the gala with you, but I'm sure if you look around, you may find someone more appealing than me to be your arm ornament. Maybe you could ask one of these girls who swoon over your "contractionless" accent or, better yet, ask the girl you're dating." Kallisto glared, turned on her heel, and left the room.

Grinning, he thought she was even more beautiful when angry. He entered the hallway behind a group of guys in no hurry to save themselves from the "fire." It took him two seconds to realize one of them was Austin, and he was talking about Kallisto.

"We went out several times over the holidays. I'm planning on giving her my class ring prom night, and I am going to f—"

Before Austin could get another word out, his knees buckled, and he crashed to the floor— again—holding his pounding head. His shocked friends helped him to his feet.

"Hey man, let's get him outside and to the nurse," one boy said.

I don't think he's okay. He doesn't look so good," another of the boys said.

Ambrose stepped around the boys and followed the crowd through the double metal doors that led to the fence line where all students and staff were to report when the fire alarm went off. It didn't take long to pick her out of the crowd. Standing with her arms crossed, Kallisto's ebony hair shone in the sunlight, and he could tell she had shed a few tears. Before he could take another step in her direction, Mr. Wright caught his arm.

"I'm glad you made it out without smoke inhalation or incineration," Mr. Wright laughed.

"I followed the crowd. Is it always this exciting here?" Ambrose asked in his thick accent.

His heart ached, and all he could do was stand there, on earth, mere feet from her, making small talk with a high school history teacher. He knew her tears were not only those of Ambrose's failing to confide in her but from all, she'd gone through over the last couple of months. He, Morpheus, a dream god, had done this to her. Was she about to break?

"Ambrose, I couldn't help but see your admiration for one of my students, Kallisto Nalani. I must tell you, being here as a "teacher," you can't see any of the students on a personal level."

"She is one of my employees from the gallery. But I must tell you, I am seeing her, or I was. I failed to tell her about this, and when I walked into your classroom, let us say—she no longer wants to see me."

"That's for the best," Mr. Wright stated without thinking.

"With all due respect, Mr. Wright, we were seeing each other before I came here to help you. If she ever speaks to me again, I will try and win her affection back. If this is a problem, I will have to leave."

"Can you keep the relationship quiet?" Mr. Wright asked.

"Simply put, I will not touch her while on campus, and I will not allow her to cheat on tests." Ambrose grinned at the teacher, putting finality on the subject. "Now, if you would excuse me, I need to go and see if she hates me."

As he turned to go to Kallisto's side, he ran straight into Amanda. Her eyes held contempt—*for me*, he thought. *This cannot be good.*

"Look, Amanda; I did not tell her because I was afraid she would not go with me for coffee or agree to go out with me again. I had no idea she had European history first period—I thought I would have time to explain."

"You need to leave. Put that cute tail between your legs and go. Give her time to deal, and she'll see you at work." Amanda stood with her arms crossed, daring him to defy her.

He could not help but notice how tired she looked. Her eyes had faint black circles around them. Ambrose gave Amanda a look of surrender and left.

The bell rang, giving the students and staff the go-ahead to return to their duties. Throughout the day, Ambrose saw Kallisto in the halls, at lunch, and once when he had deliberately entered her English class to speak with Ms. Anderson about going to her class. When he entered, Kallisto's eyes lit up like she had forgotten she was annoyed with him. A split second later, her look that said—*I hate you, go away already*—came back tenfold. Again, this made him grin—inside—he was not stupid enough to let her see it.

Kallisto was happy Austin went home. At least she didn't have to put up with him in math class. She sat through her government class, staring into space, thinking about the turn of events she had experienced over the past two days. *I've gone all these years without the trouble of a "man," and now I have three—currently all in the doghouse. Morpheus, for not being in my dreams lately; Austin, he's a jerk and will never get out of the doghouse; and Ambrose, he hurt my feelings, and I'm not entirely sure why.*

While she had her mind occupied by the irony of her life, she overheard two guys in the back of the class whisper her name in conversation. She leaned back in her seat, trying to hear all that was said. She got the gist of it and was furious. Apparently, Austin told everyone they were an item and she was not as virtuous as they thought. *Okay, forget the doghouse—he's dead.* Kallisto tried to control her anger as she continued to eavesdrop on the boys' conversation. Evidently, Austin had plans for prom or, more accurately, after prom for the two of them. *That's it. I am going to get rid of my Austin problem once and for all.*

Kallisto met Amanda outside after school. "I overheard some guys in my government discussing Austin's new girlfriend."

"That didn't take long. Who's the poor girl?" Amanda asked, not looking at Kallisto but instead glancing toward Michael, who sat with Mary Morrison, an eleventh grader.

"Me!" Kallisto yelled her answer, bringing Amanda's attention back.

"What? Surely not—he's nuts."

"If you think that's crazy, you should hear his plans. Let's say, according to Austin, I'm very loving and will be even more so after the prom."

"What a jackass. What are you going to do?" Amanda asked.

"I'm going to his house after work and set him straight."

"That won't discourage him. He doesn't care what the truth is. Unless you humiliate him publicly, he'll continue to humiliate you privately," Amanda had that look in her eyes, the one that always got the two of them in trouble. The look meant she was planning something.

"Why do I attract such strange beings? I have a Greek dream god, my boss, now my teacher, and a delusional asshole vying for my attention. The only one of the three I want to give my complete attention to is the one I can never have." *Probably the one that is just a figment of my imagination.* Kallisto looked down at her bracelet and sighed.

"I think you should publicly humiliate Austin tomorrow. Let him know in front of all his cronies that you are not his—" Amanda thought, pausing an unusually long time, trying to find a word, "—well—his anything." Amanda looked as disgusted with Austin as Kallisto felt.

"Amanda?"

"Yes?"

"Are you okay? I mean, you don't seem to be yourself today." Kallisto asked.

"I just had strange dreams last night, and when I woke up at 3:30 this morning, I couldn't go back to sleep. I'm just tired, that's all. Don't worry. Tomorrow I'll be full of my usual cynicism, I promise."

Kallisto laughed at her friend. "You know, you're not entirely cynical. You believe in my crazy fantasy world. Truth is, you believe—even when I don't."

"Or I'm just an over-enthusiastic friend," Amanda grinned.

"Well, I'm supposed to be at work in fifteen minutes, so I'd better go," Kallisto said.

"Promise me you won't go over Dumbass Delusional's house after work."

Kallisto gave Amanda a wide grin. "Now, there's my girl—I promise. I'll call you when I get home tonight. Can I use that charming endearment you just made up for Austin? What was it again, Dumbass Delusional?"

"Anytime, girl. I can give you one for Ambrose, too, if you like." Amanda winked.

"Let's hear it."

"How about Fine Ass Idiot."

Kallisto could tell Amanda was proud of herself and laughed as they parted ways.

Kallisto pulled into the mall's parking lot, dreading going to work. She didn't want to be in the same room with Ambrose, especially a room where he had the upper hand. Why didn't he tell her he would be helping the teachers? She sat in her car and thought about the best way to approach him.

Speaking aloud to the reflection in the rearview mirror, she decided, "Sunday never happened. He is now known to me as only Mr. Xanthopoulos. He'll know our relationship is only that of store owner and lowly employee."

Immediately upon entering the gallery, John introduced her to Margaret, the lady who had been on vacation the last two weeks of December.

"Kallisto, this is Margaret. She answers the phone and takes care of the housekeeping. She will be here every Monday, Wednesday, and Friday."

The two women shook hands, and Kallisto knew immediately she would like her. The woman's very kind, motherly face made you feel comfortable.

"Ambrose is in his office and asked me to have you see him when you arrive," John's face showed concern.

"Did he mention why he needed to see me?" Kallisto asked.

"No, but he is not in the best of moods. He's having woman trouble," John allowed.

"What makes you say that?" Kallisto asked. If Ambrose mentioned this to John, she would strangle him.

John snickered. "Because guys don't mope like that over spilled milk, and he doesn't have money problems, so it has to be."

Kallisto shook her head. "Are all men as observant as you think you are?"

"I don't just think, I know. He has that look. Wait, when you see him, you'll be able to tell. Remember to be on your best behavior, separate work, and personal affairs."

"What's that supposed to mean?" Kallisto couldn't believe what she was hearing. Surely, Ambrose hadn't confided in John. If he had, did he tell him all about Sunday?

"Look, Kalli; I'm not blind. I see how the two of you look at each other. If the girl he is having trouble with isn't you, I'm one of the gods we display on our walls. He's just a kid himself and has a huge responsibility put on his shoulders to get this store up and running. Cut him some slack."

"I've no idea what you're talking about." Kallisto could feel the flush rising up her neck. She was glad Margaret had been pulled away by the phone ringing and had not heard any of their conversation.

John held his hands up in mock surrender. "I'm just making an observation, that's all."

"Well, stop it. I don't need anything other than a job right now. If this is going to be an issue, maybe I should find other work." Kallisto stated.

"Now—now, let's not be that way. You have more knowledge of mythology than I could ever instill in another employee, even if they worked here for years. We need you. Our store is doing better than the one in LA, and you're a key part of that success."

"Then please stop trying to fix me up with Mr. Xanthopoulos. I'm sure he wouldn't appreciate it."

John raised his eyebrows and shook his head. "It's worse than I thought if you are going to call him Mr. and then tack on that mouthful of a last name." He walked away, still shaking his head.

Kallisto busied herself straightening paintings and asking a young couple who had just come in if she could help them. Unfortunately, they gave her the "we are just looking" answer.

"Let me know if you need anything. I will gladly tell you about some of the artwork." She continued to busy herself with mundane tasks that held no value, but she was in no hurry to see Ambrose.

The couple admired a piece depicting the three powerful brothers—Zeus, Hades, and Poseidon. Their faces were captured in their prospective areas of rule. Zeus' face was on Mount Olympus, Hades' was layered under the ground, and Poseidon's was in the ocean's waters. Engraved on a gold plate at the bottom of the painting was the title of the piece, *Brothers' Rule*.

The young woman motioned for Kallisto as she met her eyes from the opposite side of the gallery. "Yes, can I help you?" Kallisto asked in relief. She was glad to have a legitimate reason for not going to Ambrose's office and facing the "mortal god" while wanting to choke him.

"We," the lady waved her hand between herself and her husband, "like the look of this painting. Could you tell us about it, please?"

"This painting represents Zeus, Hades, and Poseidon after Zeus freed his brothers from their father, Cronus. Cronus had swallowed his children, and after their escape and Cronus' imprisonment, the three took over. They divided the world into three sections; Zeus, ruler of the Greek gods of Olympus and the lands; Hades, ruler of the dead and nether world; and Poseidon, ruler of the seas." Kallisto enjoyed her work, and as she enlightened the prospective buyers, she realized she didn't want to leave. *I'll have to make nice with Ambrose, no matter how badly he needs strangling.*

"How much is this piece?" the man asked.

"This piece is $54,000 and one of a kind." Kallisto gave the couple the price, and to her shock, they didn't flinch. She was still amazed at how much money some people had. She thought since they were so young, they would at least squirm.

"We are going to walk around for a while and discuss this piece while continuing to look," the lady stated.

"Let me know if you need anything else." Kallisto smiled as she walked back to the front desk where John was standing with a look that said *I know what you are doing, and it won't work.*

"What?" Kallisto looked like a child caught doing something they shouldn't.

"You know what. He is waiting for you, and you have procrastinated for thirty minutes." John did not want to be the one to tell the boss his employee refused to see him.

"I'll see him after I finish helping . . .," Kallisto looked up and grinned, bringing her defensive speech to a halt. The young lady in the pants suit was motioning for her again. "Looks like the customer saves me." Kallisto allowed herself a smirk and winked at John. The idea of making a sale of $54,000 had been what she needed to bring her out of her self-contained pity party.

Kallisto spent another forty-five minutes completing the sale and getting the address for delivery. When she turned around from the paperwork as the couple exited the gallery, her eyes landed on Ambrose's beautiful crystal blue ones. Kallisto forgot she was furious with him for a fraction of a second, but a second goes by fast. Her smile abruptly became a defiant stare.

Ambrose suppressed his smile as he walked to her side. He loved the look in her eyes when she was irritated—just not entirely so irritated. "I would like to speak with you in my office. John told me you made a sale," he began making small talk, keeping it work related as he placed his hand on the small of her back, nudging her toward his office.

As he walked behind her, he caught her scent, distinctly Kallisto. A rush of memories; Olympus, the Pegasus, waterfalls and meadows, Greece, all came flooding through. He had not realized they had entered his office until Kallisto spun around.

"What can I do for you, *Mr. Xanthopoulos*," Kallisto snapped. She tried hard not to admire his office.

One of Morpheus' eyebrows shot up, and he had to roll his lips inward and bite down to keep from grinning. She was not making this easy. If he had known how cute she was while spewing cynicism, he would have aggravated her before now. "Well, Ms. Nalani," he mocked her with a grin showing her that her scorn was not lost on him, "I would like to continue our discussion from this morning if you do not mind."

"And if I do mind?" she crossed her arms defensively over her chest.

"Well, instead of a—discussion— it will be a one-way conversation where I explain my actions to you, and you listen." He could not help but give her a dose of her own cynical medicine. He knew she was more hurt than mad, but until he began groveling, he could handle a little of what she was dishing out.

Kallisto glared at Ambrose, trying hard to remember he was technically her boss, and she loved her job. *But damn, why does he have to be so darn cute. Maybe if I keep my eyes closed, I won't melt. No, there is still the problem with that sexy accent. Oh well, I'll see how long I can hold out.*

"Kallisto?" Ambrose questioned.

"Huh? What? Sorry—Off in my own little world," Kallisto flushed.

"I was saying that Mr. Wright contacted me before I knew you. He only wants my help. I am not your teacher. I am just there as a resource, that is all."

"You don't have to explain anything to me, Mr. Xanthopoulos. I'm just an employee and a high school student who—" *happened to see you as more,* "needs a job, and I'm sure will benefit from your expertise in Greek mythology—at school."

Ambrose closed his eyes and took a deep breath. *Why was I finding her attitude amusing before?* "I did not tell you because I did not feel like it was relevant to our relationship, and I did not want that to be an issue when I asked you out for this weekend."

Kallisto watched Ambrose squirm, and she bit her cheek, trying not to smile at his apparent discomfort.

"Not relevant to our relationship? You're working at my school professionally; there can't be a date this weekend or for the gala. You'll have to find someone else."

"I am not getting paid by the school system; this is voluntary only. I have talked with Mr. Wright about my "other" interest in the school, you." Ambrose stated.

"You did what?" Kallisto knew she didn't just hear him say he told her history teacher they had a relationship outside of school. "You told him that I work for you?"

"Yes, he asked about how we looked at one another. So, I told him I was interested in you as more than my employee," Ambrose answered.

Kallisto's eyes widened as she went red. "You told him that we are dating?"

"In a round-a-bout way—yes." Ambrose made a defensive attempt.

"Number one, we are not dating. Number two, if we were, we no longer are, and I can't believe you told him—what did he say?"

"As for your question," Ambrose spoke calmly. "He stated school policy, and I told him if he wanted me to help him with his project, then he would have to deal with our relationship—oh—and I promised I would not touch you at school."

"You did what?" Kallisto couldn't believe her ears. *Does he plan on touching me when we're not at school? How dare he!* But she wanted a real relationship, not one in her dreams.

Morpheus was enjoying this. He loved seeing the heat radiate from Kallisto's eyes. Her irritation over the loss of control was amusing. A small part of him was sure if she knew who he was, she would take the entire situation a little differently.

"Let me get this straight before I kill you," Kallisto was making sure she heard him correctly before she laid into him. She tried to focus on the papers riddled across his desk. She saw that the words on the topmost sheet said, *The Beautiful Fates Three*, and three pictures were under the title. Momentarily she was distracted by the beauty of the women in the pictures. The delay of her tongue thrashing caused Ambrose to find the disruption. He started to change the subject to the objects of her attention before he had to withstand her wrath, but Kallisto recovered her anger just in time.

"You made my teacher believe that you and I are together? We are not together. I'm seeing someone at the moment."

Ambrose bit his lip, restraining the smile, itching to surface. After his brief composure, he managed to raise one eyebrow at her.

"If you are seeing someone, why did you say yes this weekend? And, why were you going to let me kiss you?"

Kallisto's eyes bugged. "Allow you to kiss me?" She knew she had no recourse on that one. She had admitted to him that she would've kissed him back—*crap.* "Well, everyone has lapsed in judgment now and then. Besides, I'm not exclusive with him. I'm just seeing him on occasion."

Ambrose raised an eyebrow, "Really?"

Kallisto took his look and question as skepticism, making her angrier. "Are you implying that I'm lying, Mr. Xanthopoulos?"

Now he was irritated with her; the "I'm seeing him on occasion" remark caused his stomach to lurch, but he could not tell her that. "No, not at all. Please stop referring to me as Mr. Xanthopoulos. My name is Ambrose."

"Yes sir, may I go now?" Kallisto glared.

Both brows went up at her "yes sir." Through clenched teeth, he replied. "Yes, for now, but we are not done here. I will be here until closing, and then we will finish this discussion."

"Yes sir, Mr. Xanthopoulos," Kallisto gave Ambrose a wicked grin as she turned on her heel and gracefully left the office. She knew he was watching her. She also knew he was torn between shaking her and kissing her. For the first time in her life, she felt the power of her femininity and beauty; and she enjoyed it.

The afternoon was spent with Kallisto nervously, avoiding physical or eye contact with Ambrose. As she felt the power of her effect on him, she knew she was just as vulnerable to his influence, that of a gorgeous Greek man with an accent that sent a burning desire through her body. She knew if she allowed him within feet of her, she would no longer hold control, or at least her perception of control. *What is that adage—perception is reality?*

Several times Kallisto looked up to find Ambrose with his arms crossed over his chest, staring at her; he didn't even try to hide it. Finally, Amanda came strolling in about twenty-five minutes before closing. She had changed into blue jeans and a t-shirt and had her hair in a ponytail.

"You look beat," Kallisto's eyes ran up and down Amanda. Amanda's eyes had started showing signs of dark circles. Worse, she was dressed in, well, regular everyday clothes. Amanda never went around looking "normal." She was always well put together; not that she wasn't striking in her faded blue jeans and t-shirt, but they were not what you would typically see her in while she was in the public eye. "You need to go get some sleep. Why are you here instead of in bed?"

"I wanted to make sure you didn't take any—" she looked around to see Ambrose and John both in listening range and whispered the rest, "shortcuts to kill someone."

Morpheus, of course, heard every word she said, and many she did not say. He read in her thoughts that she was concerned Kallisto would drop by Austin's house on her way home to discuss his lack of honor and maturity. Well, that was how he interpreted her words anyway. What was actually in her mind was—*If you are going to Austin's to defend your honor, I'm going too, and I'll kick his ass for you.* He also saw she was tired because of dreams. To his astonishment, he could not deduce the theme of them. He guessed she could not remember them herself. When Amanda shot him a *go-to-hell look*, Morpheus winced. He knew the best chance of winning Kallisto back to his side, besides that kiss he was dying to plant on her, was to keep Amanda on his side.

"Hello Amanda, how are you this evening?" Ambrose bowed slightly and winked at her. Amanda smiled, letting him know his "old world charm" had done the trick. All hostility had left Amanda's face; now, only a smile and heavy lids were present.

"I wanted to follow Kallisto home and visit for a while," Amanda grinned her sly smile that told everyone there was more to her story.

"Could I speak with you a moment?" Ambrose asked Amanda.

Amanda gave him a curious look, "Sure."

She followed Ambrose to his office while Kallisto stood in the gallery with her mouth open.

"Have a seat," Ambrose said in his heart-stopping Greek accent as he pointed to a leather chair.

This was Amanda's first time in Ambrose's office since he had claimed the back room as his personal space. She grinned as she looked around. In that instance, she knew her best friend and the "hunk" before her were destined to be together. Walking from the hallway into his office was like going into a Greek museum. There was what looked to be an antique table along the wall to her right that held artifacts she was sure only he and Kallisto would identify. There were old leather-bound books on the other side in an antique bookcase. Most of the writing on the spines of the books was in Greek, and some looked to be in ancient Greek. Above his desk was a painting of Greece framed in a large, intricately carved golden frame. Amanda could not tell if the frame was wood, but it was beautiful. The structure was a work of art, and she was sure the painting was worth more than any on the gallery floor. On Ambrose's desk, between bookends that looked like the goddess Aphrodite, were a few old books that looked ancient and worn out. She could make out one, *The Iliad. I don't know why Kallisto is fighting this; this man is her other half. He is physically young but, like Kallisto, contains an old soul.*

"What's up?" Amanda asked casually, still glancing around the room.

"I need to speak with Kallisto after work and try to make up for the blunder I made of the day. If you stay, she will have a reason not to speak with me. I am guessing you are here on a school night with other intentions besides going to Kallisto's house. After all, you could have shown up there once she got home from work," Ambrose paced. "Maybe you are here to enjoy watching me squirm, or maybe you are here to keep Kallisto from doing something she may regret in the morning."

"The latter, but it has nothing to do with you. I don't want her going to see Austin. He has been spreading lies about Kallisto, and she is not the type of girl to sit around and watch her reputation be tarnished," Amanda did not know why she told Ambrose that. She had no intentions of informing him of anything, but she couldn't seem to help herself.

"I know of that fool's ridiculous claims and interests. I promise he will not get away with tarnishing Kallisto's reputation and will no longer be allowed to spread lies. I have a plan of my own," the look in Ambrose's eyes made Amanda shudder. She could have sworn they turned momentarily red before flashing back to his brilliant crystal blue.

"Okay, do you have any suggestions on why I suddenly decide to bug out on Kallisto when I leave this office? She's not stupid, you know?" Amanda cocked her head to one side.

"I would never underestimate her intellect," Ambrose sounded almost offended.

"You know, Kallisto is the only person I know who would make a statement like that. Most people would say; *I know she's not stupid,*" Amanda pointed out.

"My brother, whom I know you enjoy the company of," Morpheus grinned, thinking of how mad he was about to make his biggest ally, "is coming by shortly, and you could find some reason to take him with you somewhere."

Amanda lowered her head, squinted her eyes, and crossed her arms over her chest. "You've got to be kidding. Kallisto knows we aren't the best of friends—no, she knows we can't stand each other."

Ambrose rolled his eyes. "It is only for a little while, and I am sure you can keep him entertained with the debates the two of you seem to love."

"Where...Einstein, do you propose I say we're going? And why am I doing this again?" Amanda huffed.

"I will send him on an errand, and he will invite you along for the company," Ambrose couldn't control his grin.

"Fine, anything for Kallisto, but if you hurt her again, I promise you'll have trouble performing the most basic. . ." Amanda was cut off by Christos opening the office door.

"Hey, little brother—Amanda," he bowed at the waist when he acknowledged Amanda, and she could not decide if he was being an ass or a gentleman.

"Christos, I have an errand I need you to run. Will you go to the warehouse and pick up the paintings inside the door?" Then Ambrose added in a whisper, "And I need you to ask Amanda, in front of Kallisto, to go with you."

"What?" Christos asked as if he had not heard his bother correctly.

Ambrose turned to Amanda, "Will you excuse us for a moment? If Kallisto wants to know what we were discussing, tell her I have offered you a job the night of the gala."

Once Amanda left the office, Phantasos turned on his brother like a tiger. "What is going on, and why are you asking me to go anywhere with a mortal—a mortal woman? Have you finally lost what little mind you possess?"

"Trust me, brother. I do not have time to explain. Besides, you loathe her—so there should be no problem." Morpheus gave a half grin at his brother's apparent uneasiness. He had theories about what kind of woman Phantasos liked, and Amanda was right on the money. He guessed that was why his brother found every reason to find fault with her.

"That is beside the point. A few weeks ago, I was a lost dream god who had vowed never to return to this realm. I also decided never to get involved with a mortal woman, romantically or otherwise, again. I am now standing in Hawaii by the alias Christos, working your dreams, and I am about to take a mortal woman with me as I go on an errand for my youngest brother." Phantasos stood there, letting everything sink in. "Does that about sum it up?" Phantasos looked around Morpheus' office for the first time. "Those are my Aphrodite bookends. When and why did you swipe them?"

Morpheus knew by Phantasos' change in subject, and over something as mundane as bookends, he had resigned himself to the inevitable, an evening with Amanda.

"Look, it is about five minutes until closing, and I need you to pick up some paintings."

Both men left the office to find the girls giggling with John. They were commenting on the new Greek statue of the god Apollo. The statue was anatomically correct. Morpheus could only imagine the conversation—*mental note: Chastise Apollo about the "perfect" replica.*

"Amanda?" As soon as Christos spoke her name, everyone went quiet. "Would you like to take a ride with me to the warehouse? I have to retrieve some paintings for my brother."

Amanda could not believe he had gone through with asking her. *Ambrose must have something to hang over Christos because he detests me.* "Sure, will it be okay to leave my car here until we return?"

"Yes, it should not take us too long. Ambrose will be here until we return."

"Kallisto, will you wait here for me, or will you be going home?" Amanda asked. She bit her lip enough to sting, realizing she'd just given Kallisto an out.

"I'll wait for you to return."

Ambrose could not contain his smile. He was sure Kallisto was staying to talk to him.

"Besides, Marcus from my English class came by and asked if I would go with him to get a soda. As Kallisto revealed her news, she crossed her arms and looked at Ambrose in absolute defiance.

Red was the color Morpheus saw, and the color Amanda saw his eyes flash.

"What the hell is wrong with your eyes?" asked Amanda.

Morpheus blinked three times to clear them and compose himself. Jealousy streaked through his body, and he was on the edge of losing his mind. *She is mine!*

Reading Morpheus' mind, Phantasos shook his head ever so slightly, letting his brother know he was crossing the line. Phantasos could also feel fear in Amanda. It surprised him. He had not thought of her as the type to ever fear anything. He knew he would have to go into her dreams tonight and erase her memory of Morpheus' eyes. She was not going to let it go, and he knew it. He could not allow her to figure things out before Kallisto did. There were no provisions given by The Fates or Zeus allowing the best friend knowledge of the plan.

"Are you ready to go, Amanda?" Christos waved his hand to the door in an elegant manner.

Morpheus calmed himself enough to think rationally and asked John to lock up. He then asked if Kallisto would speak with him again.

"Well, I guess I have a few minutes before Marcus arrives. I told him to come by around twenty after."

Morpheus closed his eyes, trying not to let his jealousy get the better of him. "Look, Kallisto, the bottom line is, I am sorry!" He put a lot of emphasis on the last three words. "I like you a lot, and we have much in common. Please do not hold my stupidity against me. Allow me to take you to dinner Saturday night after work, and I'll prove to you that I am not the jerk you think I am."

Kallisto thought for a minute. *Why does he have to have that accent and those crystal-blue eyes? Why does he have to make me crazy inside? Well, I might as well not fight it—*"You win. I'll go to dinner with you on Saturday, but the school situation will be awkward, so I'm unsure how we should approach it."

"I am not worried about people knowing I asked you out or that we work together."

"We don't work together. I work *for* you, and it's more complicated than that."

"How so?" Ambrose challenged.

"People will think I'm getting preferential treatment and—"

Ambrose interrupted with his half grin, "You will be getting preferential treatment—just outside of school."

Kallisto blushed and couldn't help but grin. "I'm not sure you understand how things work in this country, Ambrose."

"You worry about what people think way too much. It is none of anyone's business what we do, and I will not live my life worried about what mort—uh—" he almost said, mortals. "I refuse to let people's gossip ruin my life. *Good save, I hope.*

Kallisto came up short. He was right about gossiping people. She had never cared what others thought about her. If she had, she would not spend her free time living in a fantasy world, dreaming about Greek gods, and she definitely wouldn't be as knowledgeable about mythology as she was. "You're right. We'll see how it goes, but I date who I want to. We're only going out this weekend and to the next weekend's gala."

There was the distinct sound of someone clearing his throat. It was John. "Kallisto, there's a young man at the door waiting on you. See you two tomorrow." He walked to the back exit and left before Ambrose could reprimand him for telling Kallisto her date was waiting for her.

Kallisto heard a slight growl come from Ambrose's throat as he walked with her to the front of the gallery to open the door for Marcus. "Do not embarrass me or run him off."

"Now, why would you ever think I would do either of those things? I will have you know, I am a distinguished gentleman who would never lower himself to such things." Ambrose grinned, and Kallisto knew he would be up to no good if she didn't get Marcus out of there as soon as possible.

"Marcus, this is my boss and friend Ambrose Xanthopoulos," Kallisto introduced the men. She could have sworn that she heard Ambrose growl when she said friend and again when she used his surname, but the growl was not out loud; it seemed to be in her head. She shook her head and looked at Ambrose curiously.

Morpheus knew as soon as Kallisto looked at him, he had messed up—again. First, he allowed his jealousy to take over, and his eyes turned red in front of Amanda, and now he was using telepathy to growl in Kallisto's mind. It had been a reaction. He was so used to speaking to her telepathically and verbally as Morpheus and he had let his guard down. He just hoped that Zeus and The Fates were not watching his every move. Morpheus could tell Marcus liked her, so he listened in on his intent, pushing into his thoughts. He was pleased the boy's thoughts were pure—well—as pure as could be expected. At least he was not thinking like Austin or almost every other man who stood within fifty feet of her.

"I will see you at school in the morning, Kallisto; it was nice to meet you, Marcus. Remember, it is a school night." With that, Ambrose smiled.

Chapter XVII

Loss

Kallisto enjoyed her soda with Marcus the night before. He was a nice guy, but they had nothing in common except some of the same acquaintances. He was very nice to her, and they had laughed about memories from their junior high years, but he wasn't Morpheus or Ambrose. Kallisto got dressed, and before she went downstairs to eat her cereal, her ring became slightly warm. She looked up at the ceiling and grinned.

"You could've come about three hours ago."

Morpheus smiled. How he wished he could have. Hera called for him again. After answering her inquiries, he decided to stay the night on Olympus. Out of habit, he went straight to the orb upon waking to watch his favorite subject. At Kallisto's acknowledgment of his observation, he backed away from the orb and flashed to his car. He was heading to Kallisto's school and could not wait to stake his claim on her in front of all those hormone-crazed teenage boys whose impure thoughts were sure to drive him over the edge. He spent the first part of his night telling Hera she needed to give him a chance to go into Zeus' dreams since it had been only part of a night. He was also beginning to think she was trying to figure more out about his situation instead of her husband's sleeping issues. Hera questioned him about Kallisto, everything from who her family was to her eye color. *Why is my love life so interesting?*

"Hera, I am getting tired of your interrogations. I told you I learned my lesson where the mortal is concerned. I have been asked to help Hermes out with his latest gallery. I believe this is punishment for my escapades with the mortal." Morpheus had always been a good liar when he needed to be. "I'm sticking with goddesses and nymphs from now on. Now if you will be so kind as to excuse me, I cannot attempt to see what is going on in your husband's dreams while here answering questions about my personal life."

He spent two hours with Hera before she let him go home. Now all he wanted was to get to the school to see Kallisto. Dreams and orbs were not cutting it. He preferred being with her in this realm, where she could completely remember him. Unfortunately, it was as Ambrose. Kallisto seeing him as a mortal meant more to him than he thought was possible. He was confident she knew his *dream* self, possessed crystal blue eyes, and blonde hair, and was sure she remembered his name. Most of the time—*Damn Fates, maybe I should renounce my godhood before this goes any further.* Morpheus was ready to be with Kallisto as himself and lose the dual relationship. He also had to decide how to let Zeus know that his wicked wife was up to something, what, he was not sure, but something.

Kallisto felt Morpheus leave as fast as he started watching her. *What did I do to make him so distant? Maybe I was becoming too attached.* Kallisto's memories of Morpheus seemed more like dreams again. She found herself looking at her bracelet and ring, getting flashes of him. She could see blonde hair and Pegasus. She could feel his kiss and strong embrace, but they were not like they had been days before. The only words she could recall were *"Remember me."*

She pulled into her parking space at school and sat in her car, thinking about how strange her life had become. Suddenly, guys were coming out of the woodwork wanting to go out with her, and she wasn't prepared for the drama. She was in love with a dream, infatuated with her boss, and found the boys in her class immature but interesting nonetheless.

"Is there a sign on my head that reads, "Need a date, desperately?" or "Only virgin left on the island! Yeah, I'm now a trophy virgin who desperately needs a date," she murmured to herself. Sitting there, she watched several junior and senior kids waste time in the parking lot. She never was one to goof off with her peers, with the exception of Amanda, of course. Hanging out and talking about boys and the latest fashion trend was not her idea of fun. Yeah, sometimes she and Amanda enjoyed gossiping, usually about boys, but she had always been more mature than the kids she went to school with. It hit her then why she was not interested in guys her age. She felt like she was so much older than they were.

As so many thoughts and emotions played through her mind, she looked in her rearview mirror as a black Mercedes pulled in. Her ring began to heat. *Surely you aren't jealous,* Kallisto thought as if expecting an answer from Morpheus. Ambrose stepped from his car wearing a white long-sleeve button down with the sleeves rolled midway to his elbows, black pleated dress slacks, and his hair pulled to the nape of his neck with a leather cord. She briefly wondered what he would look like in a chiton.

Kallisto's heart sped up. *What's wrong with me? I'm drooling over a man I should be mad at?* She watched him get closer, but she only registered how delectable he looked in his dress clothes. She didn't take her eyes off him until he was no longer visible in the mirror—so she felt her reaction to his tapping on her window was unjustified. *Shit, you scared me!* That was a word she rarely used, but he had scared her.

Ambrose opened her door and tried to keep his laughter at bay. Her surprise at his "sudden appearance" was amusing. He knew she watched him when he entered the parking lot. He was a god, after all.

"May I walk you in, Ms. Nalani?"

When Kallisto stepped from the car, it was Ambrose's turn to drool. Knowing, subconsciously, of course, Ambrose would be at school; she wore her favorite faded jeans, ones that made her butt look perfectly sculpted, with a well-fitted graphic tee from D. F. O. that said, *"Wit is Educated Insolence."*

"Aristotle?" Morpheus gestured to her shirt, then reached up and tucked her bra strap underneath it, not thinking anything about it—doing what Morpheus would do. Until her eyes widened and red shot up her cheeks. "I apologize. I did say no touching. I did not want all these boys to see your hot pink bra strap," he grinned devilishly.

Kallisto was happy Ambrose couldn't read her mind. After a second, when his eyes seemed to glow, and his smile widened, she wondered if he could guess them.

"Let's not have any public displays."

Ambrose loved this. Kallisto had no idea who he was, so reading her mind was fun. He usually tried to give her privacy, but when she blushed so, he could hardly help himself.

With a broader grin, he asked, "Does that mean there will be private displays?"

"Ambrose!"

"Hey, you are the one who said public. I was just finding my boundaries."

"You're incorrigible." Kallisto could not help but smile at Ambrose's boyish behavior. She enjoyed the banter and took pleasure in his presence.

"Amanda!" Kallisto raised her voice, getting the attention of her best friend, who was walking into the school with a dazed look.

Amanda spun around to see Kallisto standing by her car with Ambrose. As she walked over to the couple, her bleary look became more focused, and a smile crossed her face.

"Well, the two of you are on better terms. At least you're being civil."

"We are, as you say, ironing out our differences." Ambrose supplied. "I am trying to convince your friend here," he tilted his head toward Kallisto and grinned, "that I have no ties to this school except for her."

Kallisto turned what seemed to be the only color she was capable of lately, red.

"Now, let's not forget your word to Mr. Wright that you would help him," Amanda smirked.

"That I can do through email," Ambrose smiled.

"Okay, you two, enough; let's go to class—" Kallisto looked at Amanda, "and you," she looked at Ambrose, "can go to—"

"Be nice," Ambrose winked.

"I was going to say before you interrupted, can go to Mr. Wright's office and let him know you are here." Kallisto pushed through her two friends and walked into the building, leaving them to follow.

Kallisto enjoyed having Ambrose in her history class. Once she got over her irritation, his godly looks, and his heart-stopping accent, she found his teachings very interesting. This was the first year her school had offered European history as an elective. If students took American history early, they could take European history and get college credit. Of course, Kallisto was all over that. She loved history; the closer she could get to ancient Greece and Italy, the better. She found the hardest part of him being in her class was trying to ignore the remarks and suggestive behaviors of the other girls. She hadn't thought herself to be the jealous type. Wrong; she was ready to rip someone's head off by the end of the day.

Ambrose didn't sit with her at lunch, for which she was glad. She was not quite ready to introduce him as anything, not even her boss. She sat at lunch looking at where he sat with the teachers. It was a strange feeling to look up at the teacher's table and have the sort of thoughts and bodily reactions she was having. *Maybe he should sit somewhere else, not by or in front of me. He should eat in his car.* As usual, whenever confused or too stimulated, Kallisto's thoughts whirled.

She caught his eyes from across the cafeteria. He winked, and she melted.

Kallisto rushed to her car once school was out, excited to see her boss. *Has he already left?*

"Everything alright?" Michael asked as he walked by Kallisto's car.

"Yeah, I'm just waiting on someone."

"Okay, see ya." Michael was polite, though Kallisto didn't feel she deserved it. After all, she never encouraged Amanda to stay with him, knowing they weren't compatible.

"What did Michael want?" Amanda asked as she approached Kallisto, who stood with her hand above her eyes, trying to block the sun as she glanced around the parking lot.

"He just wanted to know if I was okay. I guess he saw the disappointment on my face."

"Who are you looking for?"

"Ambrose."

"See, I knew you liked him." Amanda smiled.

"I do like him, but I love a god who I can never be with," Kallisto murmured just loud enough that Amanda could barely make it out. "How can I truly love Morpheus when I'm infatuated with a mortal man? I'm so confused."

"Life sucks, but at least Austin hasn't been at school, and Elizabeth hasn't killed you yet," Amanda grinned. "No pink frilly blankets."

"Thanks for trying to cheer me up, but I'm beginning to think I should quit my job and stop sleeping. Maybe then my life will get back on track," Kallisto sighed. "I've got to get to work." About that time, Kallisto's cell rang. "It's my mom," she said, puzzled.

Answering the phone, Kallisto responded to her mother. "Whatever possessed her to come? Is she okay?"

Once Kallisto hung up with her mom, Amanda finally had a chance to find out what had happened. "What's going on?"

"My grandmother decided to come to Hawaii for a visit next week. She should be here by next Thursday evening."

"What made her come out right before you are headed to Greece—and after Christmas instead of during?" Amanda queried.

"Mom's not quite sure, or she won't tell me. I don't know which one," Kallisto replied. "Hey, call me later tonight. I get off work early tonight, seven-thirty."

"Will do. I think I'm going home and taking a nap. I'm not sleeping well. I've been having the strangest dreams," Amanda took a deep breath as if to wake herself. "See ya later."

Kallisto walked into the gallery and saw who she was looking for. He leaned against the reception desk with his arms and legs crossed and a devilish glint in his eyes, giving her chills. She walked over to him as he stared at her. *Please don't let me trip!* Kallisto thought, her eyes locked onto his.

"You were in a hurry to get to work," Kallisto said, breaking the sensual tension.

"John called last period. He needed to go to the doctor."

"Why? Is he okay?" Kallisto asked.

"He tripped and landed on a rusty nail this morning. His girlfriend made him nervous about tetanus—whatever that is. He said he needed to go and get a shot. So, I am here alone, well, until now." The tension was back.

"Ambrose, I'm—" Kallisto paused before continuing, "confused by what you want from me."

"Well, I could give you the entire list—but I am almost positive it would get me slapped," Ambrose winked.

Kallisto laughed at Ambrose; he was so gorgeous, especially when devils danced in his eyes. "Well, let's stick with the part of the list that will not cause me to inflict harm on my boss."

"There you go again with the boss thing. Do I need to fire you so our working relationship will no longer be an issue?"

"You, my friend, are hopeless," Kallisto laughed. "You seem different somehow—you remind me of someone."

"I do? Whom may I ask?"

"No one you would know, I'm sure."

"Really? Well, let us narrow it down." Ambrose gave her that same wicked grin that made her blush. "I sure hope the one I remind you of is a man, but not your father."

Kallisto arched a questioning brow.

"Not that I have anything against your father, I do not even know him, but I prefer my relationship with you not to be of a paternal nature," Ambrose continued with his list. "Second, he must be good-looking," again he winked. Third, he is witty and makes you laugh, fourth he—"

"Oh, stop. You're overly confident today. Have you made any sales?" Kallisto tried to change the subject.

Ambrose smiled at her dodge of the subject and answered her question. "Yes, one, the small painting of Apollo with the sunset on the easel in the back corner."

"That's good." Kallisto paused, trying to think of something to say to keep her eyes from raking over him and her mind in check. "My grandmother is flying in next week."

"Really? The one from Greece?"

"Yes, my mother called to tell me just a bit ago."

"What is the special occasion?"

"I'm not sure. Mom assured me she was okay and was coming for her own reasons. Kinda cryptic if you ask me."

"Well, I cannot wait to meet her." Ambrose bowed slightly, which further reminded Kallisto of someone.

After they closed the gallery, the two sat in his office for over an hour, talking about life and what they wanted out of it. They spent the rest of the afternoon talking about the legends of the gods and about her going to university in the fall. They made two more sales, smaller than the one Ambrose made before she got there but large enough to make the end-of-the-day totals look good.

"I want to get my degree in history and go on to study the history of the Mediterranean. I hope to move to Greece with my grandma after two years here and finish in the only place I feel truly at home," Kallisto sighed, thinking about her dream with Morpheus. Little did she know, Ambrose was thinking about it too.

"Why are you staying here for two years instead of doing all four in Greece? You speak the language well. I heard you practicing when you read the manuscript that came with the painting of Persephone."

"I don't get to use it that often. My mom and grandmother, when she visits, are the only ones in Maui who know the language. Mom doesn't like speaking in Greek, she's afraid her accent will get worse, and she tried hard to overcome it—not that it's completely gone."

"Why does she not like her Greek accent? I hope mine does not offend her," Morpheus asked.

"No, she's just funny that way; she doesn't mind your accent or anyone else's. I lost my accent after about three years. Amanda says she can hear it occasionally, like when I am sleepy or very angry," Kallisto smiled.

"I have noticed the accent when you get angry. I prefer not to hear it again—in anger." Ambrose grinned, thinking about having heard her accent when she was sleepy; however, he could not say that.

Ambrose's beautiful Greek-inspired timepiece chimed, letting them know the hour. "Oh, it's late, and I told Amanda to call me since I was getting off work at seven-thirty, and it's now eight o'clock."

"I will walk you out to your car. Let me lock up the money first."

"I enjoyed talking with you tonight. You're a nice guy, and I'm sorry I got so upset over the school thing."

"The fault is with me, Kallisto, do not apologize for my mistake." His heart rate spiked at her thoughts. Then she stood on her tiptoes and gave him a peck on his cheek. *That was not quite what I read, but it will do—for now.*

Embarrassed, Kallisto hurried to her car, waving bye to Ambrose as he stared after her. She couldn't believe herself. She had some decisions to make, ones that would not be easy. She needed to talk to Amanda.

When she arrived, Amanda's car was parked in front of Kallisto's house. Kallisto pulled into her driveway when the feeling came upon her. She didn't know whether to grin or cry. She had decided to let Morpheus go. Here she could sit down and get an unbiased opinion, well as unbiased as Amanda could be.

➳➳➳⟶ ⟵⟸⟸⟸

Morpheus closed the gallery and flashed himself to his home on Olympus. He needed to see Kallisto tonight as Morpheus. Through the orb, he saw Kallisto get out of her car. At first glance, he was impressed by her beauty, and then he saw the sadness on her face. Knowing she felt his presence, a wave of despair shot through him. His legs felt weak, and his stomach ached. He was a god, and those were not bodily reactions a god had.

"Something is wrong. But how can it be she just left me mere minutes ago?" Morpheus asked aloud. Eager as he was to see her, he was equally nervous. Watching, he saw Amanda come to the door.

"Did dad leave early this morning?" Kallisto asked her mother as she entered the house. Amanda watched her with curious eyes. She knew Amanda could see the despair on her face, but she didn't want her to call attention to it until they were alone.

"He did. He won't be gone too long this time."

"What made grandmother decide to come? Christmas and New Year's are already over, and I'll be going to Greece in a few months?"

Thia looked at her daughter, "Are you okay, Kallisto?"

"Yes, I'm just tired, that's all."

"Your grandmother wanted to spend some time with us. You'll be going to Greece, and I won't, so she's coming here for a while," Thia answered.

Kallisto heard the hesitancy in her mother's voice, and most of all, she heard her accent shine through; she wasn't being forthright.

"It just seems strange. Don't get me wrong, I can't wait to see her, but for her to randomly come to Hawaii—it's made me worry about her."

"Just enjoy her visiting. Now, I'm going to light some candles, take a long hot bath and finish the novel on my nightstand that's been calling my name all day. See you girls in the morning before school." Thia said as she walked away.

"Kallisto, you seem a little weirded out. What's up?" Amanda asked in her *Amanda* way.

"I'll tell you upstairs," Kallisto said as she started up the staircase with Amanda in tow.

"Okay, you haven't been yourself lately, and I know the whole Ambrose is sort of your teacher thing is weird; not that crushing on your teacher is a bad thing, especially when he looks like a god," Amanda rambled. "You just need to see the humor in it and move on. In my opinion, you need to go out with Ambrose and tell Morpheus you can no longer—" Amanda thought for a minute. "You can no longer *dream* with him or of him."

Kallisto went straight to the painting of the waterfall and remembered Morpheus' scent and the warmth of his touch, but as usual, never his face. She turned slowly to Amanda, her face colorless, except for her eyes. They were red-rimmed, and her cheeks streaked with hot tears slowly inching down her face as she lost herself in mourning. A grief so profound it would change who she was and, most likely, who she would become.

"I'm going to ask to go to Morpheus tonight, and I'm going to tell him that I can never see him again." Then, through her tear-stained face, she began to laugh.

"Kalli, I'm gettin' worried about you. You're standing there crying, sadder than I've ever seen you, and then you begin to laugh like a crazy person. You're freakin' me out!" Amanda hated seeing her best friend like this. After all, Kallisto was the rational one, and Amanda was the crazy one.

"I was just thinking," Kallisto began to explain. "I just said I'd never see him again since I don't actually know what he looks like; how would I know if I ever saw him again?"

Morpheus could not believe his eyes or ears. "Phantasos," he could only whisper, and barely that.

It took his oldest brother only moments before he flashed by his side. "Man, you look like shit. What the hell happened?" Phantasos spared no punches.

"Kallisto is leaving me."

"Did she give you a reason?"

"I saw her telling Amanda through the orb. She plans on telling me tonight."

"Do not go to her. She will change her mind. From what I have seen, women of this century are different from the ones I knew. They change their mind often and wear skimpy clothes, plus they have no reservations about telling a man where to go and how to get there. Tomorrow she may decide she still likes you."

"See, man; I told you—you and Amanda are kindred spirits, maybe even soulmates," Morpheus knew how to shut his brother up.

"Do not start that again," Phantasos threatened.

"It does not matter if I go or take her anywhere. She is able to come here on her own. She has done it before," Morpheus informed Phantasos of the secret.

"What did you just say?" Phantasos asked.

"While daydreaming, she flashed herself to Olympus without my assistance."

Phantasos backed up several feet and sat, stunned. "You are telling me she brought herself here?"

"She either brought herself or a god other than me did. The only other god I could conceive of doing that would be you, and I am positive you did not."

"Only gods can breach the boundaries of Olympus, Morpheus. She could not have come here on her own. Have you told Zeus?" Phantasos asked.

"No, and I do not plan on it either. If The Fates found out, I would have Hades to pay. Besides, it is a mystery for another day. She is going to leave me tonight, and I am unable to let her go. I will renounce my godhood before I allow this," Morpheus was losing control of his emotions, and his room began to shake.

"On what terms did she leave Ambrose?" Phantasos asked.

"We were fine when she left the gallery, or I should say that she and Ambrose were fine when she left the gallery. I felt turmoil inside of her, but I never guessed this. When I saw her get out of her car at her house, sporting a similar look to the one she wore when her father went missing, I tuned deeper into her thoughts. She told Amanda we were over. So, I called for you. Maybe you will keep me from killing something or someone."

"Just because she does not want to see Morpheus anymore does not mean she does not want to see you. Maybe she is more interested in the "you" she can fully remember," Phantasos said.

"Even so, how can she let go of the feelings I know she has for me? She loves me. What if Ambrose was a different person? What if he was not me." Morpheus shook his head in hopes of clearing it. "Are you listening to me? I sound crazy. I am not only talking about myself as two separate entities, but I am jealous of one of them. This dual role has me going crazy."

"Maybe you should hear Kallisto out before you have a pity party. Remember you, as Ambrose, can give her your entire self. If you are destined to be with her, it does not matter what name you go by. Yes, for now, she sees you as two separate beings, but you are not, and she is attracted to only one person no matter what realm," Phantasos tried to counsel his brother, knowing he should tell him to let her go, but he couldn't find it in his heart to crush his youngest brother's heart.

➤➤➤ ◀◀◀

Kallisto sat on her bed, trying to get up the guts to go to Morpheus. Amanda consoled her for a while and reluctantly left when Kallisto insisted she needed to get this over with and go to Morpheus—*rip the Band-Aid off*. Now, she needed to remember how she'd gone to Olympus by herself the first time. She remembered standing in front of her painting, wanting and wishing to see Morpheus. About the time she stood in front of her painting, ready to try her fate, she felt Morpheus watching her.

She hung her head and whispered, "Morpheus, I need to see you." Instead of trying to go to Olympus on her own, she laid across her bed and waited for him to make her sleep.

Kallisto woke on Morpheus' bed. He was lying beside her, gently rubbing the bridge of her nose repeatedly with his index finger. She couldn't help but smile.

"This is how my mother used to wake me in the mornings and ironically put me to sleep at night. She refused to allow my dad to put me in a "false sleep," as she called it," Morpheus' insides felt like they were on fire. His brother was right, and he needed to hear her out before he did anything rash, like give up his godhood.

"I'm glad you came to me. I was about to see if I could go to you—again." She closed her eyes, savoring his touch and the scents of lavender and honeysuckle. *How can I do this? If only this relationship were possible, but it isn't.*

Kallisto opened her eyes and sat up. Morpheus joined her, now sitting face to face on his bed, staring into each other's eyes. Tears began to well up in hers, and she choked on her words. "I need to tell you—"

"Remember my dea femminile; I am a god—I know what you want to say." Morpheus couldn't stand having her struggle like she was doing. Even at the point of his own pain, he wanted only for her to be happy.

Kallisto broke into tears and threw her face into his chest. He, too, began to weep. This had to be the hardest thing he had ever done. How would he go on with his life without her? She was an intimate part of his world. For over three thousand years, he never found a being, mortal or immortal, that made him so aware of his emotions. Happiness and pain felt magnified since he first set eyes on her, as he sobbed in her nightmare. He did not even know her then and could not stand for her to be in pain. Now, it was almost impossible to bear.

"I love you, Morpheus, but I can't continue this way. I can't remember you how I should, and I feel half-crazy most days. If I could stay in your arms and never leave, I would, but we both know that's impossible," Kallisto pulled back from his chest. "I need to let you go."

"Does this have anything to do with that Austin boy?" Morpheus knew better but was hoping he could lead her into admitting she liked Ambrose.

"You've got to be kidding. No, I can barely stand him. But I need someone who shares my interests and whose face I can recall no matter where I am. I need someone like you; only I need them all the time."

"What if I was to renounce my godhood?" Morpheus asked as he hung his head.

"You can do that?"

"Yes, I would never be able to return to Olympus, and I would become mortal like you. We could be together."

Kallisto thought for a few minutes. She moved to sit between his legs with her back leaned against his chest, their arms intertwined over her chest. "I could never ask that of you. You can't give up who you are. I wouldn't be able to live with myself."

Morpheus laced his fingers with hers, and they sat holding each other for a long time with only the silence and the warmth of their bodies between them.

"Morpheus?" Kallisto asked, getting his attention.

"Yes."

"If I asked you to make love to me right now, would you?"

"Excuse me?" He stopped reading her mind, so her question shocked him.

"I don't want my first time to be with someone I'm unsure of. I'm sure of you, that's not the problem. We just can't be together because we live in different realities. I know I'll regret not being with you," Kallisto tried to explain what she was feeling, but no words could do her emotions justice.

Knowing he would regret his decision for the rest of his existence, he thought before he spoke, "I would love nothing more than to make love to you, Kallisto. You are the love of my life, but I refuse to do that to you. You are meant for someone; how I wish it were me. Your first and last time should be with the man you are fated to love for eternity."

"That's not what I wanted to hear, but I understand."

"Maybe The Fates will change their minds one day," Morpheus sighed.

"If they do, then—"

Morpheus did not let her finish her sentence. "Then I will make love to you for eternity." He turned her to face him and gave her a kiss filled with love and sadness—clearly saying goodbye. "I will always love you, my dea femminile."

Kallisto woke back in her bed. Her eyes were still moist, and her lips slightly swollen. She sat up and whispered, "I love you too, Morpheus."

Tears dripped onto her lap. She didn't have the chance to tell him that before he sent her back. She felt a heavy weight on her chest and couldn't stop her body from trembling. Her alarm clock said eleven-thirty.

Kallisto could smell lavender and honeysuckle clinging to her skin. She drew a deep breath through her nose, knowing that would be the last time she would ever wake with those smells. She cried herself to sleep somewhere around three in the morning.

Chapter XVIII

Truth

Morpheus **continued to lie in bed and stare** at his ceiling. His anger subsided, but if a god could be in shock, he was. Ambrose still had a date with Kallisto on Saturday. Would Zeus allow him to stay on earth since Kallisto left him—would The Fates? He decided to be proactive. Instead of waiting to find out his fate, he needed to speak with the Moirai (The Fates). Maybe if he pleaded his case, they would be empathetic.

Morpheus stood in the doorway of the three sisters who would decide his future. A daemon escorted him to the sitting room where The Fates waited. The sisters were three of Zeus' daughters whose jobs were to watch over the fate of all mortals and immortals. They also cut a being's thread of life when the time came. Morpheus knew from their dreams the Moirai could manipulate destiny. He hoped he could convince them to let him stay on earth for the month and a half he had remaining of their deal.

All three goddesses smiled when Morpheus walked in. Clotho, the youngest of the three, had long blonde curly hair and ice-blue eyes. The middle sister, Atropos, had straight auburn hair and emerald green eyes. And the oldest, Lachesis, had such black hair it looked blue and the eyes of cocoa. Even though they looked very different from one another, they were triplets. When someone speaks of their age difference, they refer to only minutes. All three were incredibly stunning and very intelligent.

They often spoke in riddles to see if the immortal or mortal was worthy of what they wanted them to change, fix, or destroy. Did the being have the intelligence to understand the consequences of their request? They did not deal with *stupid* people or crazy gods. Dealing with a god's request could be more dangerous. They could wind up in severe pain or dead if not careful and precise. Because of that, the goddesses did not deal with less-than-sensible immortals.

"Oh, Morpheus, to what do we owe this honor?" Lachesis, the oldest of the three, asked.

"My beautiful Lachesis, do you expect me to believe you do not know why I am here?" Morpheus tried to smile.

Clotho spoke up. "We know you are sad, and Kallisto has left you, but why are you here?"

"I am here to ask you a few questions." Morpheus knew not to ask a *couple* of questions. The goddesses would hold him to only two—which they would answer in riddles.

"Well then, ask," the middle sister, Atropos responded.

"Is there any hope for me and Kallisto to be together without me renouncing my godhood?"

The Three Fates looked at him, wanting him to continue his questions.

"If not, is there hope if I renounce my godhood?" Morpheus stared into the eyes of the three women who held his fate in their collective hands.

"There is always hope, Morpheus," Lachesis answered.

"Why are Zeus and Hera so interested in my relationship with Kallisto?" Morpheus continued with his questions.

"There are some things we are bound to not speak of, and that is one of them," Atropos replied. "But I will say, life on Olympus is about to get interesting."

"Who or what bound you to this *thing* you cannot speak of?" Morpheus asked.

"Fate," Clotho answered.

"May I finish my two months with Kallisto as Ambrose?" Morpheus finally asked.

"Only if you make the right decision," Lachesis said.

"I do not guess you would like to tell me what that decision is, would you?" Morpheus did manage to muster a smile this time.

"Think long and hard before you are rash in your decisions, Morpheus. Kallisto is more than what you think her to be. She is strong, and if she is meant to be with you, she will find a way. You have to have faith in those you love. If you do not, there can never be hope," Clotho said.

"Hope and persistence are the only things that can change one's destiny. You must hope and make the right decision. Your decisions will be what destine you, not us." Atropos replied.

"Thank you, ladies. I need to think and go see Zeus," Morpheus bowed.

"By the way, Morpheus," Lachesis spoke. "Tell your brother we said to be careful and not allow history to repeat itself."

Morpheus nodded his head and left the home of the Moirai. His heart continued to break, and he did not think he could handle seeing Kallisto without holding her, knowing he would want to ease their shared heartache. He decided to call John and have him pass on a message to Kallisto.

After talking to John, he flashed back to Olympus. He resisted the urge to watch Kallisto in the orb and tried to get some rest, giving the ache in his heart a break. It took a lot of control to keep his emotions in check while questioning The Fates.

⇝ ⇜

Kallisto woke to her phone ringing. Congested from her marathon of tears, she answered.

"Where are you?" asked Amanda.

"It's eight-fifteen, crap!" Kallisto jumped from her bed. When she turned, wildflower petals were lying by her pillow. She knew Morpheus placed them there when he returned her to her room. She sat back down on her bed and sobbed.

"Hey, Kalli—are you going to be okay?"

"Yes, I'll be fine. I'm just very upset right now. I'm not sure I did the right thing," she told Amanda.

"Look, I have flex next period—so I can skip out of here. By the way, Mr. Wright asked where you were. He also asked me if you went with Ambrose on his business trip. Do you know what he was talking about?"

The beep that signaled Kallisto's call waiting sounded. "Hold on, it's work," Kallisto clicked over to hear John's voice telling, who she assumed to be, a delivery man—*"to put it by the table."*

"Hey Kallisto, Ambrose asked me to call you and the school. He and his parents had to go out of town until next week. Something is wrong with the exhibit paintings for the gala. He wanted me to apologize to you for messing up Saturday and said he would call you when he could."

She could tell John was in a hurry, "Thank you for calling. Do you need me to come in this afternoon since Ambrose can't be there?" Kallisto asked, needing the distraction.

"That'd be great, if you don't mind," Kallisto felt John's relief through the telephone.

"I don't mind. By the way, where were they going?" Kallisto asked.

"Greece. I'll see you this afternoon."

"Okay, see you then, bye." Kallisto hung up. *The irony, Ambrose is headed to Greece, and my grandma is coming here.*

Kallisto clicked her phone back over to where Amanda was waiting. She laughed; Amanda sang to herself, not just any song. She was singing "Baby Shark," of all things. *You gotta love her.*

"Looks like I'm a free woman Saturday night. Do you want to rent a chick-flick and paint our nails?"

"Why, what happened to Ambrose?"

"That was John telling me Ambrose and his family went to Greece on an emergency concerning the paintings for the gala. I guess when paintings cost that much, you drop everything to get to the bottom of a problem," Kallisto tried hard not to sound too upset.

In truth, she was sure her heart was shattering. She left the one she loved for some normalcy and a chance to get to know someone she had a lot in common, guilt-free.

"Are you coming to school?"

"No, I don't think I can face people right now. I'm going to lay here on my bed and throw a pity party. I know mom has chocolate stashed somewhere. I will find it and eat it—all of it—until I'm sick."

"Do you want me to skip out of here and keep you company?"

In truth, that would be fun, but Kallisto was not in the mood for fun. "No, I want to be sad right now, as crazy as that sounds. I think it's part of the mourning process I need to get through before I can be myself."

"Okay, but promise me you'll call me if you need anything. I have no problem ditching school."

"I have no doubt you'd be here in minutes if I asked you to, school or not. Now you better get to class. Come by the gallery tonight and see me if you get a chance. I think I'm going up there around four or so."

"Alright. See ya tonight," Amanda disconnected.

Kallisto went on her chocolate hunt. After finding said chocolate, she grabbed a glass of milk, returned to her bedroom, and took out her journal. She wrote all day, putting the last three months in black and white. She even wrote about Phantasos walking in on her dream with her and Morpheus on her bed. Some of the journal pages were wet with tears from her reminiscing. She wrote what looked to be a book by the time she pulled herself from the pages. Wiping away what tears had yet to fall, she closed her journal and got ready for work.

Kallisto left by the time her mother got home. The school called Thia at work to see if Kallisto was okay since she wasn't at school. Thia, knew her daughter must have a good reason to miss, probably cramping and needing some sleep, so she didn't call her. Instead, she stopped by the grocery store and got her daughter some chocolate and a bottle of Midol.

"Kalli?" Thia yelled across the house as she entered the foyer.

When she didn't answer, Thia went up to her bedroom. Kallisto wasn't there, and her room was a mess. That was unlike her daughter, unless she was trying to find the perfect outfit. Laying on Kallisto's bed was her journal.

Thia worried over Kallisto's despair when her dad went missing; after all, she was the one who asked for a dream god to be sent to help her daughter. Once, her husband returned, Kallisto seemed to do better—until the last month or so. She'd started noticing Kallisto's tired eyes and the constant look of worry on her face. Her mothering instincts told her something was amiss.

Thia walked over to her daughter's journal and contemplated, "Okay, if I read this, am I a bad mother? If I don't read this, am I a bad mother? If I read this," she was now holding the journal with all its knowledge, "I may have a better understanding of what she's going through. Of course, I wouldn't ever tell her." Thia mused aloud as she paced the floor, trying to decide what to do.

Decision made, Thia opened the journal, surprised by all the writing labeled with today's date. She began to read, noticing the words and the smudges on so many of the pages. After she finished, she hung her head, tears in her own eyes. Thia immediately called her mother in Greece. She spent the next hour telling her mother everything she had read in the journal, from Kallisto's nightmares to how her heart broke when she decided to leave Morpheus.

"I'm moving my flight up. I'll be there by the day after tomorrow," Zenovia said to her daughter.

Thia hung up the phone, wondering what she should do next. She felt her daughter's broken heart was her fault. She brought the gods into her life or at least one of them.

"I knew better than to send my daughter unprepared into the world of gods and goddesses."

Kallisto relieved John giving him his much-needed break. "Go have fun, and if you speak to Ambrose, will you have him call me?"

"Sure thing. Thanks for coming in. I'll see you tomorrow," John said in his slight Greek accent as he walked out the back door.

Kallisto sat daydreaming about Olympus. She could hear the water falling into the fountain outside the gallery door. She closed her eyes and allowed the splashing to take her back to the waterfall on the Mount with Morpheus. When she finally opened her eyes, tears slid down her face. "Good thing no one else is in here with me. They would think I was crazy."

Kallisto cleaned herself up and busied herself with the mundane housekeeping of the gallery. She bent over to pick a paperclip off the floor and stood up to meet the eyes of a very tall, very handsome man.

"May I help you sir?" Kallisto asked. She couldn't shake the feeling she knew him from somewhere. *Where did he come from?*

"Kallisto Nalani." It was a statement.

"Yes, and you are?" *He knows my name.* The man's accent was even thicker than Ambrose's.

"I am here to ask you a few questions," The tall, dark, and gorgeous man stated.

"Well, maybe I could better answer your questions if I knew who I'm giving my answers to," Kallisto folded her arms over her chest.

"Let us just say I am here to see what your intentions toward Morpheus are."

Kallisto's eyes widened, and it donned on her where she had seen the man standing mere inches before her. He was in a painting with his mother, Hera, that hung on the gallery wall before a little old lady bought it about two weeks ago. Her hand covered her mouth, trying to hold in her gasp, and she took two steps backward.

"You're Ares." It wasn't a question.

The man grinned showing a mouth full of beautiful straight white teeth. "I see you know your gods, maybe some better than others. What are you to Morpheus?" He asked with a deep sensual voice.

"Why would the god of war come to me and ask me about a dream god?" Kallisto asked.

"Why did an Oneiroi go to you more than once or twice? How is it you know who I am?" The man's voice held uncanny persuasion.

"Who said a dream god came to me? As for you, we just sold a painting of you and your mother."

"You know who I am. You should also know I will get my answers from you the easy way or the hard way," Ares smirked.

Kallisto pushed her shaking hands into her pockets, hiding her fear. "Morpheus came to me when my father was lost at sea. He and I were friends, but I don't see him anymore. Now, it's your turn," Kallisto raised her chin, gesturing he should answer.

"My mother sent me to check on you."

Kallisto could hardly believe he answered her question so quickly and without protest. *This can't be good.*

"Why, what does she have to do with the Oneiroi?" Kallisto was teetering between fear and curiosity, not to mention awe from standing before a Greek god.

"Everything," Ares took a step toward Kallisto. "Do you know you are as beautiful as my Aphrodite?"

Kallisto saw lust in the god's eyes, and it scared her. "I don't think Aphrodite would like for you to see any woman as beautiful as she. After all, she is the most beautiful goddess of your pantheon."

"Who are you, Kallisto?" Ares cocked his head in curiosity.

"I'm no one of importance. Now, could you please leave?" Kallisto could not believe her bravado.

"You would speak to me in such a manner? Do you know who I am? Let me clarify for you. I am the god of war, the son of Zeus and Hera, and the lover of Aphrodite—never tell me to leave."

"Forgive me, Ares, but I'm not used to gods standing before me, in the flesh, at work. I'm uncomfortable."

The lines on his face softened a little. "You are not mortal, are you, little one?" Ares asked.

"Excuse me?" Kallisto asked, shocked. "Of course I am. I have an intuitive nature. Many mortals have one. Some just don't embrace it as I have," Kallisto's eyebrows furrowed. "Why would you come to such an outlandish conclusion?

"You are talking to me when you should not be able to see me. Another reason would be your appearance. Have you ever seen someone with eyes like yours and beauty like what you possess? No, there has to be something else," Ares lifted his right hand and trailed his fingertips down Kallisto's face.

Kallisto's skin crawled. His fingers were cool and felt wrong. She wanted to order him to leave again but was too afraid. Mythology was full of tales about the warrior before her. She knew enough of the stories to know for someone to send the god of war—something bad was going on.

"Why were you sent to check out the life of a mortal teenage girl? Isn't that a little unexciting for a god such as you?" Kallisto asked.

"How do you accept me as a god if you are so human?"

"Look where I work," she waved her hand around the gallery. "Besides, my mother's family is Greek, and I've seen Olympus in my dreams more than once. I believe gods were created to help mortals—when needed."

"So, you believe in all the gods?"

"Yes, but I don't like to be touched," Kallisto's boldness grew.

Ares grinned, "Or am I not the right god to be touching you?"

"I don't know what you mean. For the last time, I'm not in a relationship with any god. I'm seeing a mortal man."

"Really, who is this man you speak of, and where will I find him?" Ares glanced around the vast room as if to challenge Kallisto's word.

"Not that it's any of your or your mother's business, but he and his family are on a business trip to Greece," Kallisto quickly became irritated with Ares' questions, and her braveness grew.

"Girl, do not ever think something is not Hera's business. Because you are young and so lovely, I'll excuse that remark," Ares grinned menacingly. "I suspect I will see you again—until then," he bowed and vanished.

With her mouth open, Kallisto was left standing before a painting of Zeus and Hercules. She wasn't used to gods appearing and vanishing while she was awake. *Why are such strange things happening to me? I must be going mad.*

She tried calling Amanda, but she didn't answer.

Finally, it came time to close and go home, where she found her mother sitting in the family room on the sofa with a strange look on her face.

"Hey, mom, why so glum?"

"Your grandmother has decided to move her trip up. She should be here the day after tomorrow."

Her mom's voice was monotone, another sign something wasn't right.

"Well, I wouldn't think that was a reason to be sad," Kallisto stated. "Are you sure you're being completely honest with me? Is grandma okay?"

"Yes, dear, I was just missing your dad and worried a little about you."

That took Kallisto off guard. She had tried not to show her sadness to her mother and hoped that her parents would chalk her strange behavior to being a teenager.

"Why?"

"I can tell something is bothering you just as you can tell there is something not quite right about me. I can see the tear streaks from where you've been crying."

This was true. Kallisto cried all the way from work to the stop sign at the end of her road. She pulled into her driveway and waited, allowing her reddened face to return to normal. Her mother was a better observer than she gave her credit.

"I told someone that I like a lot, I can't ever see him again," the truth was out before Kallisto could stop it.

Thia brows shot up. "I wasn't aware you were seeing someone."

"Mom, do you believe there could be some merit to the Greek mythological tales?" Kallisto asked.

"Merit?"

"Oh, mom, my vivid imagination, along with my place of employment, has me wondering if legends are more real than we think."

She would never tell her mom she knew the gods existed. If her mother scoffed at the idea, Kallisto would pretend she wished they were real. If her mother thought there was more to the stories, she could tell her about the precarious situation she was in. Sometimes a girl needs her mom.

Thia thought for a moment. Her daughter was not eighteen yet, the agreed-upon age to tell her about the legends. Now she found, birthday or not, she needed to give her daughter something to hold on to. "Kalli," Thia patted the spot next to her for her daughter to sit. "I summoned a Greek dream god to aid you in your sleep when your father went missing—" Thia held up a hand, seeing that Kallisto was about to start questioning her. "Please, let me finish."

"Okay," Kallisto's eyes were wide, and she was glad she was sitting. She felt like someone threw a bucket of ice water over her head.

"The gods were given to us just like angels. They were supposed to aid us when we needed them or if we asked, but just like humans, they took free will a little too far. Many humans began to idolize the gods and worship them as such. I called for a dream god to help you. So, the answer to your question is yes. I believe the legends are—for the most part anyway—true," That was all Thia wanted to tell her daughter before her mother arrived. This was a conversation that needed the attention of both her and Zenovia.

"So, you're the one who sent Morpheus?"

"Yes, is he the *someone* you told you couldn't see anymore?" There was an edge to her mother's voice that Kallisto didn't understand. She just said she believed in the gods; why would she be surprised at her conversing with one?

Then it hit her. The gods weren't supposed to converse with mortals, much less have an intimate relationship. By Thia asking her daughter that question, she confirmed she knew a relationship was possible. Kallisto tilted her head slightly as she contemplated her mother's question and its implications. Her mother knew more than she let on.

"Mother, are you asking me if I broke off a relationship with a god?"

"I suppose I am," Thia lifted her chin slightly.

"What if I told you I met a god who wasn't Morpheus or any other Oneiroi?" Kallisto asked, studying her mother's body language.

Thia stiffened, "You met a god other than the one I sent?"

Kallisto shook her head. "Mom, there's something you're not telling me. What is it?"

"Yes, I sent a dream god to you. If they wish, I believe gods can be a part of our lives. What I want to know is, are you having contact with a god."

Kallisto contemplated how to tell her mother everything. *Here goes everything—*

"At first, I could only remember part of my times with Morpheus; then I remembered most everything, but never his appearance. When I wasn't with him, I couldn't remember what he looked like. I fell in love with him, and he with me, but I could no longer be with someone I couldn't have all of. Can you imagine what it's like to be in love with someone and not be able to pick them out of a lineup?"

Thia scooted closer to her daughter, wrapped her in her arms, and allowed her to cry. She spent the better part of twenty minutes consoling her baby girl. Her heart ached for her child. She never considered love when she sent Morpheus.

"Look, honey," Thia said, "I want you to tell me everything, but first, you mentioned there was another god other than Morpheus. Do you know who that god was?"

"Ares, the god of war," Kallisto answered.

"What? When? Why?" Thia asked, alarmed.

"He said his mother wanted to know more about the mortal Morpheus was so interested in."

Thia jumped up. "Look, Kalli; there are some things I need to check on. I know you must have so many questions, but please trust me and let me figure out what's going on. Have you been seeing Morpheus since your father's disappearance?"

"I'm not sure. For a couple of months, I had vivid dreams of a handsome man on Mount Olympus and would wake with the smell of lavender and honeysuckle on my body and in my room. I thought I was going crazy, but then I began working with my subconscious and realized I wasn't dreaming, not completely, anyway. I was, somehow, going to Olympus and other places, and my dream god was exactly that. Before I knew it, we fell in love. Sadness set in when I realized I could never actually be with him."

Thia saw the pain etched on Kallisto's face and heard the pain of heartache in her voice. She wanted to kick herself for sending a god into her little girl's life—she knew better. Firsthand knowledge should've been enough to keep her from turning to such drastic measures. Unfortunately, she hit rock bottom when her husband disappeared. Seeing her daughter so traumatized by his loss, she gave in and summoned a god to help. Now, Hera had what she wanted. Now, she would know where to find them.

Chapter XIX

Strange

Kallisto stayed with her mother in her parent's room all night. They cried and sometimes laughed together as she told her mother everything she could remember of her divine interactions.

Thia worried over her child more than she ever had before. In the morning, she called Kallisto's school, telling them she was sick and wouldn't return until Monday. Thia knew if Hera sent Ares, things were about to get interesting and possibly very dangerous.

Thia enjoyed spending the rest of the day with her daughter. She told Kallisto she had a lot more to discuss with her about the gods but wanted her mother to be there when she did since her grandmother could answer many of her questions.

Kallisto was beyond curious but could see the stress on her mother's face and hear the concern in her voice. She also bit back the urge to call on Morpheus. Her heart felt raw. She called John and told him she was sick. She hated lying, but honestly, she was sick. Her heart was aching and she thought she might spontaneously combust. The term *broken heart* now held profound meaning, not just emotional, but physical pain. Her heart was on Olympus, and she didn't know if she could live without it.

Amanda came over around six to give Kallisto her class assignments.

"Hey girl, how are you?" Amanda greeted Kallisto.

"I suppose I'll live. Hey mom," Kallisto called from the family room.

"Yes," Thia came to see what her daughter wanted.

"Amanda and I are going upstairs. I want to fill her in on the newest developments of my incredibly strange life," Kallisto told her mother about Amanda's knowledge of the situation earlier.

Thia wasn't concerned about Amanda knowing. She knew the friendship forged between the two girls was strong, and she'd never deny her daughter that connection. She, too, once had such a trusted friend.

"Okay, I'm going to finish dinner. I'll call you girls down when it's ready."

"Kalli, you look horrible. What's going on?" Tact wasn't a virtue Amanda possessed.

"Have a seat. This will take a while," Kallisto gestured to her bed.

"Okay, here it goes. First, Ares, the god of war, shows up at the gallery to ask me a lot of questions about my relationship with Morpheus," Kallisto started.

"Excuse me, did I hear you right?" Amanda wide-eyed. "A Greek god physically came to the gallery and spoke to you?—In the flesh?"

"Yes, but I wasn't supposed to be able to see him. Since I could, he's convinced I'm more than just a human and wanted to know *what* I was," Kallisto explained.

Amanda shook her head. "I think I need a drink. You know I need my caffeine if you insist on telling me this stuff. Do you have any soda? I got used to Morpheus, but gods coming out of the woodwork—how do I get on this list?"

"Let me finish—" Kallisto insisted. She continued telling Amanda everything.

Amanda sat in the chair, staring. Kallisto became worried after Amanda hadn't said anything for several minutes. In all the years they had been friends, Kallisto had never seen Amanda lost for words, and definitely not for that long. Amanda shook her head, sipped the soda, and shook her head again—repeatedly.

Finally, Amanda asked for confirmation, "Did you say your mother knows and understands all of this—and she has more she wants to tell you—but she is waiting until your grandmother gets here?"

"Yes, she's very worried, and I'm curious to know what she is withholding until grandma gets here. Something very strange is going on—and for me to call things strange—they have to be."

"When are you going back to school?"

"Monday," Kallisto had started her nervous rambling. "Mom's worried, though. She said Ares showing up under Hera's orders was a bad thing. That was a slip-up on mom's part. When I asked her why, she shrugged it off as nothing, but I could see the concern on her face."

"What time will your grandmother's flight land tomorrow?"

"Supposed to be around noon. You should come with us."

"I might. So—how gorgeous was Ares?" Amanda grinned.

Morpheus contemplated his next move for a couple of days. "Why can nothing be black and white? All this gray is driving me damn near crazy," Morpheus said aloud. As he saw it, The Fates were leaving his fate to him.

"Because gods would be useless if they were in black and white. Humans could figure out and fix their own problems," Phantasos popped in.

"Damn it, Phantasos, can you ever knock?"

"Well, I guess, but that would not be as much fun. When are you going back?" Phantasos asked.

"Why do you miss doing my dream work, or is it Hawaii you miss?" Morpheus managed a grin. It was his first genuine smile since Kallisto stabbed him through the heart. He had never felt such pain as when he returned her to her room.

"No, I just called John, and he said Kallisto is sick and he's working every day. I think he needs your help, plus I feel sorry for him," Phantasos replied.

"You have never felt sorry for a soul. What is the real reason? And did I hear you correctly? Did you say Kallisto is sick?" Morpheus asked.

"Yes, but I believe she has the same problem as you."

"And what problem might that be?"

"A broken heart," Phantasos stated.

"I will go back soon. I have been contemplating what The Fates were trying to say when they said nothing. I believe I should renounce my godhood and become mortal for her. Dying after eighty or ninety years could not feel worse than I do now. I feel dead inside."

"At least call John, and when he tells you Kallisto is sick, you should call her and check in to see how she is."

"I do not think I can stand hearing her voice and not go to her. And, if I go to her, in my condition, I cannot promise I will not break most, if not all, the rules given to me," Morpheus hung his head looking at the floor. His long blonde hair was not tied back, so it spilled around his face concealing tears he could no longer contain. "Damn it—I am a god; how can I be in this agony?"

"There are some things in life, my brother, that can cause even a Greek god to ache so bad he goes mad," Phantasos vanished, sensing his brother's need for privacy.

⤜⟫⟫⟫ ⟪⟪⟪⟫

Amanda stayed for supper, and she and Thia tried to keep the conversation casual and light to keep Kallisto from any more free-spirited emotional trauma. Before Amanda left, she started to tell Kallisto about her free spirited first cousin and her family's drama.

"Mom's youngest sister, you know, the one that lives in Tennessee?" Amanda asked Kallisto.

"Isn't she the one whose daughter is almost our age and has the two, much younger, twin boys?"

"Yeah, well, her daughter, Nicole, is giving my aunt and uncle a hard time. She has been missing curfews and sneaking out. Not to mention she went from being top of her class to about to fail her junior year. They're hoping I can talk some sense into her," Amanda gave a small laugh at the idea.

"They're asking you to be her role model? Oh, I needed a good laugh," Kallisto snickered.

"I guess they see me as a success because I maintain pretty good grades, I haven't gotten pregnant, and I don't do drugs," Amanda shrugged. "In my aunt's book, I'm a saint."

"So, while you are in Greece, I'll be in Tennessee trying to talk sense into Nicole. Make sure to bring me a cool t-shirt from D.F.O. and go to the docks to get me a good-looking Greek man. One who has just graduated college and has a promising career in—making lots of money," Amanda giggled and continued to describe the money maker's eyes, sun-tanned skin, and ass.

"Amanda, I now realize why I love having you around."

"Why is that? I make you look sane?" Amanda supplied.

"No, you make me smile even when smiling seems impossible. You are truly a magnificent bestie."

Kallisto and her mother slept late the next morning. They were tired from the drama of the past two days and needed to be fully coherent when Zenovia landed, ready to talk if she wasn't too jet-lagged.

On the way to the airport, Kallisto asked her mother to stop by the gallery and check in with John. She promised him she would be back to work the next day, and to be extra nice, she told him she would open and close to give him a much-needed break. While catching up with John, she found out Ambrose was scheduled to return in a couple of days and wondered why she hadn't heard from him, but she tried not to put too much thought into what it meant. After all, he was overseas, and they weren't officially dating.

Thia and Kallisto arrived about thirty minutes before Zenovia's plane landed. When Kallisto saw her grandmother, she took off running into her arms.

Zenovia hadn't changed since Kallisto could remember. She was beautiful. Her mouth and eyes still held a lot of youth. She looked to be in her forties when she was actually in her mid-sixties. Kallisto hoped she took longevity and a youthful appearance from her mother's side of the family.

"Grandma!" Kallisto squealed in delight.

"My beautiful Kalli, how I have missed you," Zenovia's English held a heavy Greek accent making Kallisto homesick for Athens, and to her surprise, for Ambrose.

"I've missed you too."

Thia embraced her mother with a hug showing how much she missed her and still needed her mother. Kallisto couldn't help but wonder again if her grandmother was okay or if they were keeping something about Zenovia's health secret.

The three women talked animatedly to one another all the way home. Amanda waited by the curb since she hadn't been able to go. She'd texted Kallisto that she didn't feel great but would try to make it later if she felt better. Kallisto noticed Amanda hadn't *felt great* often lately and always looked exhausted. Curiosity and a little nagging at the back of her brain flashed through her when she read her friend's text. She made a mental note to make Amanda spill her guts when they were together again.

Zeus' home was as captivating as ever. The daemon who answered the door was beautiful and held herself like a goddess. She had wavy blonde hair and tawny skin.

"Come in, Morpheus. Zeus received word you would be coming. He is waiting in the throne room."

Even her voice was mesmerizing.

Morpheus followed the tawny beauty remembering a time when she would have appealed to his masculine senses, now he could appreciate she was beautiful, but she was nothing compared to his Kallisto. *She is no longer your Kallisto.* Morpheus reprimanded himself as he followed the daemon.

"What brings you here? Your report is not due for days?" Zeus asked as Morpheus walked through the ornately carved doors.

"I have come to talk with you about my situation and a consort problem you have and probably know nothing of."

"I have a problem with Hera that I am unaware of. How could you know, and I know nothing?"

"Because she sent me to investigate. Of course, she made me promise not to say anything, so if you tell her and she comes after me, I will be forced to protect myself. This conversation is between you and me and no one else," Morpheus gestured between them.

It took Zeus a minute to contemplate everything, knowing he could not give Morpheus what he had come for.

"I will tell you as much as possible, but no more. I, too, am bound by The Fates, even if they are my daughters."

"Hera wants to know what has been plaguing your mind lately. She says you are not acting like yourself. You are having dreams and nightmares and once said my name while asleep. And she is as curious about my love life as you seem to be. Why?" Morpheus asked without hesitation.

"Let us just say there are issues that were set into place many years ago, and they are at work against your relationship with—" Zeus hesitated, "with Kallisto—I cannot tell you everything, but if you desire to bring her to Olympus, to live—well—that will be a problem."

"I want to know why. Who does not want her here?" Morpheus asked. "You, The Fates, my father...who?"

"That is a complicated question that I cannot answer. Just know you are playing with fires from hell by loving that girl," Zeus stepped from his throne and walked over to peer out the wall of windows overlooking Olympus. He looked sad.

"Are you telling me I cannot have her?"

"I guess I am asking you, what price are you willing to pay to love her? Are you willing to fight the powers of the scorned to have the woman you love? Are you willing to do what it takes to protect her?"

Morpheus' eyebrows pulled together. "Do you realize you are not making sense? Kallisto is no threat to anyone. She is a seventeen-year-old mortal who was having nightmares. I was called to help her and fell in love. Who could possibly have a problem with that?"

"Morpheus, who called you to aid in her sleep?" Zeus asked.

"Her mother, Thia. She is Greek and believes in the old ways. She understands we were created to aid in mortal and immortal problems and uses us to help.

"No, Morpheus, she used you to help her daughter," Zeus turned to face him. "Never before had she called out to a god. She called on a god to intervene only to aid her daughter while in despair. Ask yourself why."

"Are you saying the problem I am encountering is Thia?" Morpheus asked, more confused.

"I am saying there are underlying issues that will cause you and Kallisto great problems if you continue to seek her affection. Regrettably, things have been unlocked, and problems will follow even if you choose to forget about Kallisto. How deep you are willing to go is up to you, but if you decide to continue with her, you may have to give up your godhood."

Zeus finally confirmed Morpheus' fear. He very well may lose the only existence he had known for over three thousand years.

"Will you allow me to return for the remainder of my allotted time since Kallisto asked me to stay out of her life? She wants a relationship with Ambrose since she can remember his face. So, she rejected me so that she could be with me."

"And here I thought my life was complicated. You may have me beat. Just know, I will support you in your decisions, even though your decision may change my life," Zeus walked to Morpheus and stood toe-to-toe with him. "Is she worth it?"

"She is worth whatever hell I must overcome, even if it means the end of my godhood."

The right side of Zeus' lips pulled up to a smile. "I thought you would say that."

"I need time to absorb all this information or lack thereof. I will soon return to the mortal realm and try to convince her that Morpheus is not such a bad guy," Morpheus smiled, turned to leave, and remembered his other reason for visiting.

Morpheus turned to ask, "What would you like me to tell your wife about your sleeping habits? She is convinced they are somehow my fault."

"Say, I would not allow entrance into my dreams. The rest will be up to you. Just remember, she *is* my wife and has been through a lot because of my—life choices."

"Still no straight answers. Dealing with gods is a pain in the ass," Morpheus shook his head and vanished.

He sat for the rest of the day, trying to assemble the pieces. "What could have Zeus, Hera, and The Fates so cautious? Whatever it was, Zeus and Hera were playing on different teams, and he was not sure he wanted to know all the details.

Morpheus decided to stop hiding from his destiny and return to the gallery. He called John and told him he would be back within a day or two, unwilling to give him a set time just in case someone decided to check on the flights from Greece back to the U.S. He could imagine someone deciding to surprise him at the airport.

CHAPTER XX

ZENOVIA

Zenovia was exhausted from her trip, so as soon as they got to Thia's, she took a shower and a nap. Kallisto busied herself with cleaning her bedroom and giving Amanda tips on approaching her cousin. While dusting her dresser, she came across the ring and bracelet Morpheus gave her. Again, tears welled up in her eyes.

"Will I ever get over this?" She asked Amanda.

"You're amazing, Kalli, but not even you can cure a broken heart in forty-eight hours. Time heals, so my mom says."

Her grandmother slept a few hours before joining Kallisto and Thia for supper. She did look a lot better after a bit of sleep.

"I'm sorry I napped so long. Jet lag set in."

"That's okay, mom," Thia interjected. "We're just glad you're here. I hope you still like my cooking."

"I love anything you prepare, my child," Zenovia smiled at her daughter. "Where is Amanda, don't tell me I missed her?"

"She'll be back tomorrow. I'm opening the gallery in the morning at ten, and I think she's meeting me there so I won't be alone. She usually spends the night at some point over the weekend." Kallisto answered.

Thia cleared her throat and nervously addressed her daughter. "Honey, your grandmother and I need to talk with you. What we are about to tell you will be the turning point of the rest of your life."

"Mom, you're scaring me."

"There's nothing to be afraid of, my dear," her grandmother started. "I just want to tell you a story about my life."

That didn't seem nearly as bad as she was imagining. Thoughts of danger and disease were at the forefront of her mind. She had been worried since her mother told her that her grandmother was coming to Hawaii on a whim.

"Okay, that doesn't sound so bad," Kallisto said.

"Let me begin by asking you not to judge me too harshly. I was young and very much in love—not that's any excuse," Zenovia smiled halfheartedly.

"I would never," Kallisto shook her head at the increasingly strange conversation.

Zenovia closed her eyes as if trying to find the words and possibly even the nerves to continue. She had dreaded this day for almost eighteen years. In fact, Kallisto's birth was the day the anxiety began, as she looked into her granddaughter's trademark eyes that set her apart from the rest of the world, eyes no mortal had seen since Hercules. She took a deep breath and let all her skeletons fall out of her closet for her granddaughter to hear.

"I was eighteen and walking along the beach, watching the tide come in and change the surface of the sand as it washed back out. I remember that explicitly because I wished change could be easy. All I wanted was to travel, see the world, and settle down one day with a man who cherished me like my father had cherished my mother before she died. Unfortunately, I was engaged to a man who only wanted a trophy to hang on his arm when he was among his high society buddies from America," Zenovia paused.

Kallisto could see the memory wash over her grandmother. She felt life was about to be very different—she knew she would refer to life before the story and after. A strange vision of white columns and a vast white throne with intricate carvings flashed through Kallisto's mind. She shook her head, trying to focus.

"You never told me that before," Kallisto did the math. Her grandmother hadn't met her grandfather for at least ten years after the time she was speaking of now.

"I've never told you anything I am telling you now."

"Mom, would you like more tea?" Thia asked her mother, giving her a break.

"No, dear, I am good for now."

"Are you sure you want to tell me this?" Kallisto asked.

Zenovia continued the story in answer. "As I walked down the beach, a beautiful man appeared out of thin air before me. My mouth fell open in admiration at the apparition. He winked at me, and my knees went weak. He had the most beautiful aqua blue eyes, rock hard tawny body, and full lips that framed a set of gorgeous white teeth," Zenovia's face flushed as she described the man in her memory.

"Did you say aqua?" Kallisto interrupted. She had a mental image of a man such as the one described by her grandmother, standing on the sand wearing a chiton edged in gold. Again, she shook her head, dislodging the vision.

Zenovia nodded. "You see, right before the man showed up, I lifted my head and asked Zeus himself to help me out of my situation. I had to marry a wealthy businessman to help my family after my mother's death three years before. My father grieved so much that he became bedridden. It was up to me to see to the needs of my two younger brothers. My fiancé and I had a deal, I was his trophy, and he was my financial means to keep my siblings and me off the streets," Zenovia paused for another moment.

It hadn't gone unnoticed to Kallisto that her grandmother was fighting back tears.

"Zeus personally answered my cry for help. He was the man standing before me in the chiton."

Kallisto froze at her grandmother's words. Finally finding her tongue, she asked, "You were speaking to Zeus?"

"Yes," Zenovia answered. "He held out his hand and asked if I would walk with him. I smiled, and the next thing I knew, we were standing by the most beautiful waterfall," Zenovia paused before she finished her sentence, "—on Mount Olympus."

Tears ran from Kallisto's eyes. She could guess the rest of the story, but needing to hear it from her grandmother's mouth, she said nothing.

"I'll not bore you with all the details, but that day was the beginning of the best times of my life. Zeus and I spent hours that day talking, swimming, and feeding the animals. He told me about his children, all of them, and about his wife, Hera. For the first time, I talked about my mother's death, my father's self-exclusion, and my commitment to marry a man I loathed," Zenovia took a deep breath and a sip of her tea.

Kallisto took the pause in her grandmother's story to ask a question. "Was there a beautiful meadow covered in wildflowers by the waterfall?"

"Yes, that's where we had our picnics."

Kallisto couldn't help but notice her grandmother used the plural form of a picnic.

"So, you went often?"

"That was the first day of many. Zeus and I became the best of friends. About a month into our friendship, he told me he had made a grave mistake. At first, I was worried that he meant our friendship was a mistake. I didn't think I could take that since my feelings had gone way past friendship. I had fallen in love with the King of the Greek gods. It was not his looks; even though those didn't hurt, it wasn't his power. It was the man I loved. I couldn't take rejection from him. I was more than willing to be just friends, as long as I could be near him," now, the tears fell unchecked down Zenovia's face.

Kallisto and her mother wrapped their arms around Zenovia, and all three cried. It took Zenovia a few minutes before she regained enough composure to continue her story.

"Zeus told me his mistake was that he allowed his feelings for me to exceed his task of helping a mortal; it even surpassed friendship. That day he pulled me into his warm chest and kissed me like no other ever had and like no other ever has. He empowered me to leave my fiancé, and he, himself, provided for my family instead. That is where the family money comes from, not the restaurant business, so many assume. We spent the next year and a half loving each other. I knew it was wrong. He was married. I seared my conscience by telling myself Hera had many lovers, and Zeus, of course, had many before me, but this was different; he loved me—more than any other goddess or mortal. We were meant to be—soulmates. His daughters, The Fates, told him so when he asked them. They detested Hera and knew everything anyway, so he asked them about us and our future," Zenovia took another sip of her tea.

"Let's go into the family room, mama. It'll be more comfortable," Thia suggested.

As they walked from the kitchen to the family room, Kallisto's mind reeled at the knowledge of her grandmother in love with a god, and not just any god—Zeus. She had spent hours on end with the ruler of the Greek pantheon and obviously still loved him. Kallisto couldn't wait to hear the rest of the story. The three women sat on the plush, much more comfortable furniture, and Zenovia resumed her tale.

"Ares saw us together in the meadow one day, and before we knew it, Hera appeared before us.

"Oh shit," Kallisto exclaimed. "Sorry Yiayia, sorry mom, I just—sorry! I didn't mean to say that." Kallisto reverted to the Greek term for grandmother.

"Well, that was a fair assessment of what was about to hit the fan. Hera looked me up and down with a stare that could kill, and I'm guessing if Zeus hadn't been there, she would have. She yelled at him and told him not to bring his mistresses to Olympus. She seemed more worried that I was on Olympus than we were having an affair. I, on the other hand, was mortified," Zenovia's eyes were wide as she remembered the exchange.

"She didn't care he was having an affair?" Kallisto asked.

"Well, not at that moment. You see, gods are different when it comes to those things. She was okay with his infidelity until she realized a few months later that he was truly in love with me. He hadn't lain with her in many months, so she followed him. For him not to realize he was being followed was a sign of the depth of his infatuation. I was all he thought about most days. Even his attitude toward his pantheon changed. As Hypnos had once put it, he was tolerable for the first time ever."

"You know Hypnos?" Kallisto asked. She couldn't believe her grandmother knew the father of the Oneiroi.

"Yes, Zeus sent him to me to aid me in our separation."

"Separation?" Kallisto repeated, but as a question.

"Hera went crazy when she realized Zeus loved me. He had never loved anyone other than his children. Even between those, his love was not equal. Hercules was by far his favorite, and he held a lot of admiration for Hercules' mortal mother but never loved her. Hera tried giving Zeus ultimatums, telling him she would destroy everything he held dear. Nothing swayed him until she decided the only thing he held dear was me. She came for me and had me backed into a corner, yelling. She bound my hands behind my back with a mere thought and was reaching toward me when she heard my deepest secret—a tiny heartbeat. It was then she knew I had more advantage over her husband than she ever could, even with all her powers. I was carrying his child, a child made from love—true love. She didn't realize I wasn't like her, though. I would never hold my child over him, especially to hold him to me. She could see in my eyes and hear my thoughts that I hadn't told Zeus. The baby's heartbeat had just begun, and he had yet to pick up on the tiny beat," tears were streaming again down Zenovia's face.

She continued after another sip of tea and another minute of composure. "Hera gave me an ultimatum. Unlike Zeus, I didn't have the power to choose my own way. She said she would allow me and my unborn child to live, but I had to disappear and never call for the help of her husband again. I shook in pain and anguish. Of course, I chose my baby and life for both of us. If it had just been me, I would've chosen death. I didn't want to live without him.

Having his baby was getting him for life in a way, so I left. Hera created some magic hiding my whereabouts from Zeus. I still had access to other gods, but Zeus was no more. He sent Hypnos to help me sleep. He knew me well enough to know that I had nightmares often, and since I was not accessible to him, he wanted to keep me safe, even from my demons. Hypnos told Zeus about your mother—his daughter."

Kallisto let out a gasp when her grandmother confirmed her assumption. "That would make my mother—"

Thia interrupted her daughter, "A demigod."

Kallisto's eyes widened, her hands trembled, and her mouth went dry. "That would make me—"

"A demigod as well," Thia answered again.

Zenovia and Thia sat watching Kallisto, giving her time to absorb information bound to shake the most stable people. It took Kallisto a good ten minutes to arrange her thoughts into a coherent line. Her mind was all over the place.

"You're telling me that Zeus, the ruler over the Greek pantheon, the father of Hercules, Apollo, Artemis, and The Fates, to name a few, is my grandfather?"

"Yes," Zenovia answered her granddaughter.

Kallisto grabbed her chest and started breathing heavily. Her mother made her sit on the floor and put her head between her legs. Zenovia and Thia exchanged looks, wondering how much more she could take.

"Is there more?" Kallisto lifted her head.

"Yes," Thia answered this time.

Zenovia started again with her story. "Hera proved her point. She needed to show me she was serious. She sent her son, Ares, to kill my father."

Kallisto gasped as the danger she was in became a little clearer. "She knows I'm your granddaughter, and that's why Ares came to check me out for his mother. She knows that Morpheus and I . . ." Kallisto couldn't finish. She shook harder as her world turned upside down.

"Kalli, Hera is very dangerous, and she means business. Your grandmother is the only being to ever come between her and Zeus. She knows the love that created me will be the same love he will feel for you. She will do anything to keep you from him. Morpheus taking you to Olympus and falling in love with you has brought back bitter memories for her, and a goddess with bitter memories can destroy all we hold dear," Thia explained.

"Does daddy know?"

"No," Thia answered. "I've never told him. I've extended his mortal life beyond his natural death for twenty or thirty years. I'm immortal, I'll have to watch him die, and it aches my heart every day."

"Am I immortal?" Kallisto asked her mother.

"We aren't sure. You may have an extra-long existence. When I say that, I mean a life of several hundred years, which I think will be the case. The only way to know is by asking The Fates," Thia answered.

"I knew something was going on with me. I willed myself to Olympus and saw Ares when he said I shouldn't be able to. I see and know things normal kids don't. I'm in love with a dream god. I guess I always knew I was different," Kallisto's eyes were red and tear-filled as she looked beyond her mother and grandmother,

"I'm sorry we're just now telling you about your lineage, but the deal we made with Zeus was we would tell you when you became an adult. In mortal years that would make you between the ages of eighteen and twenty-two when we could tell you. Since Hera decided to come into the picture, things have changed; you need to know what we're up against," Zenovia said.

"Zeus knows about me?" Kallisto asked.

"Yes, we've been keeping in touch through our dreams ever since he realized I didn't leave of my free will. He and I feared Hera attacking Thia and, later—you. So we never resumed our relationship. He only knows of you through the dreams I can share with him through Phobetor."

"Phobetor is an Oneiroi, one of Morpheus' brothers." Kallisto stated.

"Yes. Due to having to share our dreams, Phobetor has kept to himself. He has always been afraid Hera would retaliate," Zenovia supplied.

"How long has this been going on?" Kallisto continued with the questions. "Since you met Zeus?"

"I met him ninety-four years ago," Zenovia watched her granddaughter as she did the math.

"You are 112 years old? How? I thought you were mortal?"

"I am, but Zeus has seen to it that I live an extra-long life," Zenovia answered.

"That would make mom. . .," Kallisto paused and pondered. "She is at least 92 years old? No way!"

"Yes, I'm 92 years old. You, though, are still only 17 until next Saturday anyway," Thia smiled, trying to lighten the moment.

Kallisto stood, needing to walk and defog the cloud forming in her head; *too much—too fast.* She paced the floor, thinking. After about five rounds around the sofa and two trips around the coffee table, Kallisto took a deep breath. The breath symbolized her resignation to the fact her family was beyond normal and her acceptance that it would never be.

"What will Hera do to us?" Kallisto asked.

"She will do whatever it takes to keep you, Thia, and me from your grandfather, even if that means keeping you from other gods and your rightful place on Olympus. Most of Zeus' children live on Olympus, even the ones that are not her children, but because of the relationship he and I had," Zenovia pointed to each of them, " you are liabilities to her status as his wife."

The three women talked and answered each other's questions all evening. Around midnight, Kallisto's eyelids grew heavy. Kallisto was so emotionally spent that she fell asleep immediately after she got in bed. Her last thought was to wonder if her grandmother would dream tonight. If she did, would she tell Zeus that she told his granddaughter about him?

⤜⤜⤜ ⤛⤛⤛

Morpheus decided to return a day early, but first, he needed to go to California because of a small shipping problem with The Fates paintings. He fought the urge to look into the orb. He flashed to Phantasos, and to his astonishment, his brother Phobetor was eating breakfast.

"Well, no one called me to the family reunion. I am hurt," Morpheus grabbed his chest in mock sadness.

Phobetor stood up and greeted his brother. "It has been a while, little brother. I hear you are in love with a mortal."

Morpheus gave Phantasos an unkind gesture showing his irritation. "I see our eldest brother cannot keep his damn mouth shut."

"Well, he asked me to check in on your dreams next weekend, and I questioned it. Are you really in love with a mortal woman?" Phobetor asked.

"Yes, her name is Kallisto Nalani."

Phobetor froze. "What did you say her name was?"

"Kallisto Nalani, why?"

"The name sounded familiar, that's all. So, when can I meet this mortal who has stolen the heart of our playboy brother?" Phobetor was abnormally cheerful.

"Whenever you want, but the only problem is, she broke up with me. Well, she broke up with the god, not the mortal me."

Phobetor's eyebrows shot up. "What the hell are you talking about, Morpheus? You sound like an oracle, or worse, a Fate."

"Since Kallisto could not remember everything about me. I went to earth pretending to be a mortal named Ambrose. She loves us both, but she broke up with me since my immortal self had so many complications. She has no clue I am also Ambrose. It is quite complicated."

"It is more complicated than you even think," Phobetor said under his breath.

"What?" Morpheus asked.

"Nothing. It sounds like our little brother has yet to lose his flair for drama. Phantasos, I will get back to you," Phobetor flashed from the room.

"Well, that was a surprise," Morpheus said.

"Yeah, he seems lonely. I think he just needed to see how we were doing," Phantasos explained. "So, what do I owe to your early visit?"

"It's not that early."

"Well, for us working dream gods, it is early," Phantasos chided.

"I am going back today, but first, I must go and fix a problem with the delivery of The Fates paintings. It is so wonderful being human," Morpheus rolled his eyes.

"You still have not told me why you are here."

"I want you to come sometime this week to visit with me in Hawaii. I need someone in my corner."

"It sounds like you are becoming a clingy little brother," Phantasos laughed.

Morpheus, once again, gave Phantasos a sign of brotherly love. "I just need someone to help out with Amanda, that is all,"

"She is a pain in the ass, Morpheus," Phantasos replied.

"I cannot go to Kallisto in dream form, and I am afraid she can tell when I invade her thoughts. Amanda is the closest thing I have to an orb. Please find out all you can about what Kallisto is thinking and how she feels. I need to know the moment she suspects Ambrose is me," Morpheus reasoned. He also thought Phantasos' secretly enjoyed her company, even though she was a pain in the ass.

"Fine—when, where, and how?" Phantasos was determined to sound tortured.

"If you could show up Monday at the gallery, and as for how, well, you are a dream god."

Phantasos arched a brow. "What in the hell does that have to do with it?"

"You have a good imagination," Morpheus vanished, giving Phantasos an evil grin. He headed to the museum, where the gallery in California kept The Fates paintings. He needed to sort out the shipping problem they were having, then he planned on going back to the gallery to speak with John.

Chapter **XXI**

Oneiroi

Kallisto **walked through the gallery doors with** an entirely different perspective. The gallery now held the faces of family. She, by blood, belonged to a pantheon, just as the t-shirt she often wore asked for. She grinned at the painting of the twins, Artemis and Apollo, gave a mocking nod to each, and said aloud, "auntie, uncle."

She couldn't wait to see the paintings of The Fates; they, too, were her aunts, not full-blooded, of course, since they had different mothers. Before she rounded the corner, she braced herself for what was coming. The largest painting in the gallery. She had seen it hundreds of times and dusted its large, carved golden frame more times than she could count. Whether the likeness of the god was accurate or not, it still represented her grandfather, which had to be why her stomach felt queasy.

Kallisto remembered what John told her before the gallery became her place of employment. The paintings and busts were true representations of what the gods looked like. When she rounded the corner, her eyes met the eyes of the god. She had never really looked at it before. His eyes were almost the same color as hers. Tears started to burn her eyes, and she felt a longing she couldn't explain. A million questions she wanted to ask him ran through her mind, but she knew she'd never get a chance to ask them.

She stood before the painting in what felt like minutes, wishing it would talk to her when the clock chimed. She realized she had been standing there for over thirty minutes. She wiped tears from her cheeks and went to splash cool water on her face. The gallery would open in twenty-five minutes, and she needed to vacuum the rugs and dust. She talked her grandmother into coming to see her at work. Now she thought about it; maybe she shouldn't have asked. Her grandmother seeing the painting of Zeus and, even worse, the new one they just received of Hera may not be such a good idea.

Kallisto, humming to herself while vacuuming, thought she heard the phone ring. She shut off the vacuum and answered it to hear Ambrose's voice on the other end.

"Kallisto?" he asked. "I heard you were sick."

"John needed a little break, and Amanda should be here any minute to keep me company. I just came in early to get the housekeeping done." If her mother found out Amanda wasn't with her, she'd be furious. *This whole Hera pissed thing is getting to mom*. She thought.

"How are you?" Ambrose asked. He got a lump in his throat when he heard Kallisto's voice. It was like a physical pull or a compulsion—he needed to go to her.

"Feeling much better, thanks for asking," Kallisto said a little formally.

He could tell by her tone she was upset Ambrose had not called and checked on her.

"I will be back in Maui later this afternoon. I am on the Big Island where my plane just landed," Oh, how he hated lying to her, but what choice did he have? He could not tell her he was in California and would be in Maui in a couple of hours or seconds. She had to think he was much closer and had already taken care of everything.

"Will you be coming here?" Kallisto meant for the question to sound nonchalant, but it sounded more like anticipation.

"Uh, not sure, but probably. I called to let John know the museum sent us the wrong paintings. The paintings they sent were ours but were not The Fates. I'm bringing The Fate paintings in with me."

"What paintings did they send?"

"I have no idea yet. You can decide when they get there to put them in the gallery or leave them in the back."

"Will do, boss," sarcasm dripped from Kallisto's lips.

"Do not make me fire you."

Kallisto laughed despite herself. "Do I need to send someone to the airport? My mom and grandmother could always come and pick you up. My grandma wants to meet my boss."

"So, your grandmother came early?" Ambrose asked.

"Yes, she's coming to the gallery for a while today. She loves the gods." *Literally*, Kallisto added to herself.

"I will see you later. I have to go," Ambrose said abruptly.

Morpheus could not wait to see Kallisto again but was not up to seeing her family. He wanted to be alone with her. He needed to ensure she was okay and desperately needed her to realize who he was. Coming up with a plan to make her recognize him was not presenting itself. Now, not only did he have to keep Amanda out of the way, but also Kallisto's grandmother.

Kallisto hung up the phone and felt a pang of regret hit her square in the chest. Memories of Morpheus filled her head. She, once again, began to tear up. "Damn it," she stamped her foot. "I've never cried so much in my life."

A tap came from the front door, and to Kallisto's delight, Amanda stood there, her hands full of lattés and scones. Kallisto gave a contented sigh as she opened the door. "Thank you so much. I saw every hour pass last night, and I need a coffee in the worst way."

"I aim to please. I made sure yours was a vanilla caramel topped with whipped cream and chocolate syrup," Amanda winked.

Kallisto took some of Amanda's burden, including her purse and a couple of gossip magazines the girls liked to read when they were goofing off together.

"Have you been cryin'?" Amanda noticed Kallisto's swollen eyes and red cheeks.

"My world just took the most unusual twist. After you left yesterday, my grandmother told me about my true lineage," Kallisto said.

"True? As opposed to your untrue lineage. Did you find out you are kin to a mass murderer or something? You look a little shocked."

"I am. You know how deep my love of fantasy goes?"

Amanda nodded her head. She gave no sarcastic comeback, and it had not gone unnoticed by Kallisto that her friend looked almost as tired as she felt.

"Well—" Kallisto began the long story of her lineage. It was rare for anyone to shop the gallery before lunch on Saturdays, so Kallisto was able to finish her story and give Amanda time to recover without interruption.

"So, you're telling me my best friend is the granddaughter of Zeus?" Amanda asked—again—for the third time.

"Yep."

"Shit!" Rarely was Amanda at a loss for words. This was one of those rare moments.

"I know. This explains so much. How I was able to go to Mount Olympus on my own, the reason I'm able to see things before they happen, and most of all, the reason Morpheus and I are so bound. We are cut from the same cloth, for lack of better words."

"Yuck, you guys are kin," Amanda had a look of disgust on her face.

"No! We're from the same pantheon. I'm not a full god, though. To top everything off, Hera hates my family because her husband loves—loved—my grandmother. That's why she sent Ares to watch me." Kallisto started her fast, non-stop rambling. "Mom has gone crazy, worried about me, and grandma relives painful memories. She still loves Zeus. I could see it in her eyes when she told me their story. She hurts."

"What about Morpheus? Are you still going to stay away from him?" Amanda asked.

"I'm so confused right now. I love him, but I'm forbidden, by my mom, to ever set a toe on Olympus again. How could there ever be anything between us?" Kallisto hung her head as the waterworks started up again. "He's still unavailable to me."

"Why don't we go kick some Hera goddess ass then?" There was the Amanda Kallisto was waiting for.

"Because she's a goddess and I'm a demigod, twice removed, plus I rather like living, and you're 100% mortal," Kallisto reasoned.

"I know, but there has to be a way. Maybe you could go to Zeus and ask him to work all of this out for you," Amanda contemplated.

"He doesn't know me. He doesn't even know my mom. Hera allowed my grandmother to escape her wrath only because she was pregnant. Apparently, not even Hera is so cruel as to murder a pregnant woman. She also told her she would kill her entire family if she pursued Zeus' affections ever again," Kallisto explained the finer points of her problem. "Not even Zeus has known where to find us. If he came to us, Hera would have us destroyed."

"And I thought my family had issues."

Before Kallisto could retort, the buzzer on the back door rang. "That must be the delivery that Ambrose told me about," Kallisto explained in conversation as she went to open the door.

Per Kallisto's instructions, two tall, well-muscled men carried a large wooden crate and sat it down in the back room. The two men looked to be in their early twenties and were faithful to the gym. Amanda nearly licked her lips at the sight of so much testosterone.

Amanda leaned over and whispered into Kallisto's ear. "Now, that would be a reason to work for airport delivery."

Kallisto rolled her eyes and giggled. "You're not right in the head."

Amanda followed the two guys out to their truck as she talked to them about job prospects. Kallisto continued to shake her head and went to start opening the crate. Once she finally opened the crate, she pulled out the first of three 30" x 40" paintings. On the bottom of the first painting was a metal plate with the inscription, "*Phobetor, Middle Brother of the Oneiroi, god of Dreams.*" Kallisto froze and then called for Amanda. The man in the painting was gorgeous. He had dark brown hair with deep golden eyes. His body was honed to faultlessness, and his eyes showed a glint of danger.

When Amanda arrived, she showed her the painting. "If this is one of three paintings in this crate, I would say it would be a safe bet that the other two are Phobetor's brothers. I'm about to see the face of Morpheus." Kallisto's hands were shaking, and Amanda was speechless. "At least a rendition of him, anyway."

"Well, here goes nothing," and Kallisto dove through the strips of packing paper to the next painting. When she pulled out the second canvas, Amanda squealed as her hands covered her mouth in shock. The inscription at the bottom of the vast work of art stated, *Phantasos, Eldest Oneiroi, god of Dreams.*

"It's—it's—" Amanda was, in shock, "—it can't be."

"It's Christos," Kallisto supplied. Sure enough, an exact replica of Ambrose's brother stood leaning against a beautiful tree with his arms crossed.

Kallisto suddenly got a funny feeling in the pit of her stomach. She approached the crate slowly. She once again dug through the paper and pulled out the last painting. She stood there transfixed, staring at the man she knew all too well, with his dark blonde shoulder-length hair, crystal blue eyes, and skin tanned to perfection.

This time Amanda was the one who spoke since Kallisto didn't seem to be coherent. "Ambrose," was all Amanda could get out.

The inscription on the painting that held the face of Kallisto's boss said, *Morpheus, Youngest of the Oneiroi, god of Dreams.*"

"Surely not; they're rich, and their father painted the Oneiroi to look like his sons. Ambrose never mentioned another brother. The way he talked, it was just him and Christos," Kallisto rambled, trying to make sense of the paintings.

"Kalli, if you're a demigod, could Ambrose not be Morpheus?"

"I suppose, but I would've known. You'd think if he were Morpheus, me seeing this painting and inscription would trigger a memory to where I could recall Morpheus' face," Kallisto's eyes began to burn again. This time she refused to give in. "Why wouldn't he tell me?"

"I don't know, maybe he couldn't," Amanda shrugged. She was trying to stay on track and help her best friend out in her time of need, but her eyes kept returning to Christos's painting.

As the girls sat there reeling over the paintings, they heard footsteps in the gallery. They both stood and went to see if it was a customer.

"Yaiyia!" Kallisto flung her arms around her grandmother, who stood transfixed before the painting of Zeus.

Kallisto let go of her embrace when she realized her grandmother was not returning it. Zenovia was engrossed in the painting hanging in front of her.

"It's him, my Zeus. This painting looks just like him. How is that? They have a real painting of him?"

"I was told all the artwork in this gallery is true replications. I may know how, though. Will you follow me, grandma?" Kallisto led her grandmother toward the back room. "Didn't you say Hypnos and his son Phobetor know of you and Zeus?" Kallisto questioned.

"Yes, they have been the ones to relay important information for us when necessary," Zenovia answered.

"Can you tell me if this is an exact likeness of Phobetor?" Kallisto turned the canvas toward her grandmother. Once again, Zenovia went still.

"Yes, that is Phobetor," Zenovia confirmed.

Kallisto's blood ran cold, "Do you know what his brothers look like?"

"No, I only dealt with Phobetor and Hypnos, never the other Oneiroi. Why all the questions?"

"The other two pictures are of my boss, Ambrose, and his brother Christos."

"Who all knows about this?" Zenovia asked.

"I assume just me and Amanda. We just now unboxed the paintings. I'm not sure, though."

"Look, sweetie, I know this is a lot to handle, but the Oneiroi are good gods. I want you to be careful, though. Where one god is, often others follow. When your boss gets here, you need to have a long talk with him. Now, I must go; your mother and I are going to the bookstore. You girls, be careful and let us know what you find out about the paintings." Zenovia kissed Kallisto on the forehead and Amanda on her cheek. As she walked toward the door, she stopped at the painting of Zeus. Kallisto could see the anguish on her grandmother's face. She could only guess how hard it must be to see the man you loved, bore a child with, and were forced never to see again standing life-size in an art gallery. Her pain over Morpheus was bad enough; she didn't see how her grandmother could stand up.

"I feel so sorry for her," Amanda commented.

"Me too," Kallisto replied.

Kallisto made only one sale. It was of a nymph standing in a large doorway. Nothing meaningful to a Greek history buff or a mythological fantasy lover. It was just a pretty painting with a pretty price of six thousand and seventy-five dollars. Time went by fast, and before she knew it, Amanda had to leave.

It was six in the evening and no sign of Ambrose. Kallisto role-played with Amanda on how to ask him about the paintings, but nothing seemed to work. How can a person ask their boss and a possible new boyfriend—no, that was not the word for him, but the best Kallisto could come up with—if he was a Greek god? *In particular, the Greek god I have fallen in love with and the one who has seen me very close to naked.* She flushed just thinking about it and giggled at the fact she had the strangest obstacles to overcome of any teenager she knew of.

Kallisto kept glancing at the clock's hands. Every second seemed to intensify her anxiety. She believed there was some connection between Ambrose and the gods. She didn't think he was Morpheus, that would be too good to be true, *but* there was something about him.

The back door opened around six forty-five. A wave of fear ran from the top of Kallisto's head to her toes. *He's here!*

Ambrose rounded the corner looking rather godly. He was wearing his hair down, which was unusual for him. Kallisto's first thought made her knees weak and desire run through her veins. *Down girl, he is your boss,* was the reprimand she gave to herself.

As soon as their eyes met, he gave her a huge smile, which made her physically dizzy. *I cannot do this! She braced herself against the desk to remain steady.*

"Where are the paintings? Did you leave them in your car?" Kallisto finally managed speech.

"I dropped them off at the museum. They put them in the vault until Saturday. One less thing for me to worry about."

"How was your flight?" Kallisto asked.

Morpheus could tell she was nervous. She was making small talk. He thought her cute when nervous, but chalked it up to being a week since they had seen each other.

"It went well," he grinned. "Did the other paintings come in, the ones sent by mistake?"

Then, Kallisto realized the paintings had to be just a family thing. They were probably made for them to put in one of their mansions, and they were sent out by accident.

"Uh—Yeah," Kallisto stumbled over her words—her sounds.

Uh, yeah? When has Kallisto ever said "uh yeah"? Morpheus was curious, no. "What were they of? Please tell me they are not some mythological porn or something," his grin widened.

Kallisto blushed. "No, but I do think you'll find them interesting. Maybe not as interesting as I did, but attention-grabbing enough."

"Well, let me take a look." Morpheus was concerned. Not all artwork made of the gods was decent enough for his eyes, let alone Kallisto's.

"Ambrose."

"Yes?" he furrowed his brow at the strange sound in her voice.

"Maybe I should go before you look at them," Kallisto suggested.

Brow, still furrowed, Ambrose asked, "What could possibly be so bad that you do not want to be present when I see what they sent over? Blood, violence, porn—?"

Kallisto blushed crimson and grinned from his use of the word porn for the second time. "Tell me something," Kallisto lifted her chin with sudden resolution.

"Okay, what?" Ambrose asked. He was confused and concerned at Kallisto's uneasiness. She had never been this apprehensive around him as Morpheus or Ambrose.

"John told me once the artwork in this gallery is allegedly true likenesses of the gods and goddess they represent, is that true?" Kallisto let out a breath. *There, I said it or asked it.*

"Well," Morpheus was wondering where their conversation was going. "That is the story."

"Fine," Kallisto turned, walked to the front doors, and locked them. It was seven and finally, closing time. She sighed and resigned herself to seeing this through, no matter how uncomfortable she felt. She walked very close to Ambrose as she headed to the back room. She felt the heat radiating from his body as she passed and for a brief moment, she could have sworn she smelled lavender. Ambrose stood there staring after her in total confusion.

She looked over her shoulder, "Are you coming?"

Ambrose followed, a little uneasy. As soon as Kallisto turned on the light his eyes found the paintings. Each one propped against the wall. Staring out from the canvases were his brothers and himself. Morpheus stood transfixed, unable to speak.

"Well, I was wondering if this was something your parents paid to have done, or are you a Greek dream god?" Kallisto let out a practiced laugh, one meant to make light of the situation but wasn't convincing.

Morpheus turned to Kallisto slowly. "Am I the Greek dream god, who?" He needed her to ask the right question.

Kallisto laughed again. "I thought this was clever of your parents. I would like to have one made of me with the name Aphrodite engraved on the bottom."

She is not asking the right questions. How can I make her see—she is so close? Morpheus decided to tell the truth, or the parts he could. "To my knowledge, my parents never had our portraits painted." He crossed the five steps to place himself directly in front of Kallisto, mere inches from her body. "I need you to remember." With those five words, the words he said to her so many times as Morpheus, he bent his head and captured her lips with his. He placed his right hand flat on her back and pulled her hips against his hard frame with his other hand as he deepened their kiss, praying for all her memories to return.

Kallisto had complete clarity as soon as her body made full contact with his. His lips were full and soft, his body warm and hard, and he smelled of lavender and honeysuckle, just like Olympus.

Kallisto pulled out of the deep kiss leaving their lips touching enough to say one breathy word, "Morpheus!"

After a few moments of passionate kissing, Kallisto pulled away and pressed her face into his chest. She held him like she hadn't seen him in years and shook in shock. She allowed herself to cry—hard.

Morpheus' tears fell into Kallisto's hair. He pressed her into him and breathed her scent in deep. He had never felt so much love and relief in his three thousand years. He had wanted this moment for months, and it was proving to be as wonderful as he had imagined. His emotions were off the charts, and slight rumbles shook the gallery.

Several minutes passed as they held each other tightly and savored the moment. "You know, I think I've always known, deep down. Why didn't you tell me?" Kallisto asked, still overcome with happy tears.

"I was bound to stay silent. I have no idea where these paintings came from, but I thank whoever painted them and sent them here. I love you, Kallisto, and it has been a special kind of Hades to be with you as Ambrose and not be able to do this, not be able to tell you," Morpheus' voice broke.

"Morpheus, I have something important I need to tell you. You may feel differently about me once I do, but I didn't know any of this until last night."

"You have bigger news than three paintings of the Greek dream gods, one being of your boss with an inscription saying the name of your lover?"

"Strangely enough, yes—yes, I do," Kallisto answered without hesitation.

Chapter XXII

Fear

Morpheus waved his hand and conjured a dark brown leather chaise. Kallisto giggled when he picked her up and placed her gently on the lounge, and joined her without letting her go. He was not about to take his hands off her. He was afraid if he did, everything would vanish because it was all too good to be real. He gave her another long, hot kiss. She giggled and pushed him back an entire inch. "Conjuring furniture, hum, this could prove to be a very interesting gift," Kallisto gave Morpheus a grin making his body tighten.

Before he could reply with another kiss, Kallisto put the palm of her hand against his chest.

"I do need to tell you this," Kallisto said, still giggling. She was happier than she'd ever been in her life.

"Okay, you talk while I—" he pressed his lips to the hollow of her neck.

Kallisto groaned in complete satisfaction. "You cannot—do that—I must tell you this."

Morpheus whimpered and stuck out his bottom lip. Kallisto smiled. "Give me fifteen minutes, and I'll just give you the highlights."

"Okay, but I am not letting you go. Here lie down." Morpheus pulled her down to lay her head on his chest. He ran his fingers through her long black hair as she began her story.

An hour later, she'd finished. Morpheus interrupted only twice; once, when she told him about Ares, he let out a few swear words and questioned whether Ares touched her or said anything inappropriate. That had taken them into a conversation about how he was going to kill Ares for scaring her. The second time was when she had told him about Hera sending Ares to kill her grandmother's sick father. That had spurred him into another tirade about Ares. That had been his confirmation as to why Ares was questioning her.

Surprisingly, he didn't interrupt when she told him about Zeus being her grandfather. When the story of her lineage was over, he told her he wondered what god she was related to, and it was no surprise to him it had been Zeus; after all, Zeus *was* a bit of a playboy.

"What made you think I was connected to a god?" Kallisto tilted her head to see the crystal blue eyes from her dreams. How could she not have known? Everything was so clear now. When she thought of her times with Morpheus on Olympus, in Greece, and in her room, she remembered his face as if it was always there. The block was removed with his kiss.

"I knew after you appeared on Olympus, by your own volition, and Pegasus let you ride without a god. That was one of the most astounding acts I have ever witnessed on the Mount. The only ones allowed to come to Olympus by their own will are gods, demigods, daemons, and nymphs. You had to be one of those. So, when you told me Zeus was your grandfather, everything made sense. You know, he reluctantly allowed me to come here. The only reason he did was to ensure you were not harmed by the repeated pull from one form of consciousness to another. I was reckless with you, and he seemed more upset about that than where our relationship was going," Morpheus put the pieces Kallisto was missing into place. "I wondered why he was vested in my relationship with a human girl."

"So, he knows some things about me then?" Kallisto was curious about her grandfather, King of the Greek Pantheon.

"Well, he knows I am in love with you, and I would do anything for you. To gain the love and trust of a young god such as I, he would have to consider how amazing you are."

Kallisto thought for a moment. "I would like to meet him someday."

"If I had to bet, I would say the Fates are the ones who sent the paintings of us. I believe they wanted you to recognize me."

"Why would they do that?" Kallisto asked.

"They detest Hera. The Fates are less forgiving than their mother, Themis, one of Zeus' first wives. When prophecy stated, Themis' son would become greater than his father, Zeus left her. They had six daughters together. The Fates are three of those six. Themis tries to get along with Hera; however, The Fates despise her and blame Hera for their mother's sadness," Morpheus continued, giving Kallisto some behind-the-scenes details of the not-so-glamorous politics of his world.

"So, it seems I have many half-aunts and uncles?" Kallisto felt a little overwhelmed. Her head ached from the politics of Olympus. "Why do you think they wanted me to recognize you?"

"I believe they would do almost anything to get under Hera's skin. It seems the only threat she ever encountered regarding her husband was your grandmother. That is the only thing I can think of anyway. It is always possible Zeus put them up to it, though.

"Hera's never been a favorite of mine," Kallisto said

"I do not know the details of Hera's blackmail, but knowing her, I am almost certain she is holding your mother's life over Zeus and your grandmother. We know she did once, but she must still be holding that card. She is a bitch, and I would not put anything past her. She adores control and will do anything to keep it.

"I went from a normal teenage life I understood to a life of confusion, and now I find I'm related to a dysfunctional family of immortal beings," Kallisto buried herself into Morpheus' arms and felt content in the only part of her life that finally made some sense.

Morpheus lay on the chaise content, holding Kallisto as he thought about all they discussed. He never mentioned he would have to renounce his godhood to stay with her. That was not an issue he wanted to think about for the moment—he was finally happy.

For the next couple of hours, Kallisto questioned Morpheus about the gods and all the changes he saw in the world over his lifetime. She had so many questions, barely letting him answer one before she popped out with another one. Morpheus laughed at her exuberance and answered every inquiry with a smile on his face—until her phone rang, it was Amanda.

"Did you realize it's almost nine at night, and I've never paced as much as I have since I left the gallery? What are you doing anyway?" Amanda asked anxiously.

"I'm lying on a beautiful chaise in the back room of the gallery, trying to hold onto what virtue I still have." Kallisto giggled. Morpheus spread kisses over her neck, around her cheekbone, and on top of her eyelids.

"Kallisto Nalani, are you getting frisky with your boss?"

"Yes, and with the god of my dreams," Kallisto giggled again.

"Are you telling me—?"

"Yes, I am."

"If he is Morpheus—then Christos—?"

"Yep, it looks like the Christos you are always complaining about is—a—god," Kallisto drove the truth straight to Amanda's core.

"Kalli, I'm happy for you. I need to go," Amanda hung up the phone without explaining her strange behavior.

"Amanda practically hung up on me," Kallisto looked from the phone still in her hand to Morpheus, who was twirling a piece of her black hair around his index finger. "She sounded shocked and possibly sad by the admission you and your brother are gods."

"Maybe it has more to do with Christos being Phantasos," Morpheus supplied, transfixed on his finger playing with her hair.

"She's been acting strange lately and always seems so tired. Not like her at all," Kallisto said.

"That is interesting," Morpheus acknowledged what Kallisto was saying and made a mental note to look into things closer when he was not quite so busy.

Kallisto's cell rang again. This time it was her mother, and she wasn't happy. She questioned her daughter's whereabouts, "You know you cannot be alone right now. What if Ares returns, or Hera, or for Zeus' sake, some other salaried god-like creature that Hera decides to deploy?"

"Mom, I'm not alone, uh—" Kallisto had difficulty admitting the impossible. "Morpheus is with me."

❧ ❧

"Oh, I see. So, he is with you in our realm. Bring him to me, now!" Thia hung up and waited the five seconds it took for Morpheus to materialize with her daughter in her family room.

Standing with her arms crossed, Thia glared at the Greek god who had stolen the affections of her daughter's heart. The same god she trusted to help Kallisto with the tragedy of her father's disappearance. Thia wasn't too pleased to see how possessively Morpheus held her daughter around her waist. To her astonishment, he didn't flinch under her scrutiny.

Morpheus wasn't about to let Kallisto go. He would not risk it after months of her forgetting him when she returned to her realm. No, he refused to take chances. He didn't think he could go back to that after the last three hours they spent together and the long road it took to get those few precious hours.

"Wow, that was incredible and could come in handy," Kallisto exclaimed, unaware of the silent exchange her mom and Morpheus were engaging in. She shook her head to clear it. She had done things like a flash from one spot and materialized in another place in her dreams, but never in her realm of consciousness.

"What do you think you are allowing my daughter to fall in love with you?"

"Mom, what are you doing?" Kallisto asked, in shock and embarrassment.

"He was supposed to help you out of a hard time, not cause one," Thia answered her daughter.

"Mrs. Nalani, I had no intention of falling in love with your daughter or her with me. Your daughter is an amazing woman who stole my heart the moment I appeared in her dreams. I had no idea of her affiliation with the gods, let alone Zeus," Morpheus answered.

"Thia, don't. He obviously loves her," Zenovia scolded her daughter as she made her way into the room, having heard everything.

"He is the reason Hera is breathing down our backs."

"How so, Mom?" Kallisto was getting angry.

"If he had just helped you and gone on his way if he had never taken you to Olympus, Hera would have no reason to look into our lives."

"If he hadn't fallen in love with me, Dad wouldn't be alive," Kallisto was not sure how she knew that, but it made perfect sense.

Thia's eyes widened as she looked from her daughter to Morpheus, "is that true?"

"Yes. I could not stand to see her so distraught. I made a deal with Hades to get your husband back. That is why he was found so far from the site of the storm, and that is why no one else was ever found. He is never to know that, though. You have to swear."

"I'm sorry, Morpheus. I—I owe you an apology and a life debt." Thia's eyes burned with the knowledge that her husband had been dead.

"You owe me nothing. I did it for Kallisto. Above all, she deserves happiness."

Thia walked to the sofa and sat, her anger gone. The past few days held more tension than all her 92 years. She finally told her daughter the truth, the family secret she had kept from her; Hera was breathing down their backs, Zeus must know his granddaughter was on Olympus, and to top it off—Kallisto was in love with a god. Thia had always thought the gods were *love 'em and leave 'em* beings. That wasn't ever Zenovia's story—that was her perception of it. She thought her mother didn't want to hurt her feelings, so she created the story of Hera backing her into the corner and then hearing Thia's heartbeat. Now she realized her mother was telling her the truth, and the guilt ate at her. Shame for how she viewed her father, guilt for not protecting her daughter, and guilt for not believing her mother.

Kallisto pulled gently away from Morpheus to console her mother. Thia cried on her daughter's shoulder. "Mom, I know this is hard, but I love him, and he loves me. I truly believe with all my heart Hera will leave us alone."

Thia gained control of her emotions and hugged her daughter. "What are we going to do, mama?" Thia asked Zenovia.

That night, the four sat up late discussing the day's events and tried to solve their Hera and Ares problem. Thia decided Morpheus could sleep downstairs on the couch, but he had to make a god-vow not to go into her daughter's room or her dreams.

That night Kallisto couldn't sleep. She felt like she was dying inside, knowing her dream god was sprawled out on her couch downstairs from her. *How could my own mother torture me this way?*

Hey, I am just glad you remember who I am and what I look like.

"Morpheus?" Kallisto whispered aloud.

Shhhh. You can use your mind to speak with me. Your mother is bound to hear you and think we are together.

How can we communicate this way?

We are gods, baby. Kallisto received a mental picture of Morpheus wagging his eyebrows and couldn't hold in her laughter.

But I'm only a demigod twice removed or something like that.

You are the grandchild of Zeus; believe me, you hold a lot more power than you think.

Mom said you couldn't come to me in my dreams, but what if I came to you? Can you do that?

I went to Olympus, why not, you are only downstairs, surely, I can make that.

Not in my house, you won't—Thia chimed in.

Mom?

As you are the granddaughter of Zeus, I am his daughter. Don't underestimate my abilities, little girl. I was once young and in love—I'm not stupid.

Good night, Morpheus, Kallisto mentally said.

Good night dea femminile.

Good night you two. Thia couldn't help but smile, but of course, she would never allow her daughter to see her amusement.

The next few days were normal. Well, as normal as they could be when your boyfriend's a dream god who happens to volunteer at your school, helping your history teacher embark on his everything Greek curriculum. When your enemy is a scorned Olympian goddess whose son is the Greek god of war, and at his mother's beck and call, and happens to be your half-uncle. Okay, they weren't as normal as the word normal would imply, but they were wonderful, except for Amanda, who wasn't at school on Monday and looked sick when she showed up on Tuesday. Not sick exactly, but something was wrong. Her eyes were red-rimmed, her hair was a mess, and she looked exhausted.

"Amanda, you look like shit," Kallisto stated bluntly.

"Thanks, Kalli. I love you too," Amanda yawned.

"I called you last night, and your mother said you didn't feel good and went to bed early, but you look like you haven't slept in days," Kallisto interrogated.

"I—I've just not been sleeping very well, and I've been—" before she could finish, the bell rang, and Amanda stopped explaining, and they headed to class.

Kallisto noticed the fear on Amanda's face when the bell rang. *What could make her look so panicked?* Kallisto followed Amanda when she felt that familiar sense of being watched. She quickly spun around to see if Morpheus was behind her. No, only a couple of juniors headed to their class. When Kallisto walked into the classroom, she saw Morpheus talking with Mr. Wright and Amanda at her desk with her forehead lying on top of her folded hands flat on her desk. *Something isn't right. Really, not right.*

Amanda kept her head on her desk the entire class, and Kallisto became increasingly worried about her friend, who was always upbeat and sarcastic, not worn out, and without comment. As Kallisto watched her friend off and on, she noticed a light bruise on her cheek. No, maybe it was the light. *My mind is messing with me,* but Kallisto couldn't shake the feeling something terrible was going on with Amanda.

Determined to get to the bottom of her friend's troubles, she pulled Morpheus to the side and told him what she witnessed, and she was pretty sure she saw the shadow of a bruise under Amanda's makeup.

"It looks like a bruise along her left cheekbone. Morpheus, I'm worried. She's not acting like herself—at all," Kallisto's voice shook with concern. "Oh yeah, were you watching me before I entered class this morning?"

"Watching you?"

"Yes, were you watching me the way you used to?"

"No, why?"

"Because I felt someone watching me. It felt just like it did when you used to watch me."

"I have no orb. Besides, I knew you were in the hall about to come in," Morpheus sounded concerned. "I noticed Amanda's behavior also. I do not know what is going on, but believe me, I will find out."

"I'm going to talk to Amanda," Kallisto looked around and saw they were alone, so she quickly stole a kiss.

He arched a brow, "Do not start what you cannot finish. I am liable to stop time and take you here and now."

"You can't do that. Can you?" Kallisto looked a little worried.

"Kiss me again, and you will find out."

"Ambrose, could you come with me to the library?" Mr. Wright walked in and asked.

Kallisto whispered, "Saved by the bell—or teacher, rather."

"Damn it," Morpheus uttered under his breath as Kallisto left the room.

Kallisto found Amanda and took her by the arm, "Come with me."

"Where to?"

"We're ditching classes for the rest of the day and going to the coffee shop on Main Street. You look like you could use a latté," Kallisto, still holding onto Amanda's arm, led her out the senior door, into the parking lot, and to her car.

"Why don't I follow you?" Amanda suggested.

"Amanda, don't take this the wrong way, but you don't look fit for anything, including driving. I'll bring you back or have Morpheus bring your car to my house."

"He doesn't have keys," Amanda protested.

"He's a god. He doesn't need keys."

There was silence between the girls all the way to the coffee shop. Kallisto knew Amanda needed to get her thoughts in order. Amanda had to know she was about to be interrogated. Kallisto's thoughts strayed to her mother and grandmother.

"My treat, find us a seat, and I'll get you a coffee and a pick-me-up dessert," Kallisto directed.

Kallisto brought a tray of fruit-topped pastries and two very large lattés to the table, where Amanda stared out the window, her mind far away. Kallisto placed all the tray's contents on the table and cleared her throat before Amanda finally looked up.

"Okay, Amanda, spill it; what the hell is going on with you?" Kallisto's tone held a mixture of demand and worry.

It seemed like minutes went by before Amanda answered with her own question. "What did you say Ares looked like?"

"Who?"

"Ares. What did he look like when you saw him at the gallery?" Amanda's voice was faint. Kallisto had to strain to hear her.

"Why do you—?" Kallisto didn't get her question out before Amanda looked her square in the eye and repeated herself.

"What does he look like?"

"Tawny skin, ice blue eyes, bright white teeth, hair as black as a raven's wing, and a chiseled body you can see through his clothes. He is gorgeous and very dangerous," Kallisto gave her the basics, but what she hoped would be enough to get her to explain why she was questioning her about Ares. Surprising Kallisto, Amanda began crying. *Amanda, crying? Not normal at all!*

Amanda spoke through her tears. "It started a week or so ago. One night, I fell asleep on my bed but woke up in a mostly dark chamber. It was so cold and damp. Fear shot through me, and I went back and forth between being afraid and thinking I was in a dream. So, I ran my hand down the chamber wall, and it was too real, not dreamlike at all. There was a man on the other side of the room. I couldn't quite see him, he was concealed in a shadow, but I could tell by his silhouette he was well-built and super tall. It was his voice... he had a deep sultry voice. He questioned me all night about you. As I said, I thought I was dreaming or hoped I was dreaming."

"What else happened?"

"Nothing, but when I woke up the next morning, I was so tired and sore, like I'd run for miles."

Kallisto started putting two and two together. "Are you saying you think the man in the shadows was Ares?"

"Well, there's more, a lot more." Amanda took a sip of her latté before she continued. "Several days went by, and I forgot about my dream. Then it happened again. I tried to wake myself up, but the man just laughed. He said I was awake and I would stay in the damp chamber unless I answered his questions. Again, I woke from my nightmare tired, sore, and with the smell of that damp cellar on my skin. It smelled like—like death. This time I was terrified."

"What questions did he ask?" Kallisto inquired, her mother's warning coursing through her mind.

"I don't remember—well, I only remember one," Amanda looked like she didn't want to tell Kallisto the one question. "He asked me what my, and I quote, "slutty ass" was doing with Phantasos."

Kallisto's eyebrow furrowed, "What? That makes no sense. Why would he ask you about Phantasos?"

Amanda took a deep breath and answered. "I'd had sensual dreams about Christos. This was right before we uncrated the paintings. But I hadn't dreamed of Christos since I found out. So, I knew my dreams of him were just dreams. Unlike you, I remembered everything when I woke up, his face and all—besides, in real life, we can hardly stand each other." Amanda was talking fast, the way Kallisto did when she was nervous.

"Why haven't you told me about all of this?"

"Let me get it all out, then I'll beg for forgiveness," Amanda said.

"Sorry, please continue."

"I don't know why he was asking about Phantasos, but he sounded almost—jealous, which freaked me out even more. I hadn't even seen his face at that point."

Kallisto heard the "at that point" and waited, holding her breath for the rest of the story.

"He left me alone, in the dark chamber, for hours. Then you found out about your family and Morpheus, which led to my realization about Phantasos. Who I haven't heard from since."

Kallisto expected that Amanda had a thing for Phantasos; she always had a thing for a good-looking man, and he was definitely handsome. However, she denied any interest in him, which was unusual.

"This weekend, I went through hell," If possible, Amanda looked even more drained. "He came for me after I went to bed Saturday night. I wasn't asleep this time, so I knew all the *dreams* of that chamber, filled with the air of death, and the man in the shadows was real. This time he didn't take me straight to the cellar. He loomed over me while I was on my bed. He stroked my cheek and told me to stand. I tried to scream, but he put his hand over my mouth and pulled me straight from my bed to his body." Amanda stopped, and her eyes filled with tears.

Kallisto put her hand on Amanda's, "You can take a few minutes. Don't force this if you need a little time. I'll be with you."

"No, I need to finish," Amanda took another sip of her coffee and continued. "He pulled me to his body, still covering my mouth. He smelled of lavender and honeysuckle, just like you described Olympus. I knew then I was dealing with a god or an entity that wasn't quite human. He made me promise not to scream by threatening my family. I nodded, and he removed his hand but didn't let me go. Instead, he spun me around, and I looked into the ice-blue eyes of one of the most gorgeous beings I'd ever seen. A gorgeous man who threatened to kill my family, so even my hormones were pissed. I found him completely repulsive," Amanda took another sip of her coffee. She was no longer on the brink of tears. Instead, she was looking more like herself—brazen.

"He flashed us to a beautiful room that glowed warmly with candlelight. The smell of lavender and honeysuckle increased; I was in shock—literally, I pinched myself," Amanda showed Kallisto the bruise on her arm where she had indeed pinched herself—hard.

"You were on Olympus," Kallisto stated.

"The man, god, whatever," Amanda continued, "told me he had been watching me for some time and wanted me. And when I say wanted—I mean *wanted*," Amanda went from brazen back to distress.

Kallisto's eyes widened as she gasped.

"I told him to kiss off. Well, that wasn't the word I used, but the word I used was not meant to be repeated. So, he hit me. See?" Amanda pointed to her cheek, to the exact spot Kallisto suspected to be a bruise.

"He did what?" Kallisto's stomach turned.

"Yes, he hit me. Then he told me, my little girlfriend, meaning you, would regret her decisions, and so would I if I didn't start giving him the information and—" Amanda hung her head, stopping momentarily, not wanting to say it, "and the other things he wanted."

"What did he say he wanted?"

"He didn't. He left the room and didn't come back for almost twenty-four hours. I don't know how he managed to keep mom from knowing I was gone, but she didn't know when I returned. I came back last night. I was in shock and only managed a shower before I finally fell asleep for a few hours."

"So, you think the man was Ares?"

"Yes, the man you described to me was the same one I was with yesterday, the one who wanted me and threatened you. He's a nutcase. Kallisto—I'm scared."

Kallisto laid her hand across the bracelet Morpheus gave her to let him know she needed him. Their bond had grown inexpressibly over the last three days.

Morpheus and Thia guessed that now Kallisto knew of both her lineage and Morpheus' identity, her powers helped forge a tighter bond.

"Kalli?" Amanda spoke very softly. "Ares is crazy, and so is his mother. If he can take me to Olympus, threaten my family, try to seduce me, and hit me—all in a matter of minutes—he's capable of anything."

"Does anyone else know about this?" Kallisto asked.

"No, I don't think so. I didn't see anyone else—but hell, he took me from my own home for more than twenty-four hours and was able to keep it from my mom. Who knows what all the gods are capable of." Amanda stated as she stood.

"Where do you think you're going? We haven't even begun to eat our desserts," Kallisto asked.

"To the restroom; that coffee made a beeline to my bladder. I'll be right back."

Amanda retreated to the restroom right as Morpheus showed up in response to the silent summons. Kallisto set in giving Morpheus the rundown of what Amanda told her. The more she spoke, the tighter his hands fisted. Before Kallisto finished, Morpheus took off running like a madman to the restrooms. He yelled for Amanda as he burst into the ladies' room to see Ares standing with Amanda in his arms, his hand over her mouth. Ares grinned, and before Morpheus could reach them, they vanished.

Chapter XXIII

Abduction

Kallisto burst into the restroom as Morpheus turned back to the door. He looked pale and in shock. "He—he took Amanda."

Kallisto didn't have to ask who he was. She knew by the look in Morpheus' eyes. She let out a scream, "NO!"

With speech barely above a whisper, Morpheus cradled Kallisto to his chest and said, "we have to remain calm. I will call Phantasos, and he can call others to aid us. You should call your mother." Morpheus' eyes were full of worry. If anything were to happen to Amanda, Kallisto would blame herself.

"Why is he messing with Amanda?" Kallisto asked.

"I am not sure, but he waited until I saw him, so he is expecting retaliation. I felt the spell he spun over the coffee shop, masking his presence from mortals. He knew I was here." He pulled his cell phone from his pocket and called his brother. Morpheus relayed the information Kallisto told him. When he got to the part about Ares taking Amanda, Phantasos flashed himself to the coffee shop, even knowing the possible ramifications. If a mortal saw him, there would be hell to pay from Zeus.

Phantasos looked angrier than Morpheus had seen him in over a century; he was shaking. Kallisto found the anger a little strange but said nothing. She only wanted Amanda back, and his rage seemed to suit his overall demeanor, but anger over someone he didn't necessarily like seemed odd.

"Where did he take her? Did he say anything at all? Why are we standing here?" Three questions ran from Phantasos' mouth without a breath or a pause for answers.

"I believe he has her on Olympus, maybe at his place," Morpheus answered.

"Again, what are we waiting for?" Phantasos repeated, gritting his teeth. Kallisto realized Phantasos was angrier than she first thought. His muscles rippled under his long sleeve shirt, bunching up and preparing for a fight.

"He waited for me to see him take her. He is taunting us, and I think this may be a trap to get to Kallisto and her family," Morpheus said.

"If that is so, then why did he not take her, her mother, or her grandmother instead of Amanda?" Phantasos asked.

"I'm not sure that's his only motive here," Kallisto answered Phantasos' question.

"What do you mean?" Phantasos turned his attention to Kallisto.

"When Amanda told me about Ares, well, he hit her because she rejected him—physically," Kallisto didn't know Phantasos well enough to go into detail.

"You did not tell me he hit her. So, her cheek *was* bruised."

By this time, Phantasos was red with anger. Kallisto could've sworn his eyes flashed red.

"He hit her?" He bit the question through clenched teeth.

"Yes, he wants her for information on me, and he *wants* her for himself."

"I am going!" Phantasos looked at Morpheus, then flashed from the coffee shop, still not caring if he was seen.

"Shit!" Morpheus exclaimed.

"Go. I'll tell Mom and Grandma what's happening. Please, Morpheus, don't do anything crazy," Kallisto gently kissed him on his lips and pushed at his arm, "Go!"

Morpheus, not wanting to risk being seen, went to the men's room and flashed himself to his brother's side.

Phantasos was in his bedchamber, changing clothes and putting on the knives he carried whenever the need presented itself. The need often presented itself before he fell in love with Marissa. He had not done anything with them since her death. He donned black leather pants to protect his legs and a black long-sleeved t-shirt. He strapped knives to the insides of both forearms. He had a dagger concealed in his boot and a larger dagger strapped to his thigh. The blades were not only lethal to mortals but immortals alike; forged from the metals of Atlantis, they were lethal to all beings.

Phantasos was a cunning warrior. A millennia ago, creatures formed by an evil deity invaded the dreams of mortals. The creatures were large, hairy, and very intelligent. Phantasos and Morpheus, along with their brother Phobetor, hunted them down in the dream world and exterminated each one. It took the better part of three hundred years to eradicate the evil beings, but the three dream gods proved themselves warriors. Morpheus was the one to take down the evil deity who created the foul beasts, earning him the allegiance of all the gods of Olympus. Phantasos and Phobetor killed thousands of the creatures making the two brothers powerful in their own right. Since then, no god has ever tested the Oneiroi's ability to uphold justice—until now.

Morpheus manifested his weapons just as Phantasos. Both brothers carried swords, which were fabricated by gods to be wielded by gods. The blades were 14 inches long with blood grooves running their lengths. Swords would only be used against Ares if they could get close enough. The gods usually fought each other a little differently than mortals. They each wielded their own unique powers with a mere thought; even so, it would still be a bloody battle.

"Phantasos, you should let me go. He wants information about Kallisto. I am sure he is acting on the orders of his mother. I will go to her and put a stop to this," Morpheus suggested.

Ares is a bastard and needs his ass kicked for hitting a woman, especially a mortal woman—Especially Amanda, my—" Phantasos paused. "He will be punished." "You go meet with Hera. I am going to get Amanda," Phantasos' maddened eyes glared, and his nose wrinkled in a snarl.

"And here I thought you could hardly stand to be in the same room with her. Just be careful," Morpheus accepted he would not be able to convince Phantasos to let him go to Hera first. The brothers grasped each other by their forearms, a sign of respect between warriors, and they went their separate ways to battle their enemies.

Phantasos arrived in the great room of Ares' mansion. He walked, covering the first floor, and found no one, not even a servant. He made his way through the next three floors to no avail. *Could she be in the dungeon?* He hoped not. He tensed and quickly made his way to the basement, dreading what he would find. That was where Ares was known to keep prisoners who he tortured.

Morpheus was shown to Hera's throne room by a male daemon. He grinned, thinking about Amanda and what her assessment of the daemon would be.

He had to bring her back to Kallisto. He knew Kallisto would die with grief if anything were to happen to her best friend.

"Well-well-well, Morpheus, to what do I owe this honor?" Hera sneered.

"You know what brings me. You have Amanda, Kallisto's dearest friend. Where is she?" Morpheus growled.

"I do not have her, but I have someone who may bring you more interest. It would be best if you worked with me. I had to seek out Zeus' dreams from another," Hera gave Morpheus a wicked grin, making his skin crawl.

"Who do you have, Hera?"

With a wave of Hera's hand, the mirrors on the wall showed a vast room with a figure curled on the floor. The figure was small and had long, silky black hair. Morpheus swallowed; he knew that sweater.

"Kallisto!" Morpheus ran to the mirrors screaming.

"She cannot hear you; she cannot hear anyone except who I say she can hear. You should have known better than allow her out of your sight. She did not make it out of that quaint coffee shop's parking lot," Hera looked blissful.

"You bitch, where is she?" Morpheus' eyes went black, and the room began to shake.

"Now, now, Morpheus, calm yourself." Hera mocked, "I have a deal to make with you."

"I am going to kill you, and then I am going to kill your son," Morpheus was trying to control the tremors shooting from his body through the floor, causing everything to shudder.

Hera gave a high-pitched laugh, exuding evil. "I do not die so easily. You see, even if she is the grandchild of my husband, her life will never mean as much to him as mine does. If you kill me, she will die, and so will you and your two menacing brothers."

"Why are you doing this?"

"I told them to stay away. I told—" Hera stopped as a bright flash pierced the room.

Thia appeared before Hera.

"What have you done with my daughter?"

Hera was momentarily stunned by the unexpected turn of events; she had not reacted in time to stop Thia's hands from wrapping around her neck. Once Hera gained her bearings, she flashed from Thia's hold.

"How dare you touch me! You are nothing but a bastard daughter created by mistake—a demigod. You cannot harm me."

"Never underestimate the power of a mother. I promise if you do not release my daughter, I *will* kill you with my bare hands," Thia's eyes turned crimson.

"Like I told your daughter's lover," Hera pointed an elegant finger at Morpheus, "if you kill me, she will die. You can see her—look." Hera's finger went from Morpheus to the image on the wall of mirrors.

Thia ran to the mirrors and pressed her palms to the solid cold surface, begging her daughter to hear her.

"Let me speak to her," Thia demanded.

"I am quite sorry, you see, she cannot speak; she is in a dream state, one not even her hero can break," Hera's laugh echoed through the marbled room.

"Where is Amanda?" Morpheus questioned. The room was still shaking from his anger. He needed to calm himself to think. There had to be a way to get to Kallisto and find Amanda.

"She is with your beloved. Well, she is on one side of the clear wall begging her to wake—much like the two of you are. Funny, is it not? If your mother had not put her hands on my husband," Hera glared at Thia, "then you would not exist, and your daughter would not experience the pain she is about to start going through."

Those words spurred anger so deep in Morpheus that the pillars holding up the staircase to the throne began to shake harder and crack. Worry briefly crossed Hera's face. She flashed herself from her throne as the platform crashed to the floor. Large chunks of marble, diamonds, and dust flew everywhere.

"You should have controlled that anger of yours better, Morpheus. You know Kallisto will be the one to suffer for your lack of control," Hera looked from the rubble that was once the beautiful throne Zeus had given her.

Phantasos flashed beside his brother. "Amanda is not at Ares'— and neither is he."

Morpheus nodded toward the mirrors where Kallisto's body lay curled on a hard floor.

"She is on the other side of the wall beside Kallisto. She is alive and screaming for Kallisto to wake. When I brought Kallisto here, I breached a deal we knew nothing of."

Morpheus' head jerked up when he heard the sound that pierced his soul. Kallisto was screaming, still curled on the floor in pain.

"Stop this!" Thia screamed as she ran toward Hera.

Hera raised her hand to release power. To Hera's disbelief, the power never left her hand. "No, this cannot be."

Thia gave an evil laugh this time, making her sound like she was on the border of insanity. Thia drew back her fist and knocked Hera fifteen feet into a trembling column.

"Give her to me, or I'll kill you, Hera. I don't care if Zeus kills me for it. Give me my daughter."

"STOP!" Zeus appeared, placing himself between his daughter and his wife. He took in the chaos. Thia's pupils were dark red, the room shook under Morpheus' anger, and Hera's mouth was bleeding. "Stop this madness."

Thia couldn't believe her eyes. Her father was standing in front of her. She was looking at him for the first time.

"I'll kill her if she doesn't give me my daughter."

Zeus spun on Hera. "Where is my granddaughter?"

"She is being taught a lesson. She came to Olympus more than once, and one of those times was on her own. She is going against the deal I made with your mistress. I have the right," Hera met Zeus' anger-filled eyes with her own.

"You will give her back to her mother—now!" Zeus' voice boomed, commanding and full of authority.

"She has Kallisto *and* Kallisto's best friend," Morpheus spoke up.

"The spell is complete. I cannot give her to her mother or you," Hera grinned as she glared into Zeus' eyes.

Zeus turned to Thia with visible concern.

He was as handsome as her mother had said. She gasped when she saw her daughter's eyes on his face. "Your eyes! Kallisto has your eyes." Tears ran down Thia's face, and her knees buckled. Before she hit the floor, her father caught her and carried her to a golden chaise that manifested before him.

"Hera used old magic on the room Kallisto is in. Not even I can break the spell, but Morpheus can." Zeus turned to Morpheus.

"How?" Morpheus asked.

"Remember when I asked you if you would be willing to do anything for her.? Are you willing to suffer, lose your godhood, or even die to protect the woman writhing on that stone floor?" Zeus pointed to Kallisto, who was now in so much pain her body jerked uncontrollably.

"Of course. She means everything to me. Tell me how?"

"You must leave this realm and go to the one she is in," Zeus answered.

"Which one is that? How do I get there?"

"Follow your heart."

With a triumphant male voice came, "What is the problem? They are only human?"

"Ares," Phantasos said.

Morpheus stood, confused, and turned to see his brother flash from his side to the other side of the room before Ares, who had just entered the fray and plunged his sword through Ares' side.

"No!" Hera cried.

Thia was on Ares faster than even the gods in the room could see. She manifested a weapon and held it to Ares' neck. "Hera, send Morpheus to my daughter and Amanda. If you don't, I'll kill him. By the way," she continued coldly, "this is a knife forged from nightmares and Atlantean steel. It can kill a god if it so much as touches their blood. So, hold still, big brother," Thia bit the usually endearing term from between her teeth.

Now sister, is this any way to meet your older brother?" Ares strained to speak.

"Quiet!" The booming voice of Zeus came as he pointed his index finger at Ares, rendering him speechless. "You are an idiot. She has a god killer at your throat."

"Move, Thia. I have him," Phantasos commanded.

"No, Phantasos, you are coming with me," Morpheus commanded above the commotion. He wanted Kallisto and Amanda returned, and he knew Phantasos would give up his godhood or die to save Amanda.

Morpheus walked over to his brother and grasped his forearm. As he did, he morphed into vapor taking his brother with him.

"I didn't know he could do that," Thia said as she held Ares around the throat.

"Hence the name he was given at birth—Morpheus. He is more powerful than anyone knows," Zeus turned to look at his wife and then back at his daughter, who continued to hold a knife to his son's throat.

"Thia, release him," Zeus commanded.

"No, he'll not be free until my girls are free," Thia growled.

"Ares will cause you no more trouble. I assure you, he will be dealt with accordingly. Now drop the knife and come here to me."

Thia thought about what she should do. By keeping the knife to Ares's throat, she made sure Hera stayed put *and* Zeus didn't retaliate. After all, Ares was their son, and Zeus had spent thousands of years with him and only five minutes with her. True, Ares was an asshole, but still, he was Zeus' son. She and her father didn't have a bond; they just shared DNA. Adrenaline ran through her veins, and she knew if she allowed herself to falter, she would be useless against an attack. With her knife to Ares' throat, she had the upper hand.

"How do I know you'll not harm my daughter or me?" Thia asked the god-king.

How could I harm you—you are my daughter, Thia. I loved your mother deeply. That is why Hera is doing this. You have to trust me.

Zeus' mouth hadn't moved, only his eyes, but Thia heard him answer her as clearly as if he had spoken aloud.

Thia let Ares go, and his body crashed to the floor. He was hemorrhaging from where Phantasos' blade had sunk into his side, and he could no longer stand.

Hera rushed to his side to stop her son's bleeding. "How dare you harm my son, he is a god, and you are nothing,"

"How dare you harm my daughter, a goddess," Thia shot back.

"She is no goddess, a demigod at best, which is one step from human," Hera sneered.

"No, the love was so great between my parents, I bypassed demi and went straight to god."

Thia chose to wield her power when she felt the pull from her daughter as she was taken from the parking lot. She willed herself to Olympus for the first time, guided by that pull. She felt the power she kept leashed when she appeared in the throne room. She held the power captive, not wanting to be found by Hera. The gloves came off when her daughter was placed in harm's way.

"That cannot be," Hera denied continuing to heal her son.

"It is true, Hera," Zeus answered.

Chapter XXIV

Aftermath

Morpheus appeared with his brother on the lawn of a great, dilapidated mansion. "Do you know where we are?" Phantasos asked. Morpheus slowly shook his head, "No, but I am not liking it."

"My gut tells me they are in there. We need to stay together. I do not like this either," Phantasos said.

The two brothers entered what appeared to be an abandoned structure. They started on the bottom floor and worked their way up the levels. After searching three floors, Morpheus paused, "Did you hear that?"

"Yes, it sounds like growling," Phantasos said.

The brothers rounded the corner to find a giant sphinx guarding a massive, mirrored door. Her lioness body was positioned to spring, as her eyes of different colors looked her intruders up and down. She had a light blue, almost white eye and an eye the color of blood. Morpheus and Phantasos pulled their swords at the same time.

"Let us by sphinx, my consort is in there, and we are here to return her and her best friend to earth."

"Earth, oh," the sphinx gave a shrilling laugh. "I did not know those two females were of so little value. And to think, I have been so hungry and did not eat them for fear they may have been worth something." The sphinx laid her feminine head down as she lowered her winged lioness body and serpent tail to the ground."

Morpheus walked forward, ready to attack the beast blocking his way. "Move."

"Why should I? The females are under my command, and I wish them to remain sleeping."

The sphinx's shrill feminine voice pained their ears.

"She is the granddaughter of Zeus and is not asleep; she is in pain. He has sent me to bring her home. Not even the sphinx wanted Zeus' wrath. Do you deny the ruler of the Mount his own flesh?"

"I suppose you may pass, but you only have ten minutes. If you go over that, you will be stuck here in my home with your women." The sphinx grinned.

She rose from the ground onto her padded feet, stepping to the side so the brothers could enter. "Remember, ten minutes, not a second more," the sphinx taunted.

Phantasos followed Morpheus into the damp, dark corridor. Lit torches hung on the walls, casting ominous shadows. It took the brothers at least three minutes to find the correct room where Morpheus finally felt Kallisto's presence.

She is here," he pointed to a chamber on his left.

"That means Amanda must be in the corridor on the other side. You get Kallisto, and I will get Amanda," Phantasos said.

Morpheus concentrated and once again turned to vapor. Phantasos watched as his brother went under the door of the corridor where they thought Amanda was being kept. He came back under the door mere seconds later and confirmed her presence.

"She looks bad, Phantasos."

Again, Morpheus turned to vapor and entered the room he knew held Kallisto. Crumpled on the ground groaning, she looked so tiny. Morpheus drew in a breath, almost afraid to look at her face, especially since he had just seen Amanda's. He gently rolled her onto her back to survey the physical damage. She, to his huge relief, looked as beautiful as ever.

"Morpheus?" Kallisto questioned in a whispered voice. "Is it really you?"

Kallisto's body tightened and jerked as pain ripped through her veins.

"I am going to help you, and then we are getting out of here," Morpheus clenched his teeth to keep the profanity from flying. He could not stand to see his beloved Kallisto in so much pain.

"You have to leave; they'll kill you," Kallisto begged through her pain.

"Shhh, you are about to feel extreme heat enter your body. It may be uncomfortable, but we do not have time for me to take this slow. I have about two minutes before we have to head out of here, or we will not make the time limit."

Morpheus placed one hand on Kallisto's forehead and splayed the other over her heart. As he spoke words in ancient Greek, he released heat through

Kallisto's body, making her writhe even more. As the heat subsided, Morpheus slumped slightly, and Kallisto sat up.

"What did you do, Morpheus?"

"I gave you the greatest gift I could—my godhood," Morpheus sounded weak. He sounded—human.

"You did what?" Kallisto sounded strong.

"We do not have time to talk. We must get through the tunnel. Phantasos should be waiting outside the door," Morpheus directed Kallisto with a nod.

"How do we get out of here?" Kallisto asked.

"You, my love, just concentrate on the door and imagine it off its hinges."

Kallisto did as Morpheus said, and to her astonishment, the door flew off its hinges to the other side of the room.

"How did I do that?"

"My powers have been added to those you possess as a demigod. You are very powerful now, so be gentle," Morpheus, despite the danger, made Kallisto smile with his sexy half-grin.

They met Phantasos in the hall, where he was cradling Amanda's barely conscious form. To Kallisto's horror, Amanda looked like she had been beaten. Her right eye was black, almost completely swollen shut, blood dripped from her nostrils, and bruises started showing across her arms. She moaned mostly intangible words; sometimes, you could make out Kallisto and Phantasos' names.

"What happened to her?" Kallisto asked as anger surged through her.

"Ares must like hitting women," Phantasos said through gritted teeth, "so when I return to Olympus, I plan on hitting him—a lot."

"We need to go—Now—we have two minutes—at most, to make it back through a maze that took us three minutes to get through," Morpheus turned and led the way down the hall.

By the time the four reached the entrance, the sphinx was standing on all fours, blocking their escape. "You are thirty-seven seconds late. It looks like I will be having guests for a long time," the sphinx let out a shrilling laugh.

Kallisto looked at Morpheus for confirmation—he nodded. She raised her hands above her head and shot the sphinx across the room with a bolt of red lightning. The sphinx lay unconscious or dead; none of the party wanted to find out. Phantasos gave Morpheus a questioning look and started to ask, but Morpheus explained before he could.

"The only way I knew to heal her from the magic so we could take her home was to give her my godhood. She is now more powerful than any of us, and when I say any, I mean all gods except her grandfather.

Phantasos blinked back his shock. "You are no longer a god?"

"Nope," Morpheus replied, "and that means that you," he looked at Kallisto, "will have to take us back to Olympus, as I cannot go there unless taken by a god."

"Why can't Phantasos take us?" Kallisto asked.

"Uh, I am holding Amanda, and—you wield more power than me," he said under his breath.

"Imagine Olympus and your mother. She is there now; take us to her," Morpheus answered Kallisto's questioning look.

"My mother is on Olympus?"

"Yes, she—well, she is a lot more powerful than we thought—she is not demi. Turns out, being the daughter of Zeus means she is a full-blooded goddess," Morpheus answered.

Kallisto's eyes widened, "Why is she on Olympus?"

"She was going to kick Hera's ass," Phantasos supplied.

Kallisto had so many questions but was more worried about her mother fighting a goddess as conniving as Hera. She closed her eyes and willed herself and her companions back to Olympus. When she opened her eyes, she stood before her mother in a room that looked much like a war zone.

"Oh, baby! Are you okay? How's Amanda? Where were you?" Thia wrapped her arms around Kallisto's neck, unable to hold back the tears.

"I was so scared, and I went through some pain, but I'm okay. Morpheus saved me, and Phantasos has Amanda. She doesn't look so good, though. Ares hurt her very bad this time," Kallisto said.

"This time?" Zeus asked, surprised by the revelation.

Kallisto turned to the voice, and her eyes went wide. She knew who the tall, handsome bearded man was. He looked just like the paintings hanging in the Gallery of the gods. She stared into eyes identical to her own, amazed he was real.

"Yes, he's been harassing her, and the time before, he hit her across her cheek because she wouldn't see to his carnal needs," Kallisto sounded disgusted.

Ares was the god of war with a bad reputation. Stories were full of his cruel exploits. His looks earned him popularity among women, mortal and immortal. Women loved catching his eye, but if they rejected his advances once his eye was caught, he would take advantage of their weaknesses. If the woman was strong-willed, the rumor was he beat them into submission. It was no longer a rumor; it was now a fact.

"He will pay for his misdeeds, I assure you. How are you?" Zeus asked Kallisto.

Kallisto was surprised. He sounded concerned. "I'll be okay. I now seem to have the power to do anything. I just don't know how to use it," Kallisto cut her eyes to Morpheus.

"I see," Zeus answered and turned to look at the youngest dream god. "So, you told the truth. You were willing to do anything for her."

"Yes, and I would do it again," Morpheus answered unceremoniously.

Everyone in the room looked puzzled. Hera stood over her son, who was still unable to speak, finishing the healing as Phantasos glared, waiting for her to move. He had his own plans for making the god of war pay.

"Well, I know of none other I would entrust my heart to. Thia and her daughter hold much of my heart, even if I cannot be with them. I am leaving you to care for them from this time forward," Zeus spoke aloud but only to Morpheus.

"I am unable to protect them anymore; they are both more powerful. I am no longer a god. I became mortal when I transferred my power to Kallisto. She now wields her powers along with mine—she is very powerful," he glared at Ares and Hera as he spoke, "I do not advise attacking her ever again."

"No, my son," an endearment Zeus often used with the gods of his pantheon. "From this moment on, you will have your powers back, just as they have always run through your veins. I will make a change in Kallisto, though. She will no longer have your powers."

"What, how could you?" Thia was shocked her father could take the only safeguard her daughter wielded. "She needs all the power she can wield with your wife and son going after her. It wasn't her fault you had an affair with my mother. She's not to blame; you are. You can't do this to her!" Thia was yelling. She couldn't believe the man her mother loved so dearly was about to leave his granddaughter without the power to protect herself.

Zeus grinned, amused at his daughter's fiery outburst. "Not many of my children have ever spoken to me the way you speak to me now."

"Well, I'm not your other children. I'm Zenovia's daughter."

"Well, daughter," Zeus grinned even wider, "if you will allow me to finish, you would find out that I am giving Kallisto the powers that are rightfully hers. The power all of my offspring wield, the powers of a god—forever."

"Forever? You mean, she's—?" Thia couldn't complete her sentence.

"Yes, she is forever a goddess—immortal," Zeus confirmed.

Everyone stared at the intimate happenings between Zeus, Thia, Kallisto, and Morpheus. Hera had healed Ares enough to keep him from bleeding out. She was glaring in disgust and growling in displeasure.

Zeus rounded on his wife and his son. "The two of you have conspired to harm my daughter, granddaughter, and her best friend. You will never go near or send anyone to harm them again. You are not to seek out Zenovia, either. Because of you," he pointed at Hera, "she and I will never be together again. That is enough; you are to leave this madness be. Understood?" Zeus then looked past Hera to Ares. "You are my son, and I love you, but you will be punished for harming my granddaughter and her friend. I will not allow your wound to heal completely, and you will face Phantasos—wounded."

Phantasos grinned, "Can I kill him?" He thought he should ask since Ares was Zeus' son.

He gently placed Amanda on a small bed that he manifested while watching the family adversity play out. Without realizing what he was doing, he sat beside her with both hands wrapped around one of hers. She went in and out of consciousness while moaning the name Christos.

"You may not kill him nor leave him to die, but you may make him regret his actions," Zeus said. "He needs a good ass-kicking, and you look like you can provide that service."

Zeus turned back to Thia. "Daughter, you are welcome on Olympus whenever you want. Rest assured, Hera will leave you alone." With that, Zeus flashed Thia, Kallisto, Morpheus, and Amanda back to earth to the warmth of Thia's living room.

Amanda was on the couch with a blanket over her while she slept. Kallisto shook her head, then ran to Amanda's side. Flashing from one place to another always made her dizzy.

"I'll get a warm cloth and clean the blood off her face," Kallisto left the room.

"I will get my father, Hypnos. He can give her healing sleep, and I can make sure she does not have nightmares," Morpheus flashed from the room.

Zenovia sat in a high back chair, waiting for explanations. "Tell me," She ordered her daughter.

Carrying the warm cloth, Kallisto entered the room in time to hear her mother telling her grandmother what had happened. Kallisto was especially interested in how her mother ended up on Olympus.

"My daughter was in danger. I felt her abduction in every fiber of my body. So, I flashed myself to Olympus. I always expected that I could, and when you said you had," Thia looked at Kallisto, "I knew for sure that I could. I wasn't about to let those—" she paused, not wanting to get herself worked up again. "I wasn't going to allow anyone to harm you. It wasn't until I appeared on Olympus that I found out Ares had taken Amanda too."

Kallisto listened to the rest of her mother's side of the events, and when Thia finished, Kallisto filled in the gaps. She told them of her abduction and how Ares laughed about Amanda's situation. She told them about Morpheus and Phantasos coming for them and how Morpheus gave, without thought, his godhood over to her.

By the time both women finished their stories, Morpheus had reappeared with a gorgeous man by his side. He looked like Phantasos but with Morpheus' eyes. *Damn, are all gods this good-looking?* Kallisto thought to herself. Morpheus glared at her. *Oops!* Then he grinned. She forgot their bond was stronger, and sometimes her every thought was his, and now she suspected vice versa.

"This is my father, Hypnos, the god of sleep. He has agreed to help Amanda through her discomfort. When he is done, I will ease the memories, making them seem more dream-like," Morpheus supplied.

Hypnos sat on the sofa next to Amanda. He placed his hands on her forehead and closed his eyes. Within minutes her cuts and bruises vanished. Even the bruise from the first time Ares hit her faded before their eyes. Amanda slept deeply.

"She will wake in the morning ready for explanations. If I were you, Morpheus, I would allow her to decide if she wants you to aid in easing her memories. Not everyone wants their memories tampered with. A lot of people want to deal with them on their own." With that, Hypnos said his goodbyes and vanished.

Epilogue

Gala

The doorbell rang, and Kallisto sprinted downstairs. Her new gifts, that's what everyone referred to them as from her grandfather, changed her life in many ways. She was faster and more agile than before, plus she radiated an otherworldliness she hadn't before. She no longer destroyed her bedroom to find an outfit, she just manifested her fashion desires onto her body, and on this night, she manifested her and Amanda's dresses. She wore an elegant red, *'oh my gosh'* dress, and Amanda wore a baby blue dress that set off her blonde hair. The girls each wore four-inch strappy stilettos accentuating their shapely legs.

Kallisto opened the door and smiled at Morpheus, "Do you like it?" She twirled for him.

"Oh yes, I like it," he grinned back, eyes dilating as he looked her up and down and back up again.

Phantasos covered his mouth and gave a cough that sounded like *'shit.'* "Are you going to allow her to wear *that*?"

Kallisto shot Phantasos a look that could kill, but Morpheus answered. "Why would I object to such beauty?"

Kallisto giggled and flung her arms around his neck, "I love you, you know?"

"Well, maybe because of the plunging neckline or the skirt that practically shows her ass," Phantasos was an over-protective brother.

"All will look, yes, but only I will have," Morpheus winked.

"I cannot believe you would let—" Phantasos stopped, and his mouth involuntarily fell open.

Amanda was standing on the top landing of the stairs when she caught Phantasos' eye, and he stopped his scolding. He quickly shut his mouth and looked, well, he looked hungry—starving. As fast as the desire and longing spread over his face, he bit it back.

"Oh, I see Barbie is coming with us."

Amanda couldn't hear his comment, and Kallisto hoped he would be nice. It was true, her external injuries were gone as soon as Hypnos placed his hands on her forehead, but the internal injuries weren't healing as fast. Morpheus had heeded his father's words and given Amanda the choice about her memories. She, of course, decided to keep everything the same, wanting to work things out for herself. Kallisto didn't know if she would ever get her friend completely back. Amanda was different.

Amanda stopped on the top ledge, watching her friends. Mostly she watched Phantasos. He hadn't been to see her since that day on Olympus. That was four days ago. She was shocked that he was still escorting her to the gala. Kallisto told her he had stabbed Ares wanting to kill him for taking her. Kallisto also told her that he held her to his chest and sat with her hand cradled in both of his, but she thought Kallisto was mistaken by the look he was giving her now.

"Well?" Amanda twirled in front of the group.

"You look beautiful, Amanda," Morpheus acknowledged.

Amanda looked from Morpheus to his brother. Phantasos eyes seemed to go from desire to anger and back.

You are—pretty," Phantasos murmured.

"You don't have to take me. We can go in separately, and maybe I'll spark someone else's interest," Amanda's eyes were glassing over.

"No, we are going together," and he held out his arm, waiting for her to take it.

Amanda did, but only to keep from punching him. Kallisto looked at Morpheus, rolled her eyes, and shook her head. The two couples climbed in Phantasos' Mercedes and headed for the museum.

"Hey Amanda," Kallisto began, "when is your cousin coming to stay?" Amanda's mother and aunt told her that her cousin, Nicole, would come to live and complete her junior year.

"Apparently, hell finally broke loose, and my aunt can't take it anymore, so she is sending Nicole back with us in a few weeks. Mom and I are flying to Tennessee so she can fly back with us."

The conversation was animated between the four on their way to the gala. Phantasos seemed calmer but kept looking over at Amanda whenever she wasn't looking at him. Amanda seemed to be back to her old self, momentarily anyway.

Once inside the gala, Phantasos took a protective stance in front of Amanda.

"What the hell are you doing?" Amanda shoved at his arm.

"Those men are looking at you," he nodded at a group of tuxedo-clad twenty-year-old men standing next to the bar.

"Maybe they think I look good, even though my date doesn't," Amanda crossed her arms and looked more like herself than she had in two weeks.

"I—I never said you do not look good. You need more on," Phantasos replied.

"You aren't my dad. In fact, all you are to me is a pain in my ass," Amanda sneered, arms still crossed.

Phantasos pulled Amanda to the balcony. She went reluctantly, only because she didn't want to make a scene.

"No, I'm not your father, thank Zeus, but you are here with me, and I won't have some guys licking their lips at the sight of *my* date."

Amanda had been pushed around enough, and she was tired of it. Before she knew what she was doing, she drew back and slapped Phantasos across the face. "You need to learn some manners."

Phantasos grabbed her wrist and glared hungrily into her eyes. She raised her other hand to slap him again. He caught that wrist before she made contact with his face. While holding both wrists, Phantasos pushed Amanda, with his body, against the wall of the building and kissed her hard and deep.

Her tight ready-to-fight body melted underneath his raw power. She gave as good as she got and felt peace for the first time in weeks.

Phantasos pulled from the kiss, still holding her wrists and with his body still pressed to hers. "I never said you were not beautiful," He let her go, took two steps back, and vanished.

Morpheus and Kallisto worked the room, and he kept his arm around her waist the entire time. Someone familiar sitting at the bar caught his eye.

"Give me a minute, Kallisto. I need to talk with someone."

Kallisto saw Amanda standing against the rail of the balcony, alone. "Okay, I'm going to check on Amanda."

"Morpheus dear, I see you made your own destiny after all," Lachesis, the eldest Fate, smiled.

"You know your face is one of the three faces on display here tonight. You may get mobbed if you are not careful," Morpheus smirked.

"I just wanted to see the dream god that gave Hera her just desserts. She has been groveling at Zeus's feet and has even been nice to my sisters and me."

"Lachesis, you told me to tell Phantasos not to allow history to repeat itself. Are you saying that he may repeat the affair he once had with a mortal?" Morpheus asked.

"He came to us the same day you did, trying to find out what we told you. I gave him the warning myself. You no longer have to deliver the message if you have not already," Lachesis stated as she watched the room full of people marveling over the paintings. "Those paintings are amazing. I remember sitting for them about 350 years ago. And I still look the same," Lachesis raked a hand through her black hair and winked.

"Will he be okay?" Morpheus asked, a little concerned.

"I would be more concerned about Phobetor. He and your father relayed messages between Zenovia and Zeus."

"Can you, for once, give me something more to go on?" Morpheus asked.

"Fate is a funny thing, Morpheus. If I tell you, you change things—things could worsen. You have to live to the best of your abilities and try to stay on the right path," Lachesis winked and, to Morpheus's irritation, vanished.

⟿ ⟾

"Hey, where's Phantasos?" Kallisto looked around the balcony.

"He vanished after he pinned my body, with his, against the wall and kissed me."

"Uh, he what?" Kallisto's eyes widened in disbelief.

"Yeah, we fought, and he kissed me and left."

"I'm confused; why did he leave, and why did he kiss you if you were fighting?"

"Because we hate each other," Amanda finally turned and looked at Kallisto. She had been crying.

"Shit, what's his problem?" Kallisto asked. The girls stood there for a few minutes looking at the city lights twinkling from the balcony.

"Maybe he needs to get la—"Morpheus walked out onto the balcony beside Kallisto before Amanda could finish.

"What is going on?" he asked.

"Your jerk of a brother pinned Amanda to the wall, kissed her, then vanished," Kallisto was irritated.

"He does not need to repeat his past," Morpheus whispered to himself.

"What?" the girls asked in unison.

"He is afraid and a little confused. Please do not think too harshly of him. He has good reason to be so standoffish," Morpheus pleaded.

"Let's join the party and have some fun," Amanda dried her eyes and smiled as she turned and walked toward the twenty-year-old men by the bar.

Morpheus pulled his hand from behind his back, and in it was a black rectangular box with a gold bow on top.

"Happy birthday, you did not think I forgot, did you?"

"I would've forgotten if Mom hadn't woken me to an off-key, Thia version of Happy Birthday," Kallisto smiled and took the black box. Her hands shook when she saw the most gorgeous diamond pendant she had ever seen. Around the diamond were the words Dreams are Divine engraved in platinum.

Morpheus removed the pendant from the box and placed it around her neck. It hung next to her heart.

Morpheus smiled and laid a finger on the pendant, "That is where I want to be. Kallisto, I love you, and I want to love you for eternity. I would never have asked for my powers back. I gave them freely, because you are my heart," Morpheus bent his head and gave Kallisto a world-rocking kiss.

The End
Or is it?

Dream Healing
Chapter I

Tennessee

"Damn it! How could you?" Nicole shouted at her mother from across the living room. "I'm your daughter. You can't just send me away!"

The shouting was usual; the reason behind Nicole's outburst, however, was new. Kellie and her husband, John, finally made a decision. They decided to send their daughter to Kellie's sister to finish her high school career. The decision had not been an easy one to make; after all, their daughter had once been a straight "A" student, on the math team, a regular volunteer at the hospital, and president of her sophomore class. Now it was the second semester of her junior year; her grades, on a good day, were "C" averages, she no longer volunteered anywhere, and no one in her junior class spoke to her, not since she dyed her light brown hair black and purple, pierced her tongue, nose, navel, and eyebrow, and developed a mouth that could make a sailor blush. She went from "miss congeniality" to "miss, wouldn't want to meet you in a dark alley" practically overnight.

"You can't keep going on this way, Nicole. You've been sneaking out of the house doing goodness knows what. You even look the part of a juvenile delinquent, and your grades are horrible. We told you that if you didn't start controlling your actions, we would send you to live with your aunt. What did you think—that we were bluffing?" Kellie yelled back, trying, with volume, to convince her daughter sending her away was for the best.

It was true; she had been sneaking out of the house for the last year. At least once a week, she crawled out of her bedroom window. She had also taken on the stereotypical characteristics of a juvenile delinquent, she once had been so pretty, but now she just looked scary—and liked it that way. As for the grades, well, what was the point in making good grades when your life was over?

"I hate you!" Nicole stomped up the stairs and slammed her bedroom door.

Kellie sat on the edge of her brown leather couch, dropping her head into her hands, and cried—again. That was all she seemed to do lately. She was forty-two years old with three children. Her twin, five-year-old boys had curly blonde hair and blue eyes. They actually looked like Nicole, except Nicole had brown hair before her gothic makeover. Kellie was making the hardest decision a parent could, but she knew Nicole needed to get out of Tennessee and start over. She and John had cried together over their decision to send their only daughter thousands of miles away, to the middle of the Pacific Ocean, but at this point, they would try about anything to save their daughter from the self-destructive path she was on.

I need to get out of here. Nicole paced her bedroom floor, trying to calm her shaking hands. She went to her window and tried frantically to lift it. "Shit," her father had nailed it shut. "So much for fire safety."

Her father had threatened to do it ever since he caught her sneaking back in the previous weekend.

Amanda looked at the airline magazine in the seat pocket in front of her. She was accompanying her mother to Tennessee to retrieve her cousin. She didn't know how she was going to be of any help. She had not been the same person since her abduction three weeks ago by the Greek god of war, Ares. Her best friend Kallisto and she had escaped the clutches of a scorned goddess and her son, but not before Ares, the war god, developed an infatuation for her, and when she denied his advances, he beat her unconscious. Kallisto's Greek dream god, Morpheus, and his brother, Phantasos, saved them. *Phantasos—Amanda closed her eyes and remembered the last time she had seen him.*

Yes, Amanda's life was all but ordinary. Her best friend happened to be the granddaughter of Zeus, the Greek god-king. If that wasn't strange enough, the "person" she loathed, obsessed over, hated, lusted over, and despised was the Greek dream god who had saved her—Phantasos.

She was now flying over the Pacific Ocean to bring normalcy to a teenager who had gone through a tragedy that had changed her very core. Amanda was a lot of things, but a miracle worker was not one of them. She was not the "good girl" of the Kallisto/Amanda duo and certainly not a person known for tact. She was heading into new territory. To top everything off, she couldn't tell anyone about her divine dealings. She was not sure how to keep such things from her cousin. Amanda was an only child, so there had never been any chance of someone finding out.

John arrived at baggage claim as Amanda and her mother, Kathryn, did. "How was your trip?" he asked.

"Long, but without delays. How's Kellie?" Kathryn asked in return.

"She's not doing so well. Nicole thinks Hawaii is an empty threat. I'm sure when Kellie tells her I came to pick you two up—all hell will break loose." John lifted Amanda and Kathryn's luggage into his Escalade. "I hope you're up to the challenge Kathryn. Nicole's not the person she was before the accident. She's, well, beyond depressed and perpetually pissed."

The ride from the airport to Amanda's aunt's house seemed relatively quick. John continued to fill them in on Nicole's new outlook on life as they drove, making the trip move along faster now they were on land.

"Kathryn!" Kellie hugged her sister and immediately began to cry. "Thank you so much for coming. This is the hardest thing I've ever had to do."

John took their suitcases inside. The plan was for them to stay a couple of days before returning to Hawaii in the hopes of persuading Nicole that leaving was in her best interest.

"Can I go see Nicole?" Amanda asked.

"She's in her room. She stomped her way upstairs, cursing when she found out her father went to pick you two up at the airport; second door on the right, good luck."

Amanda knocked on Nicole's door. Nothing. She knocked again—still nothing. "Nicole, it's Amanda. May I come in?" No answer.

"Uh—she's not answering her door," Amanda announced as she walked back downstairs.

John and Kellie looked at each other and ran upstairs. They took out a metal key and unlocked their daughter's door. To their horror, but not surprisingly, their daughter was gone. "How could she? I nailed her window shut?"

"I bet she went out the twin's window," Kellie supplied.

"Where would she have gone?" Amanda asked.

"She usually goes to the graveyard where she weeps over Chase's grave. I don't know where she goes when she's not there," Kellie answered.

"If you give me some keys and directions, I'll go look for her." Amanda put her coat back on and held her hands out for keys. John gave her his keys and wrote down directions to the graveyard and the mall, just in case.

Amanda's idea of a good time had never included graveyards. In fact, she hated graveyards; they freaked her out, but here she was on her way to a cemetery at twilight—*shit.*

"Now would be a good time for my "all-powerful" friends to join me," Amanda said, looking at the ceiling of her uncle's SUV.

Nicole sat by Chase's grave with black mascara streaking down her face. No one understood how much she hurt, how painful the last year had been. The only person who could have ever understood died the night her world changed. He had been her best friend, confidant, and lover. The latter was part of her distress.

"Chase, all I ever think about is that night. How wonderful everything was before the wreck. Why did we go that way? Why was that man driving drunk? Why did you leave me?"

Nicole beat her fists on the grass beside his grave. Tears fell to the ground as she leaned over and wept. She imagined those tears absorbing into the earth, closing the distance between her and the boy who lay motionless. This was the kind of pain that compelled her to pierce her body; each piercing seemed to give release. This was the pain that separated her from the world. She was alone in the grief, alone in the despair. The week following the wreck was lost to her, well, mostly. The anguish was there, even in her unconsciousness. How could anyone understand? No one but he could, and he was gone.

Amanda pulled up to the front of the graveyard. The entrance had two brick columns with an iron gate hinged to each. When closed, the top of the gate said, Rest in Peace. Just past the brick columns inside the cemetery was a large oak tree, and next to it was a sign showing the layout of the grounds.

"I can't believe I'm about to go in there," she said aloud. Amanda could see past the entrance just inside the gate.

As she stepped from the vehicle, she got an eerie familiar feeling, like she was being watched. The last time she felt that was when Ares watched her through an orb. If Ares watched her now, she was unsure what she would or could do. Fear gripped her chest.

"Whoever's there, show yourself."

Phantasos appeared by her side, scaring the hell out of her. He caught her around the waist before she slipped. Amanda was shocked and pushed at his chest. Phantasos had made it clear that they would remain—well—nothing.

They weren't even friends. The fact his hands burned a sensual caress down her spine enraged her. At that moment, she hated herself for the feelings he invoked in her—except the ones of hate.

"Let me go. You scared me so bad I couldn't even scream. What the hell are you doing here?"

"You told me to show myself," he sounded irritated.

"Okay then, why were you watching me?"

"Kallisto asked me to."

"She did what? Why I'm fine? Why would she send you anyway?" Kallisto knew she struggled when it came to the god standing before her. He made her crazy, mostly with loathing but also with a sexual intensity that overrode the desire to kill him.

"She felt your distress, and because her father was sitting with her and Morpheus, neither could check on you, so here I am. It was not my idea. I would rather walk across hot coals." He folded his arms and glared.

"Well, as you can see, I'm fine. Now leave," Amanda demanded.

Phantasos looked around and realized they were standing at the front gate of a graveyard in—"Where are we?"

"I'm in Tennessee, getting my cousin. There's no we because you're leaving."

"Why are you standing at the entrance to a graveyard?"

"I'm meeting a man. What's it to you?" Amanda was hurt by his "rather walk on hot coals" remark, so she decided to twist the knife a little herself.

With a glare, Phantasos inclined his chin, "Really? Why would he want to meet you in a place of the dead?"

"He thought it would be cool to *do it* in a graveyard." Okay, she knew better than to go there, but she could not help herself.

Eyes widening, Phantasos turned on his heel and walked into the graveyard.

"I was kiddin'," Amanda *whispered* loudly. "I'm looking for my cousin. She ran off, and she's known to come here to grieve."

Phantasos stopped, "Is this the truth?"

"Yes, not that it's any of your business. You can't go in there. If she's there, you might frighten her, and if she thinks we know each other, she'll be suspicious."

"Very well, I will watch from a distance."

Amanda rolled her eyes and saluted her nemesis with her middle finger. Phantasos grinned and vanished. Amanda felt his gaze on her, wishing she could *choke or kiss him. Shit, I forget he can read minds.*

Amanda saw her cousin leaning over the grave of her boyfriend. She could hear the sobs wrenching out of her. The sight was painful to watch. *How could someone so young feel so much?*

Nicole felt the presence of someone. She jerked her head up to see her beautiful blonde cousin walking slowly toward her.

"So—you found me." Wiping at her face and eyes, Nicole stood to greet her cousin.

"Your parents are worried about you; I'm worried about you."

"Why, I haven't seen you in over two years. You never call or text, and suddenly you're worried about me. Save us both the trouble, stop lying, stop pretending, and leave," Nicole voiced, scratchy from sobbing.

The truth was that Amanda hadn't been worried until Nicole had not answered her bedroom door. Then, she became very worried when she saw the anguish tearing at Nicole's soul while she lay over the grave of a boy she loved.

"I see now I should've been more concerned. I thought your parents were exaggerating. Truthfully, I don't think they know how bad off you truly are."

"What the hell do you know about it?" Nicole stood and began to walk away.

"More than you know. Where are you going?" Amanda had no intention of going any deeper into the graveyard.

"I'm going where it's less crowded."

"Nicole," Amanda ran up to her cousin and grabbed her arm, turning her so she could look into her eyes. "Please, talk to me. Tell me about that night."

"Why should I? I wouldn't want to mess up your perfect life."

Amanda laughed. "Well, I'll make a deal with you. If you tell me about the night Chase died, I'll tell you how wrong you are about my life." Amanda could still feel Phantasos' eyes on her.

"I don't know you well enough to tell you about that night."

"Fair enough. Will you let me get to know you better then?" Amanda asked.

"I don't want to go with you and your mother. I want to stay here."

"Come back with me, and let's talk about it. I'm from Hawaii, and it's freezing out here. Please, come back home with me." Amanda looked up to the darkening sky and admitted to Nicole, "graveyards scare the hell out of me."

To Amanda's surprise, Nicole laughed.

Nicole did not want to fight with her cousin. The two had not seen each other in a long time but had always gotten along well enough. She remembered when Amanda beat the snot out of a boy on the playground when they were about seven and eight years old. The boy was mean to Nicole on several occasions, and when Nicole pointed the bully out on the monkey bars, Amanda saw red. She marched her eight-year-old little badass self up to Johnny and kneed him right in the crotch. Then she made him apologize to her. Nicole had never forgotten that, and that's why she turned and left the cemetery with her cousin.

ACKNOWLEDGEMENTS

I want to thank God for giving me the gift of gab and perseverance; it definitely took both to finish this book.

Second, I want to thank so many women whose encouragement and hard work got me to this place, Nikki, Kellie, and Jacque, for reading the raw first draft of Dream Divine and encouraging me to continue and publish. It was HORRIBLE, but they endured. My editor, Fran, who survived the second, or was it the third, draft. And Jacque for rereading it, fifteen years later, as my proofreader.

Third, JoAnna for awesome merch and inspirational words.

Fourth, Rowan Magennis for the best cover art an author could ask for.

Fifth, my daughter, Allison—she is my biggest fan.

Last but not least, my husband—Ty, thank you for putting up with me for the last several months as I race to the finish line.

Thank you for helping make my dream come true!

L. W. Phillips is a businesswoman with a secret—well, with everyone reading this, she had a secret. For years she figuratively wrote all day. Once she went through each day thinking of her actions and reactions and those of others as scenes in books. Finally, she decided to write things down--okay, she typed them out. Those things turned into more things, and one day, she woke with a full-length novel—okay—four months later, she woke with a full-length novel.

Sometimes her musings are more cartoonish, especially living with three Schnauzers. Please don't get your hopes up; no comics from her--she can't draw a stick figure. Along with her pups, she has a husband and three children—two grown and one teenager. She breeds crested geckos and runs a dental company. When does she sleep, you ask? She doesn't.

Her escape is the world of fantasy. Reading and writing relax her. Young adult fantasy is her favorite, with adult fantasy and historical fiction following close behind.

Her motto is never give up and always follow your dreams!